PICK ME

MAY ARCHER

Cover Art: Cate Ashwood Designs

Cover Photo: Michelle Lancaster

Cover Model: J.J. Michaels

Editing: One Love Editing

Beta Reading: Leslie Copeland, Lucy Lennox, Chelsea Bell

Proofreading: Victoria Rothenberg, Lori Parks

A big, huge thank you to Lucy Lennox, who kept me motivated and smiling throughout the writing of this book, despite all the vagaries of life.

Lucille, I don't remember how I wrote books before you, but I know it was never this much fun.

Chapter One

GAGE

After two weeks, I was beginning to think moving to Vermont had been a miscalculation. I blamed the lumberjacks.

I'd decided to leave Whispering Key on the spur of the moment for the same reason most small-town guys probably left home. First, because my town was rich in pretty vistas and quirky people, but a wasteland for new jobs... and new men. Second, because Florida island vibes were overrated IMO, and I craved the structure and bustle of a city. And third (but most importantly), because my extended family had been driving me utterly batshit—by which I meant even more batshit than the usual low-level batshit—since I'd graduated from college and moved home for the summer.

"Seeing anyone, Gageling? Because a friend of a friend just became single and... wait, how do you feel about guys who sob quietly during sex? Is that a deal breaker?"

"Why not consider grad school, Gager? Programming phone apps sounds boring as fuck. Not too late to trade computer shit for something more interesting."

"You know, precious, you should have just continued backpacking around Europe all summer instead of limiting yourself to a couple weeks! After all, you're what the kids call a 'cheddar baby.' You know, young and wealthy? The opposite of a sugar daddy? It absolutely is a real thing, look it up!"

"You know, Gage, my boy, what you need is some time on the open seas to really find yourself. Your mother and I named you for a treasure hunter, after all…"

I figured this extra batshittery was because both of my older brothers *and* my cousin *and* my dad had all gotten happily paired off within the last year or two. Evidence suggested that people in relationships couldn't resist poking their noses into the lives of perfectly content single folks like me, and I hypothesized that this was due to the lack of sexual variety making their lives so epically boring.

So when I'd gotten a random LinkedIn request from a family-owned orchard in a tiny town in Vermont—less than an hour from the capital city of Montpelier! Two-ish hours from scenic, gay-friendly Boston! A mere three and a bit hours from New York! But a solid *seven* hours from Whispering Key, even if you used the fastest combination of commercial flights and rental cars—I hadn't let the rural location put me off.

My potential new boss—a chill dude named Webb—said Sunday Orchard needed their systems updated, optimized, and automated via a custom app that would allow him and his brothers to control everything. It'd be a monthlong project, he figured. Maybe two? But since I'd need to be on-site in Vermont to handle things, they'd be happy to pay my room and board locally for as long as it took, *plus* pay me a monthly salary that was really fair for a recent grad whose only job experience—besides unpaid work with my professors—was working on my dad's tour boat.

I'd been sorely tempted.

I didn't need the money, per se, but I sure as heck needed the experience and the reference Webb Sunday would provide. Not to mention, Vermont was light-years closer to the cities where I planned to end up than Florida was. And, when Webb described the town of Little Pippin Hollow—the closest town to Sunday Orchard—he'd made it sound like something out of the fairy-tale TV movies my mom used to watch: sweet and simple, culturally diverse and friendly.

So I'd dragged up their ancient, shittastic website—a relic that had clearly been designed during the days of the dial-up modem—to get a feel for the place. There'd been all sorts of shit about heirloom varietals, and sustainable practices, and farm-to-table. There'd been pictures of apples and picturesque barn-type structures. And then there'd been a picture dated five years before of the whole Sunday family and their "crew" standing in the orchard under a bright blue sky.

And that had been that. I'd agreed to take the job that day with no additional questions asked.

What? I was a sucker for trees, okay?

Ugh, fine. *Fine*. I was actually a sucker for tall, dark-haired muscle bears, and at least five men in that picture fit that description, complete with jeans that had been lovingly painted over their thick, *thick* thighs, plaid, flannel shirts rolled up to their elbows, and grins peeking out from behind dark beards.

I don't know how my fascination with lumberjacks began. I mean, it started with porn, obviously, since lumberjacks aren't exactly thick on the ground in beachy Florida. But whatever specific porn I'd stumbled across had long since faded from my memory bank, and in its place was a very broad-ranging love of all things lumberjack. I could not stop this obsession, I could not subdue it, and I didn't bother trying. Beards were my kryptonite. Flannel was my siren song. If the Sundays had been wearing knit hats in the photo, I probably would have come on the spot.

As it was, they'd been hatless, so I'd waited until that night before I'd jerked off to the mental image of one of the guys in the picture, the Sunday brother who stared at the camera—at *me*—with a quirk to his brow and a happy-go-lucky smile on his face, like he was laughing at a joke no one else could hear.

I figured, as vices went, my lumberjack obsession could have been way worse. I mean, I could have been free-jumping off buildings, or huffing glue, or sending weekly Instagram DMs to Zac Efron and sobbing when he wouldn't follow me back, like my freshman roommate Nick.

So, if fate was offering me the chance to live in the Land of Lumbersexuals, to bring them home to the quaint bed-and-breakfast accommodations I'd envisioned and lick maple syrup off their solid bodies before they went out and slaughtered trees, where was the harm?

I'd signed my contract with Webb Sunday, invested in a wool sweater that my almost-but-not-officially brother-in-law Toby solemnly swore made my dull brown eyes look *amber*, and headed north with a kind of desperate optimism, figuring I'd known all I needed to know.

Spoiler: I hadn't.

For example, I hadn't known that, beginning in September, all the roads around Little Pippin Hollow, which called itself "small in size but big in charm" on its town website, would be absolutely *clogged* with tourists. I'd later heard Webb's best friend, Jack, refer to this scourge as the "damn flatlander leaf peepers," and after watching them pull into *every. single. one.* of the scenic overlooks on the way to Sunday Orchard, making me arrive ninety minutes late for supper and so hungry and tired I could cry, I understood the sentiment.

I hadn't known that the orchard, a place that grew *apples*, would also inexplicably have cows—loud, menacing, territorial, possibly violent cows—loitering like a group of thugs near the orchard's pea gravel parking area so they could taunt me with their bellows and rolling eyes as I exited my Prius.

I had for sure not known that Webb's offer of "room and board" would mean eating all my meals with the Sundays in their farmhouse kitchen and *sharing* a converted apartment over the orchard's barn turned gift shop—an apartment whose cutesy sliding barn doors offered zero privacy for lumberjack shenanigans, even if a guy could find an amenable lumberjack, which I hadn't.

I hadn't known Sunday Orchard's systems would be quite so firmly entrenched in the Dark Ages, or that when Webb had said he wanted to automate "things," he meant literally *all the things*, from irrigation, pruning, and fertilization schedules, to tracking retail prices for apples, to the processes in his Uncle Drew's cider press, to time and personnel management for the farm stand and the jam kitchen, all of which would take until Christmas, minimum.

But the widest and most glaring gap in my knowledge? The gravest miscalculation? My biggest rag-ret?

I had not counted on Knox Sunday.

"Are you even listening, Goodman?" the man demanded. "Blink twice if you're aware of my presence."

I stifled a sigh. Aware of his presence? Was he kidding?

The Sunday Orchard office might have made a good-sized tack room back when the building had housed horses instead of the gift shop. But when filled with two desks pushed front-to-front, a couple of file cabinets, and one incredibly sexy, incredibly annoying, incredibly cranky man who was constantly jabbing his keyboard like it owed him money, or making frustrated noises as he squinted at the paper ledgers where his Uncle Drew had kept the orchard's accounting before he'd broken his ankle and let Knox take over, or glaring at me while he pontificated on my latest failings as a roommate—specifically my inability to *"wash out a damn coffee mug if your damn life depended on it, Goodman"*—the space felt incredibly cramped. It wasn't really possible to ignore someone.

And I knew this, because it made pretending to ignore him that much more satisfying.

"Hmm?" I looked away from my computer screen and blinked innocently at Knox. "I'm sorry, did you say something?"

Knox's gorgeous face went red, and his jaw clenched. "Hard at work, were you?" His biting tone suggested he thought the opposite.

"Oh, no. I finished my work for the day fifteen minutes ago," I lied, conveniently forgetting the two additional hours of work I'd need to do that evening to stay on track. "But you were being really boring, so I started daydreaming."

Good. Lord. The look the man gave me could have turned Whispering Key into an icy tundra.

It was a little thrilling but mostly baffling.

Have you ever had someone take an instantaneous and irrational dislike to you? I had *not...* until I'd arrived at Sunday Orchard.

When I'd finally, *finally* pulled down the long driveway from the road, it had been the golden hour. The place had been gorgeous in the early evening light—menacing cattle aside—and very nearly empty, since the orchard was closed Tuesdays and Wednesdays. Webb had greeted me with a handshake and introduced me to his uncle Drew, his sister Emma, his son Aiden, and his younger brother Hawk, all of whom had been welcoming and friendly and *lovely*. He'd shown me briefly around the office and given me a plate of dinner they'd kept warm for me. Then he'd helped me drag my big suitcase up to my new barn-apartment.

I'd been so tired from the drive that I'd nearly been sleepwalking at that point, so I hadn't seen Knox emerge from the apartment's tiny bathroom dressed in nothing but a low-slung towel until I'd walked smack into his naked chest and bounced off it. He'd been startled, obviously, and he'd reached out his hands to steady me, while I'd tried very hard not to chub up right then and there, because *ohmyflippingGod*, he was the guy from the picture.

That guy from the picture.

The happy-go-lucky one with the devilish grin that made my stomach fizz like pop rocks. And he was standing right in front of me, close enough that I could watch the lucky little water droplets cascade from his beard down his thick, muscular shoulders.

I would swear to you until my dying day that when I first glanced up at his face, his fingers had clenched around my biceps for half a second and his eyes had flared with interest—with *want*—like Webb hadn't even been in the room with us. And at that moment, you could have told me that Vermont contained nothing but rabid tourists and homicidal cows, and I would have told you it was all worthwhile, because *holy shit*, lumbersexuals were even hotter in their natural habitat.

But then Knox had taken a step back, given me a single up-down, from the toes of my worn Birks to my Mordor Fun-Run T-shirt, and proclaimed, "This *child* is the programmer you're paying an arm and a leg for, Webb? The one you expect me to *share an apartment with*? For fuck's sake, the kid was supposed to be here hours ago. He can't even tell time."

Then he'd stalked off to his bedroom, leaving me gaping after him while Webb stammered out a lame-assed explanation about Knox's "minor health issues" forcing him to leave his "dream job" in Boston, and how he was having a "tough time adjusting" and blah blah blah.

Like that was an excuse to be rude to someone? *Please.*

The old expression says to never meet your heroes, right? The real trick is to never meet the hot guys you've randomly jerked to because, trust me, the disappointment was epic.

Sadly, that had been the high point of our relationship, and it had all gone south from there.

Later that night, I'd knocked on his sliding door to apologize for showing up late and explain about the traffic, but even though his light had been on and I'd fucking *heard him* moving around in there, he hadn't acknowledged me.

It was so nonsensical, I was confident that there'd been some kind of mix-up, so I'd tried talking to Knox again the next day. I'd rocked up to the office promptly at eight, taken my seat at the empty desk Webb had shown me the day before, and smiled at Knox so hard it hurt my cheeks. Then I'd done the whole "I think we got off on the wrong foot" thing.

Knox had looked calmly back at me and said nothing.

So I did what I always did when I was feeling uncomfortable in a situation—I'd started talking. And talking. *And talking.*

I'd told him I was excited to be in Vermont for the first time. I'd told him about my love for caramel-flavored coffee. I'd told him I had two brothers, plus a cousin who was like a brother, and wasn't it a strange coincidence that we were all gay? I'd even told him a crazy story Toby had texted me from home, about how Gerry Twomey had started a photography business taking intimate boudoir shots, and how Lorenna and George McKetcham, Whispering Key's favorite sex-positive octogenarians, had loved their pictures so much they were turning them into Christmas cards. I'd told Knox I couldn't wait to see an actual covered bridge and shared that cows really freaked me out. I'd gotten *vulnerable*, for fuck's sake.

Then I'd asked him—begged him, really—to grab lunch in town later.

The man had remained quiet through my entire recitation, and only when I'd run out of shit to talk about had he said, "Jesus Christ you talk a lot, Goodman. Are you done now? Because work begins promptly at eight." Then he'd focused on his laptop for the next four hours like I wasn't even there.

That had been *it*.

That had been *all*.

Not a single word about lunch, and the smile that had made my knees weak from the website picture? I'd only seen it *twice* in the past two weeks, and it had been aimed at his adorable little nephew each time. It was like Knox had had a smile-ectomy. A surgical removal of his sense of humor.

He acted fine with everyone else. I mean, for sure no one would describe him as happy-go-lucky anymore, but he was polite at the dinner table, he colored pictures with Aiden, and he was forever making dry little observations that sent his brothers howling. He and Drew helped their neighbor Marco tie fishing lures for hours when Marco's arthritis flared, while listening to Marco's stories about his daughter and toddler granddaughter who lived a couple of hours west in a town called Poultney. He was endlessly patient when his sister sat in front of him and explained every single facet of some young adult book she'd read while he was just trying to eat his morning oatmeal.

It was only *me* he didn't like, and for no reason I could fathom.

I'd deadass never had that happen to me before. My face was in the dictionary beside the word "delightful," for fuck's sake, and nearly a dozen inhabitants of a small Florida island would attest to it. People didn't just *not* like me. I was *undislikable*.

So, fuck him. If he didn't want to be friends, then we wouldn't be, obvs.

But it still hurt, damn it. And not in a boo-hoo-the-hot-guy-rejected-me kind of way, because it wasn't about attraction or the lack thereof, but in a way that made me wonder if I had some big internal flaw that only he could see. And *that*—the fact that Knox Sunday, with his bottle-green eyes and his need to treat me like he was my paid babysitter, made me doubt myself when I'd spent years and years not giving a shit what people thought of me—pissed me off.

Which was why I made it my job to annoy him just a little bit every single day.

I mean, I was being paid to make sure *all* the systems at Sunday Orchard worked better, after all. So theoretically, bringing Knox down a peg or two so that he could be a better human was *kind of* in my job description. Right?

"Daydreaming," he repeated in a warning voice, drawing my attention back to our convo.

"Hmm? Oh, oops! Kinda slipped away again for a minute there. Not sure why, but the sound of your voice just makes me zone out," I lied. "Weird, huh? Maybe 'cause it's kinda got that vibratey, white-noise thing going on, like a swarm of bees in my ear? You start talking and I just hear *bzzzbzzzbzzz*, you know? Oh! Oh, dude. Dude!" I gasped and pointed a finger at him. "Have you thought of recording a sleep video? 'Cause you could just sit in front of the camera and be all, 'Goodman, you need to wash your coffee cup right away and not leave it in the sink for five minutes while you go get dressed,'" I said in a monotonous, robotic voice, "and people would wake up eight hours later feeling super refreshed! And didn't Webb say you needed to relax more? I'm basically your life coach over here!"

If we were being accurate, Webb had told me privately that Knox left Boston because he needed a slower pace of life. His stressful career in finance had taken a toll on his health, so he'd quit his job, was selling his condo, and had moved home earlier in the summer to focus on his health and happiness.

He seemed perfectly healthy to me—the very fuckable picture of good health—but the man needed some remedial tutoring in being happy.

And that was *not* in my job description.

Knox sat forward, making his chair squeak. A shaft of sunlight coming through the high window burnished his dark hair white. "Goodman, I swear to God—"

Ugh. So unfair.

That deep, growly, commanding voice—the kind that gave me sexy, schmexy vibes—should not be attached to such a patronizing, workaholic, stick-up-his-ass-and-not-in-a-fun-way individual.

"Ooh, hey! Has anyone ever told you the vein in your temple throbs sometimes?" I frowned in mock concern and drew a finger down the center of my own forehead. "You should get that checked out."

I leaned back in my chair, propped my feet up on the

desk, and focused on the fading tan line where my shorts rode up my thigh. God, I needed a hookup. It had been precisely forty-seven days, and if I was going to work with Knox Sunday and not kill him or myself, I needed relief.

"Could you listen to me for two minutes, please? As your *boss*, if nothing else?" Knox growled, pushing himself half out of his chair.

"First, you're not my boss. Webb is. You told me so the first day when I asked you what the timeline for this project was. Second... Like, I can try to listen?" I sighed dubiously. "But also, I'm really hungry. So. Probs gonna be daydreaming about dinner again."

He frowned, like I'd caught his attention against his will, and sat back down slightly. "Dinner."

"Yep."

"You had two *enormous* burritos at lunch, plus rice."

"Awww." I tilted my head to one side. "Yes, I did! Sweet of you to notice." Probably keeping an account of all that I ate to make sure he got his money's worth.

"And a peanut butter banana sandwich two hours ago."

"For I wither without protein," I confirmed with a nod.

"So how can you possibly be thinking of eating again?" He folded his arms across his chest.

"Well." I blinked at him again. "You were talking about coffee cups—*yawn*—which made me think of coffee. And that made me think about the giant pear muffins with streusel topping over at Panini Jack's—you know the ones?"

I moved my fingers in the sprinkling gesture that was the universal sign for streusel topping to stress my point and watched in delight as Knox's nostrils flared in exasperation.

"—because Hawkins brought me some of those

muffins last night after his shift. And thinking of Hawk made me think *sweetie pie*, because really he is one—"

"If this devolves into your fantasies about my barely legal brother—"

I held up a finger. "Hawk is twenty-three, a year younger than I am. He's not just legal, he's *super* legal. Also, *knock knock*."

He rolled his eyes. "Who's there?"

"Interrupting homicidal cow."

Knox scowled. "Wha—?"

"*Moooooo, motherfucker*! Now, stop interrupting me before I shank you. Ahem."

Knox's mouth dropped open in disbelief. God, I was good at making him insane, and God, I enjoyed it. There was nothing as satisfying as having your talents and your passions overlap, was there?

"Where was I? Oh, right. So *pie* made me think of your Uncle Drew and how he said at breakfast that he was going to the market today for the last summer plums to make a plum ginger tart—which is *not* a pie, but is pie-adjacent, and sounds fucking life-changing—"

"Pie-adjacent is not a word." Knox rubbed both hands over his face tiredly. "And your mind scares the shit out of me. Look, I am trying to have a simple conversation in which I explain—"

"But *that* made me remember that Drew also said he'd pick up the last of the summer sweet corn," I went on blithely. "And *that* sort of distracted me because I don't think I ever noticed that corn had a season before. I mean, strawberries, sure. We have a strawberry festival not too far from my hometown in Florida, and literally everyone in the world loves it—" I broke off to inspect Knox's scowly face for a second and wrinkled my nose. "I mean, *you* might not."

Knox shook his head like he wasn't sure what he'd done to deserve this fate.

I'd have happily reminded him.

"But then thinking of corn made my stomach growl, and I remembered your sister said she was making turkey burgers with the butterkase cheese that Mr…. uh…" I closed my eyes and snapped my fingers. "Your neighbor with the mustache who makes the cheese?"

"Norm Avery," he bit out, like it pissed him off to answer my question but he couldn't help himself, 'cause he was a know-it-all like that.

"Right! Yes. Him." I popped my eyes open. "I remembered Emma's making turkey burgers with the butterkase Mr. Avery brings, and then my stomach growled, and I felt a little faint, and I thought how sad it would be if I died of starvation before I ate one last meal, and I resolved to keep myself alive just for the butterkase." I shrugged again, inviting him to see reason. "And so, you see, I couldn't actually pay attention to your talky talk."

Knox stared at me for a beat, like he couldn't quite believe I was a real human. Then he tipped his head back so he could speak to the rafters.

"Is this guy some sort of punishment, Lord?" he demanded. "An eleventh plague? Because, I have to ask… why not locusts? Locusts are a classic."

Despite the insult, I had to bite my cheek to keep from smiling, which was another thing that was extremely unfair. No one who irrationally disliked me was allowed to have that dry, quirky, seriously appealing sense of humor, damn it! But Knox's all-day conversations with God—which were the opposite of prayerful—made it hard to remember that.

"I'm way cuter than a plague of locusts." I smiled and batted my eyelashes winningly.

Knox stared at me again. "You're perpetually hungry,

selectively hard of hearing, and incapable of rinsing a coffee mug and putting it directly in the dishwasher, even though that's by far the most efficient way to do things."

I peered at him over the table and nodded solemnly. "What I hear you saying is that you think I'm cute," I lied.

A flush hit Knox's cheekbones, and my gut tightened. Annoyance looked good on him, damn it. This meant that torturing him resulted in me torturing myself, and *that* was the most unfair thing of all.

Knox opened his mouth to retort and then shut it again. "Some of us still have work to do, Goodman," he muttered after a beat.

"Emma says *dinner*, you guys!" Aiden Sunday announced, throwing open the office door hard enough to bang against the wall behind it. "And," he added with seven-year-old solemnity, "she said to tell Gage there's baked beans."

"Oooh." I let my sandaled feet fall from the desk to the floor with a slap and resolved not to think about Kno —*anyone* anymore. "Baked beans sound good."

Aiden's smile turned crafty. "I maybe ate some because I'm Emma's taste tester, and they're *really* good. She makes them with maple syrup."

"Then I'd better go get some before you gobble them all up, huh?" I grinned as I pushed myself to my feet, then groaned and slapped a hand on the desk to steady myself when my back twinged.

"Y'okay, Gage?" Aiden demanded.

Knox snorted. "Old age stalks him."

I wanted very desperately to flip the man off, but I couldn't in front of Aiden. Webb seemed like a cool guy, but I didn't think he'd enjoy me teaching his kid bad manners.

"I'm fine. Supremely youthful. Just sore from sitting still too long." I ignored Knox and directed my remark to Aiden as I stretched my arms to the ceiling so far my hoodie rode up before bending over to touch the floor. "I need to get back to working out. Maybe get some fresh air." I was way too young to be falling apart.

"Yeah, proba-ly." Aiden nodded sagely. "Uncle Drew says fresh air cures all a man's problems." The boy turned around but paused in the doorway. "You comin', Uncle Knox? You need fresh air, too."

"Coming, bud." Knox's expression softened momentarily as he reached out a hand and ruffled his nephew's hair. "But I already got my fresh air today. I ran a couple miles before I helped your dad milk Pattie and Muriel this morning."

Really? Knox the Cranky Lumberjack had gone for a run, milked a cow, *and* gotten to his desk before 8:00 a.m., when I knew for a fact he hadn't closed the door to his room until eleven the night before? He was either lying or a robot who didn't sleep.

We walked out of the office into a little hallway and then out the side door, bypassing the orchard's gift shop, which was closed for the night. Even in the hallway, though, the air was pungent with the scent of fresh apples and cinnamon sachets, and that smell drifted out into the chilly yard. Vermont was like no place I'd ever lived before, and I both liked it… and didn't.

The scenery was pretty but alien. And the people were a mixed bag, too.

Aiden skipped on ahead, and Knox strode quickly past me, but I walked slowly, struggling to figure out what I was feeling.

16

Faintly dissatisfied. Annoyed. Disappointed. I was probably genuinely hungry.

My phone chimed in my pocket, and I grinned as I pulled it out and looked at the display.

"Heya, Toby." I wandered over to a grassy area by the weathered wood fence. This was just the distraction I needed.

"Gagelet, my precious! I was sitting by the pool waiting for the Party Planning Committee to come by, and I heard on the news that your area might be getting frost tonight. I wondered if you'd turned into an icicle yet."

I tucked my tongue into my cheek. "Vermont weather made the Suncoast news, huh?"

"Well." He sniffed. "It's possible that I downloaded weather alerts for your area. It's possible that the entire family did, in fact. It was Jay's idea."

I smiled, though he couldn't see me. My brothers might annoy the crap out of me from time to time, but Rafe and Beale had done our family a solid when they picked men to fall in love with, because Jay and Toby were two of my favorite people on the planet.

"Goodman, you coming?" Knox called impatiently, like I'd once again inadvertently annoyed him with my existence.

I pressed the phone to my chest. "Call from home. I'll catch up. Sorry about that," I told Toby when I'd put it back to my ear. "What were you saying?"

"You okay? You sound... annoyed?" Toby's voice was puzzled. "You're so rarely annoyed unless Rafe's driving you crazy. Or your dad."

"Yeah." I sighed. "Rafe, Dad, and now you can add Knox Sunday to that list." I watched him climb the steps to the back porch. "Cranky asshole."

"Knox Sunday." He chortled. "If your mother blessed

17

you with a name like that, you might be a cranky asshole, too."

I snorted. Maybe if I hadn't seen that picture of him grinning, I'd believe Knox was just cranky by nature. But instead, despite his antagonism, I wondered what had happened to change the guy in that picture to the guy who wanted to lecture me over a coffee cup.

"So, what's he done? Tell Toby everything," he went on. "Many people say I'm an excellent advice-giver."

"Yeah, right." Toby gave the *worst* advice. "He's done nothing really. He just… doesn't like me." It sounded even stupider when I said it aloud. I drew in a chilly breath and looked around the yard, but it was empty. Just me and the dark shapes of the pine trees silhouetted against the sunset. "He thinks I'm a child, and he treats me like one. Little cutting remarks. Sour looks. He's always watching me, and when I catch him at it, he makes a snide comment. That sort of thing."

"Ahhh. And how old is he?"

"Thirty-nine. He's the oldest of the six Sundays. Older than Webb by a couple years. Older than Emma, the youngest, by like…" I winced and ran a hand through my hair. "Twenty-one years, I guess?"

"Mmhmm, mmhmm. So, older than *you* by fifteen years. And is he gay?"

"Um. I think?" I said, confused at this line of questioning. "I mean, I can hardly ask the guy, and he hasn't introduced me to a boyfriend or anything, but…" I thought back to our first meeting, to that hungry look. "Pretty sure."

"Well, there you go, then." Toby audibly swallowed, and I imagined him on his lounge chair, sipping his adult beverage. "Mystery solved."

"Is it? You're gonna have to elaborate, Scooby-Doo."

"He wants you, precious Gagelet," Toby said simply. "And he's a cranky asshole because he thinks he can't have a sweet, young employee like you."

"Nah." I shook my head and leaned my shoulder against the wooden fence so I could watch the reddish light of sunset playing over my bedroom window above the gift shop entrance. "No. That's stupid, and Knox is not a stupid person. It's not the 1900s anymore. Age is relative, especially for hookups. And I'm a temporary contractor, not an employee. And—"

"Don't convince *me*, angel—convince *him*. And, just some friendly advice, maybe don't start by slagging on the 1900s," he added, his voice thick with laughter. "Some of us actually remember parts of that century fondly."

"I'm not convincing anyone of anything, because you're wrong. If he was interested in me, *really* interested, I'd know." Wouldn't I?

I thought back to that first moment we'd met, and I wondered.

"Uh-huh. Then forget about Mr. Sexually Frustrated. Tell me about your job search," Toby demanded. "Do you have any interviews lined up?"

"Nope." I sighed and launched into an explanation of all the letters of interest I'd sent and how I still hadn't heard back from any of them. "That's why I need *this* job at the orchard," I concluded. "I need experience."

"Or you could start your own company," Toby suggested. "It's not like you lack startup capital."

"No, but I lack contacts," I said impatiently, since we'd had this exact conversation before, more than once. "I lack a real understanding of the market. I don't want a vanity project. I'm capable of doing things the right way, even if it's hard."

"Easy, killer. I hear you," Toby soothed.

But I wasn't sure he did. Not really. I wasn't sure anyone did.

"Don't take things too seriously, Gagelet," he continued. "Your time in Vermont was supposed to be partly a vacation. A chance to get all kinds of experience, not just stuff that goes on your resume. Have you done anything fun at all?"

"Uh. Does binging Scandinavian dramas on Netflix count?"

"I'm gonna let you answer that on your own, sweetness. Get out and do something, for heaven's sake! Find a hot guy. Take some scenic pictures for the 'gram. Tip a cow. Whatever counts for fun up there."

I shuddered. The very idea of getting close enough to a cow to tip it was horrifying.

But I was pretty sure Toby was right about the rest.

"Thanks, Toby. Love you. Love to everyone, okay?"

"Check in soon, honeybunch."

Once we disconnected, I took a deep breath and logged in to Grindr, which I probably should have done the second I reached the Vermont border.

No wonder I was so out of sorts. I needed sunshine and loud music. I needed to stop trying to impress the unimpressible Knox with my work ethic and remember all the reasons I was here.

I'd just started scrolling when a shuffling noise behind me in the empty yard startled the hell out of me. I whirled around and threw my phone like a projectile at the shadowy figure looming in the half darkness.

"Jesus Christ, Goodman!" Knox easily batted the phone away, and it landed on the ground with a bounce. "It's bad enough Emma sent me out here like your personal servant to fetch you in to dinner. Now you're attacking me?"

"You *loomed* at me!" I cried. "You crept up behind me and *loomed*."

"I didn't creep. I was specifically trying not to interrupt your conversation, if you were still on the phone. That's what we call politeness." He rolled his eyes. "Now get your damn phone and come eat before all the burgers are gone."

I looked from the farmhouse—where the food was—to my phone, lying face-up and still shining on the far side of the fence—where the cows were—and bit my lip.

Knox folded his arms over his chest. "Are you trying to call it back to you with the power of your mind?"

"No! I'm… I'm strategizing."

"Strategizing. M'kay. I'll let the others know your plate is up for grabs." He turned on his heel and walked two paces, but when I didn't follow, he groaned and walked back to me like it was literally costing him two arms and a leg to do it. "Fine, then. What are you strategizing?"

"We don't have cows where I'm from. I mean, we do. Obviously, there are cows in Florida. But I've never had to meet one. So I'm trying to think about the best way to get the phone back… but, like, respectfully."

"Respectfully?" He tilted his head and looked at me fully.

"You know." I swallowed. "Being respectful of the animal's territory. Not provoking the predators to aggression."

Knox rubbed his palm over his mouth. "You… are aware that cows are vegetarians?"

I blinked. "Obviously, yes." No. I'd had no idea. "But they could still gore me." I made horns on the top of my head in demonstration.

He made a strangled sound. "Is it true that you graduated at the top of your class in college?"

"Yes, but I don't think my intelligence is going to keep them from stampeding me, Knox." I rolled my eyes. *Now* he wanted to do the whole getting-to-know-you thing? The man had shit timing.

Knox closed his eyes and shook his head slowly before opening them again. "Okay, brainiac, here's a lesson in cows. First, cows are female. They don't have horns. A bull might chase you. A single cow generally will not, unless she's got a calf she's protecting or you act particularly stupid."

"Hey! Unfair."

"For example, this cow here—" he went on, motioning behind me.

I twisted my neck and saw an enormous bovine face mere inches from mine. "Gah! No! Go 'way!" I yelled, jumping around Knox so I could use him as a human shield. My heart beat wildly in my chest.

Knox looked back over his shoulder at me, and the muscle at the corner of his mouth twitched. "Excellent example of stupid behavior. As I was saying," he went on mildly, "this cow is Stella. She's maybe a week away from going into labor, so she's not chasing anything these days except a decent night's sleep. Isn't that right?" He stepped toward the fence before I could stop him and rubbed the top of her head.

Stella gave a little huff that might have been agreement... or a warning of an attack.

But Knox didn't seem to recognize the danger because, after another over-the-shoulder look at me, he reached right through the slats of the fence, picked up my phone, and handed it to me. His fingers brushed my palm, and it felt like I'd stolen something—a little illicit and a little delightful.

"Still working?" He nodded down at the device.

"Huh? Oh. Screen looks fine." I unlocked it… and gave both of us an eyeful of my Grindr "nearby" dashboard before I immediately turned the phone off again and shoved it in the pocket of my shorts.

Damn it.

I felt my face going hot for no good reason. Who cared if I had Grindr? Who cared if I was chatting with a million guys?

He wants you, precious Gagelet.

Except he didn't.

"Er… yeah. Seems no worse for wear," I said belatedly.

"Uh-huh." There was a distinct thread of amusement in Knox's voice, which gave me all kinds of conflict-y feels. "*Now* can we eat?"

I nodded silently. My cheeks burned as I followed Knox to the house and then into the big kitchen with its hardwood floors, white cabinets, butcher block counters, and giant oak farmhouse table. Sally Ann, the Sundays' golden retriever, shook herself up off the floor and showed her love for Knox by nearly tripping him.

"Evening, Gage," Uncle Drew said cheerfully from his spot at the head of the table. He had his broken ankle propped up on the bench next to him, but otherwise the man was so healthy and fun, he could have passed for Knox's slightly older brother… if Knox had exponentially less hair, significantly more belly, and a penchant for Jerry Garcia T-shirts. "You remember Marco, right?"

"Sure. Hey, Marco," I said with a smile.

Marco, who was Drew's absolute inverse with his thick, dark hair, deep-set laugh lines, lean frame, and sometimes fussy nature, smiled back a little primly.

Knox and I took turns washing our hands at the sink, and then I sat down while Knox hung back for a moment, leaning against the counter.

"You coming?" Webb gave Knox a look of concern. In his blue Sunday Orchard T-shirt that strained across his biceps, he was every inch a farmer and caretaker of both humans and animals. "All good?"

Knox shook his head like he was coming out of a trance. "Yeah, I guess. Depends on your definition of good. Narrowly saved your new employee from being attacked by Stella," Knox said blandly, taking the seat opposite him. He stroked a hand over his beard. "Almost got impaled by a phone in the process."

I rolled my eyes and took the guest chair at one end of the table, and Uncle Drew winked at me from the other end.

Hawkins, the Sunday brother closest to my age, elbowed Knox lightly. "Don't tease Gage about the cows. Imagine if you had to go to Florida and live with alligators," he said earnestly. "It's the same for Gage coming here."

"Thanks, Hawk." I appreciated his defense too much to point out that most Floridians didn't actually attempt to corral and domesticate alligators. Let alone milk them.

Emma brought a platter of burgers to the table that was nearly as big as she was and set it down before taking her spot next to Drew. "There." She smiled at me, and her dark ponytail swayed. "I knew better than to put the food out before you got in here, Gage, or there'd have been none left. Though I just realized I'm still cooking as much as I did when Reed and Porter were home over the summer, so maybe not."

"Please. This guy eats as much as Porter and Reed together," Knox commented before passing the platter to Marco, Drew's friend from next door.

"*This guy* has a name," I retorted. Marco passed the

platter to me with a wink, and I took two burgers because why not? "And a girlish figure to keep up."

"Me, too," Aiden piped up from my right, reaching for a second burger, even though he still had half of his first one in his chubby hand which, frankly, was the correct and smart way of doing shit when you shared a table with a bunch of guys who were bigger and hungrier than you.

I stretched out a fist for a bump, but he bumped me back with his elbow rather than surrender either of his burgers, and I covered my laugh with a cough.

Webb took a giant bite of his burger and groaned happily. "God, that's good. Remind me why you don't cook every night, Ems? We'd pay you."

"Because conforming to some patriarchal expectation that I, as the only female in this household, should shoulder more of the responsibility for cooking, cleaning, and care-taking, would be massively unfair to all of *you*, who deserve to achieve self-actualization, and part of that is learning to make food that doesn't suck." She grinned and flipped her long hair again. "Also, I'm student body president, captain of the girls' lacrosse team, and I work the orchard on the weekends all fall. Truth is, you couldn't afford me, Webb."

"That's my girl," Drew said proudly.

"Oooh," Hawk laughed. "Tell him, sis."

I lifted my water glass. "From one youngest sibling to another, I salute you."

Emma winked down the table at me before her gaze turned speculative. "So, Gage," she began in a carefully neutral voice.

"Oh, jeez," Hawk said under his breath.

"Beware," Webb mumbled.

"Nonsense," Emma sniffed innocently. But even after two weeks, I knew their warnings were correct. Emma

Sunday was two hundred pounds of persuasion crammed into a five-foot, hundred-pound package, and she proved it when she continued. "I was just thinking you might like to come to the fundraising auction dance with us tomorrow night. It's being put on by the Averill Union Athletic Association to raise money to cover sports fees at the high school." Her big green eyes—the same eyes all the Sundays at the table besides Hawk had—went wide and limpid. "You *do* want to help underprivileged children, don't you?"

"Er." Red flags were popping up all over the place. "Isn't tomorrow night a school night?"

"Nope! The high school is off Thursday and Friday for teacher in-service days." She beamed, smelling blood in the water.

"Oh. Um. What do I have to do?"

"Show up," Emma replied promptly. "That's all. Dance a little, the same way the other guys will." She smiled innocently. "Be your usual charming self."

Knox snickered, and I tossed the lumberjack look-alike a dirty look. I was charming! I could contribute! I could *dance*.

"Sure," I said easily. "I'd be happy to. I mean…" I hesitated. "It's not a party for high school kids, is it?"

"No way," she assured me. "Half of the Hollow will be there, along with half of Two Rivers, and probably all of Keltyville—all the towns that send their kids to Averill Union. Webb's going. Knox said he might come. And Hawk is coming, too, aren't you, Hawk?"

"I said maybe." Hawk spoke to his plate. "I'm not good at… you know. All that stuff."

Aw. My brother Beale hated socializing, too.

"If you go, I'll go, too, and we can stick together since I won't know anyone but you guys," I offered.

Hawk's gaze flew to mine, and I felt the weight of

26

Knox's stare on me, as well.

"There'll be lots of pretty girls there," Drew observed apropos of nothing.

Hawk frowned. "I'm gay, Uncle Drew."

"I'm well aware, Hawk," Drew confirmed gently. "I'm just mentioning it in case Gage is interested."

"Oh. Thanks." I shrugged and smiled. "But I'm not. At all."

Drew smirked down at his burger, like he wasn't surprised to hear it.

"If Gage and Uncle Hawk are going, I'm going also," Aiden announced, licking burger juice off the side of his hand. I picked up his napkin and casually handed it to him. "My teacher Mr. Williams says boys can dance."

"They can, for sure, but you're not coming this time, bub," Webb said. "You're staying home with Uncle Drew."

Aiden looked like he might argue, but Drew cut in. "My ankle's still awful sore, so I need a babysitter, and Marco tries, but he doesn't know how to make Sunday Sundaes the right way. He always gets the ratio of peanut butter to pretzels and chocolate sauce wrong." He shook his head sadly. "I've only taught my secret recipe to _you_."

"This is true," Marco said in a voice that made it sound like there was an unspoken "…thank God" at the end of the sentence.

"Mr. Williams says it's important to help people with a happy heart or not at all." Aiden sighed. "So I'm happy to help you, Uncle Drew… I guess."

I pressed my lips together against a smile.

"Wonder if Jack'll be there," Webb asked the table at large, but based on the way everyone darted glances at Knox's face, somehow it felt like he was speaking mostly to his older brother.

Knox must've thought so, too, because he swallowed

his bite of burger and scowled. "You'd know better than I would. He's *your* best friend. Or ask Hawk. Hawk works for him every day."

"*Or* you boys could head over to the diner tomorrow and ask him yourselves," Marco suggested.

Webb gasped like he'd never heard such an amazing idea. "Yes. Yes, we should. Hawk is working, so Knox and I can go grab a bite for lunch and visit."

Knox made the discontented grumbling noise he usually reserved for me. "You're as transparent as glass, Thomas Webb Sunday."

Aiden leaned toward me and giggled. "Oooh, Daddy just got middle-named."

"Don't know what you mean," Webb said breezily. As breezily as a man built like a mountain and with a voice like a bass drum could, anyway.

"I *mean*," Knox said, setting his burger precisely in the center of his plate, "I won't be conforming to your fraternal expectation that I, as a single bisexual male, am ripe for a setup with someone simply because he is also a single male. That would be massively unfair to Jack, since I hardly know the man. And furthermore, I have neither the time nor the inclination to date anyone right now, male or female, since I'm busy trying to sort out the orchard's finances and my time is valuable." He paused for a beat, and then his lips tipped up slowly. "Truth is, you can't afford to set me up, Webb."

The whole table collapsed into laughter, even Aiden, who pretty obviously didn't get the joke. Webb ran his tongue over his front teeth and dipped his head in silent acknowledgement.

And Knox...

Knox grinned *that* grin. The happy-go-lucky one. The one that had made me weak-kneed. The one that made me do stupid things. It was twenty times as powerful in person, and I found myself staring at him, even though I tried to make myself look away.

Then Knox's gaze clipped mine, and his smile died just as suddenly as it had been born.

Ouch.

Toby was seriously the *worst* at advice. I had no idea why I ever listened to him.

He cleared his throat. "I'll go out to lunch with you tomorrow, though, Webb," Knox volunteered. "It'd be good to get to know Jack, since he's your friend and all."

Webb grinned conspiratorially. "Excellent."

"Maybe…" Hawk began suddenly. "You know, maybe I *will* go to the fundraiser tomorrow night. You sure you're up for it, Gage?"

Against my stupid will, my consciousness swung toward Knox. He stared at his plate like he had no interest whatsoever in my answer, but I could practically feel the "*say no, Goodman*" energy coming off him in waves.

Was I up for a few hours where I wasn't looking for smiles from a guy who very clearly and stubbornly didn't like me?

"Yeah," I said breezily. "Looking forward to it."

Chapter Two

KNOX

I was not looking forward to this.

"Why do I keep letting the man provoke me?" I muttered to the heavens as I stalked down the sidewalk on Stanistead Road. The morning rain had slowed, but groups of elderly tourists still clustered close to the shop windows, where the awnings protected them from the drizzle, meaning my late ass had to practically walk in the street to get around them. "For fuck's sake, why can't I just behave like a man who's about to be forty damn years old?"

My life had been a circus before Gage Goodman had shown up, it was true. But it had been a rational, well-organized circus. Three tidy rings, safety nets all around, and the shit had been shoveled regularly.

Then that... that... *kid* had come to the orchard two weeks ago, all sunshine-smiley and messy-haired and smelling like the ocean, taking over every single one of my spaces with his sly smile and his hilariously awful T-shirts and his dark eyes that showed his every emotion, and suddenly my life was a chaotic shitshow run by rabid twin monkeys called *lust* and *frustration* that made me do stupid things like re-download the Grindr app in the dead of night just to check out who might be located twenty feet away from me—seriously, LumberjackLuvr? What kind of a username was that, Goodman?—and blurt out things like, "Sure, I'll go to lunch at your best friend Jack's restaurant with you, Webb," which was tantamount to me agreeing to Webb's nosy matchmaking bullshit with his friend, and Webb knew it.

I nearly mowed down a lady with a walker in my haste, and I blew out a breath, forcing myself to slow down. To take a deep breath that smelled like wet autumn leaves and maple taffy, and count the beats of my heart, and appreciate the chill in the air that denoted the changing seasons.

"I am in control," I lied to myself in a slow, soothing voice. The voice was important, because it made superhealthy meditation mantras out of statements that would otherwise be really worrisome self-delusions. "All is well with me."

Dr. Travers would be so proud.

"Hey, hon. Table or stool?" a friendly, blonde thirty-something called from behind the lunch counter as I stepped into Jack's restaurant. Other than the new name emblazoned on the doors—Panini Jack's Diner—the place looked a lot like it had back when it was our high school hangout, but at a quick glance, I hardly recognized anyone.

Before I could answer, her eyes tracked behind me, and her grin widened flirtatiously. "Webb Sunday! Well, hey there, cutie!"

"Katey." Webb stepped up just behind me.

"This another brother of yours?" She nodded at me and cracked her gum. "Never mind—I can see the Sunday all over him. Grab your usual booth, honey, and I'll let Jack know you're here." She tossed him a wink as she moved off.

"Thanks," Webb said with an easy smile.

"*Honey*," I whispered under my breath.

Webb shoulder-checked me as he moved toward a booth at the left rear corner of the restaurant, beside the swinging door to the kitchen, and I headed in that direction without comment.

"Nice place, eh?" He slid onto one of the benches.

I grunted, shrugging out of my windbreaker. "Been here before plenty of times."

"Ages ago, maybe. Jack did an amazing job on the place, huh?"

I glanced around the restaurant, at the dull gleam of the wood floors and the red pleather booths. "Wasn't it always like this?"

Webb tilted his head to the side. "You are seriously unobservant. No, it wasn't. It was getting worn down before you went to college, remember? By the time Jack bought the place when he moved to town six or seven years ago, it was falling apart. He redid all the booths, and I helped him do the wainscoting a couple years ago with reclaimed shiplap from the Cauffeys' old barn. Em did the drawings." He pointed up at the framed drawing of a dancing sandwich on the wall.

"Ah," I said. "Cool."

It was a little disorienting to think that the diner had had time to not only fall apart, but also be restored since I'd been gone, and that the random guy I'd only met a couple of times in passing at Aiden's birthday parties was Webb's best friend. I hadn't felt like I belonged in the Hollow twenty years ago, which meant I definitely didn't belong now.

"You'd know all this if you bothered coming to lunch

with me any of the times I've invited you this summer," Webb noted. "I'm here all the dang time."

"Yes, you are. And I naively thought it was for the sandwiches. *Cutie.*"

Webb's cheeks went pink. "No. That's not... No. That's just Katey being friendly." He darted a wary glance over his shoulder toward the counter. "She doesn't mean anything by it."

I begged to differ, but I restrained myself to another grunt.

Webb leaned over the table, and his green eyes narrowed the same way mine did when I was at the end of my patience. "Look, I know you're not feeling sociable these days, Knox. And that's—*ugh*." He ran a hand through his hair in frustration. "You know, I could kill you for putting me in the position where I'm the one trying to get you to talk about your feelings, right?"

"Then you could just *not*. That would work well for me."

"Nope. Em said it had to be either me or Drew, and he'd probably make you do sun salutations and smoke weed first, so." He sucked in a breath like he was preparing to dive underwater. "You've gotta stop holing up in the office all damn day every day. Now you've got poor Gage doing it, too, and it's not healthy for either of you. Okay? I'm worried. *We're* worried."

"You don't have to worry about *poor* Goodman," I scoffed. "Me doing something is more likely to make him *not* do it, and the kid is plenty well rested, too. He leaves his desk to eat literally fourteen times a day. And if he wants to go out, he can go. No one's stopping him."

Webb shook his head. "You're *so* blind. He's trying to make a good impression, Knox. He's doing what you do."

Yeah, right. "Has he complained to you?" I demanded. "About his work hours or… anything?"

"Anything? Like the way you alternately pretend he doesn't exist and bite his head off? Don't bother denying what *all* of us have observed," he said blandly when I shot him a look.

I shrugged. I wasn't sure what he wanted me to say. I knew I wasn't overly nice to Goodman—and, yes, on one or two occasions, I'd been downright curt—but the man was obnoxiously flirty and knife-blade snarky and unprofessionally cheerful.

And drop-dead gorgeous, though that wasn't something I blamed him for.

Much.

In any case, assholery was the best defense, because otherwise…

"No," Webb continued, plainly exasperated. "Gage hasn't said a word to me. But then, he doesn't strike me as that kind of guy."

I shrugged again. The man-child was perfectly capable of complaining to *me* about all sorts of shit, but I supposed Webb was right. Goodman didn't seem the type to tattle. Why should he when it was so much more effective for him to just give me an angelic look and then spout off for twenty-two minutes and twelve seconds (of course I'd timed him; it was either that or *listen* to him) about which cover of "Landslide" best captured the essential pain of the original, while I contemplated the many, many pleasurable ways I could shut him up?

It had been years and years since I'd wanted something with an all-consuming passion, and longer still since I'd wanted some*one* that badly, and the whole thing set me off-balance. I wasn't entirely sure whether I wanted to wipe the smile off his lips with my own or just sit beside him and bask in his presence like he was sunshine—and, Jesus Christ, that right there was a more flowery sentiment than I'd expressed about anything in over a decade.

I hated the *compulsion* of him. The way he'd swooped in and taken up rent-free space in my head within seconds for no good reason whatsoever. My inability to swiftly evict him felt like a sign of my weakened mental state.

One more sign I wasn't in control.

Rick and my colleagues at Bormon Klein Jacovic would laugh their asses off if they ever got wind that their steady-handed head investment auditor had turned into a caricature of a middle-aged man going through a midlife crisis, behaving like a moody-assed teenager over a man nearly half his age.

Webb cleared his throat, and I startled guiltily. I hadn't been paying attention.

Goodman's wandering brain was infectious.

"Knox, I know it hasn't been easy for you, moving back here. And I know you like to pretend you're invincible, so it's hard for you to wrap your mind around the fact that you have certain…" He broke off as Katey came over and deposited two giant plastic cups of ice water and a couple of menus on the table, then continued. "…certain health issues—"

"Panic attacks, Webb," I interjected. "That's all. Mental bullshit. Not cancer, okay? I'm not dying here."

But even as I said it, I remembered how I'd felt the first time I'd had one. The sickening lurch in my stomach, the iron band around my chest, the feeling that I was endlessly falling—through the floors of the building, through the sidewalk, through the entire earth, and out into the stratosphere on the other side—and no force on earth, especially me, could stop it.

It had *felt* like I imagined dying might.

"You ended up in the ER twice." Webb toyed with his straw wrapper, an uncharacteristic show of nerves.

"The first time was a massive overreaction because my coworkers thought it was... something else." I waved a hand, dismissing my colleagues' heart attack concerns. "And the second time, it was because my dumb ass hyperventilated, passed out, and concussed myself. But there was zero blood, and they discharged me almost immediately. And now I have a therapist and good coping mechanisms, so I'm good."

All is well with me. Or it would be, anyway. I was making sure of it.

"Right. Yeah. I'm not sure why I'm making such a big deal about your silly little panic attacks and *concussion.*" Webb huffed out a breath like he was trying to remember where he'd put his patience. "Have you slept a full night yet?"

I set my jaw. No, I had not. *Yet.* But that was only because things were still so up in the air.

Obviously, I understood my brother's concern. Dr. Travers said my panic attacks were probably triggered by my "stressful environment"—the bustling city, the constant work and too little sleep—which meant sleep was a priority, but every medication and supplement I'd tried left me groggy. Sometimes I felt like I was locked in a delightful little catch-22, where sleeplessness amped up my anxiety, and my anxiety made it difficult to sleep.

But I also wasn't going to say that, because then Webb would ask how often I had telehealth visits with Dr. Travers, and whether I'd been honest with the doctor about my sleep issues, and he probably wouldn't understand if I explained that I was handling things just fine.

"Never mind," Webb said. "I'm not trying to pick a fight. I'm just saying, I know it's hard leaving your work and your routine behind, selling your condo and all that. I guess there's a kind of…" He hesitated, then forced himself to go on. "…a kind of *grief* to it, isn't there? Even if you know it's for the best? Like when Amanda and I split." He cleared his throat and studied the shiplap. "All of which is to say, I get it's not easy, but I'm damn glad to have you back for good. We missed you."

I fought the urge to squirm. I was confident I'd never said I was back for good. Yes, I'd maybe *suggested* it, but only because that had seemed like the easiest way to get around Webb's pride so I could take over the books and give Sunday Orchard an infusion of cash from my savings while I was taking the mental health sabbatical my bosses at Bormon Klein Jacovic had politely but firmly suggested for me.

But I hadn't actually *promised* them anything.

And also, sweet, tiny baby Jesus, preserve me from Webb Sunday when his affable farmer facade cracked and his genuine, deep emotions started peeking through because I was a sucker for it.

"Missed you, too," I admitted.

"And I'm not saying that because you've been a life-saver with the financial stuff—though, you know, just to reiterate, you paying for Porter's school and putting aside the money for Em's was more than anyone expected. I don't know why the hell you felt like, on top of all that, you should sell off investments so you could 'buy in' to Sunday Orchard when you moved home. The land and the legacy belong to all of us, no matter whose name is on the deed. And the only reason we were in debt at all was because of me and my divorce—"

"Webb," I warned. "Drop it."

"I know you don't wanna talk about it. Neither do I. But we *did* need the money, and I *do* appreciate it," he admitted. "And I appreciate you taking over the books, since fuck knows when Drew would've been able to get out there to sort through that tower of receipts with his ankle all fucked up."

"It's not a big deal. Although, honest to Christ, I've never seen such a chaotic pile of paper. There's stuff from 1995 mixed with stuff from this April. Anyway." I squirmed. "Can we be done now?"

But Webb wasn't finished. "Even more than I want your help with the books, I want you to be happy, Knox. All the way happy. I've been reading up on panic attacks—"

"No." I shook my head. "Nope. Seriously, Webb—"

"—and there are a lot of relaxation and breathing techniques, and I know you know them, but taking care of your overall physical and mental health is an incredibly important component. And a part of that, I think, is just... getting out a little. Making friends. Having fun. Having a purpose. And maybe... love."

"Oh. Dear. God." I lifted an eyebrow. "You look at me and think, 'There's a man starving for romance,' do you? No, thanks. You remember what happened to Dad after Mom died, right? And how Dad and Porter and Hawk and Em just fell to pieces when Cara walked out? And how Amanda tried to take you for a ride? Romantic love is like a whirlpool, Webb. It doesn't just hurt the people involved, it sucks everyone around them into the vortex of bullshit, too."

Webb flushed a bit. "Not love, then, but... companion-ship. A relationship. Sexual intimacy. Whatever you wanna call it."

"Fucking?" I suggested, as saccharine-sweet as Goodman ever had been.

I'd been trying to make Webb uncomfortable, but

thinking of Goodman and fucking at the same time back-fired wildly on me. Suddenly that was all I *could* think about, and I had to grab my water and chug a little.

Goodman was an employee.

He was a child.

He was a pain in the ass.

He was...

"Permanence," Webb corrected firmly. "A home."

I nearly choked on my water. I did not want to have a conversation about making a permanent home in Little Pippin Hollow. I didn't want to lie.

"Look, I do *not* need you to find me a date, Webb Sunday. So you take all those well-intentioned match-making instincts of yours, fold them up really tiny, and then crush them under your big fucking boot heel like one of those beetles you pick off the apple trees. If I wanted a date, I could get one. I wasn't living like a monk in Boston. I had many a hookup. Plenty of friends with benefits when I needed to scratch an itch, too. And I like it that way."

"But—"

I held up a hand. "And if I ever felt a need to make something permanent..." I blinked, trying to envision such a scenario. "Well, first I'd take my temperature. Then, I'd google 'Have I been brainwashed question mark.' Then, if after reading six WebMD articles about how eating too much kale can mimic the effects of brainwashing, I was still convinced that the urge didn't stem from a disease but from a genuine desire, I'd pick from one of the people I've already fucked—a man or woman who's sexually compat-ible and understands what I can and cannot offer. But under no circumstances—and this is crucial, Webb, so please hear me—under *no* circumstances would I ask my brother to be the Lumberjack Yenta of Little Pippin Hollow and make me a match. Do you understand?"

Webb sighed. "You're annoying."

"That doesn't sound like agreement."

"Doesn't it? Hmm. Anyway, I was also thinking that taking care of the orchard's finances isn't gonna be a full-time job for you," Webb went on—correctly, because he wasn't an idiot. "It's probably disorienting to go from being a high-powered… financial person—"

"Investment auditor?" I supplied, amused.

"Exactly… To being your family's bookkeeper."

That was the damn truth.

"But people around here invest in shit, too," he went on. "And Drew can take the bookkeeping back once he's healed, especially if we move stuff online—"

"Good luck with that," I murmured. "I offered to tutor Drew on the software myself, and he won't hear of it. I guess he enjoys toiling over his ledgers with his feather quill by the light of a single candle."

Webb snickered. "He's not *that* bad. But my point is, once you've caught up on the backlog, you'll have time to do other stuff. Maybe open some kind of financial consulting place here?"

I shook my head. Everything in me flinched at the idea. It would be like serving myself a steaming plate of failure. It would be shrinking my life down to meaningless-ness. My job was who I *was*. "Let's just see how things go, okay?"

In other words, let's see how fast Drew got better, and how fast *I* got better, and how quickly I could escape back to the city.

He coughed. "In the meantime, maybe you could help us set up retirement accounts for our employees? Gage mentioned the idea offhandedly the other day. I thought—"

"Of *course* it was his idea," I said flatly. I finally flipped open the menu, though I couldn't make myself concentrate on the words.

Webb threw up his hands. "I don't get why you dislike him. It's... there's no logic to it, Knox. He's a nice guy. A *really* nice guy."

"I don't dislike him... exactly. He's just annoying. He's got a brain like a demented chipmunk, and he chirps at me constantly. No one should be that cheerful. I lived alone for a long time, you know? And now he's... in my space." Wearing nothing but ramen-printed boxer shorts slung low over his hips as he walked through the living room on his way to the bathroom in the mornings, so I could almost feel the warmth and sleepiness coming off him. I cleared my throat. "And? Not to be Debbie Downer, but he's fucking expensive, too. My buy-in money paid off all the orchard's debts, and you'll be turning a decent profit, but if you want to do those irrigation updates and regrade the roads up to the back of the property, you can't go crazy."

"But the updates Gage is doing will improve yields and save money in the long term," Webb interrupted.

"No, I know, but—"

"I look at Gage and see someone young and ambitious, just like you were. His professors say he's smart and reliable, he just needs room to run. I like him, Knox. He fits. He brings an energy to the place—or at least he does when you're not side-eyeing him and putting him down. Give the guy a chance, would you? Just... be friendly. The last thing I want is for him to walk out before he finishes the work because you're being an asshole. That *would* be expensive."

"Yeah." I rolled my lips together. "You're right."

"I'm not saying you have to be besties." He snorted. "I mean, he's half your age."

"Right."

"He's almost the same age as Porter."

"Yep."

"Your driver's license is older than this guy." Webb snickered. "You probably lost your virginity before he even—"

"Yes! Yes, thank you, Webb, I'm aware of how ages work."

"Just sayin', I know you won't be friends, but you can be friendly. And if he's in your space too much, move back into the farmhouse."

God, wouldn't that be great? The icing on the failure cake. "Sure. Maybe you and I can sleep in bunk beds like we used to."

Webb snorted. "No way. You snore."

Not anymore, I didn't. These days I didn't sleep long enough to snore.

"Hey, you guys." Hawk slid onto the bench beside me in a fluid motion, still wearing his Panini Jack's T-shirt and half apron, knocking into my hip. The Brother Code compelled me to shove his head until he squawked. "Nice of you to let me know you were here. D'you order yet?"

"I figured you'd find us when it was time for your break." Webb grinned. "And no."

"What's good?" I demanded.

"Panini of the day. Havarti and apple with honey mustard. Smells delicious, and I've been dying for one all day. I might even have two," Hawk said.

"Done." I closed my menu. "I'll have the same."

But the two sandwiches comment had made me think of Goodman, who'd been heating a burrito when I'd left the office at noon, and that made me say acerbically, "Webb's such a softie I bet he'll be getting his favorite employee a couple, also. Pretty sure Goodman only had two breakfasts and elevenses before lunch. He'll be wasting away."

"You know what?" Webb said challengingly. "Maybe I will. And I'll tell him it was my idea, 'cause I'm a great boss."

"He wouldn't believe you if you said it was Knox's idea." Hawk's voice was amused but also faintly disapproving. "Don't know why you don't like him, Knox."

"Exactly what I was saying before you sat down," Webb agreed.

"I didn't say I didn't like him!" I said, exasperated. "Do we have to talk about him constantly? For fuck's sake."

"You brought him up," Hawk reminded me, and the worst part was that he was right.

Motherfucker.

"Gage is great," he went on stoutly. "Stop being a dick to him, okay?"

I blinked at Hawk for a second. He and Goodman were nearly the same age. It would probably make sense if Hawk had a crush on him. And maybe Goodman… My mind stuttered out before completing the thought.

"*Okaaaaay?*" Hawk said again. He tried to make this sound like a warning, and his thin arms were folded over his chest, but as the smallest, slightest Sunday, this made him look about as menacing as a Keebler elf at cookie time.

"Down, boy. Yes, fine, whatever. I'll be nice," I assured him with an eye roll.

"Meaning you'll make an *effort* to be nice?" he demanded. "Which is different from not actively being a dick?"

Webb was staring at me, too, with one eyebrow raised, like if I said no, he'd want to know why. "Yeah, okay," I said grudgingly.

"And you'll be approachable and talkative? You'll ask him how his day is going and make him feel welcome?"

I envisioned a scenario where I actually *asked* Goodman to tell me the random trivia about his day, which was akin to *asking* someone to slap you repeatedly.

"I said yes. He'll be my new BFF, okay? We'll do each other's hair and tell secrets." We absolutely would *not*, but Hawk was right. Being rude to Goodman was uncalled for when my main complaint against him was that he was illogically appealing and my inability to ignore him was driving me insane. "Seriously. I'll apologize to him today, okay?"

"Good," Hawk said firmly.

But then a deep voice behind us said, "Hey, Webb," and Hawk nearly jumped out of our booth.

Webb grinned and held out a hand to the owner of the voice, a guy about my height and build, with light hair and blue eyes.

"Jack! How's it going, man?"

"No complaints." Jack shrugged as he shook Webb's hand and smiled, which turned his face from fairly good-looking to genuinely handsome. Deep creases at the corner of his eyes suggested he smiled often.

Honestly, a man could do a lot worse than being set up with Jack... *if* a man were in the market for a hookup, which I was *not*.

Especially not in the Hollow.

"Did you need me to do something, Jack?" Hawk's brown eyes went wide, and he set his palms flat on the table like he was ready to abandon his lunch if his boss needed him.

Jack put a restraining hand on Hawk's shoulder. "No way, dude. It's your break. Besides, I need to feed my right-hand man so he doesn't collapse on me, eh?" He shook the shoulder under his hand, and his friendly gaze swung to me. "Knox. Hey. How's it going?"

I nodded in acknowledgement. Then, remembering Webb's warning to be sociable, I added, "Good. Yeah. Nice to see you. I, uh... I like your wainscoting." Never let it be said that I wasn't suave.

Jack grinned.

"Hawkins, move over here so Jack can sit by Knox," Webb instructed.

All three of us stared at him. I maybe stared a little harder than the others.

"But... Can't he sit next to you?" Hawk asked, bewildered.

"He *could*," Webb shot back. "But there's more room on *that* side of the bench."

Oh my God. Like sitting next to the guy was going to make me want to jump his bones or vice versa?

Stop it, I mouthed at him.

Jack took the seat next to Webb, across from Hawk. "So, Knox, how do you like being back in the Hollow?"

Not a question I was ever going to answer honestly. "It's great," I said. "Fine."

"He's spent the last couple months working on the books all by himself, even on the weekends, poor guy—" Webb said sadly.

I rolled my eyes. "I'm not an abandoned puppy, Webb."

"Still," Jack said kindly. "That's dedication."

"He's *so* dedicated. *Too* dedicated," Webb said in that same sad, *terrible* voice that made me wish the idiot would go back to forcing us to talk about our feelings. "Especially when he'd much rather be... *hiking*."

Hawk and I stared at Webb like he was insane—I hadn't hiked since I was a Cub Scout, which had been long before Hawk even *existed*—but Jack's face broke into a cheerful smile.

"Oh, cool. I love hiking, too. Hawk and I have gone out together a time or ten, haven't we, Hawk?" I felt Jack's booted foot tap Hawk's under the table companionably. "We've done Tremblay Peak. The J. Arthur Trail. Montagusset…"

Hawk's lips quirked up a little. "Don't forget that eight-mile-long *ice skating* trail you made us do last winter," he said softly, in a teasing tone I'd only ever heard him use with family. "That was an adventure."

"*Made* you do," Jack scoffed, but his eyes laughed. "Knox, your brother is a pain in the ass. Frankly, both of them are. But since I don't have any brothers of my own, I'm stealing Hawk."

"Sounds fair," I agreed magnanimously. "I have plenty."

Jack's eyes came to mine, and his smile warmed like I'd said something exceptionally witty. "You'll have to come out with us sometime. I've been meaning to get back out to Stratton and down to the Long Trail—"

"Jack?" Katey scurried over, looking harried. "Sorry to bust in, but Felice wants to know whether you use gluten-free potatoes, and I keep trying to tell her—"

"On it." Jack pushed up from his seat. "Lunch is on the house, Sunday brothers. Sit and enjoy it, Hawk. No rushing back, you hear? And welcome back to the Hollow, Knox. I'm sure I'll see you around soon." He winked.

"Hey, you're coming to the fundraiser tonight, right?" Webb asked before Jack could escape.

"Eh." Jack rubbed the back of his neck. "I dunno. Wouldn't subject anyone to dancing with me. I'm not much of a dancer."

"And you think I am?" Webb demanded, rolling his eyes. "But Em's involved, so we're all going."

"All of you? You dancing, Bird?" Jack lifted an eyebrow at Hawk, who turned bright pink and shrugged.

"Maybe." He shrugged self-consciously. "Don't know if anyone'll ask me to."

Jack nodded slowly. "Well. Remember you don't have to if you'd rather not."

Hawk's cheeks went redder. "Yes. I know."

"That's, like, the third time someone mentioned dancing like it's a horrible thing," I said, confused. "Is the Hollow becoming that town from that movie, where dancing is forbidden?"

Webb snorted. "No, this is not *Footloose*. It's a regular dance," he said, like adults in the real world went to "dances" regularly, "but it's also an auction. They've been doing it for a few years. People bid money to dance with you to a specific song of their choice, and everyone else dances, too. You're allowed to say no, of course. It's all in good fun."

"Like last year, when Katey paid a hundred dollars to dance with Webb to 'Man! I Feel Like a Woman!'" Hawk traced a pattern on the tabletop and pointedly didn't look at Webb. "That was *great* fun."

"Stop. Katey just cares a lot about underprivileged children." Webb darted a glance over his shoulder and said more softly, "Wait, doesn't she?"

Hawk and I snickered, and even Jack grinned.

"Jack?" Katey called impatiently.

"Later." Jack rapped the table with his knuckles before he left.

A second later, Webb leaned toward me. "You're ridiculous. Jack was flirting with you. Would it have killed you to flirt back?"

I shook my head. "One convo about feelings and suddenly you're a relationship expert? I will not be a casualty in your quest for a Matchmaking Merit Badge. Besides, if that was flirting, he's terrible at it. He was being friendly."

"Hawk," Webb demanded. "Tell him I'm right. Tell him he and Jack would be great together."

Hawk stood up. "I'm gonna go put our order in since Katey's busy."

I frowned as I watched him walk off, wondering if I'd imagined his changed mood.

"Knox—"

I turned back and regarded my brother with something like amusement. "I promised I'd come here and see Jack, and now I have. We've seen each other. Let it go, Elsa. Whatever's gonna happen will happen without your intervention, okay? I appreciate your concern—all your concerns—but I'm a big boy, and I can take care of my own shit. I've been doing it for years."

"More like you *haven't* been," Webb shot back, his eyes intent on mine. "You got a serious wake-up call a couple months ago, Knox. A hard reset. A do-over. You get to choose what happens with the rest of your life, whether you wanna suffer through it or actually enjoy it. So what are you gonna pick?"

That was a damned good question.

Chapter Three

"Alrighty! Are we enjoying ourselves or what?" the portly, middle-aged guy who'd insisted we call him "DJ Tony" yelled through his mic. "What an amazing turnout!"

The crowd of maybe five hundred people assembled in the school gym—a solid mix of high school students, their parents, and some twenty-somethings like me who'd been lassoed into this nightmare with a rope made of *pure guilt*—cheered politely, just as we had the last seven times he'd said this.

"That was 'Love Shack,' requested by Jeriann Gerstner for her sweetheart, Eddie Gerstner! And thank you, Gerstners, for that fifty-dollar donation to the Averill Union Athletic Association! Fifty dollars for the dance, but their love is priceless, folks!" DJ Tony shouted. "Remember to place your auction bids at the front of the gym, everyone! The boys' gymnastics team is volunteering this hour, and they'll be *bending over backwards* to help you out!" He snort-wheezed at his own joke. "Get it? Do you get it? Because… gymnastics?" The crowd groaned, and he sighed happily. "*Anyway*, next up, let's rock out to a fun

49

Rick James number that Michael Herzog requested for his wife, Traci! Traci, if you accept Michael's hand for this dance, he'll give the AUAA twenty-five dollars!" Tony hesitated. "But, uh… I'm sure his love for you is priceless, too."

There was more polite applause and good-natured laughter as Traci pretended to reluctantly accept her husband's hand—except, judging by her expression, it wasn't entirely fake.

I winced and ducked my head so only Hawk, propping up the wall to my left, could hear me. "Does anyone else feel like Michael should have consulted with Jeriann so they could coordinate their pledges for Traci and Eddie? I have concerns that there might be a hard freeze happening tonight in the immediate vicinity of the Herzogs' house."

Hawk clapped a hand over his mouth to cover his snicker. "It's like you know them."

I did, sort of. Silly as it sounded, it was weirdly comforting to know that people were people, wherever you lived.

"She accepts!" DJ Tony screamed, like that was a big surprise. "Let's dance, Averill Union! Everybody on the floor!" His voice boomed so loudly through the mic that my brain shook inside my skull even before the music began blasting and the residents of the three towns that sent their students to Averill Union started dancing.

Ordinarily, I'd be out there with them. I'd had a shit day, and if you couldn't cut loose with your terrible dance moves when you were thousands of miles from home among people you'd just met and weren't likely to know for very long, then when *could* you, really? But at that moment, I was feeling sorry for myself, and annoyed at myself for feeling sorry for myself, and then feeling sorry for myself because I was so annoyed at myself for feeling sorry, and anyway, nobody had asked me to dance. So instead, I told myself I was better off being a wallflower.

I was selfishly glad that no one had asked Hawk to dance either, since that meant he'd stayed by my side since we'd arrived with Webb in his truck.

"Hey, I'm grabbing another water," Hawk said, shaking his empty bottle at me. "You want?"

I shook my head.

What I *wanted* was to get over myself and restore my equilibrium. But the tensiometers for the irrigation system, which I'd ordered literally my second day in town, were sitting at a warehouse in Massachusetts due to some shipping malfunction. And the app prototype I'd been working on kept crashing. And, worst of all, I'd discovered that the only thing more lowering than obsessing over Knox Sunday when he was sitting a foot away from me was obsessing about the man while he was out enjoying his lunch with Webb and *Jack* and I was stuck in the office with Aiden, who'd miraculously recovered from the stomachache that had kept him home from school just in time to scarf half my burrito and beg me for help making a robotic dog-treat dispenser for his science fair project.

I'd agreed, obviously, because Aiden was adorable, and chilling with him was the highlight of my day every day, but it hadn't totally dispelled my frustrated mood.

Contrary to popular belief, optimism was not an innate characteristic for me. I'd worked *hard* for that shit. My oldest brother was perpetually salty, and my middle brother was a Disney princess, but I liked to look at things more practically. If I didn't like the way things were, it wasn't because life was out to get me or because the universe was trying to teach me a lesson, it was because there was an *action* I could take that I hadn't taken. For example…

I took my phone out of my pocket and tapped it against my thigh. I *could* just pull up Grindr right now and make plans to burn off my frustrations later. Heck, statistics suggested I might even find a guy here at the fundraiser. The idea didn't inspire me, but maybe what I needed was to stop waiting for inspiration. Maybe I just needed to hook up *medicinally*, to cure myself of this weird... lumberjack fascination thing that I had for Knox.

Before I could decide, an old lady in a long, flowered dress who propped up the wall to my right leaned in my direction and sighed at me loudly. "The problem with society today," she said severely, "is that kids don't know the right way to have fun."

"Oh?" I smiled politely, slid my phone away, and wondered when I'd crossed that shadowy line between being a "kid today" and being someone who was expected to commiserate about "kids today."

Rest in peace, Gage's youth.

"Older folks know better," the woman went on, waving a hand. "We spend our free time in the great outdoors, not packed into a gym that smells like sweat socks."

I nodded pleasantly. "Sounds lovely."

"It *is*. If you haven't had an orgy under the stars while drinking hooch and listening to Jimi Hendrix, young man, you haven't lived." She turned her head to give me a wink. "You're welcome to come try it with me sometime."

I choked on my water a little bit and turned to look at her fully. The woman had a gray bob, snapping blue eyes, and a smile that turned sly when she saw she'd surprised me.

Fortunately, a lifetime spent with the McKetchams of Whispering Key meant that I was able to quickly wallpaper over the mental image of elderly people having drunken outdoor orgies and say, "Oh. Wow. Thank you for the kind invitation, but I'm more of an… indoorsy sort of person? Also… gay."

She laughed delightedly. "Oh, we're going to get on just fine. I'm Helena Fortnum—innkeeper, nature photographer, former schoolteacher." She leaned toward me confidingly. "Unrepentant gossip."

"Nice to meet you, Ms. Fortnum. I'm——"

"Gage Goodman, the new gent over at the Sundays' place. I know! Drew Sunday gave me the skinny on you when I cornered him in the cereal aisle at the Spence, and I feel like we're already friends. You can call me Helena. How are you getting along out at the orchard?"

For a moment, I was tempted to tell her the truth.

Well, Helena, I felt an instant attraction for Knox Sunday, who had an immediate and opposite reaction to me, and now my boy bits don't seem to want any other eligible men in the area, and it's making me cranky. What kind of hooch would you recommend for that?

But what I ended up saying was, "Oh, you know. It's great. Pretty scenery."

"Uh-huh." She nodded like she guessed some part of what I'd left unsaid. "Lot of personalities out there, aren't there? You know, I went to school with Drew Sunday, and I taught third grade for thirty-five years before I retired, so I had every one of the Sunday kids in my class, too," she said conspiratorially. "I've got all the tea, if you're interested."

"Oh, wow." I tried to imagine Knox or even Webb as an eight-year-old, but I couldn't. I was pretty sure they'd been born with thick beards and broad shoulders, just maybe a little shorter. "You know, I might just take you up on that offer, Helena," I told her. "'Cause I've been sharing an office with——"

"Knox Sunday!" Helena interrupted, hands on her

hips as she smiled at someone over my shoulder. "Well, well. The prodigal son's come home at last, eh?"

"Hey, Ms. Fortnum," a deep voice behind me said, and my whole damn body vibrated like a plucked bowstring. "Good to see you."

Don't turn around, I warned myself. *It'll only make the compulsion worse. Don't be that idiot. Don't turn around. Don't…*

"Webb and Emma finally dragged you out of the orchard and into town?" Helena teased.

"Not dragged." He paused for a second, and I could almost hear his lips tilting up—a glacially slow transformation. "You know Em would never use brute force when she could convince you to come under your own power, right?" He paused. "So, I see you've met Goodman."

"Oh, yes! He's adorable."

Because I was weak as hell, I turned my head to check Knox's reaction to this comment and caught Knox's eyes surveying me from heels to head like he was trying to assess whether I was adorable or not.

I knew I looked good. I'd spent thirty minutes selecting my outfit that afternoon, just in case I decided to do more with Grindr than contemplate its existence. My navy sweater was dressy without trying too hard, and Toby had once told me my jeans—the one and only designer pair I owned—screamed "fuck me" in denim.

Knox didn't seem to be picking up on this message, though, because after casually looking me over, he sipped his apple cider and watched the crowd like he'd dismissed me entirely from his thoughts.

"I don't know about adorable, but he's something alright," he agreed with heavy irony.

Knox, meanwhile, wore the Sunday brothers' uniform of a button-down shirt over dark jeans and boots, except Knox's shirt was well tailored to his tapered frame. I had no idea how a numbers guy had maintained a physique like that while living in the city. I imagined him belonging to one of those gyms that had people flip tractor tires instead of doing simple squats, and a pang of something deeper than longing made my stomach clench.

Confession time: I had jerked off to the mental image of Knox's laughter the night before.

And, yes, that might actually have been the weirdest, least sexual thing I'd ever jerked off to.

And, yes, thank you, I found that concerning also.

Particularly since the object of my lumber-crush was about as into me as I was into the 1970s game show reruns that my stepmother watched for hours each day. Survey says, not at all.

Which was why I was probably almost definitely for sure going to find a random guy to hook up with tonight, before I was tempted to beat DJ Tony over the head with his own microphone for the good of Little Pippin Hollow.

"Thank you, Herzogs! That was… beautiful," the man in question yelled, ignoring the feedback screech that made us all flinch. "Now! Marianne Palmer? Marianne? Where are you, Marianne? Ah! Marianne, Christina Miele has pledged $40 for the pleasure of your company as you dance to Meatloaf's 'I Would Do Anything For Love.' What do you say? Are you going to tell her you *won't do that?*" Tony laughed at his own joke so hard that I rubbed my forehead and made a pained, whimpering noise.

"*Tsk*. Anthony Rivera," Helena said with a sigh. "I swear that boy hasn't had new material since high school. Now, what were we talking about?"

"Actually, do you mind if I borrow Goodman for a minute, Ms. Fortnum?" Knox interrupted, shocking the hell out of me. "I need to speak to him for a second."

I frowned. Since when did Knox speak to me voluntarily?

I couldn't imagine what offense I'd committed this time, but I was in no hurry to hear my crush tell me what an irredeemable person I was, and that must have shown on my face.

"Actually, I do mind. I was just about to tell Gage tales about having you as a student, Knox Sunday," Ms. Fortnum teased. She added to me in a low voice, "Do you know, Gage, in nearly four decades of teaching, I never had another like him? Knox was an original. On his very first day of third grade—"

"Oh, wow! Okay, then! As fun as *that* conversation promises to be," Knox cut in, "I really need to—"

"Is this an emergency?" I demanded.

He hesitated. "No. Not exactly."

"Then I'm sure you can wait. Be polite."

Knox looked up at the Averill Union Beavers' basketball championship banners hanging from the steel rafters. "Now would be a great time for an intervention, FYI," he told the ceiling. "Avalanche? Fire alarm? Alien invasion?" He flicked a lightning-fast glance at me and added, "Stampede of Orwellian cows hell-bent on revenge for millennia of oppression? Any interruption, really. I'm not picky."

I narrowed my eyes and told myself he was *not* funny. "Don't even joke about the cows." I leaned closer to Helena. "You were saying?"

Knox tipped back the last of his drink and scowled. "They don't put nearly enough alcohol in these things."

Helena peered at him curiously. "It's a high school fundraiser, dear. I don't believe there's *any* alcohol in them."

"That would explain it," Knox muttered.

The level of enjoyment I obtained from his discomfort

probably made me a bad person… and I was okay with that.

"So what did third grade Knox do?" I wiggled my eyebrows. "Did he shake fifth graders down for their ice cream sandwich money?"

"Oh, no. That was Emma," Helena said fondly. "But it was usually for charity, of course. Save the dogs, save the bees, save the wild spaces."

"Hmm." I stared up at Knox's handsome face and tapped my lip thoughtfully. "Did he eat paste with a Popsicle stick? He has the shifty-eyed look of a paste eater about him."

Knox rolled his eyes and said in a bored voice, "Takes one to know one, Goodman."

"No, no, the paste eater was Reed, the third brother. Bit of an odd duck, that one." Helena chuckled. "He still down in DC, Knox?"

Knox nodded. "Still working for a think tank down there. He gets home less often than I do."

I looked Knox up and down thoughtfully. "Then Knox must've been the tattletale. The rule follower always making sure the other kids stayed in line."

"Wrong again!" she crowed happily. "The tattletale was Porter, the fourth Sunday. But he wasn't a rule follower so much as a… a… what's the word I'm looking for?"

"Con artist," Knox supplied grimly. To me, he said, "When he was *five*, he threatened to tell our dad that he'd caught me and Reed drinking out on the roof of the back porch. I was over twenty-one, and Reed was like sixteen, and this kindergartener wanted to shake us down for candy money to keep quiet."

I laughed out loud. "You totally paid up, didn't you?"

"What do you think?" he asked, and maybe he meant

it as a challenge, but it came out softer, like a question. Like he really wanted to know my opinion.

His green eyes met mine, and it was like a shot of adrenaline to my system. My heart swooped down into my belly before getting stuck in my throat.

Fuck. This man twisted me up so badly.

"You know," Helena went on before I could get myself un-stuck, "I sort of imagined that if TruCrimeTV ever came to my house to interview me about a former student, it would be because Porter had been living a double life, pretending to be a lost Latvian prince." She almost sounded disappointed that she might not get the chance. "But then the man decided to go to college."

"Yeah, well, don't give up hope just yet," Knox said, breaking our staredown so he could focus on Ms. Fortnum. "He's majoring in English Lit, so I'm thinking he might need to pursue a life of crime if he wants to make a decent living."

Helena gave a high-pitched huff of amusement before turning her attention back to our original conversation. "Before you ask, Gage, the animal-loving Sunday was Hawkins. He used to take our class hamster home with him every weekend, because he was so very afraid that our class snake, Pansy, would somehow get loose and eat her."

I laughed. That sounded exactly like Hawk.

"That's because Webb was an animal lover also, so we had a whole huge collection of Nature Planet DVDs by the time Hawk was old enough to watch them," Knox explained. He smiled lopsidedly. "I remember coming home for summer break when I was in college, and Cara— Hawk's mom," he added as an aside to me, "would plunk the kid down in front of a video. He wouldn't move for *hours*. And some of the videos were cute, but some of them were very circle of life, if you know what I mean." He lowered his voice and made a respectable attempt at David Attenborough. "'And soooo the mighty stork stalks the baby bird who's fallen out of his nest...' It used to scare the crap out of him. But every day, he'd ask for more." He shrugged.

"Because he's brave," Helena said. "Takes a brave person to be sensitive and unafraid."

"How are we doing, Averill Union?" DJ Tony squawked into his microphone as the song ended, and Knox and I jumped at the same time.

"We've been better," I muttered, rubbing my ear.

Knox's eyes found mine, and we shared an amused glance—one single glance—that made my whole body go warm.

Since the cider wasn't spiked, I had no idea what made him so peaceable that night. I didn't expect it to last—I figured any minute, Knox was going to cut in with something about how I'd hung the dish towel in our shared efficiency kitchen on the *left* side of the sink when the only correct, precise, efficient way to live was to hang it on the *right*—but in the meantime, I was going along with it because everything about the guy sucked me in like the Enterprise's tractor beam. The person he'd been in that photo, the guy he was now; the way he was cute when he was cranky and downright beautiful when he smiled; and Jesus Christ, the *shoulders* on the man were—

"Excellent! Thank you, Marianne and Christina! Aren't they adorable, everyone? That's right, give 'em a nice round of applause. Okay, our next song is a personal favorite of mine from way back, friends. Webb Sunday? Where are you, Webb? Ah! I see you hiding behind the apple topiary! Don't be shy now, buddy! Come on out here! Katey Valcourt requests the pleasure of your company as you dance to..." He paused dramatically.

"REO Speedwagon's 'I Can't Fight This Feeling'! And —*whoa-ho-ho*!—she's pledged an unprecedented $200 to Averill Union! That makes her tonight's Big Pledger! Whaddya say, Webb? Can *you* fight the feeling?" Tony guffawed at his own joke.

"Oh my God," Knox breathed, closing his eyes in satisfaction. "Karmic payback is real."

"What?" I demanded.

"Good grief," Helena groaned. "Excuse me, boys. I need to see this." She pushed her way through the crowd to the dance floor before I could catch her.

"What song is this?" I demanded. "Is it cringey?"

"How do you not know this song?" Knox darted a distracted glance at me before searching the dance floor over the heads of the crowd, probably trying to spot Webb. "It's… it's required knowledge, Goodman. It should have been in your history book."

I shook my head slowly. "You're a strange man. In the past fifteen days, the only two things you've felt true passion for are the location of my coffee mug and this song."

"Not true." Knox flushed. "Definitely not true." He stood on his tiptoes. "Now, hush. I'm trying to watch Webb so I can mock him relentlessly later."

As a man with a bunch of brothers, I understood this, even if I thought it was ridiculous that he needed me to be silent in order for him to *see*. As a man who'd spent more than two weeks trying to have a civil conversation with Knox Sunday, I had no idea where this level of friendly adorableness was coming from. I literally hadn't known whether Knox—this version of Knox that had replaced the guy in the picture—had it in him.

"Knox!" Hawk hurried over, looking worried. "You and Webb aren't answering your messages."

"Huh?" Knox turned away from the dance floor and dug out his phone. "What's going on? Shit. Four missed calls from Drew? Is Aiden okay? Is Drew?"

"Yes," Hawk said firmly. "Everyone's okay. Breathe. Murray got a little banged up, but he's fine, too."

I frowned. I was pretty sure Murray was the redhead who helped out with chores around the property part-time. I'd met most of the farm crew and the seasonal workers only once or twice, since they tended to work outdoors and be gone by supper.

"Banged up how?" Knox demanded. "I made sure the equipment was all put up for the night and the store was locked before I left. All he had to do was milk Pattie and Muriel, put the milk in the cold room fridge, and check Stella for signs of labor. Did Pattie kick him?"

"Nah." Hawk shook his head. "Stella got him."

"Stella?" Knox sounded confused. "But—"

I full-on gasped. "Stella's gone rogue! Holy shit. *Holy. Shit.* I fucking knew it. It's okay, you guys. I've been training my whole life for this. I'm gonna need some soap on a rope and a roll of aluminum foil to—"

"Shush," Hawk chided, nudging my arm. "When Murray went to check her, he saw her water bag emerging. Because she's almost ready to deliver," he explained when I stared at him blankly. "Deliver *her calf*," he added when I kept staring.

Ohhh.

"So Murray took out his phone to call Webb, but the field was all muddy from the rain earlier. Stella side-shuffled, Murray slipped, she head-butted him, then shouldered him into the wooden fence, and he went down hard. He's okay," Hawk reiterated. "Sitting in the kitchen with Drew and Marco, eating leftover plum tart. But he's never helped during calving before. Drew can't really get out there on his ankle, let alone help pull a calf if Stella needs help, and Marco says he's allergic to unhygienic tasks, so they need reinforcements."

"Oh." Knox straightened. "Yeah, I can handle that. Did Drew call Dr. Reemer? I don't have her number."

"No. Webb doesn't call the vet in usually. He says it's an unnecessary expense since the cows don't need it most of the time." Hawk hesitated. "He has it down to a science. I'd go myself, but Mrs. Hendelmann cornered me, and I promised I'd stay and help the cleanup crew. Maybe I should go get Webb—"

"Webb's busy." Knox tilted his head toward the dance floor. "So we'll do it the Knox way—" He held up a hand to forestall argument. "I'll get the job done." He glanced at me. "And Goodman will come with me."

I huffed out a slightly panicked laugh. "Goodman will go with you? What Goodman? *This* Goodman? Nooo. No way. For what possible reason would I put myself in the path of a cow on purpose? Knox, seriously. It's probably hard to tell from my blinding smile and my *joie de vivre*, but I'm actually a fairly risk-averse, realistic person—"

"Call Drew," Knox repeated to Hawk, ignoring my protests.

Hawk nodded. "On it."

"Come on, Goodman. I needed to talk to you anyway." Knox wrapped one big, warm hand around the back of my neck and squeezed gently, and I sucked in a shocked breath I couldn't quite hide. Then he led me out of the gym and into the big Sunday Orchard pickup.

And that was how I came to spend my evening *not* finding a hookup but instead sitting on a metal rail inside the

Sundays' cow barn, watching the miracle of life happen right in front of me.

Sadly, the beauty and majesty of my fuck-me jeans were entirely lost on my companions in this endeavor. Knox wouldn't have noticed if I'd been wearing a cancan dress and fishnets just on principle. Uncle Drew was busy trying to stay upright on his crutches. Marco was busy muttering baleful warnings about how Drew's FOMO would lead him to break his other ankle. Murray the Farm Chore Guy was too young and too incredibly straight to appreciate my pants. And Wendy Reemer, the vet, was too busy using a device called a calf-jack on Stella, who had a condition called dystocia and needed Wendy to help "pull" her calf. She swore this process didn't hurt Stella or the monster calf baby, but judging by the cow's pissed-off expression, Stella would be staying away from the vet *and* from smooth-talking bulls for the foreseeable future.

The whole experience had been simultaneously miraculous and horrifying—maybe a little heavier on the horrifying—and even a half hour later, after the vet had left for her next emergency and Knox had driven Murray home just to be sure he was okay, I was still kinda stunned.

"They say zombie movies are gory." I wrinkled my nose as Stella licked a bunch of viscous yuck juice from her calf's coat. "*Resident Evil*'s got nothing on this."

Drew laughed and leaned his weight more fully against the fence. "I see you haven't immediately been converted to the wonders of farm life, eh, Gage?" He grinned. "Don't feel bad. Marco's lived next door for years now and he still doesn't know if he likes it." He clapped Marco on the shoulder. "Do you, honey?"

Honey?

Oh. *Huh.*

I had not clocked that at all, but it sorta made sense

when I thought about how they were with one another. I wondered why Marco didn't live at Sunday Orchard, but I supposed that was none of my business.

Marco made a tsking noise. "Hush. I admit it took me maybe a year... *and* a couple gallons of stain remover... *and* an industrial snowblower... before I got on board with rural living, but I realized a long time ago that the beauty *is* the mess around here. Can't have one without the other. Fortunately, the beautiful parts more than make up for it."

As if on cue, Stella's calf raised itself up on shaky legs, unaware that three grown men were holding their collective breath watching her.

"Oh my word, would you look at her?" Drew breathed. "Beautiful little girl."

"This cuteness is how the cows lure you in to slay you later," I reminded all of us.

Knox appeared on my other side just in time to hear my comment—because of course he did—and leaned both forearms on the gate to watch the mother and baby.

"Goodman, you cannot possibly be afraid of cows after watching one give birth," he informed me.

"Oh, that's where you're wrong," I said with confidence. "My capacity for cow-related fear is basically unlimited."

But then the baby calf made a surprisingly loud bleating noise, like she was as pissed at the universe and all the useless humans in it as her mother was, and I felt a kind of kinship with her. After all, she hadn't *asked* to be jacked out into the cold October air, had she?

"She *is* pretty cute, though," I admitted. "Just this one particular miniature cow. The rest are still killers just biding their time, but she might be the exception."

We heard a car door slam outside, and running feet

announced Emma's arrival, with Webb's measured tread coming up behind.

"Oh my gosh!" Emma whispered. She climbed up to sit on the rail beside me. "I can't believe we missed it. Last time Pattie calved, it took hours and hours."

I shuddered lightly. "This was plenty long enough. The veterinarian had to use a *calf jack*."

"Wide shoulders on this baby," Knox explained. "I wouldn't have been able to deliver her myself, even if I weren't so out of practice."

"Gage, if you're still here when Muriel calves in a couple months, you can help out next time," she offered. "You and Knox."

While I wasn't opposed to spending more time with my moody roommate within stampeding distance of any number of bovine assassins, this plan didn't sound like something worth noting on the calendar. "Mmmm, I'll probably be down in Boston or New York by then, but you can text me about it."

Meanwhile, Webb elbowed Knox hard. "Why didn't you get me, fucker? I looked around the gym for you for half an hour before I tracked Hawk down and he told me what was going on. I would have come home, and you could have stayed. I wouldn't have minded leaving."

"Oh, I bet you wouldn't." Knox's lips twitched. "How was your dance with Katey? Gosh, she really *loves* under-privileged athletes, huh?"

"Asshole." Webb elbowed him again for good measure, then turned to Drew. "Aiden okay?"

"Oh, yeah. Perfect," Drew assured him. "Not sure what his stomachache was about this morning, but he ate a huge dinner tonight."

"And some plum tart," Marco added. "I told him

Sunday Sundaes would be too hard on his digestion. All those pretzels, you know?" He winked.

Webb smiled, gratitude in his eyes. "Was Wendy concerned about anything with Stella? Should I give her a call?"

"Nope," Knox said. "Stella came through it like a champ. The doc got another callout, but she said to keep an eye on Stella for a couple hours, call her if you need her, and she'll bill you."

"And what about——"

"Murray's fine," Knox said. "His pride was injured more than anything."

"Oh. Good. *Great.*" Webb nodded like he was trying to get his bearings. "Right. Well, I'll go check on Aiden, I guess, and then I'll come out and watch over Stella for a bit——"

"Nonsense." Drew pushed himself off the fence and got his crutches under him. "I'm going up to the house, so *I'll* check on Aiden. Marco would've fireman-carried me back to the house ten minutes ago if I wouldn't flatten him like a pancake. Everything's going just fine, Webb, even though you weren't there to oversee it. You have help now that Knox is home, remember?" He patted Knox on the arm, and Knox smiled back, but it seemed forced to me.

I mean, not that I'd know. Not that I'd made a whole mental catalog of his smiles.

Damn it. Had I?

"I, ah… I can stay out here and keep you company, if you want," Knox offered. "I'm not tired."

"Neither of you guys have to. I'll watch over Stella," Em said.

Both of her brothers looked at her dubiously, and she rolled her eyes. "I promise, I'm a fully functional human capable of exercising good judgment, despite my ovaries and lack of beard. And there's no school tomorrow, remember? And how old were you the first time you were expected to help with chores around here, Knox? Webb?"

Knox and Webb exchanged a look. Knox shrugged, and Webb sighed, "Alright, then."

"So what are you naming it… uh. I mean, *her*," I wondered, gesturing at the calf.

Em straightened and gave me that brilliant smile of hers—the one I'd started to fear. "I think *you* should name her, Gage."

"Me?" I shook my head. "Heck no. I'd give her a ridiculous name. Like Stanky. Or Monster. Or Kow-tnee Kardashian."

"All of those are cute," Em shot back, calling my bluff. "So which will it be?"

"I…" I blinked down at the calf, whose legs were like matchsticks and whose body was shaking like a leaf. Her eyes were the same brown as mine. Like maybe we shared some ancestors way, way back.

I cleared my throat. "Not Monster," I said grudgingly.

"Right," she said brightly. "Well, you think about it and tell us in the morning, then. I'm gonna go grab a sweat-shirt. Back in a second."

"I… feel like I'm being managed by a teenager?" I said to no one in particular after Em ran toward the house. "Why is she so diabolical?"

"After nearly eighteen years of living with this many stubborn, grumpy, know-it-all Sunday men?" Marco pursed his lips and shook his head sadly. "A person's got to adapt to fit their environment, son. You know, once upon a time, folks called me charming. Then I moved next door."

Knox's lips twitched.

"Folks said that? What folks?" Drew demanded,

managing to sound stubborn, grumpy, and know-it-all all at once.

"See?" Marco demanded.

I snort-laughed, but he wasn't wrong. Not *at all*. After two weeks, I'd found myself in the same boat. And clearly, I didn't want to be saved very badly since I *still* hadn't gotten on Grindr.

"And on that note, I think I'm going to bed." I swung around so I could jump down on the safe, cow-free side of the railing. "See you in the morning, folks. Oh, Webb, I might need to borrow your truck sometime this week to fetch the equipment I need for the irrigation system."

"Sure," Webb agreed. "Let's talk tomorrow."

I nodded, and after exchanging waves with everyone, I pulled out my phone as I walked across the chilly yard to the gift shop barn. It wasn't late, technically. I could still get on Grindr, and in twenty minutes I could...

"Hey." Knox jogged a couple of paces to catch up, then walked alongside me. "So, your first calf birth and you hardly fainted at all, Goodman."

"Was this your plan?" I demanded. "Were you hoping it would get me over my fear? Or make me faint and decide to leave Vermont for good?"

"Yes," he said blandly.

I rolled my eyes and walked a bit faster. "Well, joke's on you, because I'm not doing either," I bit out.

"*Shit.* Wait. Goodman, wait. I was kidding." Knox jogged to catch up to me again, and I couldn't imagine why he was hurrying since we were going to the same place. "That wasn't the reason at all. Webb was leaning on me pretty hard over the Jack thing earlier today, and I wanted him to get a taste of what it was like to be a victim of someone else's hard sell, so I didn't want to give him an excuse to cut out of the dance early. And I brought you with me because... because I needed to talk to you."

I blew out a breath and stopped short. "Fine, then. What is it this time? Did I hang the toilet paper *over* when it should have been *under*?"

"No." Knox ran both hands through his hair and looked uncharacteristically uncertain. "Fuck. Look, I... Look. It's come to my attention that I might inadvertently have been... less kind to you than I could have been."

"Inadvertently." I slowed my steps and folded my arms over my chest. "That came to your attention."

He narrowed his eyes on the light illuminating the stairs to the barn-apartment. "Hawk said I was being a dick."

Hawk had defended me? He was so cute.

"Yeah, well." I folded my arms over my chest. "That's 'cause you have been."

"Okay. So, then, I'm sorry. About that happening. Inadvertently."

I shook my head. "But... why? What did I do that pissed you off?"

"I don't..." He darted a look at me and sighed. "It's about me and my reactions, not anything you did, okay? I'm not used to being in Little Pippin Hollow anymore. I'm not used to sharing a space. I'm feeling like there's a lot of stuff in my life I can't control, and I don't know what to do about it," he concluded with unmistakable honesty. "And all of that sort of... coalesced. And I took it out on you since you were handy... and maybe also because it feels like you have a lot more freedom than I have."

I squeezed my eyes shut for a beat. Well, so much for Toby's theory that Knox wanted me, eh? But I'd known all along that was a long shot. I opened them again.

"You know, we actually have a lot in common," I said

wryly. "I'm *also* not used to being in the Hollow, and my life is *also* completely up in the air. I need to look for another job, but first I have to finish *this* job, and I don't really know what I'm looking for or where. Being in my midtwenties means I've gotten fat off a diet of possibilities for two decades, and now people are telling me to pick a tiny box to shove myself into and acting shocked when I tell them I don't fit. I have so much freedom, I've got decision fatigue." I shot him a teasing look, like I hadn't just tossed all my very real fears into the evening air. "Also, I'm perpetually horny."

Knox choked on air. "Horny?"

"Er… yes. That emotion you feel when you wish to have sex but have not had any," I explained.

Knox hip-checked me, then cut around me to jog up the stairs. "Yes, thank you, I know what the word means."

"Do they call it something different when you get older?" I called, following him. Then a thought occurred to me. "Because my brother's boyfriend is thirty-seven, and he and Beale go at it like a pair of gay bunnies, so I know they still feel it."

"It's still called horny no matter how old you are." Knox opened the door and placed his keys precisely on the hook hanging beside it. "And of course you still feel it. But after a certain age, you stop throwing your horniness around willy-nilly."

"Oh, I don't think that's true." I stepped in behind him and flipped on the overhead light so it glinted off the hardwood floor and the countertops in the open kitchen area. "Or else someone should inform the truly concerning number of Crypt Keeper leather daddies down in Florida who are ready to stick their willies in any old nilly at the slightest provocation."

Knox snorted and unlaced his boots before placing

them precisely by the door. "I *meant*, now that I'm older, I don't just hook up with any old meat sack with a dick. The guys I hook up with have similar goals. Similar interests. They're educated and ambitious."

"Ahhh, I see what you're saying. You want your meat sacks to calculate torque while you're railing them, and you want their dirty talk in the form of a haiku. Welp, far be it from me to yuck your yum—"

"Oh my God, you're infuriating," he said, though he seemed close to laughter. "The men I pick to hook up with don't call the next day whining for attention or expect a repeat."

"Okay, that makes sense." I set my hands on my hips. "So, you want a meat sack with no self-esteem."

"The exact opposite. I want someone who lives their own life and lets me live mine. Someone who understands the rules at the outset and doesn't expect more than I can give."

I nodded slowly. "So you don't *date* anyone."

"Correct."

I toed off my own shoes and purposely kicked them into a haphazard pile next to his. "Okay, same. But *I'm* talking about hooking up. Having bizarrely high standards when you're hooking up is like asking the guy at the McDonald's drive-thru to see their wine list. You're going for french *fries*, not French *cuisine*. You feel me? Both are tasty as fuck, but only one can be served up piping hot and sliding down your throat in ten minutes or less." I opened my Grindr app and shook my phone at him in demonstration.

Knox shuddered at the visual. "Thank you, Professor Horndog. I have so much to learn from you about how to have casual sex." He rolled his eyes and flopped onto one end of the little red sofa in the center of the living area. He unbuttoned the top few buttons of his shirt before he began rolling up the cuffs to expose his forearms.

Merciful fuck. I blinked, then blinked again, imagining those hands on me and those arms wrapped around my...

"Actually... Actually, maybe I *could* teach you a thing or two," I offered.

He snorted... and then he sobered instantly and shot me a panicked look. "Oh, wait. Goodman... no. I mean, you're good-looking and all, but—"

Ouch. I'd thought I'd reconciled myself to it, but that little comment reached out and pinched my heart.

"But I'm not your French cuisine? Good thing I wasn't offering, dumbass," I scoffed like I wouldn't have climbed on top of him right that minute and damned the consequences. "I was offering to help you overcome your debilitating insistence on only fucking guys who pass your twenty-point compatibility assessment. I could tutor you in..." I paused dramatically. "The Art of the Modern Hookup." I slid onto the arm of the sofa facing him and pulled my feet up onto the cushion. "What do you say?"

"I say fuck off because I've been hooking up since before you were toilet trained. Literally."

"Yes, but humans have evolved in the current millennia," I told him pityingly. "How many hookups have you had in the last year?"

He hesitated. "I've had some health issues—"

"Okay, then, the last three years. How many partners?"

"I don't know. Three?"

"Oh, dear God." I ran a hand over my face. "This is more serious than I thought."

A pillow whacked me on the forehead. "Shut up. I told you I prefer—"

"Guys who know the score, yeah. But you lived in *Boston*, man," I wailed. "There have to be a bajillion delectable gay men there who legit don't even wanna know your *name* 'cause they'll be calling you *Daddy* when you make them come, and you were all, 'But mah high standards!'"

Knox buried his face in his hands, and his shoulders shook with laughter.

"I'm serious! This is a tragedy. It's like you were living dead center of an all-you-can-eat buffet and spent three years saying, 'No, I'm perfectly fine with this small fruit cup and this sprig of parsley.' Nobody is handing out bonus points for how little enjoyment you derive from life, Knox. You do know that, right? But fine. *Fine*! We begin from where we are." I waved a hand like I could magic away his short-sightedness and moved on with what I felt was considerable maturity. "Now, get out your phone, and let's do this thing. Time for lesson one."

He shook his head. "Not only no, but hell no. I'm not interested. Besides, why in the world would you want to help me with this? Forgive me if I don't trust your sudden generosity."

"For the good of humanity? Because I'm just that kind? No?" I sighed. "Okay, fine, it's because I've been lazy about seeing what the dating scene around here is like, myself, and I'm going to regret it nearly as much as you will," I told him honestly. "I deserve to have fun while I'm here. Also? Not to dredge up our painful history since you apologized so nicely and all, but you've been a bear to deal with the last two weeks, and frankly, things are only gonna get worse now that Stella got stompy and Sunday Orchard has to adjust their OSHA sign for 'days since your last incidence of cow-related violence in the workplace' back down to zero. Think of my helping you get a stress-relieving fuck as a form of self-preservation."

More laughter—that easygoing, happy laughter—

bubbled out of him, seeming to startle him as much as it did me. "Goodman, you are…" He broke off and shook his head.

"A fool?" I said darkly. "Yes, so you keep saying."

And he wasn't wrong.

I had it bad for this man, I could admit that to myself, and that was beyond foolish because Knox was the literal definition of Never Gonna Happen.

But at least now I knew there was no point in walking around the barn-apartment wearing my fuck-me jeans, which, in retrospect, were not very comfortable. And I definitely didn't need to stop annoying him constantly, which was handy since I'd kinda gotten into it.

I just needed to approach this ceasefire with Knox the same way I'd gone into *Game of Thrones* when I'd started watching it last year, approximately a billion years after the rest of the world had seen it and spoiled it all over the internet. When you knew there wouldn't be a happily ever after, you knew not to let yourself get too invested.

"I swear to God, I'm gonna make sure you get laid one of these days. And when you're stress-free and smiley, I'm going to be smug as fuck." I threatened Knox sunnily. "Watch. It. Happen."

Chapter Four

KNOX

I walked across the frosted grass to the farmhouse the next morning with my hands in my sweatshirt pockets and a spring in my step.

This lightness was not, it was important to note, because of Goodman's ridiculous offer the night before—which I would not be taking him up on, since I had been sourcing my own hookups ever since MaryPat Fishbaugh and I had spent three minutes in the janitor's closet outside the gym at Averill Union Junior-Senior High School on a dare back when I was thirteen, *thank you very much*.

Instead, my good mood had everything to do with an early morning email I'd gotten from my boss at Bormon Klein Jacovic, saying my leave extension had been approved through the end of the year, and they'd be sending me forms to sign to make it official.

"Work will be here when you get back," Rick had written. "Take all the time you need to get healthy."

If you'd told me last spring that receiving an email from my boss saying "Nah, we won't need you for three months" would make me happy, I'd have called you a dirty liar. Even now, there was a definite undercurrent of anxiety underscoring my relief, because I hated being seen as the unhealthy weak link.

But it mostly felt like a stay of execution. That email meant I had three more months to get myself back to a hundred percent mentally. Three months to get my family back on their feet. Three months to remind my siblings that we were all better off with me living a few hours away.

Plenty of time.

Breakfast was already underway when I opened the door from the porch into the back hall, the air thick with the smell of coffee and cinnamon and the sounds of laughter and silverware scraping plates. My whole family —everyone I loved in the world, minus Reed and Porter— was gathered around the big table laughing at something Hawk was saying, and I took a minute to stand there in the doorway and watch it. Aiden, squeezing a thick layer of honey on his oatmeal. Webb smiling over at Em, while also typing something on his phone and pretending not to notice what Aiden was doing. Uncle Drew, dressed in bright blue leggings and an oversized tie-dye shirt, surveying everyone with the loving, semi-bewildered, and semi-paternal air of a guy who'd spent ten years acting as guardian to his brother's kids and still wasn't sure what the heck he was doing there.

And then there was Goodman, sitting right in the middle of the fray today, Sally Ann by his side waiting for him to accidentally-on-purpose drop some oatmeal where she could get it. His eyes pinged from one person to the next, that sunshine smile on his lips, as he put away enough oatmeal to feed four Olympic athletes.

It was strange how easily he'd slotted into place here at the orchard, while I was still trying to remember how I fit.

"Poor Cinder-Hawkins!" Em ruffled Hawk's hair, and

tiny sparkles fell like rain onto his shoulders. "Your fairy godmother didn't explain that at midnight you'd turn into a human glitter bomb?"

"It's not funny!" Hawk groaned. "Nobody explained there was gonna be a confetti cannon! Someone spilled a gallon of apple cider by the refreshment table, so I was kneeling down trying to clean it up, and then freakin' DJ Tony set off the dang cannon when I was *right there*, and now I have glitter in places where glitter doesn't belong. Not to mention"—Hawk's voice went louder as he tried to speak over the peals of laughter—"have you ever tried to scrape a mass of congealed sugar cookies, apple cider, and confetti off a floor? I reek of apples, and I have sprinkles permanently lodged under my nails."

"You do have kind of a scented-candle vibe." Goodman leaned over to sniff him. "I'd call your flavor… Autumn Dance-Auction Enchantment. It's very wholesome."

"Great." Hawk rolled his eyes. "Just what every boy wants to hear."

"Have you considered showering?" Drew asked gently as he stirred his tea.

Hawk gave Drew a narrow-eyed, pursed-lip look that was a little like a bunny rabbit trying to look intimidating. "I showered last night *and* this morning. This is what's left." He added in a mumble, "Last night, I looked like a human disco ball. And my bed looks like I've been fuc— um." He darted a look at Aiden, who watched the exchange with delight. "Like I've been *having sleepovers* with a unicorn."

Goodman laughed so hard he had to clap a hand over his mouth to prevent an explosion of oatmeal, but when his dancing eyes met mine across the length of the kitchen, his expression turned wary like he wasn't sure whether our cease-fire was still in effect.

He straightened a little, bracing himself. "Heya, Knox."

I pushed myself off the doorframe. "Morning, Goodman. Everyone."

"Knox!" Uncle Drew said happily. "I might possibly have unearthed a few more receipts I forgot to give you… by which I mean a few more boxes full of receipts. So… happy Thursday?"

"Lucky me," I grumbled.

"And more importantly, help yourself to the baked oatmeal on the stove. My assistant helped me prepare three trays of it last night." He winked at Aiden, who beamed.

"Hey, Gage," Aiden said, scooping up a spoonful that was at least as much honey as oatmeal. "Can we work on my science project this weekend?"

"Oh yeah," Goodman muttered around a mouthful of oatmeal. He swallowed and continued. "I already ordered us a treat dispenser that's supposed to be delivered today, and I had some ideas about how we can program it."

"With the pressure pad?"

"With the pressure pad," Goodman agreed.

"Yesss! I'm ready!" Aiden fist-pumped in the air and gave Goodman a gap-toothed grin.

"Morning, Knox," Em said way too breezily for someone who was up most of the night. It made me feel a little old and a little jealous. I'd been surviving on four hours of sleep a night for a long while, so you'd think I'd be used to it, but I was never that perky. She stood and put her plate in the sink. "Heading back out to the barn."

"Yeah? How's the new calf?"

"Brilliant! Gorgeous." She rocked on the balls of her feet excitedly, and I couldn't help but smile.

"Did Goodman name her yet?" I darted a glance at the man in question.

Goodman endeavored to look very innocent and got busy eating his oatmeal.

"No, I don't think so," Emma said, smiling at Goodman fondly. She lowered her voice to a stage whisper. "But he did go out and visit her this morning. He *voluntarily* got close to the cows. So… progress."

Goodman snorted and took a sip of his coffee to wash down the oats. "Not because I like them or anything," he said after swallowing. "I keep my friends close and my enemies closer, that's all." He made a hand gesture that looked like he was jabbing his fingers in his eyes, then jabbing them in the general direction of the barn.

Christ, he was adorable.

And so freakin' young.

And so very off-limits, especially for a guy who couldn't trust his own brain these days.

"I sleep easier knowing we have you to be on top of all cow terror plots," Em assured him before she laughed her way out the door. "Later, everyone!"

Meanwhile, I got a bowl and dished myself out some baked oatmeal Drew had made with leftover plums. It smelled amazing.

"Wait, so." Hawk frowned and looked back and forth between me and Goodman. "You two are getting along now?"

Goodman lifted an eyebrow. "Sure thing. That's why Knox wants to come and sit across from me."

"Absolutely. Thrill of my day," I agreed. I stole Em's seat next to Hawk at the table. "Someone eloquently instructed me at lunch yesterday to stop being a d—" I stole a glance at Aiden and cleared my throat. "*Doofus.* And I value my life too much to disobey. So yes, we're getting along."

"You were gonna say *dick*," Aiden said matter-of-factly. "Dad would've middle-named you for sure."

Goodman made a startled, snort-laugh sound that had Hawk and Drew laughing in response.

Webb looked up from his phone. "Oh, would I, Aiden Andrew?"

"Oops." Aiden blinked innocently down at his oatmeal.

I snorted softly, and Webb's eyes swung to me. "Proud of yourself, Edwin Knox?"

"Don't try it." I shook my head, closer to laughter than I'd been in a while. "You've got the Dad-voice, and I respect that, but I'm two years older than you. You can't middle-name me. It subverts the natural order of things."

Webb rolled his eyes.

"Let's back up," Goodman demanded. "*Edwin?*"

I lifted an eyebrow at his teasing, trying hard to pretend that his smile aimed in my direction wasn't warming me inside more than the oatmeal. "I was named after philosophers, okay? What's *your* middle name?"

"Spence." He shrugged sheepishly. "I was named after treasure hunters."

"The Spence is the name of our grocery store in town," Aiden informed him excitedly. "You were named after a place that sells Genessaro's Frozen Custard. That's way cooler than a philosopher."

Goodman held out a fist, and Aiden bumped it.

"Do you even know what a philosopher is?" I asked him.

"Nope. Which is why it's gotta be uncool," Aiden retorted smugly. "Sorry, Uncle Knox."

I had no comeback for that.

"Gage, I know what you should name the calf," Aiden continued. He paused dramatically. "*Diana.*"

Goodman turned to face him, his forehead pinched for

a second like he was thinking about it. "Like the Roman goddess?"

"No, like Wonder Woman, because she's the best superhero except Captain America, and Steve's not a good name for a heifer."

"Ohhhh." Goodman nodded. "Yup, perfect. Write that down, people. She's Diana."

He slapped the table like a judge with a gavel, and I *willed* myself not to smile at the way Aiden puffed up importantly under Goodman's approving smile.

I wasn't a kid-oriented person. They were very cute, and Whitney Houston was right when she'd said they were our future, but I'd never understood how people would steal and cheat and die for them until the first time I'd held Aiden.

If I hadn't already let myself start to like Goodman as a person, watching the way he gave Aiden a hundred percent of his attention would have done it. The sunshine in Goodman's grin could have powered cities, and Aiden blossomed beneath it.

Aiden pushed up from the table and put his bowl in the sink. "I'm gonna go see the calf again!"

I looked at Webb, expecting him to shut that down since Aiden didn't have the day off like Em did, but he was frowning down at his phone and not paying attention.

"Didn't you tell me yesterday that you'd be doing soccer sprints in gym today, Aiden?" Goodman asked. "You need your gym clothes, right?"

"Oh, shoot." Aiden winced. "I forgot. Thanks, Gage." He ran off toward his room.

"Yeah, thanks, Gage," Webb said, belatedly glancing up from his phone.

Goodman shrugged. "Sure. Hey, Webb, remember I was saying that I might need to borrow a truck this week? I ordered tensiometers and some other parts for the new irrigation system—you know, to measure the soil wetness?—and they arrived at the warehouse in Boston, but they're having a huge issue getting them packed and shipped up here, so I told them I'd try to arrange to pick them up. I could take my car, but my car's tiny, and I'm honestly not sure how big they are."

"Oh, sure," Webb agreed. "No problem. You can drive a standard, right?"

"I…" Goodman hesitated. "Technically yes. My cousin Fenn forced me to learn. I haven't done it in a hot minute, and never on crowded mountain roads, but how hard could it be? It's like riding a bike, right?"

"Oh, sure," Drew agreed. "Like a two-ton bike. A bike with a clutch, if you will. Just take it slow and you'll be fine."

I bit the inside of my cheek. Drew was right—the only way to learn how to drive these roads was to do it, and Goodman was probably a competent driver, so he'd be fine. Plus, the roads were so busy around here these days, he wouldn't be going above a crawl until he hit the highway.

Still, the idea of him going alone gnawed at me for reasons I couldn't put a finger on. I envisioned him going down one of the steep embankments just five or ten miles outside of the Hollow in a soaking rain—I mean, sure there was no rain in the forecast, but you never knew—and stalling out or sliding.

The thought made my chest go tight.

All is well with me.

I am in control.

It would be ludicrous for *me* to take him, obviously. I wasn't his boss. But someone else really should.

Webb was frowning down at his phone again, so I kicked him gently under the table.

He looked up. "Huh?"

"Goodman doesn't have much practice on a standard, and parking might be tricky in the city. What do you think about that?" I lifted an eyebrow significantly, trying to convey what I *thought* he should think about that.

"Oh. Uh. I'll drive you, Gage," Webb offered.

"No, I don't think that's necessary—" Goodman began.

"It is, though," I interjected, despite no one asking my opinion. "Route 26 around here is like one giant pothole. And do you know how many moose-related driving accidents there are in Vermont each year? Moose are like incredibly tall cows, Goodman. Cows on steroids. Like, if The Rock and a cow had a hungry, aggressive baby, it would be a moose."

"Oh." Goodman's jaw dropped.

Drew snorted. "In no realm is that accurate, Ranger Rick, and you know it. Besides, this time of year, that part of the drive is thirty minutes of flatlanders creeping along at five miles an hour. And once he's on the highway, he'll be fine."

This was almost definitely true.

And yet I found myself saying, "What about when he's coming back in the evening? Moose are out a lot at dusk."

"So, Gage will be cautious." Drew shrugged like he didn't get my problem. "Right, Gage?"

We both turned to Goodman, who nodded vehemently. "Yeah, no, I... yeah. I'll be fine."

"Webb," I said sharply again.

"Huh?" Webb blinked up from his phone again. "Oh. Totally. Yeah, I agree with you," Webb said, clearly not understanding what he was agreeing to. "Sounds good."

Drew shook his head and smiled. "And people say *I'm* the strangest Sunday." He set down his mug and pushed up on his crutches. "Come on, Hawk. Best way to remove glitter is with baby oil, and I just happen to have a bottle kicking around my bathroom drawer from the last rave I went to."

"So, when do you need Webb to take you to Boston?" I asked as the others left.

Goodman scraped up the last of his oatmeal. "Anytime. Today's great. Tomorrow's fine. Monday's good. I don't know if they're open on the weekend."

Webb opened his mouth to speak, but then his phone vibrated audibly, and he scowled down at it.

"Oh, shoot! Dad!" Aiden called breathlessly, rushing back into the kitchen. "I forgot Mr. Williams says I need a show-and-tell thing that starts with the letter *V*! What do we have that starts with *V*? Dad?"

Webb glanced up distractedly. "What? Sorry, kiddo, I wasn't paying attention."

"I've got this. I have a perfect idea for you, Aiden," Goodman piped up. He grabbed his bowl and jumped up from the table. "Come look in the fridge with me."

Webb began typing on his phone and barely noticed when they walked away, which wasn't like him.

Damn it all.

I looked around the table for someone—anyone—who was better qualified to have a feelsy conversation with my brother than I was, but of course, the *one time* I wished someone else was around was the one time the kitchen table was absurdly empty.

"Hey." I leaned over, plucked the phone from Webb's hand like the annoying older brother I was, and set it facedown. "What's going on with you?"

"Huh? Nothing. Just…" He licked his lips, looked to

make sure Aiden was still occupied with Goodman, and said hesitantly, "Amanda might come to town this weekend."

"Amanda? Your ex-wife Amanda? For fuck's sake *why?*" I hissed in a low voice.

Nicely done, Knox. Nothing says nonjudgmental listening like hissing.

"Because she has friends here? That's what she says anyway," he whispered bitterly. "But while she's here, she wants to stop by and see…" He jerked his head toward the refrigerator significantly. "And I told her no. Flat out. She's not happy about that, and she's letting me know it."

I grimaced. "Can you stop her from seeing him, though? Legally, I mean? What were the terms of your custody agreement exactly?"

"When we divorced, we signed paperwork saying we have joint custody, though I have primary physical custody because she moved out of town. Technically, I'm supposed to make reasonable efforts to ensure she gets time with him when she's around if she gives me proper notice, but… *Fuck*, Knox, I don't want to. The last time she blew through town, almost two years ago, she took him out for ice cream and fed him a bunch of lies about how she desperately wanted to see him more often, but *I* wasn't allowing her to. For weeks after that—after she'd fucked off back to Philadelphia or Moscow or Timbuktu—my son, my *baby*, cried like his heart was breaking every night and promised to be a good boy if I'd just allow her to come and see him. And I didn't have the heart to tell him she'd left town of her own free will."

"Damn." I winced. "I had no idea."

"I know," he said tiredly. "It wasn't your problem. I didn't wanna bother you, and I thought I had it under control. I sat Drew down one night after Aiden was in bed and explained it all, mostly so he'd understand why the kid was being such a pain in the ass those first couple weeks after her visit, but he's the only one I've told." He sighed, a heavy sound. "Drew thought I needed to go to court and officially get sole custody, but the lawyer I contacted wanted eight thousand dollars just for the retainer, *and* he told me that unless Amanda was a convicted felon, she'd probably still get visitation, so I didn't bother. I couldn't justify spending the money, and I hoped she'd just... stay gone. But now she's back, at the busiest time of the year for the orchard—which she *knows*—and my choices are letting her see Aiden and fill his head with trash again or else legitimately being the asshole she says I am by not letting my son see his mother." His jaw firmed. "So I'm going with the option that protects him."

"Yes!" Aiden cried. "Gage, you rock!" He ran around the island to Webb's side, brandishing a zucchini the size of my forearm. "Dad, look. Vegetable starts with *V*! Gage suggested it."

"Wow," I agreed solemnly. "Great job with letters, Goodman. Someday, we'll teach you about *numbers*, and then there'll be no holding you back, buddy."

If Goodman was startled by my teasing, it only showed for half a second before his mouth curved in a grin, and he rubbed his eye with his middle finger behind Aiden's back.

I started to smile in return, but my amusement died when Webb's phone buzzed again on the tabletop.

He made a frustrated noise but managed to summon a smile for his son. "Aiden, get your backpack, okay? I'll drop you at school."

"M'kay. Mr. Williams says punctuality is super impor-tant. Punctuality, honesty, and respect," he singsonged.

Webb rolled his eyes. "Yeah. Mr. Williams is a paragon of virtue who clearly knows every-flipping-thing." He raised his voice and snapped, "You know who *else* says things you should listen to, Aiden? *Me.* So get your dang backpack right this dang minute, and don't make me repeat myself, or you won't see Diana until next year. Understand?"

Aiden looked confused for a moment, clearly not used to being spoken to so sharply. Then his eyes widened and filled with tears, and he ran for the stairs to his room.

Goodman and I exchanged a glance, and then he followed Aiden.

"Webb," I said as gently as I could.

"I know! I *know*." He blew out a frustrated breath and slammed his palm down on the table. "I didn't mean to snap, but I'm just one person. Christ."

"How can I help? What can I take over for you? Or do you need to talk about feelings? Because… we can," I offered with a distinct lack of enthusiasm. "If you want."

"No. Fuck no. You've done too much already," he said shortly. "Giving the orchard the cash, working on the books, being here when I know you'd rather be… *Shit*." He pushed his chair back and stood up to pace. "Look, I'll figure it out. I have lots of help. Jack's been great. Drew and Marco, too. Take care of *yourself*, Knox. I've got this handled."

I ran my hands through my hair, feeling helpless and hating it. "There has to be more I can do, Webb, to help fix this permanently. I have the eight thousand if you want to contact a lawyer, and I can't think of a better use for the money than keeping Aiden safe. So can I call around and find you an attorney?"

"No, I… *No*. I told you, I've got it handled. Nothing's changed as far as the lawyer is concerned, and it's still a waste of money, whether it's your money I'm wasting or my own." He snorted. "But if you know a good ex-wife filter for my email... Surely such a thing exists by now. The damned woman won't stop cursing me out electronically."

"Are you taking screenshots of this?" I demanded. "Because I think—"

"Yes, Knox," he said with strained patience. "Not my first rodeo, dealing with her shit. She talks a lot, but she's not a danger."

"Right, no, I didn't mean to imply—"

I broke off when Goodman hesitantly made his way back into the room.

"Aiden's all set and out on the porch, Webb. I'm gonna go out for a run. Unless... Do you want me to take him to school for you?"

"Nah. Thank you for offering, though, Gage." Webb stood up and gave him a tilted smile. "I need to talk to him. Maybe middle-name *myself* for biting his head off."

"Meh. Seeing his dad act like a fallible human's probably good for him." Goodman grinned back. "But maybe the promise of a Sunday Sundae wouldn't go amiss? Just saying."

Webb slapped Goodman on the bicep. "Good idea."

"Hey, Webb, I'll take Goodman to Boston today if it's all the same to you," I called fake-casually before I gave myself time to think about how taking Goodman to Boston meant *being alone with Goodman*. Breathing his scent, hearing his voice, stopping every twelve seconds to buy him provisions and pretending I wasn't more attracted to him than I'd been to anyone in years. *Gah.* "I have a couple things I've been meaning to do down there, and I can get them done in person tomorrow."

"Yeah?" Webb looked over at me, his attention caught. "What kind of things?"

"Oh, this and that. Friends to visit. A condo to check

on. Colleagues to catch up with." *HR documents to sign*, I mentally added.

Webb nodded slowly.

"I'm gonna need to stay overnight since I'll probably have an appointment tomorrow," I said, thinking about how early I could set up a meeting with HR the next day. "But we'll be back tomorrow afternoon in plenty of time to help with the afternoon crowds in the U-pick orchard. Does that work for you, Goodman?"

"Sick! Heck, yeah, it works." Goodman's eyes widened. "I've never been to Boston. Can we do a duck boat tour? No, no." He waved a hand. "That's probably lame. Is it lame? Or maybe we could just walk around. Although I'm sure you've seen it all a million times—"

He bit his lip like he was waiting for me to say something cutting, and... okay, maybe his chirpy personality was growing on me, because I really regretted being an asshole to him for the past two weeks.

I also deeply regretted letting myself see that the guy wasn't just sexy but likable, too, because it made it that much harder to keep my thoughts platonic, which they absolutely *needed to be*.

The man's goddamn enthusiasm was contagious, though, and made me think dangerous things... like maybe this road trip wouldn't end badly.

"Yeah, fine, we can walk around," I agreed gruffly.

———

"How many more questions are on this BuzzFeed quiz?" I demanded.

I had not expected my regrets over this trip to be so swift or all-encompassing.

Goodman, who was sitting pretzel-legged on the

passenger's seat of my truck and should not have looked so damn comfortable, glanced up from the phone in his lap. "Like… six. Why? You have somewhere else to be?"

"No. But I'm sitting here fondly remembering the days when you pretended to ignore me."

He snorted. "Who said I was pretending?"

"You did. Your eyebrow twitches when you're lying."

"No, it doesn't."

I bit back a grin. It really did. "We're half an hour into this drive, and we've only gotten through four questions because you've questioned me about every answer, including this one," I shot back. "I've never met anyone who needed to talk so much."

"We're getting to know each other better, since we're being *friendly*." Goodman crossed his arms over his chest. "I don't care so much about what shape you want your sandwich cut into, I care about *why*."

"And you keep correcting me."

"Only when you're wrong," he shot back. "I want you to lead a fulfilling life, Knox. I'm a giver that way. And to hear you say that you've been eating your sandwiches in rectangles all these years and decades and you can't even tell me *why*…" He sighed, then bent down and rustled in the backpack at his feet, pulled out the largest bag of Twizzlers I'd ever seen, and shoved them in his mouth four at a time. "Vuh unezzamined wife iv noh worf wivving."

"Thank you, Socrates. How do you eat that junk?"

Goodman swallowed and glanced over at me. "Happily." He grinned. "You know, Knox, I feel like I'm saving you in a way. Because *weawwy*—" He paused to ingest more strawberry plastic and swallow. "—*really*, this is how evil geniuses are born."

I blinked. "Watching you eating Twizzlers? I concur."

"No, by failing to consider the tiny changes you could

make to become happier, like the triangular sandwich. Because if you live your life long enough wondering why other people seem so much happier than you, then eventually you *snap*. You build a freeze ray on top of an abandoned paint factory and start filling a vat with stingrays you've armed with throwing knives."

I shook my head sadly. "You make it sound so easy, but sourcing an army of trained stingrays is harder than you think."

He threw back his head and laughed in delight, which made my stomach clench pleasantly.

"You know, it's funny to me that a man can get so pissed off when I suggest empirically proven methods for efficient dishwashing—"

"*Efficient*," he snorted.

"—yet can have such nonsensical opinions about sandwich shapes."

"They're not nonsensical. It's about the ratio of bread to filling to crust, combined with the shapely aesthetic magnificence of the right triangle." He sketched a triangle in the air with a Twizzler, like maybe I'd forgotten what triangles looked like. "The secret to happiness has been sitting right in front of you all this time."

I shook my head. "It's clear that our parents named the wrong one of us after philosophers, Goodman."

"Maybe so." Goodman grinned. "But I'm still *way cooler* than you," he said in an Aiden-voice. "So, what time's your appointment tomorrow?"

I blinked at this topic change. "Uh… I dunno. Probably early, but we haven't set a time yet."

He nodded. "Oh, so not like a doctor, then."

"No." My occasional calls with Dr. Travers were plenty, thank you. "An appointment with a… colleague. Why do you want to know?"

I worked hard not to sound guilty.

Apparently, I failed.

Goodman laughed. "Oh my God, why are you so squirrelly? Are you and your colleague robbing a bank? Murdering someone? Soliciting a prostitute?"

"Please," I scoffed. "I'm stopping by my office, and we're going to grab coffee whenever he can squeeze me in, okay, Nancy Drew?"

"Yeah, I have no idea who that is," he said with a happy grin, and I couldn't tell whether he was lying. "You mean your *former* office, right? The investment place?"

"Obviously. Yes. My former office." The lie tasted like sawdust. "Bormon Klein Jacovic."

Goodman nodded. "Do you miss it?"

"Can we go back to talking about sandwiches?"

"Nope. We're getting to know each other. It's this or the BuzzFeed quiz."

I rubbed my neck. "That's... a big question," I deflected, but when he stayed silent—because of course, *that* was the one moment Goodman didn't have a million thoughts and opinions to share—I found myself saying, "There are parts about it that I miss. Lots of parts. I started working there fifteen years ago, and I'm really good at what I do. I turned my position into what it is today," I said proudly. "I literally wrote the training manual the company uses. I supervise a whole team of auditors, and I'm responsible for some really crucial, high-level decisions. So."

"Sounds boring, but okay."

"Boring?" I snorted. "No way. I love working in finance. I like risk analysis."

"But you just said you weren't really doing that," he pointed out. "You were watching other people do it."

I floundered for half a second. "Well, yes, but that's

how corporate hierarchy works. If you want to make good money, you have to stretch and supervise. Maybe it's not thrilling, and maybe it's a little more demanding—" Or *a lot* more demanding, I mentally revised. "—but that's how careers work."

"Yeah, I dunno." He shook his head doubtfully. "I don't think it's supposed to work like that. And hey! You wipe that '*because you're a naive child, Goodman,*' look right off your face, Edwin Knox."

I shut my mouth because I *had* been thinking exactly that.

"I'm *not* a child," he went on. "I just don't understand why people associate maturity with getting the soul sucked out of your body on a daily basis. I know life is full of hard days, hard seasons, difficult clients, and all that, and you have to work hard to get rewards. But when the majority of what you do every single day is a total slog, I just don't get why anyone would think it was more mature to keep slogging than to put yourself on a better path, even if that means you don't end up having a fancy title or a corner office. Not to say that's how you felt about your job at all," he added quickly. "If you enjoyed supervising, then that's cool. I just… I keep hoping I won't have to compromise like that."

"What did I do to deserve three and a half hours stuck in the car with this youthful idealist who refuses to compromise yet somehow landed his ass working at an orchard in rural Vermont?" I asked the roof of the car.

"Hey! I like the orchard. As first jobs go, it could be way worse. Webb's giving me a ton of freedom in the way I structure things. Way more than I'd get at most other places. And it's fun."

"Except for the cows."

"Well, yes," he allowed. "But even the cows add a little

adrenaline boost to the day. You can't get bored with them around."

"Goodman, just so you know, I get paid a *lot* of money to do the same shit every day. The boring bits are what pay the bills."

"I know! And I know I'm really privileged, because most people don't get to hold out for a perfect career and are *fine* with doing a job that's boring if it means they have money to take care of their families, or travel, or fill their houses with cat figurines, or whatever their passion is." He frowned and twisted in his seat to face me, his eyes earnest and his dark hair flopping over his forehead. His shorts hiked up his thigh, showing a lighter band above his tan line dusted with coarse, dark hair, and I had to grip the steering wheel against the urge to *touch*. "What *do* you spend money on? What do you do for fun?"

Had I actually been thinking before that it would be *nice* to be the object of Goodman's total attention? Because it wasn't. It felt like standing naked in a field.

I cleared my throat. "I, ah, have a condo in the city. It's a great investment. And I support local charities." Mostly monetary donations for the tax write-offs, it was true. "I read." Business and productivity books. "Part of the problem with being good at things is that it's hard to take vacation time, so I don't have hobbies per se."

Goodman frowned and nodded once again. He was so obviously trying not to pity me that I felt his pity sinking into my skin like Hawk's glitter.

"I invest in small businesses, too," I told him. "That's fun for me. And I put money aside to help my younger siblings pay for school and to pay the orchard's debts. And…" I broke off and shook my head. Was I really trying to impress this guy with how exciting my life was when it definitely wasn't? "Whatever. I *am* boring. I do my boring job because I'm a boring person. I accept this."

"Helping small businesses is not boring," Goodman said with surprising vehemence. When I glanced over, his cheeks were flushed. "And neither is helping your family. When I was growing up, my folks had no money. A lot of the time, it was a fight to stay optimistic, even before my mom died a few years ago. My oldest brother, Rafe, helped me as much as he could with the college expenses that scholarships didn't pay for, and as much of a pain in the ass as he can be, I'm grateful to him every single day because I wouldn't be where I am without him. He gave me choices when I didn't think I had any. So. Yeah. Not boring." He cleared his throat. "Really good. Maybe the best investment."

Something about him saying that, about the thread of real, honest emotion in his voice as he said it had been a *fight* to stay optimistic, got to me, and I found myself talking more, spewing stuff I would ordinarily never dream of saying.

Goodman and I were like strangers on a bus, in a way, headed in the same direction only for this one tiny fragment of our life journeys. And his brown eyes were frank and compassionate, making him shockingly easy to talk to.

"I feel bad sometimes that I haven't been around more." I bit my lip. *Shit.* Where had that even come from?

"Yeah?"

I shrugged. "I get back here a couple times a year, but only for a few days at a time. Reed's worse. I don't think he's been back more than a couple times this decade. Webb was the one of us older kids who wanted the orchard —the land, the trees, the legacy. He went to Hannabury College, the same place Porter is now, but he came right back here when he was done. He kept our family together, and he improved the hell out of the place, too," I said proudly.

"What happened with your parents?"

"My dad died eight years ago now, but he'd kinda checked out a few years before that. My mom died when I was nine. Freak aneurism. Dad was devastated. Swore he'd be alone forever. But then the summer before my junior year of high school, he met Cara at the State Fair. She was twenty-two—only six years older than me—and he was forty-five."

"Okay."

"So, she ended up getting pregnant with Porter and moved here, and they got married. Popped out a couple more kids. Dad was thrilled, I think, since he thought he'd save himself the pain of losing another spouse, but life in a town like Little Pippin Hollow is an acquired taste, and she was too young to know what she was signing up for. She bailed when Em was three."

"Damn. That's awful."

"Yeah, kinda. I mean, yes, it sucks. But she deserved to have a chance to be happy, right? And unlike Webb's wife, Cara stayed in touch with all of her kids, she just didn't want to live in Vermont anymore."

Goodman was quiet for a long moment. So long I felt like an idiot for oversharing.

"Anyway—" I began.

But then he said hesitantly, "My dad is obsessed with treasure hunting. When I was a kid, he couldn't keep two dollars in his wallet without investing it in some salvage operation that never panned out. My brother used to say that at least if he'd bought magic beans, we could have eaten them. Sometimes my mom would cry. My oldest brother still hasn't totally forgiven him."

"And you?" I asked gently.

For a minute, there was no sound but the low hum of tires on asphalt.

"No, I don't blame him," he said, like it was a thought he'd been holding for a long time without releasing. "I think we're all just trying to hedge our bets on happiness. Sometimes you just really misunderstand what's gonna get you there."

"Because the answer is triangles," I said lightly, cutting through the tension.

He looked at me sideways, his eyes warm on mine. "*Yes.* Now you get me."

"Now I get you," I agreed softly.

And I did. Sort of. The night before, Goodman had said that we had more in common than I thought, and he was more right than I'd believed possible.

None of which was in any way helpful when I was trying to stay away from him.

Chapter Five

GAGE

"Oh, thank fuck!" I threw myself down on one of the pristine white beds in the two-room hotel suite, arms and legs spread out like a very tired snow angel. "That. Was. Awesome. I'm exhausted."

Knox tossed his keys on the little desk in the living room area with a clatter before appearing in the doorway. "It's eight o'clock."

"So?"

"So, aren't teenagers like yourself supposed to be night owls?"

I lifted my head so he could see me roll my eyes before flopping back down on the bed. Knox had decided we were on friendly-chatty terms now, and that was awesome. I wasn't complaining. Sure, it was a huge step down from what I would rather be doing with him—which would have involved us being a lot more friendly and a lot less chatty—but it was light-years better than the Cold War we'd been engaged in before.

And yet, for some reason, the man had insisted on reminding me ten times an hour all day long that I was *so very young* in a voice that made it sound like an insult. I was officially over it.

"Not when we've woken up at the literal crack of dawn, summoned all our bravery to confront two cows—or, like, a cow and a half—in their natural milieu, put up with some middle-aged dude's incredible ignorance on important life topics as determined by BuzzFeed, single-handedly hunted and gathered a crap ton of tensiometers, seen the birthplace of the American Revolution, eaten our own weight in cannoli, and strolled all the way from Boston Common to Chinatown because that same dude didn't remember where he was going. I might sparkle like a unicorn, but I do occasionally get tired, Knox."

I rubbed a hand idly up and down my stomach over my T-shirt—a retro Godzilla one Fenn had gotten me two Christmases before that was soft from a billion washings. The guy behind the counter at the cannoli place had complimented me on it and then schooled me on all things Godzilla while a line had formed behind me, which I'd found hilarious. It was fun seeing people geek out over something.

"In retrospect, that fourth cannoli on an otherwise empty stomach probably wasn't a great idea." I groaned. "Getting older sucks. When a man finally has the freedom to eat all the cannoli he wants, it's a travesty of justice if his stomach refuses to get on board."

Knox leaned against the doorframe. "Welcome to adulthood," he said wryly. "Where you learn the benefits of self-restraint or pay the consequences."

His voice was extra deep for some reason, so I lifted my head again to see him better. He seemed relaxed enough, with his slouchy posture, but his eyes followed my hand as I made a slow circle from my waistband to my breastbone, almost as if he…

I swallowed hard, acutely aware of the two-inch gap where my shirt had ridden up because I felt Knox's stare linger there. Then his green gaze lifted to mine, and the air in the room went electric in an instant, alive with chaotic possibility like a storm on the horizon.

Holy shit.

Holy shit.

Despite the half second of maybe-attraction I'd gotten from him the day I'd arrived at the orchard, I had not fore-seen this. I'd caught zero sexual energy from him in the last two weeks, and I had for damn sure been looking.

I didn't know what had changed on his end to get us here. But since not a damn thing had changed for me, I knew exactly where I wanted us to go.

"They were really good cannoli," I whispered, trying to sound offhanded and probably failing. "Worth it."

I bit my lip and let my pinkie finger catch on the hem of my shirt as my hand continued circling, widening the gap.

Knox glanced down and blinked once, and when his eyes came back to mine, they were molten hot and shim-mery—exactly as they'd been that first day, I realized triumphantly. Everything that could be between us—all the laughter and passion and the gorgeous relief—passed through my brain in a single heartbeat, and then Knox closed his eyes and turned away, shutting it all down.

"I'm going out," he said, heading over to the second bed, which he'd claimed after we'd checked in earlier.

"Out," I repeated stupidly. "Out?"

"While you were busy flirting with Shane, I texted a friend and told him I was in town."

"Shane." I frowned hard, trying to remember flirting with anyone. "Shane?"

"Cannoli guy." Knox extracted a button-down shirt—

one from his extensive collection—from the bag and put it on the bed next to a fresh pair of jeans.

"That wasn't flirting! God. That was just a guy being enthusiastic over his hobby."

He snorted without turning around. "You're delusional."

"Me?" I scoffed. "Me?" I was not the one of us who wanted someone and was pretending I didn't.

Oh. Shit. Maybe I was. Well, damn.

"Stop repeating words. It's annoying." Knox flipped the suitcase lid closed and then hesitated. He half turned, like he wanted to look at me but wouldn't let himself, and darted a glance at the bathroom door.

As if I had a front-row seat inside his head, I knew the precise moment when he decided it would be more awkward to go into the other room to change—like it would make that unguarded moment between us real and un-ignorable—and sure enough, he shucked his shirt and pants in the next second, leaving him wearing nothing but black boxer briefs and acres and acres of gorgeous, freckled skin dusted with light brown hair.

Since Knox had clearly closed the road to Hookup Town, whether he wanted me or not, I tried to pretend I was unaffected by the sight—even as I also contemplated how far up the Creeper Scale I would be if I just took a tiny, quick picture as a memento.

Yes, yes, I know. That would make me a Level 10 Creeper.

So, I tried very hard to memorize the image instead.

Casually.

Not creepily.

Like, Level 5 at most.

But when he bent over to pull on his new jeans and his

underwear pulled tight over the globes of his truly majestic ass, I couldn't help sucking in a quick breath.

Knox paused with his pants halfway up his broad thighs and did that half-turn thing again, but he recovered fast and worked his jeans up the rest of the way.

Yes, I said *worked*. Because these were not just jeans, they were fuck-me jeans, and apparently Knox had a pair, too.

Fucking. *Fuck*.

"So, um, where are you and your fuck buddy going?" I asked when the silence started to feel oppressive.

Knox shrugged into his shirt and finally turned his head in my direction, though he still didn't meet my eyes. He did not correct my interpretation of *friend*. "Myles said we'd hit up a bar in his neighborhood first. Then... who knows."

"Ah." I was pretty sure I knew what came after the bar, and it made my stomach hurt in a way that had nothing to do with the cannoli.

I was so stupid.

When we'd been walking down Long Wharf by the harbor earlier—just to say I'd seen it—I'd been a little shocked at how that choppy, green-gray water was in any way connected to the clear turquoise waters around Whispering Key. It was like it had gotten a total makeover on its way north and turned itself into something different. Something full of potential and secrets.

But the truth was, it was still *water*, no matter where it was. Still a couple of hydrogens and an oxygen. Still salty as fuck. Just like I was still the same geeky guy who'd left Whispering Key because there hadn't been anything for me there, because I hadn't fit... and lo and behold, I still didn't.

Which just meant I had to try harder to get over this crush. Or try *at all*.

I put my feet flat on the bed and pushed myself backward until I was propped up on the pillows, and then I took out my phone.

A second after I opened my app, my phone trilled with a tap from a guy called Diccrater, and I snorted. A guy named uNoUwanna sent me an unsolicited picture of an erect penis that I was 97.64 percent sure wasn't his, and I made a gagging sound.

"What?" Knox demanded. "Is it someone from back hom—I mean, the Hollow?"

I shook my head. "Nah." I scrolled past a guy named Blue4You and shook my head. "These names. Sweet Gay Jesus. If a guy calls himself Diccrater, does that mean he wants to rate my dick? Or like... he wants to put his dick in my crater? Because either way, I am *not* turned on. Wait until *after* I click your picture to try to play mind games with me, thanks."

"Is that right, LumberjackLuvr?" Knox mocked, and then he froze.

My eyes flew to his in shock and more than a little horror. "You know my profile name?"

Knox finished buttoning his shirt so *efficiently* he almost seemed angry. "Yes. So? Was it a secret? If I open the app, I can't help but see you on my Nearby page since you're practically on top of me at all times— I mean..." He paused and swallowed. "You know what I mean."

"You saw my dick pics?" I demanded.

"What? You don't have any—" He closed his eyes and sucked in a breath as he saw how neatly he'd fallen into my trap.

"You clicked on it," I accused. "You clicked my profile."

"Curiosity." He waved a hand and tucked his shirt into his jeans, though a flush climbed high on his cheekbones. "And I saw nothing I haven't seen before, since you waltz around with your abs on display constantly."

"Constantly? *Constantly?*"

"Why, Jesus?" he demanded of the hotel's popcorn ceiling. "Why, if I'm forced to spend time with this man-child, must he also have developed this tendency to repeat himself? Is it because I teased Webb yesterday? Is it payback for the sandwich rectangles?"

"Don't try to be cute." I sat up straighter and swung my feet onto the floor. "Here I was, attempting valiantly not to be a creeper—or, like, not an *excessive* creeper," I corrected, "while I watched you changing, and meanwhile, you've been looking at pictures of me on Grindr!"

"I… you were watching me change?" He sounded bewildered.

"Of course! Jesus Christ. Your mouthwatering ass was perched there, two feet from my face, defying fucking gravity, and as you keep reminding me, *I'm twenty-four.* Do that math, Knox." I shook my head. "But I was trying to play it cool, since you weren't interested." I paused, eyes narrowed. "Right?"

"What? No. Or… yes?" He looked exasperated. "Learn to structure a question, for God's sake." Knox ran one big hand through his hair. "You and I are… we're colleagues, Goodman. Sort of. So this is not a discussion that we should even be having. And aside from all that—"

I coughed, "*Bullshit.*"

"Aside from all that," he repeated—and he was right, people repeating themselves *was* annoying—"there's a significant age difference between us, and with that comes a significant gap in experience. Nothing will ever happen between us because I'd be taking advantage of your youth, and I—"

I burst out laughing. "Oh my God. You're a walking, talking logical fallacy. Age does not equate to experience, Mr. High Standards, because I have plenty of experience. Like… *plenty*."

Knox's eyes flared, and his jaw worked from side to side for a minute. "I'm not having this conversation," he said at length. "And I am not having sex with you."

I made a squawking noise that would have been embarrassing if I hadn't been too outraged to care. "Who asked you to?" I challenged. "I said I liked looking at your ass. I didn't say I wanted to claim it."

He huffed out a laugh. "No, because you want me to claim *yours*. Not happening."

I put on my pity-face. "Your loss." I jumped off the bed, whipped off my T-shirt, and grabbed my own suitcase from the floor so I could heave it onto the bed.

"What are you doing?" he demanded.

"Seducing you, obviously." I rummaged through the bag until I found a polo shirt and yanked it on, then turned to the mirror and ran a hand through my wavy hair until the mess looked just-fucked instead of fucked-up. "Later." I grabbed my phone and patted my ass pocket to make sure I still had my wallet before heading into the living room.

"You're going out." Knox made the words sound half-questioning and half-accusing.

"Ding ding ding. Don't wait up. Oh!" I wrinkled my nose. "And don't bring anyone back here to fuck, okay? It'd just be awkward with four of us here."

"Where are you going?" he asked as I wrenched open the door.

"A bar first." I grinned, quoting his own words back at him. "And then who knows?"

I realized pretty quickly that there were several problems with my plan for "I'll show Knox how fuckable I am" vengeance sex.

For one thing, though the number of available Grindr gays in Boston was exponentially higher than anywhere I'd ever lived, that just made weeding out the weirdos that much more time-consuming. By the time I'd had my second drink in the hotel lobby—and, yes, watched Knox walk out the front door of the hotel, because I was a sap like that—I'd decided that Grindr was not for me. Not in this town. Not at this juncture. I was going to have to do things the old-fashioned way.

So, I'd googled "gay clubs Boston," picked the top search choice, and called a ride share, but before we'd left the curb, my driver, Nazim, had taken one look at me and pronounced that I was "way, way underdressed, sweetie" for Club Giraffe. Instead, he'd suggested a gay bar in Dorchester called Bar-Z, which sounded far away—much further than Knox would have gone—which was about the time I realized that vengeance sex required Knox not only to know I was having the sex, but to *care*, and neither of those things would be true.

"Yeah, sure, wherever," I'd agreed half-heartedly.

And that was how I'd ended up at a place that was less of a raucous hookup spot and more like a laid-back Irish bar with a DJ—one who knew how to use a mic, thank God—who spun increasingly up-tempo songs for the folks on the nearly empty dance floor. I perched my ass on a stool next to a slightly heavyset, very drunk, bearded man named John, whose roommate Teagan had broken his heart by receiving love texts from *another* guy named John, except first-John didn't get how Teagan could have feelings for other-John when Teagan spent all his waking hours with first-John, and Teagan should know first-John loved him even if he'd never spoken the words and even if other-John was the one who'd written him love texts, and... well, by that point I'd been working on my fourth drink of the evening, and I probably looked like that meme of Zach Galifianakis counting cards, but I nodded along very seriously.

The best way to deal with the shit state of your own sex life was to worry about someone else's, and I believed that sincerely.

"Have you tried talking to Teagan?" I suggested when he finally wound down. "I mean, I'm no expert on relationships since I've never had one, but I think I'd want someone to spell things out for me. Loudly. In tiny words that are impossible to misinterpret. Like, 'I want to fuck you over the kitchen counter, Teagan, because you're the hottest thing I've ever seen,'" I nearly yelled in demonstration, making heads swivel in my direction.

John snickered, then sighed. "Yeah, but... I was afraid of losing our friendship."

More quietly, I continued. "But you kinda lost it anyway, if he's with other-John now. And it's better to be honest about what you're feeling."

"Maybe."

"*Definitely*," I said with the confidence of four heavily poured gin and tonics. "Better that than having someone be all 'lemme give you this look that's so hot it's like my eyeballs are made of molten green glass and then accuse you of being an immature *teenager* who wants things he shouldn't want.'"

I signaled the bartender for another round.

"Men are assholes," John said loyally, even though he had no idea what I was talking about.

"Men are assholes," I agreed, proving that I really did have a repetition problem *and* that I was rather inebriated.

John nodded vehemently for two beats, and then his eyes got suspiciously shiny, and he sniffled a little. "Except they're not always, though, are they?"

I deflated. "Sometimes not," I admitted, thinking of Knox opening up about his family on the car ride from Vermont and his happy-go-lucky smile in that picture on the orchard website. "They're like cows that way, when you think about it. They lure you in, then *bam*. Murdered. Cold as ice."

"You're a little odd," said John after a beat. "Would you like to dance?"

I was about to tell him I refused to be the only person out on the floor, but when I turned my head and looked—whoa, those strobe lights were *something*, huh? And when had they turned off the overhead lights?—it had gotten surprisingly full while I'd been talking with John.

Besides which, John was kind of cute with his lumber-jack-adjacent vibe, and I felt like we were besties now.

"Sure." I stood up and swayed a little, which was a sign I needed to slam back my fifth gin and tonic and then suck on the lime for good measure. "Let's go."

It had been a minute since I'd been drunk on the dance floor, and I'd forgotten how much fun it could be. The press of sweaty shirtless bodies against mine, the flashing lights, the loud beat of the music that pounded through me like a primal heartbeat.

It turned out John was a really good dancer. His hips swayed against mine in perfect tempo, but he didn't try to get handsy at all, which was great since I didn't want him that way, and it was easy to let my mind float away on the rhythm to a place where I wasn't thinking about the future, or my career, or the dizzying array of life choices in front of me and how badly I could fuck everything up.

"Oh, my God," John cried in a panic, grabbing my arm hard enough to hurt and startling me out of my happy drift. "Don't look over there. No! I said *don't* look! That's *Teagan*."

"How am I supposed to know who I'm not supposed to look at, John?"

"Oh. Right. Redhead, navy shirt, and *hoooly fuck*, he's heading this way! I don't want him to see me." John attempted to hide himself behind my considerably smaller frame.

"Dude, he's looking right at you. Why are you hiding?"

"Because he must be here with John," John moaned, which made the calculus in my brain start up again. "This is going to be awful."

"It's going to be fine—" I began, but then suddenly the redhead was right in front of me, peering around me to see John's head buried between my shoulder blades.

"Hey! You must be John's roommate Teagan!" I said super enthusiastically.

Teagan's eyes flashed to mine for half a distracted second. "Yeah. John, are you—?"

I elbowed John lightly, and he straightened up and gave Teagan a bright smile.

"Teagan, hey! I didn't see you there!" John leaned against my side, which was dangerous since I wasn't feeling a whole lot steadier than he was, and draped his arm around my shoulder. "This is Gay."

"Gage," I corrected.

"Are you sure?"

I nodded. "Entirely."

"Gage," he agreed. He squeezed me against him more tightly. "He's my new boyfriend."

"I'm what?" I demanded.

"He's what?" Teagan demanded.

"John," I began, shaking my head, but Teagan interrupted.

"Did you get him drunk on purpose?" Teagan's angry voice was loud enough that people around us began backing away. "Are you trying to take advantage of him?"

"What? No! *No, no, no.* God, no. He and I just m—"

"Goodman," a voice way too close to my ear said. "What the hell are you doing?"

Jesus. Christ. Of all the gin-and-tonic joints in all the world…

I suddenly understood why Knox talked to God so much, because I was having a very strong urge to ask the laser lights in the rafters *why me?*

"Knox!" I plastered on a bright smile as I turned. "Hey! Meet John! I'm… He's… We're… boyfriends!" My voice was a little strangled and breathless with what I hoped sounded like excitement. "So you should probably go back to whatever—*whoever*—you were doing. Where *is* Myles?"

"Myles had a work emergency."

"Aw." I grinned. "How sad. No fuck buddy for you."

Knox shrugged. "We'll see each other again in a couple of weeks. So you finally caught a lumberjack." His nostrils flared. "And you're *boyfriends*, are you? Here I thought you were a master of the Grindr hookup."

"John! You were on Grindr?" Teagan looked like he couldn't decide whether to vomit or punch me. "You said you weren't doing that anymore. You pinky promised!"

"I…" John, on the other hand, looked miserable. "It's…"

"We didn't meet on Grindr. We met at the bar earlier tonight. The specifics are all a blur," I lied smoothly. Semismoothly. Probably not at all smoothly. "But we're very committed. Aren't we, honey bear?" I hooked my arm through John's.

"Committed," he agreed sadly.

"Goodman, what's John's last name?" Knox demanded because he was an asshole like that.

I rolled my eyes. "John and I were *dancing* before you rudely interrupted us. Come on." I nudged John and half dragged him a few feet into the crowd before I hissed, "*Boyfriends?*"

"I panicked," he whispered back. "God, did you see T's face? Did he look upset? He looked upset, didn't he?"

What was upsetting was the way I hadn't noticed any damn thing about Teagan after Knox showed up.

"We're dancing," I informed John. "We can have a shocking breakup at the end of the night." I swayed my hips to the beat and grabbed John's hands in mine to make him do the same.

"Yeah, okay. And it's Curran, by the way. My last name," he explained when I peered at him blankly.

Oh.

The music was still good, and the rhythm was still infectious, so I tried to get lost in it... but as was always the case when I tried really hard to do something, it became kind of impossible. One part of my brain was very centered on Knox, wondering why he was here, at this random bar. And more pertinently, why he was angry at me.

I glanced back at the last place I saw him and nearly jumped out of my skin when I realized he was right next to me on the dance floor... and that he was dancing with Teagan.

The two of them were... okay, they were kind of beautiful together. Teagan was short and sort of lithe, and his navy blue crop top showed off his lean stomach. He lifted his arms in the air and swayed his hips in a way that made his thick red hair fall over one eye like a curtain. Knox braced one hand on Teagan's hip and moved in time with him, incredibly graceful for someone so big, and every movement made his ass flex in those tight, tight jeans.

"Spin me," I told John impulsively. Anything to distract me from this show.

John did better than that. He grabbed my hand and spun me so my back was to his chest, then put his other hand on my hip and held me that way, not quite grinding, but almost.

I flicked a glance at Knox to see if he'd noticed and found him looking right at me. God damn, the way his eyes glowed in the purple club lights was so unfair.

He pulled Teagan closer, front to front, so that Teagan had to brace his hands on Knox's big, broad shoulders.

Mother. Fucker. I had a very brief but satisfying vision of ripping Teagan's hands off his arms, which was concerning since I wasn't normally prone to violence. Once again, I blamed my uncharacteristic behavior on Knox the Cranky Lumberjack.

I bent over slightly, hoping John would get the message and go along with it, and he did, pulling me more tightly against him and moving his hips in a simulated grind. It was approximately as sexy as dancing with a chair, but I didn't care as long as it looked good, and the way Teagan's eyes flashed as he stared pointedly at all the places John and I touched suggested that it *did*.

It also suggested that, despite whatever fuckery had transpired with other-John, this John was very much the John that Teagan was invested in.

John pulled me upright, put his face in my neck like he

was biting me or something, and said, "What the fuck are we doing right now?"

"Go with it," I told him. I lifted my arm over my head to wrap around the back of his neck and whispered in his ear, "Teagan is giving us jealous eyeballs, dude. I think you misunderstood some shit."

"Yeah? Well, your friend looks like he's thinking about where to dump my body."

And the crazy thing was… John was right. Knox did look faintly murderous. Though I was pretty sure it was aimed at me more than John, which figured.

The dance floor got more crowded, pushing everyone closer together, and suddenly I was grinding on John right next to Teagan, which was uncomfortable on many levels.

Teagan went up on his tiptoes and wrapped his arm around Knox's neck.

"Oh, oops!" I said as I knocked Teagan with my hip. "My bad."

He glared daggers at me and very deliberately ran his hand through Knox's hair.

I sucked in a breath and spun around to face John. "Dip me."

"Dip you? Do I look like Fred Asta— Oh, *Jesus*," he exclaimed and hurried to brace me with his hands as I wrapped my arms around his neck and force-dipped myself nearly into a backbend.

It was approximately the least sexy thing I'd ever done. My brother Beale had been trying to get me to do yoga for years, but I hadn't practiced *nearly* enough. When John lifted me back up, though, our whole bodies were aligned from chest to pelvis, and some random dude yelled, "Get a room!" which in my drunken brain meant I was winning.

At least, I thought that until I looked over and saw that Knox and Teagan had nearly stopped moving. Knox's hand was on Teagan's waist, Teagan's hands were fisted on Knox's shoulders, and their cheeks were pressed together. And whatever Knox was whispering made Teagan's eyes slide shut as he bit his lip.

Shit. I felt nauseous. All the euphoria and competitiveness I'd felt drained out of me, leaving me empty. I moved and swayed, but I couldn't even feel the rhythm. Knox was going to kiss him. Knox was…

Suddenly, John let go of me. "Sorry, Gage, but I've gotta—" He broke off with a shake of his head, then reached over and grabbed Teagan's wrist where it rested on Knox's shoulder.

"T, can I speak to you please? Right now? Outside?"

Teagan's eyes opened, and for a second it looked like he was going to refuse, but then he looked away and nodded almost imperceptibly. Knox gave him a wink and let him go.

For a moment we just stood there, Knox and me, not dancing, not talking, just staring at each other. His green eyes were stormy. Wary.

And even though I knew for a fact that it was stupid—ridiculous, pathetic, hopeless, and maybe legit uncool since he'd said he wasn't interested—I took a step toward him and slowly brought my hand up to his cheek, ghosting my fingers over the softness of his beard.

I waited for him to push me away. To step back. For his eyes to shutter as he shut me down. I knew I was risking my job and our tentative almost-friendship for a solitary moment of connection. But if this was how it all ended, how my all-consuming crush went down in flames for the final time, at least I was going out in a blaze of glory, and I was okay with that.

Except… he didn't step back.

In fact, he stepped forward. Right into my space. Right

into my embrace. And he settled both hands on my hips like he'd been waiting all night—or maybe even longer—to do just that.

I leaned back a little so we could maintain eye contact and lifted my other hand to his face also.

Knox lifted one eyebrow.

"What? I like the beard," I whispered defensively, stroking his face with my fingers. And there was no way he could have heard me over the music, but his fingers tightened on my hips, and he pulled me in closer anyway.

He trailed a hand up my arm to grab my wrist and move it back so I was clutching his neck. He spun me around in a quarter turn, and suddenly we were dancing again, the two of us like a tiny, perfect island in a sea of bodies.

Unlike with John, though, there was nothing platonic about this dancing. My cock was hard even before Knox widened his stance and pulled me against his thigh. And when I felt his erection—a very proportionately sized erection, which was to say *huge*—I couldn't help but moan.

He wanted me. He un-misinterpret-ably wanted me.

Yes, fucking yes, I thought, and I only realized I'd said it out loud when Knox's eyes flared and his hand dipped from my hip to the upper curve of my ass.

I undulated my body against his, breathing in his air. His natural scent was overlaid with the faintest tinge of Scotch and sweat and maybe smoke, all of which should have been off-putting but was not. I wanted to climb him like a tree. I wanted to fuck him hard and imprint myself on his brain. I wanted to sit on his…

My thoughts short-circuited as Knox bent his head just the tiniest bit and his lips hovered over mine, so close that his beard tickled my chin. So close that I could feel every particle of air between us buzzing with the electricity we generated together.

Knox was going to kiss me. Knox Sunday was for real going to kiss me. And if I never won another thing in my entire damn life, at least I'd have this.

His mouth touched mine, and my stomach swooped. His tongue darted out to trace the seam of my lips, and I shivered convulsively.

Then Knox blinked and pulled back. "You taste like lime," he growled.

"Yeah. Gin and tonic." I grinned up at him, but he frowned. Did he have a problem with citrus fruits?

He pulled back just slightly, though his arms remained around me. "How many gin and tonics?"

What? He wanted to talk about this *now*? "Um... four. No, five? I'm pretty sure. Plus a couple at the hotel, but that was ages ago. Why?"

He closed his eyes and pressed our foreheads together. "Seven drinks." He groaned just a little. "Goodman, what am I going to do with you?"

There were a million answers to that question. A billion. And if Knox had the time, I had the stamina and organizational skills to make sure we did every single one of them.

But before I could express that, my stomach did a funny kind of dance move of its own, and my head spun in a way that had nothing to do with Knox's closeness. "Knox, I think... I maybe don't feel so great?"

"No shit." Knox snorted and wrapped an arm around my waist. "Let's get you home."

Chapter Six

KNOX

"Yeah, if you can resend that invoice tomorrow, I'll be sure it gets paid Thursday," I assured our feed vendor, making a note on my calendar to follow up in the morning. "I apologize for the misunderstanding. Things have been a little crazy here the last few months. I've been wading through a backlog of receipts, and—"

A flash of movement caught my eye, and I looked up to find Goodman standing behind his desk with his arms stretched toward the ceiling in a Sun Salutation. The move made his T-shirt ride up and his shorts ride so far down they barely caught on his lean hip bones and revealed the thick black band of his boxers.

I adjusted myself surreptitiously under my desk.

Goodman had gotten incredibly fond of yoga in the four days since we'd been back from Boston. These days, he stretched constantly—leaning over couches and countertops to stretch his lower back, bracing himself on doorframes to stretch his pecs, lunging up the stairs to our shared apartment when I was right behind him so he could "stretch his quads."

And for a twenty-four-year-old, the man was a mess of aches and pains, from the trapezius muscles he'd asked me to knead in the kitchen Sunday morning to his "old hamstring injury" flare-up—which, in a weird anatomical twist, was located in the *front* of Goodman's thigh, though most humans kept their hamstrings in the back.

He'd also developed a strange insecurity about his clothing. He'd asked me at least three times to check the fit of his T-shirts over his shoulders, he'd begged me to tell him my *honest* opinion about the way his ass looked in his tight jeans, and—my personal favorite—he'd made me solemnly swear to give him "friendly erection checks" on a daily basis to make sure I couldn't see a dick print in the loose basketball shorts he wore around the apartment so he didn't "make you uncomfortable, Knox."

Seriously.

From a guy with a degree in applied mathematics, you'd expect at least a subtle nod toward logic in his attempts to drive me insane, but no.

I knew exactly what Goodman was up to. This was payback for putting his drunk ass to bed *alone* Thursday night after his gin-tastic hurl into a trash can outside Bar-Z and then leaving him to wake up alone while I'd grabbed a very quick cup of coffee with Rick, who'd been way too distracted by some problem at the office ("Nothing you need to worry about, Knox! You're on leave, for fuck's sake") to actually tell me how things were going.

Did knowing it was payback mean that I could stop my eyes from tracking every single movement Goodman made as he dipped into a Downward Dog or stop my dick from responding to it? Did it mean that I hadn't jerked off liter-ally every single night since then, thinking about Good-man's eyes on me as I'd changed clothes at the hotel and the feel of his body undulating against mine on the dance floor?

That would be a solid no. Goodman was un-ignorable, and reciting all Dr. Travers's mantras couldn't change that.

I knew because I'd tried.

The good news was, all the orgasms were working better than any medication ever had to help me sleep. Five or six hours at a stretch made me feel like a new man. I hadn't thought about the situation at Bormon Klein Jacovic much at all since we'd gotten back either, which had probably helped, too.

"Knox?" the voice in my ear said.

Fuck.

I squeezed my pen more tightly in my hand. "Sorry, Wayne. I was just contemplating that backlog of receipts and feeling sorry for myself." I forced a laugh. "I appreciate your patience and your continuing to supply the hay despite the mix-up."

"No worries, Knox. You know we've been supplying Sunday Orchard since your dad's dad was running the place. My wife can't get enough of Webb's heirloom apples. Let me know if I can help with anything."

Goodman let out a restrained groan as he bent over and touched his toes—facing away from me, naturally, so I had a prime view of his ass—and I had the bizarre urge to laugh.

Well, Wayne, since you asked… what would you advise me to do when my extremely young but painfully sexy officemate and roommate wants me to have sex with him, which is a thing I also want, but which feels irresponsible for reasons that are probably incredibly important even though I forget them whenever he walks in the room?

"Yeah, I'll do that," I told him, averting my eyes from Goodman's luscious ass once more.

"Good to have you back, Knox."

"Good to be back," I replied automatically.

But as I disconnected the call, I realized that the words weren't just polite; they were kind of true. I was kind of enjoying my time at the orchard. More than I had at first, anyway.

I felt good. Truly calm. I hadn't had even a fluttering of a panic attack in a couple of weeks. I wasn't foolish enough to think I'd never have another one, but I was definitely getting better.

And even though Goodman was the bane of my existence—and I was still almost positive I wasn't going to sleep with him—his open, cheerful nature made life fun. I couldn't remember the last time I'd woken up interested to see what the day held like I had recently.

"*Hnghhhhhhhhh,*" Goodman moaned, lifting his flip-flopped foot onto the edge of the desk and leaning his body weight into his leg.

I wasn't sure what *that* move was supposed to stretch… besides my self-control.

"Y'okay, Goodman?" I demanded without looking at him. I shuffled some papers on my desk and grabbed one at random so I could pretend to be making crucially important notes.

"Yeah, no, I'm great. Never better." His eyebrow twitched. "I actually got a huge chunk of the scheduling software customized this morning, and Webb is thrilled. But for some reason, my muscles just feel so… *hnghhhhh*… so very, very *tight* these days."

"Dehydration from last week?" I suggested sweetly.

"What? No!" His outrage was adorable. "I wasn't even hungover."

"You sure? 'Cause you vomited a lot. Like, a *lot,*" I lied. "I wasn't sure someone could puke that much and live."

Goodman let his foot fall to the floor. "It's not dehydration." He sounded sulky, and I felt the urge to laugh bubble up in my throat.

"Maybe it's the change of seasons, then," I said mildly. "Gammy Sunday used to be a slave to her arthritis, especially when she was underdressed. She used to wear a scarf religiously come fall, and she swore by her raw-onion liniment recipe. I think Webb might have some of Gammy's liniment in the cow barn if you're interested."

"I'd literally rather die." He jumped to his feet and began pacing the length of our front-to-front desks. His gorgeous, bare, golden-tanned legs ate up the short distance.

"Or you could put on warmer clothes, maybe." I tugged at the drawstring of my Hannabury College hoodie. "Protect yourself from the chill. Maybe a blanket for your lap. Maybe not wearing shorts when it's fifty degrees, or—"

Goodman rolled my chair back from my desk and inserted himself in the space he'd created, his bare knee an inch away from my jean-clad one. "Why don't you want to fuck me?" he demanded.

I blinked. *God damn.* Was he actually asking me that flat out? "Goodman—"

"Don't do that. Don't *Goodman* me. Look, I told myself it'd be fine if you weren't interested in me. Plenty of people aren't. But then the other night at the club, you and I danced, and it… you… We kissed, Knox," he blurted. "You kissed me. I didn't imagine that." He frowned. "Wait, I didn't imagine that, did I?"

"No," I agreed softly. "You didn't imagine that."

"And you were *hard*," he accused.

I sighed. "I was."

"And you were jealous of John."

I rolled my eyes. "Did I tell you about the text I got

from Teagan? About what happened between the two of them?"

"Yes. And stop trying to change the subject."

I tapped my pen against my thigh. "Yes. I was jealous."

"So, then…?"

It was hard to think clearly when he was so close, so warm, and smelling so damn good.

I slid my chair back further and stood up. "Come with me up to the Pond Orchard," I said impulsively. "Gil suggested regrading the access road out there this year, but Webb's hoping we can get away with just another load of gravel until after next year's harvest. I told him I'd give him my opinion."

"But…"

"Please, Goodman."

"Are there cows up there?"

He wasn't nearly as afraid of cows as he'd once been. I was pretty sure he and Diana were besties. But I couldn't tease him about it anymore.

After all, my attraction to Gage scared the shit out of me every bit as powerfully and irrationally as cows scared him, so who was I to judge?

"Not a single bovine. I promise."

"Yeah." He sighed lustily, waving an arm. "Yeah, okay, fine."

We didn't speak a word as we walked to the big garage on the far side of the farmhouse, got one of the 4x4s, and headed up the long access road that led to the orchards at the rear of the property.

The sky was the perfect blue that only ever happened in Vermont in autumn, and the hardwood trees were a riot of color as we bounced up the road. I went faster than I needed to, mostly for the thrill of it but partly to see the way Goodman's eyes sparkled as the wind whipped his hair and T-shirt. Only when we crested the rise that overlooked the farm did I slow down a little.

"Is this still Sunday Orchard?" Goodman asked. "We've been driving for miles."

"More like half a mile as the crow flies, though the road is loopy. The original place was just over three hundred acres, and my parents added another hundred seventy when they married. Not all of it's cultivated—a good bit of it is wooded. I'm not sure how much of the place you've seen so far—"

Goodman counted off on his fingers. "The barn, the farmhouse, the U-pick areas, the pumpkin patch, and the area near the road that the elementary school manages for the kids' science classes."

I nodded. "Yeah, all that's the front half of the property. The public areas. Back here, there's a larger orchard that Webb leased out to a company that makes organic juices." I pointed to the northeast. "And our little Christmas tree farm down that way near the red barn." I pointed left.

"Wait, is that orange building over there a house?" He leaned in close so he could peer over my shoulder, and I definitely did not sniff the beachy, saltwater scent of him. "Does someone live out here?"

"It's a house," I confirmed. "Growing up, we used to call it the Pumpkin House. My grandfather's brother raised his family there, but it fell out of use for a few decades. Then my dad fixed it up when Webb and Amanda got married, and they lived there when Aiden was a baby, but it's been empty again for a few years now since Webb moved back to the farmhouse. Sunday Orchard has a few old houses like that on it. Houses for the second and third sons. The ones who didn't inherit," I explained when Goodman looked at me curiously. "Up until my dad's time, all the land passed to the oldest boy."

"That's not fair."

"Sure, but necessary. If my great-great-great-grandfather hadn't done it that way, by now the Sunday Orchard would be a hundred one-tree plots, each managed by a different great-great-great grandchild. Things just run more efficiently when there's one person in charge."

Goodman pondered this for a moment. "But you're the oldest son."

"Mmm. True," I agreed. "But Webb was always more interested in the orchard than I was. The science of it, the magic of it. So I told my dad a long time ago that he should leave the place to Webb. It's still not a totally fair solution. I mean, four of our siblings didn't get a say in the matter at all. But this is the way that kept everything together best and made sure all of them had a home. With Webb."

Goodman blinked at me, a curiously soft expression on his face like he was thinking thoughts about me.

I hurriedly continued. "It's not like the second and third sons were banished. Plenty of them stayed on and raised their families here over the years. But *their* kids didn't have a reason to stay, so most of them followed the jobs to the city, and these houses were abandoned. Nobody wants to live out this far."

Goodman snorted. "Yeah, right. You've heard of agricultural tourism, haven't you? I bet there are thousands of people right now who want to spend a weekend working in the crisp autumn air, picking apples for free."

I frowned. I hadn't thought of that. I wondered if Webb had.

"Anyway, through those trees to the left, you can see

Pond Pond, so called that because it's a pond that was owned by my mother's family. The Ponds."

He snorted. "Of course it was."

"Over on the far side of that hill, past the Sunday Christmas tree farm and the road to town, there's another body of water called Pond Lake, for maximum confusion. And the meadow next to it is called—"

"Pond Meadow?"

"It's like you've lived here all your life, Goodman." I let out the brake and got us moving again.

"Small towns, man." He shook his head and grinned. "The next island over from the island I grew up on is called— Well, never mind. Suffice it to say, you'd need to see it to believe it, but I'm down with the weird names."

I wanted to ask him about it. I wanted to hear all his stories, or just to hear him talk about nothing at all—which made me remember a moment not far back when I'd thought I'd rather be smacked in the face repeatedly than ask Goodman to talk to me. That had certainly changed.

But what hadn't changed was that I *shouldn't* want it. Couldn't afford to want it. I had a job to go back to, a life in the city, that definitely didn't include an over-inquisitive, way-too-sexy, underdressed Goodman.

I cleared my throat. "So. This orchard up ahead, Pond Orchard, is kinda special. A few years ago—or, *shit*, must be going on ten years now—Webb started grafting antique apples from scionwood. That's what you call the twigs of the apple trees that you graft into the existing trees," I explained. "Webb has some Rhode Island Greenings, and Hubbardston Nonesuches, and my personal favorite, the Westfield Seek-No-Furthers."

The front tire of the 4x4 hit a deep rut in the road and launched us into the air a little. Goodman braced a hand on my shoulder to keep his head from hitting the roof.

"I vote for regrading the road," he said.

"Mmm, I'm not sold. It'll cost a ton, and worse than that, it'll be disruptive."

"Know what's disruptive, Knox? Decapitation."

I snorted. Christ, the man was funny.

I also noticed that his hand lingered on my shoulder, tracing over the muscles there. It felt way too pleasant.

I moved to the side of the road, shut off the engine, and stepped out onto the gravel. "Come check out the graftings."

Goodman sighed again as his hand slipped off me and thunked his head back against the headrest. "I would be a lot more excited about this if I didn't think you *actually* intended to show me *actual* graftings."

"Pardon?"

"Nothing. Coming, O Bearded One." He got out and folded his arms, nearly hugging himself when a chilly breeze blew across the mountain. "Fuck, it's cold. How is it this cold when it's still only September?"

"Because we're in Vermont," I reminded him. "Where autumn is generally a time when we put *more* clothing on our bodies, not less—"

"Yes, yes. Show me your graftings so we can get back indoors." He waved a hand imperiously.

Despite his words, he seemed content to stroll slowly down the neatly mowed grass paths between the rows of apple trees with me as I pointed out the various neatly labeled branches Webb had grafted onto the trees over time and explained grafting techniques and why it was so important to preserve these heirloom varietals. I even picked him a Seek-No-Further so he could try it.

After a first reluctant bite—literally the first time I'd ever seen him look dubiously at food—Goodman ate the rest with relish.

"Oh my God," he groaned. "It's tiny, but it's tart, and it gets sweeter as I eat it. It's really good."

"Right? The legend goes that two hundred years ago, a gentleman farmer in Western Massachusetts was looking to add trees to his orchard. He wasn't satisfied with the yields of the trees he had, though, and he wasn't convinced that his apples were the tastiest either. So, he wrote to friends all over the Northeast and offered an exchange: a bushel of their best apples for a bushel of his. People from all over sent him options."

"And this is the one he picked?"

"No. This is the one he was already growing." I grinned. "Can you imagine? He collected all these apples from all over the place and decided he liked his own the best, so he'd Seek No Further. But he wouldn't have known that unless he'd tried them all, right? That's the moral of the story."

I threw the remnants of my apple core into the shrubbery on the edge of the orchard.

Goodman licked apple juice from his lips and frowned. "Look, this is all fascinating, Knox—and, surprisingly, I really mean that—but I'm freezing my ass off out here, and my testicles have climbed up into my spleen." He threw his apple core after mine and shoved his hands in his shorts pockets. "It's become clear that you didn't bring me out here to ravish me." He darted a hopeful glance sideways at me. "Unless this is all some kind of weird apple foreplay? Because I could get on board with that." He clasped his hands under his chin. "Fuck me under the Rhode Island Whatjamacallits, Knox Sunday!"

"Yeah, no," I said with way too much reluctance. "That's not gonna happen. I'm very physically attracted to you, Goodman. You know that. But it's complicated. You work here, and—"

"And you think I can't keep things casual? We've been over this, Knox," he groaned, walking backward so he could face me. "Dude, I'm not looking to become your next of kin here. I don't want you to make me promises. I just want to fuck around. To have *fun*. To relieve this tension between us. To someday have a funny story I can tell my friends about the time a hot lumberjack fucked me against a tree so thoroughly that I'd get spontaneous erections anytime I ate applesauce after that. It doesn't have to be complicated."

I shook my head stubbornly. "We work together. We eat dinner together daily. That *makes* it complicated, because I'm going to see you across the office every day. And I'm not in a position to offer you or *anyone* a relationship yet."

"Yet?"

Figured he'd caught that.

"Or maybe ever. I dunno. I've never been a relationship person. But then Webb said something at lunch the other day, and I started thinking…" I hesitated. "It's conceivable that at an unspecified time in the future I could want one. And on that potential future someday, I could see myself picking one of the guys I've fucked around with to be something more… you know. Permanent. But that time hasn't come. It might never come. And I don't want you to get hurt."

"Pick someone," Gage said slowly. "*Pick* them. Like… like they're fruit in the orchard of life and you can just reach up and grab it? Like love is an ice cream flavor and you just point to the one that looks tasty? Like love doesn't just happen, you just… pick?"

"Why not? It's logical. It's convenient. It's smart."

"We—you and me being together—that's convenient and smart. Heck, I *like* you, Knox Sunday, even when

128

you're a grumpy asshole. I prefer to bottom, but I can get toppy if that's what you're into, I can deep-throat like a champion, and… Okay, now it sounds like I'm reciting some kind of sexual resume, and that's just weird." He fluttered his eyelashes at me. "Look, I told you I'd help you find a hookup, right? It just turns out that the perfect candidate was closer than you thought. Pick me, Knox. Just… pick me."

It would be so easy to give in. To lick the tart apple flavor from those dark pink lips, to slip my hands into that too-messy hair and hold him exactly where I wanted him, to take the light and happiness of him in my arms.

But then what?

The sad truth was that I didn't trust my own brain anymore. I didn't trust my judgment. I didn't trust myself not to overreact to stress and collapse on a sidewalk. I didn't trust myself to not make a stupid rash decision, like the one that had led me back to Vermont and landed me in an even bigger mess with my family that I still had to fix before it was time to move back to Boston. And I sure as hell didn't trust that I was feeling some kind of way about this gorgeous, wild, inappropriate man-child, when I'd never felt such overwhelming feelings for all the entirely appropriate people I'd dated in the past.

And, for the first time in—God, maybe *ever?*—I didn't want *myself* to get hurt. I'd never been as instantly, powerfully, against-my-will attracted to someone as I'd been to Gage Goodman. The terrifying truth was, if he and I were fuck buddies and then stopped, I wasn't sure *I* could handle seeing him across the desk from me and not want to fuck him. I couldn't handle him trying it on with me and then leaving to go live his big life.

The only way to stop that was to never set off down that path.

It was right to be cautious. It *was*.

I looked away, and the words felt like they were being dredged up from the deepest part of me. "I can't."

Goodman deflated. "I swear to God, if you tell me one more time this is because I'm your 'employee' or because you'd be taking advantage of my innocent, naive little ass, even though my ass hasn't been innocent since sophomore year of high school—"

"No," I said, a little more sharply than I'd intended because I was remembering the way he and John had slid together on the dance floor, all sweaty and breathless. Because I knew that saying no to him meant that he'd be saying yes to some other lucky bastard sooner than later. "No. It's me, okay? I couldn't handle it."

"Ugh." He turned around so he was walking— stomping—beside me. "Because I don't score highly enough on your compatibility checklist."

"No. Stop putting words in my mouth. I like you, too, Goodman, even when you're a relentlessly cheerful muppet. We're just…" I ran a hand through my hair. "We're at different places in our lives. You were telling me all about your ideal job while we were driving the other day, remember? And then you started applying for positions in New York and Chicago—"

"And Boston," he confirmed with a nod. "While you're gonna be here at the orchard. So?"

"So, I…" I swallowed the urge to disagree about my future plans—to tell him I'd be going back to work in the city—and I told myself that an omission wasn't a lie, exactly. "You should be focusing on the future. You're here for only another few weeks. And meanwhile, I have so much shit on my plate, this face is in the dictionary next to the word 'obligation.'" I squeezed my own chin lightly. "So. Yeah. That's why, even though it's not what I *want* exactly, and even though the other night was the most turned on I've ever been while fully clothed, it can't happen again."

Goodman opened his mouth like he wanted to argue, but then he shook his head. "Okay, then," he said in a small, disappointed voice. "I don't agree with you. In fact, I strongly disagree. I think we could have the hottest, most satisfying sex ever and that your face is actually in the dictionary next to the words 'pointless self-denial,' but whatever. I respect your decision. I appreciate you explaining it. Good luck finding another candidate as enthusiastic as me, but if you do——"

I rolled my eyes. "There are no other candidates right now."

"——I suggest you don't drag them out into the tree fields and subject them to hypothermia before you condemn them to a fuckless existence." He sighed lavishly, and even though I was so frustrated I could scream, he made me feel like laughing, too.

"God, you're such a drama queen." I stuck my hands in my pockets, mirroring him, so I wouldn't be tempted to reach for him. To comfort him. Or *myself*.

"I feel foolish," he admitted. "I thought you just maybe needed me to be clear that I wanted you even when I wasn't drunk, so I've been throwing myself at you the past few days, while you…" He broke off. "Anyway. Sorry."

"No!" I felt weirdly heartbroken. Like he was the one putting a stop to things, not me. "Goodman, no. I…" I stopped myself, literally biting my tongue against the urge to tell him that I'd felt exactly what he felt. Maybe more. "It's *fine*. I promise. A gorgeous twenty-something guy being attracted to me is the most validating thing I've experienced since *I* was a twenty-something guy. Believe it."

"I appreciate you being cool about it, but seriously,

sorry for the lack of clothing and the, um…" He looked up at a puffy cloud ambling across the sky, clearly embarrassed. "The massages. And the erection checks. *Jesus*. And the yoga."

"Come on. Do *not* apologize for that stuff. Especially the yoga." I knocked my arm into his. "I kept waiting for you to bend yourself into a shape you couldn't get out of. The anticipation was what got me out of bed this morning."

Goodman snort-laughed, then darted me a searching look. "So we're good, you and me?" he asked.

"Yes. We're great. We're… friends. At least I hope we are."

He nodded down at the ground, then shivered again as a stiff breeze shook the leaves on the trees.

I took off my sweatshirt and dropped it over his head.

"Hey!" he squawked.

"Friends don't let friends lose their testicles to frostbite," I said casually, pretending I didn't notice the way my shirt fell nearly to the backs of his thighs.

Pretending I didn't love it.

Pretending that the *right* thing was also the *easy* thing.

"Thanks, Knox." Goodman laughed. "My testicles appreciate your friendship."

I knocked my arm into his again. "You want my no-sexual-innuendos lecture now or later?"

"You're adorable, pretending I have a choice," he mused. "You're dying to speechify me, Knox. You're fully engorged with annoyance and thrumming with the need to lecture me… to lecture me *hard*. You're turgid with the desire to pound all those words right into my tiny, tight little—"

I burst out laughing. "Christ, you are such a shit. Who uses the word turgid?"

"I do," he said, grinning smugly. "If you're feeling tense, you might try some yoga stretches. I could show you my forward bend—"

I grabbed for him, but he leaped away, laughing.

And then my cell phone rang with a call from Webb... and neither one of us felt much like smiling after that.

Chapter Seven

GAGE

I'd learned back when my mom died that nothing brings a small community together like a tragedy.

But until the Tuesday afternoon that Aiden Sunday went missing, I hadn't realized how a community could completely mobilize itself so that every man, woman, and child was actively pulling together to help one another. It was kind of a beautiful thing— or at least it *would* have been, if everyone hadn't been too sick to their stomachs with worry to really appreciate it.

My hands shook as I measured out coffee grounds for the tenth pot of coffee I'd brewed in the past five hours. The Sundays' happy kitchen had become a mini command center—a place where family members, law enforcement officers, and the entire boys' and girls' soccer teams had stopped by for snacks and to coordinate search efforts, while Drew, Marco, Knox, and a few others manned the phones, trying to find someone who'd seen Aiden since school let out.

At least two kids were absolutely positive that Aiden had been on the bus home that day but couldn't remember what he'd been wearing or whether they'd spoken to him.

Mac, the bus driver, was slightly less sure. "I think I remember stopping at the end of the driveway like every day," he'd said when he'd come by earlier, his face drawn and haggard-looking. "But every day's a little like the day before, isn't it? And I got so many kids I drive… I couldn't swear to it. I'm sorry, Webb."

Webb had stormed out then without saying a word, and I understood why. I felt bad for Mac, and I didn't blame him, but I also couldn't imagine how anyone could spend a minute with Aiden and not see that he was special. The boy's infectious smile and mini-adult brain that had made me like him immediately—he was sweet and earnest and confident and happy, and I wanted to be like him when I grew up.

Hawk walked in the back door to the Sundays' kitchen just as I flipped the switch to get the coffee brewing, and he knelt to scratch Sally Ann's head. The old dog had been keeping vigil on the braided rug by the back door all evening, not interested in food or attention, like she sensed that something was wrong. That someone was missing.

"Barns and paddocks are completely clear, including the haylofts," Hawk announced. "Chicken coop, too, not that I thought he'd be there. Gift shop was closed up, but I checked there anyway, just in case. The sheriff's got a dozen people on 4x4s checking the orchards." He ran a hand over his face, looking impossibly young. "I don't know what to do next… but there has to be something."

"I'm sure there is. Sit down and wait for the guys to get off the phone," I instructed, pushing him toward the table. "Refuel for a second, and we'll figure it out. Coffee or tea?"

"Tea," he said tiredly. "Thanks, Gage."

"Sure." In truth, I was glad I had some task to

perform. I'd be more of a liability than a help when it came to actively searching for him since I didn't know the area as well as everyone else, but this was something I could do.

"No, Miss Ethel, Aiden hasn't run away," Drew said loudly, his voice brittle and strained. "He's missing, which is different. Yes, I'm positive… Oh, yes, I remember the stories about Carl Justis from years ago, but that was— Uh-huh. No, it was a very different thing. Yes, of course Webb's extremely worried. Yes, he called Sheriff Carver right away when we realized Aiden hadn't— Yes, ma'am, I've heard that the first forty-eight hours are the most important. I've watched *Law & Order: SVU*, too. No, Aiden doesn't have a cell phone. He's six. Why in the world would he? No, thank you, we do not need you to crochet us a prayer shawl," he said impatiently. "Yes, I'll keep you posted. But when you call Betty Ann and the rest of the Little Pippin Hookers, please tell them to call us or the police directly if they've seen anything, okay? Alrighty, then."

"*Ugh,*" he pronounced as he jabbed the button to disconnect the call. "That woman, I swear. But all the octogenarians, busybodies, and fiber artists in the area have been alerted now. Helena Fortnum and Norm Avery sent messages to all the artists and the farmers in the Little Pippin Vendor Co-op respectively. And Emma texted that she's already hit up the library, Scoops, and Wing Factory, and she alerted all the moms she babysits for, who're spreading the word, too. No one's seen him in town. Which is *good,*" he said mostly to himself. He looked at Marco. "It *is* good. Right?"

"Sure, honey. Tells us he's around here somewhere. Poor kid took a nap in a loft or built a fort someplace, and he's gonna wake up and wonder what all the fuss was about." Marco leaned over and patted Drew's shoulder sympathetically, then nudged a plate of banana bread at him that some kind soul had dropped by earlier. "Eat, old man. You need fuel just like Hawk does."

Drew wrinkled his nose, which was maybe the only time I'd ever seen him turn down a baked good since he enjoyed them as much as I did. "I'll fuel up when Aiden gets home." He pushed himself up from the table and looked toward the pantry cupboard. "Do I have pretzels for Sunday Sundaes? I should get some——"

"Marco's right. You should eat," I suggested, bringing him a cup of yerba maté when I brought Hawk his tea. "That way you can be alert and steady and ready to make sundaes when he's home. Do you want banana bread? Or I could make you a sandwich?"

Drew grunted but sat back down and took a piece of the bread.

"Aiden's not at the McMahons' house." Knox tossed his phone down on the kitchen table and scrubbed two hands through his thick hair so forcefully that his biceps strained against the fabric of his flannel shirt.

"Should we call Reed?" Marco asked. "Your brother's got friends who are politicians, right? Maybe he knows an FBI agent, too."

"Maybe," Knox agreed unenthusiastically. "But let's keep that in our pockets for now. Goodman, any luck getting the student contact list from the school principal? I've run through the list of classmates Webb could remember."

"Yeah. I couldn't get in touch with Ms. Oliver. She left town right after school for some family thing. But I got a hold of Luke Williams, Aiden's teacher, a couple minutes ago, and he's emailing me his class list. He also said he thinks we should 'check with Aiden's mom.'" I looked from him to Drew and then to Hawk. "Does she live around here?"

"Nah. She hasn't been back in town for ages," Drew said.

Knox winced and squeezed his eyes shut.

"What aren't you telling me?" Drew's eyes narrowed.

"She texted Webb a few days ago," Knox admitted. "Thursday morning, I guess. She wanted to see Aiden, Webb said no. Repeatedly. But as far as I know, that was the end of it."

"Good," Hawk said with uncharacteristic venom in his soft voice. "She's toxic sludge. And don't get me started on her boyfriend." He shuddered.

"No kidding. But why didn't Webb tell the rest of us?" Drew demanded.

"Why didn't I tell you what?" Webb demanded. He strode in the back door with Jack right behind him, bringing in the cold night air on their jackets.

"That Amanda's back in town." Hawk folded his arms over his chest.

Webb stopped short, and his eyes flew to Knox's accusingly. "She's *not*. And what's she got to do with anything?"

"I brought her up," I said. "Luke Williams suggested talking to Aiden's mom—"

Webb's eyes flashed with anger. "Yeah? What the fuck does Aiden's teacher know about it, Goodman? Amanda texted that she was passing through last week, I told her I didn't want her here, she argued, I held firm, and she finally said 'whatever.' Last I heard, she was headed to Vegas for the weekend, okay?" he snapped.

"Yeah, okay." I held up my hands in surrender.

Knox stood up from the table and moved to stand in front of me. "Webb, I know you're in hell right now, but don't yell at Goodman. He hasn't done a damn thing but try to help."

I bit my lip against a groan. It was nice of Knox to defend me, but I almost wished he wouldn't. I'd been too consumed with worry to fully process my disappointment from our conversation in the orchard, and my brain still reacted to this unexpected behavior with, "*Fuck. Yes. Hot. Grr.*" when I knew it should be, "Oh. Nice. Friend. Kind."

I'd heard all the words he'd said about us only being physically compatible and not all-the-other-ways compatible, and blah blah, so I was for sure not gonna throw myself at him anymore, but it was hard to really understand his position when he was so very much exactly what I was looking for.

Hot. Funny as heck. Smart. Occasionally really, exceptionally kind. And, it must be repeated even though this was the worst time for my traitorous brain to remind me... *hot.*

Webb blew out a breath and deflated. "Yeah. Sorry, Gage. That wasn't about you."

Jack clapped him on the shoulder from behind and gave me a small, distracted smile. "I'm sure Gage understands you're not at your best right now."

"Of course I do," I said.

"Come on and sit down," Jack said.

Webb let himself be guided to the table and pushed into a seat across from Hawk while Jack took the seat between him and Knox.

I brought Webb a mug of fresh coffee, and he looked up at me with a devastated expression. "I really am sorry, Gage. I just..." His normally stoic face crumpled, and his eyes went shiny. "I just don't know where my boy could be. And it's cold and dark out there. Rand says—that's Sheriff

Carver—he says they, ah…" He broke off with a shake of his head and stared down at the mug in his hands.

"He said if they don't get any leads in the next hour or so, they're going to get the boats out and look up at the pond," Jack finished quietly. "I think that's unnecessary, 'cause Aiden's too smart to go up there on his own, but—" He glanced at Webb and shrugged.

"But now that he's brought it up, it'll give Webb peace of mind to eliminate that possibility," Hawk said firmly.

Jack looked at him fondly and nodded. "How're you holding up, Bird?"

"Me?" Hawk shrugged. "Oh, I'm… fine. Worried."

Jack gave him a look that said he knew Hawk was feeling something closer to terror, but he didn't call him on it.

Jack bumped Knox's arm with his own, just the way Knox had done to me in the orchard. "How about you, big guy? You hanging in there?"

Knox looked surprised to be asked. "Yeah." He pushed a hand through his hair. "Just wish there was more I could do."

"You're doing it." He grasped Knox's shoulder and shook it. "It's good that you're here."

His hand lingered on Knox's shoulder for a beat longer than strictly necessary—and heck yes, I noticed. I was pretty sure Hawk did, too, since his eyes caught on Jack's hand and stuck there—and it reminded me how just a week ago at dinner, right at this very table, Webb had teased Knox about setting him up with Jack.

At the time, I hadn't thought a thing about it except maybe, "Good luck to Jack dealing with the cranky lumberjack." Now, though, I was feeling all proprietary about Knox's shoulders and contemplating hand-ripping violence for the second time in a week.

This was ridiculous. *I* was ridiculous.

So ridiculously besotted by this man, with his bottle-green eyes and his sly humor that I'd started thinking of him as *my* cranky lumberjack.

I'd never been a jealous person, and of all the people to start being jealous over, I'd picked a guy who was insanely attractive and not at all interested in me. If I started ripping the hands off every guy who wanted Knox, I'd have a trophy collection to rival any serial killer, and I *still* wouldn't be any closer to finding someone in Vermont who could help me get over my sexual frustration.

Besides which, Jack was probably exactly the kind of person Knox *should* end up with. Jack had seemed friendly and fun the couple of times I'd been to the diner. He was in his early or maybe mid-thirties. He owned his own business and was settled in Little Pippin Hollow. He probably wasn't the sort of person to drink too many gin and tonics, or if he did, he'd handle them without vomiting in front of Knox. He wouldn't talk and talk and *talk* endlessly or throw himself at someone who wasn't interested in him sexually. He probably had his own opinions on efficient dishwashing, and he and Knox could have thrilling discussions about the best ways to fold socks or whatever. Maybe he was precisely the right sort of person to put that happy-go-lucky smile back on Knox's face.

I cleared my throat and forced myself to look away. "I just forwarded you that list of classmates, Knox."

"Thanks, Goodman. I'll get started on that." Knox picked up his phone again.

"And I guess I'll text Amanda, just in case," said Webb, with the same enthusiasm one might use when volunteering to remove their own appendix.

Sally Ann lifted herself off the rug by the door and

shook herself, making her tags jingle. She gave a single bark and then whined at the door.

"You need to go out, baby girl? Poor thing's probably worried, too." Marco sighed, preparing to push himself up from the table, but I held up a hand.

"I've got it," I said quickly. "I could use the fresh air."

I opened the door for the dog and followed her out onto the porch and down the steps to the yard. The evening air was cool against my overheated cheeks. Every exterior light was on, and the visitor parking area was filled with searchers' cars. Past the barn, down in the largest of the U-pick orchards, I could see lights and movement as the police officers searched. But the area immediately around the house was silent. Peaceful.

I stuffed my hands into my sweatshirt pockets—*Knox*'s sweatshirt pockets—and took a deep breath. The air smelled like woodsmoke and apples, which had become really familiar and comforting over the past week or so.

Where the hell was Aiden?

"What's this? We gonna tour the yard?" I asked Sally Ann. She was usually happy to do her business on the grass behind the house, but tonight she seemed to want to stroll the perimeter, trotting a little ways up the drive and over to the gravel parking area before circling back to me, like she wanted to make sure I was following. "Guess you didn't get enough exercise today, huh?"

I followed along after her because I'd heard Webb talking about the coyotes in the area a couple of nights before, and the last thing the Sundays needed was something else to worry about.

"Hey! Slow down!" I called as Sally Ann sped up past the fence where the cows grazed and headed toward the gift shop barn. "If you lead me to the cows, I'm letting them have you first. You hear me? I will not be trampled for your amusement, Sally Ann."

A familiar childish giggle filled the quiet air, and I froze, looking around at all the places where shadows congregated.

"Aiden," I called quietly, my heart beating crazily as I wondered if maybe I was going crazy.

A soft, sad "Yeah" came back, and my heart beat even faster for a whole other reason.

I followed the sound—and Sally Ann's running feet—past the gift shop barn to the outside stairs that led to my barn-apartment, and then up. Aiden was perched on the top step, clutching his backpack, his face full of Sally Ann's fur.

"Oh, holy sh—*shoot*." I was so relieved, I pressed a hand to my chest to keep my heart from bursting out of my rib cage. I stopped two steps away and scooted the dog out of the way so I could touch the boy's knee, just to reassure myself he was really there. "Aiden! Dude, are you okay? Everyone is looking for you."

"I'm okay," he whispered. He tilted his head up so I could see his face in the spotlight, and I saw that his eyes were big and frightened. "Am I in trouble?"

"No," I said immediately. "No way. Everyone is gonna be so *glad*, buddy. But where did you go? You didn't come home after school, and your Uncle Drew freaked—"

"My mom was there," he whispered, wide-eyed like he still couldn't believe it. "I haven't seen her in months and months—only because she lived far away for her job and couldn't come back to see me. But when I was about to get on the bus, her car was parked right there in front of the school, and she got out and hugged me. She wanted to hang out with me, Gage. Just like she said on the phone."

"On the phone?" I knew Aiden didn't have a phone… but I was pretty sure Sunday Orchard had a landline.

He squirmed a bit in discomfort. "Yeah? She, um… she called me one time when I was home sick. And then, um… she maybe told me which days to pretend I was sick so I could be home to talk to her," he finished in a whisper.

"Ah." That explained his constant stomachaches.

I tried not to look as angry as I felt and to remember that Webb's ex-wife had a story in all this, too, but encouraging a kid to lie to their parent… *Ugh.*

"What happened today?" I prompted. "After she showed up."

"Well." Aiden's words tumbled over themselves in his excitement. "Mr. Williams was worried and said we should call Dad, but Ms. Oliver said it was fine. So we left! And my mom let me ride up front in her car without a booster because she said I was plenty tall enough, and we went for pizza, and she said I was so much smarter and more grown-up than I'd been last time she saw me, and she let me order a sundae that wasn't on the kids' menu and drink as many sodas as I want. She told me about her new house, too! It has a big giant pool and a room that can be *my* room, and I can decorate it however I want, and I told her about my science fair project you're helping me with, and she said she was so proud, and…" He took a deep breath and seemed to run out of steam all at once. "I didn't call Dad. I didn't know how without making her mad."

I closed my eyes and grimaced. Yeah, I was definitely not feeling positive thoughts for Aiden's mother.

"When she dropped me off, Mom said Dad was gonna be upset at me for not coming home because he's jealous of Mom and doesn't love her anymore and because he's an unreasonable… um." He winced. "Bad word. So I came up here because I was thinking maybe I could live with you and Uncle Knox until he calms down." Aiden hesitated. "Dad yelled at me the other morning, remember? I didn't like it."

I shook my head wordlessly. I was completely unqualified to give Aiden any answers, and I didn't envy Webb *any* of the shit he was about to have to deal with. "I think the only thing you have to worry about is your dad squeezing you so tight your head pops off." I ruffled his hair and held out a hand. "Come see."

Three hours later, I finally padded down the farmhouse stairs and through the darkened living room to the kitchen.

Aiden had begged me to stay with him until he fell asleep—which was adorable but kind of odd, since at least five of his relatives, including Webb, were keeping watch in the kitchen, and I would have imagined he'd have picked one of them.

Webb had made it clear he hadn't been angry at Aiden at all. What he *had* been was devastated, and guilty, and so furious at his ex-wife and everyone at the elementary school who hadn't stopped Aiden from going with Amanda —though, from what I understood, this was technically allowed under their custody agreement so long as Amanda gave "proper notice" to Webb, which she had not—that Jack had taken Webb's phone away to stop him from yelling anymore.

"She didn't notify me," I'd heard him whisper to Jack, sounding tormented. "The school didn't notify me. And Aiden didn't have a phone. Am I supposed to put a GPS tracker on my kid now? What if she just forgets him someplace?"

By the time I'd glanced up from the fantasy book about

warrior mages I'd been reading aloud—one of my favorites from when I was a kid—and saw that Aiden was asleep, the farmhouse had fallen silent, and it seemed like everyone was in bed.

But when I got to the kitchen, I found Webb sitting in the same spot where he'd sat earlier with his head in his hand, looking like a man with the weight of the world on his shoulders.

"Webb?" I said softly.

"Huh?" His head jerked up in alarm. "Does Aiden need me?"

"No, not right now. He's out cold."

"Oh." He settled back down.

"Where's Knox?"

"I don't know. He took off about the time Aiden was conning you into eating sundaes with him, and I called him after you went up to read Aiden his story, but he hasn't answered." He chuckled softly. "I wanna say I don't have the brain space to worry about him right now, but that would be a lie. Not that anyone will let me help them, anyway."

I shifted uncomfortably. I almost wanted to apologize for being the person Aiden had wanted to put him to bed. "Can I get you anything before I go? A snack or tea or…?"

"Absolutely not. You've done enough for this family today, Gage," Webb said, his voice friendly but kind of empty, like the night had hollowed him out. He sat up straighter. "Being an emotional support human for a bunch of Sundays was not what I had in mind when I offered you this job. Not what you had in mind when you took it either, I bet."

"This is a great job," I said firmly. "With an amazing family that's been nothing but welcoming and wonderful. There's nowhere else I'd rather be."

I was a little bit startled to realize this was absolutely true. No matter what happened with Knox, I was glad I was there.

"Plus," I added slyly, "I'm getting a really generous salary, don't forget."

Webb's mouth pulled up at one corner. "For forty hours a week of actual work. Add in another thirty of attending charity dances, babysitting my kid, volunteering in the jam kitchen when Brenda hurt her wrist, helping with Aiden's science project, running the cash register at the U-pick last Sunday, and dealing with the occasional child abduction," he said grimly, "and you're the biggest bargain ever. Next time I need our systems upgraded, I'll try to be more honest about what someone can expect while working here."

Next time. My heart twisted just a tiny bit at that idea, even though obviously he was right. It was the beginning of October already. In just a couple of months, I'd have moved on, and they'd have moved on from me, too.

Knox would remember me as that ridiculous child who'd bugged him for a few weeks one autumn. And I... hell, I'd be too busy in the city to remember him at all by then.

Wouldn't I?

"I like the Hollow, even though I keep seeing the signs for violet fudge and I'm not sure where to buy it. I like the roads with their fourteen billion scenic overlooks. Rand Carver is the friendliest police officer ever. Your pal Jack is..." *A handsy bastard who needs to keep his paws off my lumberjack.* "...lovely. Really lovely. And Ms. Fortnum is terrifying in the best way. Any programmer would be lucky to live here." I hesitated. "Though you might want to clarify a bit about the proximity to *cows.*"

Webb snickered and rubbed a hand over his tired

eyes. "I'm heading to bed. I'll lock up behind you." He stood and clapped a hand on my shoulder as I headed toward the door. "I'm gonna be sad to see you go, but when you're ready to move on from the Hollow, you know I'm gonna give you a hell of a reference, right? You're a good man, Gage. Thanks for being someone my kid can trust."

Oh, wow. I sucked in a breath and tried not to look as stunned as I felt, but in my whole life, I wasn't sure anyone had ever said anything like that to me. Taken me seriously that way.

I had one older brother who was competent and in charge and another older brother who was the sweetest human to ever exist. They were both taller and stronger and funnier than me. People counted on them for things all the time.

My only gift was being more tech savvy than most people, and on an island with terrible internet and spotty cell service, that hadn't been particularly useful. It had made me stick out rather than fit in. Somehow here in the Hollow, where the cows outnumbered the humans—a terrifying reality I pondered almost every day—I felt more useful than I ever had at home.

"Don't thank me. I've never been so popular in my whole life as I am with Aiden," I said, which was true. "Thanks for letting your kid chill with me."

"I heard you two are winning the science fair with some robotic dog-treat dispenser."

"I'm afraid I can't discuss the specifics while the patents are still pending, Webb," I said archly.

He laughed.

"Hey," I added impulsively, "if you ever need to talk—"

"Thanks, Gage, but I'll be okay. If you need an impossible task, try getting my brother to talk. Good luck with that."

But it turned out I didn't need luck at all, because when I got back to the apartment, Knox was sitting on the sofa, deep in a bottle of vodka and ready to chat up a storm.

"See this?" he called in lieu of greeting before I'd even closed the door. "This bottle was a gift from Bormon Klein Jacovic. A get-well present. Because what every person with mental health issues needs is top-shelf vodka, right?" He snickered. "Grab another glass from the kitchen, Goodman, and let's toast to oblivious coworkers and to mothers who kidnap their own children."

Wow. *Okay, then.* Not just chatty but drunk-chatty.

And unhappily drunk-chatty, at that.

I approached with caution.

"None for me, thanks. Still dehydrated from last week, remember?" But I took a seat on the far side of the couch and hitched up my knee to face him. "I guess this answers the question of where you disappeared to, huh? Webb was worried. And what do you mean 'mental health issues'?" I added belatedly.

"No one told you?" Knox's green eyes were a little unfocused but not totally glassy. Buzzed, then, not drunk. "I get panic attacks. The stress of my life in Boston was too much for me, or so my doctor says." He rolled his eyes. "But all is well with me now that I ran home to Vermont, so Webb doesn't need to worry. *All is well with me.* You know, I've repeated that phrase often enough, it almost felt true? At least, it did this morning."

"Okay," I said lightly, like my heart wasn't squeezing at the pain in his voice. "I guess that explains the health issues Webb mentioned when I first got here. He never specified."

Knox snorted. "He didn't specify, and you didn't push for an explanation? That's not like you."

I got that he meant the comment mockingly, but he was right. It wasn't like me. "I didn't really think about it." I frowned. "I guess maybe because you seemed so healthy. My bad. Is there something I can do to help? My college roommate took meds for his anxiety, and it really made a *huge* difference. Meditation helped, too. And therapy. And I know it's almost a joke between us, but yoga—"

He huffed out a laugh. "Yeah, no yoga for me, thanks. My therapist suggested reciting mantras, and I do that sometimes. I wanted medication, but he said I'd need to be monitored for side effects and do *weekly* talk therapy, too." Knox wrinkled his nose, and his bright green eyes were almost vulnerable as they met mine.

"And you… don't want to do weekly therapy?"

"It seems…" He hesitated. "Excessive."

"Does it, though?" I peered at him. "Therapy is a perfectly normal, healthy, *responsible* thing to do. There's zero shame in needing mental health—"

"Yes, I know," Knox said in a voice that said he absolutely did not know, or maybe that he believed it was true for *other* people but not for himself.

I sighed. "You think it makes you weak to talk about your feelings?"

"No! Not at all. I just…" His mouth firmed and he shook his head once. "It does no good to dwell on negative shit. You've gotta push through. Keep looking forward. Remember people are counting on you. You know?" He sipped his drink. "That's a life lesson for you, Goodman. Free of charge."

"Wow." I leaned my head on my hand. "That advice is worth about as much as I paid for it."

Knox didn't seem to notice my sarcasm. "So, I turned

down the meds, and Dr. Travers said another option was to remove the stressors from my life temporarily." He spread his hands wide, like it was plain to see which option he'd chosen. "And lo and behold, I haven't had a full-on attack in weeks." He curled in on himself again and stared morosely down at the glass in his hand. "Until tonight."

"Yeah?" I tilted my cheek against the back of the sofa and watched him. The golden glow of lamplight caressed his beard the way I wished I could. "You should've said something. *All* of us were worried about Aiden, Knox."

He shook his head. "I was holding it together fine until Aiden came home. But then…" He swirled the liquor in his glass but didn't continue.

"Did the relief throw you for a loop?"

"Not exactly. The thought occurred to me that this could have happened while I was in Boston. Webb might not even have called me. I wouldn't have been able to help. And this whole terrifying possible scenario where Aiden was hurt played out on an endless loop in my brain, and my chest got tight, and I…" He cleared his throat. "It took half an hour to talk myself down, but I'm good now."

God, the man was so sweet. And so frustrating.

"That sounds awful. I wish you'd told me or someone else. I wish you hadn't gone through that alone. But those intrusive thoughts are something you could, you know, *talk to your therapist* about. You don't have to white-knuckle your way to being okay, Knox. In fact, I don't think you can. Wasting your time trying is inefficient," I teased gently.

Knox shrugged. "I'll mention it next time we do a telehealth visit. It doesn't matter, though. I *was* here, Aiden is fine, all is well," he recited. "And I'm gonna make sure it doesn't happen again." He finished his drink and winced at the burn. "Webb needs a lawyer. He can't afford it, and he doesn't want to accept my help to pay for it, but good lawyers aren't cheap, and I need him to have the best. Whoever represented him during his divorce must operate their law practice out of the back of a Ford Pinto, because Amanda cleaned Webb out financially *and* he didn't even get sole custody of Aiden."

"How are you going to make him change his mind about you giving him the money, then?"

"I'll reason with him. *Strongly.*" He shrugged. "Webb's my younger brother."

"Oh, Lord. What does that mean?"

Knox's sideways grin was a little bit wry, a little bit mischievous. Not quite his happy-go-lucky smile, but one that made my heart pound nevertheless. "It means I'll do whatever it takes to make sure he and Aiden are okay."

Seriously, *so* sweet. And so goddamn frustrating.

"Whether Webb likes it or not? And yet you think that *Webb* should simply stop worrying about *you?*" I sighed. "You are the biggest of all big brothers. It's a two-way worry-street, Knox."

I fetched him a bottle of cold water before coming back to prod at his beefy shoulder until he stood. "Plan your strategy tomorrow, Genghis Khan," I instructed. "For now, sleep."

I followed him to his room and set the water bottle on his little nightstand. "You need anything else? Puke bucket? Bedtime story? I've got one about a warrior mage that'll knock your socks off."

Knox sat on the edge of his bed, ran a hand through his thick, dark hair, and looked up at me solemnly. "You know, all this was so much easier when I told myself I didn't like you."

"Yeah?" I set my hands on my hips, torn between decking him and kissing the life out of him. I didn't have to ask what *all this* was. I knew because I felt it, too. "You want me to start ignoring you again? 'Cause I can do that for you."

And I meant it. I was so fucking annoyed at the big lummox for denying us what we both wanted that if he'd said yes, I vowed I'd ignore him so powerfully he would fucking *glow like nuclear waste* from the force of it. I would ignore him so loudly his ears would ring, and he'd get no rest by night or by day. Legends would be told about the magnificence of my ignoring.

But instead, he shook his head slowly and said in a soft and totally un-Knox-like voice, "Nah. I don't think I could make myself believe it anymore. I don't think I believed it then. Night, Goodman."

Ugh. What kind of utter asshole took away a man's anger by saying something sweet like that?

I wanted to punish him for it. I wanted to push him down on the bed and do unspeakable things to his lumberjacky body. I wanted to bite his incredible ass like it was a damn Westfield Seek-No-Further and taste the salt of his skin on my tongue. I wanted to reach out a hand to his face like I had at the club just a few days before to erase the serious little pucker between his eyebrows. I wanted to curl up beside him and rest.

Instead, I clenched my hands into fists and stuffed my fists into my pockets, vowing to give him the space he said he wanted.

"Night, Knox," I said just as softly, and then I turned and fled.

Chapter Eight

KNOX

"Morning, Goodman." I leaned back against the counter in the efficiency kitchen and sipped my coffee as Gage shuffled out of his bedroom. He wore flannel pajama pants, a T-shirt bearing a picture of a beaver above the word "dam," and a pair of heavy woolen socks he'd "borrowed" from me when the first October cold snap had hit.

It had been nearly two weeks since he'd last worn shorts and done his stretches right in front of me, since he'd casually informed me that we would have the hottest, most satisfying sex ever, since he'd last given me a flirtatious look or let his eyes linger on me.

Instead, he now gave me polite but distracted smiles when I joked with him. He'd thrown himself into his work, getting to his desk before I finished helping Webb with chores each weekday morning, and returning to his desk after supper nearly every evening, except for the nights when he helped Aiden with his science project. On Saturday, Gage had let Em talk him into wearing a green Statue of Liberty toga and body paint for some historical society presentation she was running—which I'd naturally had to attend due to my deep love of history and for no other reason—and on Sunday he'd greeted customers in the orchard gift shop like he'd lived here forever and wasn't the closest thing to a tourist himself.

The whole time, he'd been sweet and friendly, not cranky or sulky in the slightest. He'd put his coffee mug directly into the dishwasher each morning without fail. He didn't chatter at me incessantly anymore.

In short, he'd done everything I'd ever asked him to do. Become exactly what I'd wanted him to be.

And I was contradictory enough to miss every single part of the way he'd been before.

"*Mhmmnfh.*" His grunted reply went straight to my dick, but the jaw-cracking yawn that followed made warmth blossom in my chest. His hair stuck up from his head like he'd suffered a terrible electric shock in the night, and his big brown eyes were still mostly shut. I had an almost uncontrollable urge to open my arms wide so he could burrow into me and I could inhale that saltwater scent that seemed to have seeped into his skin, which was so far from what I should want that it shocked me.

I was not a man who'd ever wanted those sorts of things. I felt like Sally Ann, chasing her tail in a circle.

I had become my own biggest problem.

Then again, this was not a huge surprise. There was nothing like waking up at 3:00 a.m. from a vague dream about a tsunami hitting Vermont—still a landlocked state, last time I checked—and not having enough hands to save everyone to really get a man's blood pumping in the morning.

I'd sat on my bed in the dark for long, long moments while my heart pounded out a crazy rhythm, telling myself that *all was well* while counting my breaths—in, hold, out, in, hold, out—feeling the panic threaten to swamp me.

But when I'd finally been able to draw a deep breath, I'd heard Goodman's teasing voice in my head reminding me that it was inefficient to keep trying to white-knuckle my way through my mental health struggles... and that was when I'd finally emailed Dr. Travers about what was going on with me and asked if I could make our telehealth visits more regular.

I was doing better than I had been last spring. I *was*. So much better that it was tempting to believe I didn't have a problem anymore. But it was just possible that I'd be better for real if I took my mental health more seriously and actually engaged rather than doing the bare minimum.

I turned toward the counter and the coffeepot. "I see you need to be jump-started this morning. Coffee?"

"Please." He took a too-big gulp from the mug I handed him and sighed appreciatively. "Mmm. Thanks. Just the right cream-to-sugar ratio."

I rolled my eyes and moved around him to snag my own mug from the counter so I could keep my hands busy. "It's not that hard to achieve when your preferred ratio is ninety percent cream and sugar to ten percent coffee."

"Lies," he squawked before taking another deep gulp. "I'm very badass, and I drink only the highest-octane fuel. *Grr.*"

"If I melted coffee ice cream in a cup, you wouldn't know the difference."

He grinned, marginally more awake. "Okay, you're not entirely wrong. But then, what is life without cream and sugar, Knox?" he mused philosophically.

I took a sip of my black coffee. "Healthier? Simpler? More efficient?"

"Tragic." He pushed his hair back out of his face, and I saw his golden-brown eyes glinting with humor.

I grabbed a towel so I could wipe nonexistent crumbs

off the counter, mostly for an excuse to turn away from him. "Late night?"

"Eh." He seesawed his hand. "Pretty late. Had a breakthrough and almost finished a side project I've been working on, though, so it was worth it."

"Side project?" I abandoned my towel. "Which one?"

"Mm." He swallowed more coffee. "I'll show you guys next week. Speaking of which, any luck getting Webb to take your money?"

"Not yet. Stubborn ass. And short of pretending our distant cousin Rockefeller died and left Webb a lawyer on retainer, I'm out of ideas for now. But I'm gonna keep trying. Has Aiden heard from Amanda again?"

Gage shook his head. "Not that I know of. I reminded him he's got to ask permission from his dad before he goes with her or she could end up in trouble, but who knows if he's listening. I mean, that's his mom." He blew out a breath. "Anyway. Aiden and I ran late last night because we're trying to finish his project so he can bring the prototype to school next week—"

"Prototype." I snorted. "You guys gonna mass-market these? To all the dog owners who don't want to feed their dogs treats by hand?"

"Hey! You never know." Gage took a loaf of bread from the freezer and put two slices in the toaster before leaning a hip against the countertop. "The guy who first sold pre-sliced bread to the masses was laughed at, too. 'Who'd ever want to buy their bread *sliced*, Otto? What a stupid idea, Otto.' *His* genius wasn't recognized either."

I snorted. Only Goodman would know the name of the man who invented sliced bread. Only Goodman could be cute about it.

"I mean, I know it's not life-changing shit," he went on, "but it *is* kinda cool. It dispenses a treat when the dog uses a pressure pad or button. Showing Aiden how to use it to train Sally Ann—or any other dog—is the fun part. I don't need the money, just the inspiration." He extracted a jar of Marco's apple butter from the fridge and a spoon from the drawer.

"Oh, really?" I teased. "We're independently wealthy now, are we, Goodman?"

"Kinda." He shrugged casually as he spooned the sweet mixture onto his bread. "Not like I could buy my own rocket and pretend to be an astronaut, you know? But I can get by."

He stuck the spoon in his mouth and licked it clean so thoroughly and distractingly it took me a second to realize what he said.

"Wait. I thought you said you didn't have a lot growing up."

"True. But our circumstances changed a year or so ago."

I blinked, then blinked some more. "Like you won the lottery or something?"

"Something," he agreed.

New Gage did not volunteer information, and I fucking hated it.

"So are you saying you can afford to invest in tiny projects here and there, or—"

"Could I be sitting on a beach somewhere and never work again?" he asked in a hard voice. "Theoretically, yes, assuming a good rate of return. But I have goals, and—" He broke off with a head shake. "I really hate when people suggest that I shouldn't be motivated to do something just because I have money in the bank. Is money the only reason a person works? How much money do *you* have in the bank? Should we talk about *your* motivations?"

Touché. "You're right. Of course you are. I just

thought…"

I'd thought that he wouldn't understand that. That someone so young and sunshiny couldn't also be serious and goal oriented.

When was I going to stop underestimating him?

Gage folded his toast in half and shoved the piece in his mouth, a signal that the conversation was over, at least for now. "Wonder what Drew's making for breakfast," he asked around the mouthful.

I stifled a smile and shook my head. He and I had discussed his consumption of "Breakfast Appetizers" several times before, and he knew my thoughts. Just like I knew better than to get him started on the supplementary meals he referred to as Breakfast Dessert, Lunch Dessert, Dinner Dessert, and Second Dinner Dessert.

My cell buzzed on the counter, and I grabbed it. "Probably eggs and bacon. It's Satur—*oh*. Hmm." I read the text through twice. "Interesting."

"What is?"

"You remember me mentioning my friend Myles?"

He swallowed his toast with a gulp. "Your fuck buddy."

"My friend with occasional benefits. He's having a party tonight at his apartment in the city, and I'm invited." I glanced up. "He wants you to come along."

"Me." Gage wrinkled his nose. "Me?"

I shot him a look that said *not this repeating thing again*, and he rolled his eyes.

"How does he even know I exist?"

"Because I mentioned you the night I saw him." I'd had a couple of drinks myself that night—though not nearly as much as Goodman—and I vaguely remembered mentioning Gage's name kind of a *lot*.

An embarrassing amount, really.

"You did? What did you say?"

I shrugged casually. "That you were creating an awesome integrated app for Sunday Orchard. That you were looking for a job with a lot of upward mobility and interesting projects you could sink your teeth into." I was pretty sure I'd also used the words *relentlessly sexy* and *infuriatingly adorable* and *so fucking young*. "His company has some job openings, and our other friend Jason is doing the hiring. Jason's going to be at the party tonight, too, so this would be a great opportunity for you to network."

Gage frowned. "But... they haven't seen my resume or anything. How will they know I'm qualified?"

"Jobs are more about who you know than what you know, Goodman. Ask anyone."

"Hmm." He took another huge bite of toast, unconvinced.

"Did I mention that Myles and Jason work for Rubicon?" I asked casually.

"Wu-ba-cawn?" He coughed toast crumbs onto the counter and struggled to swallow his last bite. "I mean, *Rubicon*? As in... as in... the company that creates applications for half the Fortune 500 companies? The one that, along with Seaver Technologies, has been voted the best tech company to work for in Boston for the last five years? The one that won the Safe Transportation grant for improving railway safety *and* won a Stevie for creating the OneUS voter education app?" His voice hummed with excitement.

Whatever the hell a Stevie was.

"Probably? They're a huge company, and the headquarters is in Cambridge. Myles works in finance there, and Jason works the tech side. And if the networking's not enough to convince you, Myles throws great parties, catered by the best restaurants in the North End. Tons of Italian food."

"Damn. You're speaking my love language." Gage bit his lip.

"And there'll be dancing, probably."

I wasn't sure why I was trying so hard to convince him. I didn't particularly want to drive down to Boston again so soon. These last few weekends of the season would be packed at the orchard, and Webb probably needed the extra help. And frankly, I hadn't been in the mood for socializing since last spring.

But for some reason, I wanted to do this for him. I wanted to be the one to help him, even if he didn't really need my help.

"Dancing. So, like." He shot a look at me from under his lashes. "There'll be guys? Good-looking, single men?"

Oh. *Wow.*

No good deed went unpunished, huh?

"I… guess? It's a party, so there'll be all sorts of people. Men, women if you're into that."

"Which you are." He said it as a statement, but the look he gave me made it sound like a question.

"Sometimes," I agreed, though I hadn't been attracted to a woman in… Damn, had it really been *months*?

And double damn, how long had it been since I'd been attracted to anyone but Goodman?

I cleared my throat. "You know, the more I think about it, we don't need to go to this party. I can just ask Jason to—"

"Nah. Let's go."

"What?"

"We should go to the party. I'm game. And we can get separate hotel rooms this time. For privacy."

"Oh." My fingers twitched to touch him. "Yeah. Okay."

Remember he's a billion years younger than you, idiot.

He's barely figured himself out.

He's starting his career, and you're trying to cling to yours.

He's hot, you're horny, that's all this is.

Remember all the reasons you put a stop to this weeks ago.

But the words of reason refused to sink in.

"You can see if Myles or one of your other acceptable fuck buddies is free tonight. Because, I'm telling you as your friend, you totally need to get laid, Knox—" Gage laid a sympathetic hand on my bicep, and it sent a bolt of lust to my balls so sweetly painful I had to grip the counter.

I snorted. He had no idea.

"—and so do I."

Oh.

By the time Gage and I stood on Myles's penthouse balcony that night, I recognized that the enormity of the punishment had fuck all to do with the size of the good deed.

I also regretted that I hadn't tied him to the bed in my hotel room or conveniently lost Myles's address when Gage had shown up at my door in a pair of tight as fuck green trousers, a fitted patterned shirt with the sleeves rolled up, and his hair even more mussed and just-fucked than usual.

If we'd still been doing friendly erection checks, I would have told him honestly that his dick print was very, very visible, and I was extremely uncomfortable.

"You look… nice," I'd gritted out instead, because never let it be said that being almost forty had taken away my awkwardness.

"Yeah? Okay, good. It's thanks to Toby, my almost brother-in-law," he'd explained, running a hand down his shirt over his flat, toned abs. "When I told him what I'd

162

worn out the last time we were in town, he'd immediately FedEx'd me this outfit and a couple more." He'd grinned slyly. *Sexily.* "He says that while he admires the 'youthful insouciance' of my T-shirt collection, wearing them in public makes it impossible to take me seriously. So what do you think?" He'd spun in a circle. "Does this say serious?"

Oh, indeed it did. As in, he was *seriously* sexy, which made me *seriously* horny, *seriously* distracted, and *seriously* jealous.

I had also *seriously* not considered the consequences of taking Goodman and his dick print to a party where a bunch of sex-starved, forty-something jackals would salivate over him like he was filet mignon... until it was too late.

They'd attacked in a pack the moment we arrived, thrusting a drink in my hand and pulling Gage onto the makeshift dance floor until he'd finally begged off to catch his breath. We still hadn't made it out onto the balcony where Jason was, though I'd sent him a text to come and find us.

"So, Gage, you're from Florida? That's *adorable*," my gym friend Rodney purred. "I was in Miami Beach for Pride last month. Maybe next time you could show me around."

"Oh, cool." Gage smiled tentatively. "But Miami's kinda far from—"

"You mean you and your *sugar daddy* were in Miami Beach, Rod," Curt corrected snidely. "How is Gandalf these days? Still suffering from arthritis of the dick? Now, Gage, sweetheart, I was telling you about Madonna's early years—"

"Curtis, you're embarrassing yourself." Dustin shook his head sadly. "Gage doesn't give a shit about Madonna, and at least Rod can *get* a sugar daddy. You might as well get the Louis Vuitton logo stamped under your eyes because that's the only way to make *that* baggage attractive."

Forget Goodman finding a guy to leave the party with. I was afraid he'd get caught in the jackals' mating display and be torn limb from limb.

"He's actually here to see *Jason*," I muttered. "About *business.*"

I watched Jason stroll across the floor, eager for him to arrive… except then he did arrive and immediately greeted Gage with a warm smile and a hand on his upper back and a "Hey, Gage, let's chat about Rubicon outside, where we can hear ourselves think," and I was not a fan of *that* at all.

When they left, the others made outraged squawks and trailed after them, and I debated going, too… But Gage looked back at me and shrugged happily enough, and I refused to be one of the pack of assholes clamoring for his attention anyway, so I forced myself to look away and focus on my drink.

"Evening, handsome," Myles said archly, coming to stand by my side. "I thought you'd never get here."

"We've been here half an hour. You've been busy doing host-y things."

"Remind me to have someone else host next time." He shook his head. "Anyway, what have I missed? Where's this kid you're unofficially headhunting for? And what's your cosmopolitan done to deserve the scowl you're giving it?"

My gaze strayed from my drink to the balcony.

"Oh ho! I see I've been upstaged at my own party. Who's the sweet young thing with the fine ass? Wonder what his face looks li—"

I made a noise of disagreement that possibly sounded like the growl of a feral animal.

"No, wait! Never say that's your infant job applicant? How is it fair for someone to be a technological wunderkind *and* have a rear view like that?" Myles made a *tsk*ing noise and turned his too-knowing gaze back to me. "But I thought you'd decided he was far too young. Since when do we make calf's eyes at hot boys we're not planning on dicking down, Knox?"

"Hey! He's not just a piece of ass, okay? He's smart, too. Sweet." I had no right to sound so defensive, but I couldn't help it. "And a hard worker."

God, I sounded like a lovesick idiot.

"I see." Myles laughed softly. "And have *you* been working him hard? Or just wishing you had?"

I bristled. "Neither. He's too young to know what he wants."

"Dear God. Did you see the look he just sent you?" Myles's laughter was a little harsher than I remembered. "Didn't seem indecisive to me."

"Not the point."

"Yes it is. Don't be that asshole, Knox. When we were young, we knew exactly what we wanted. If you like him, *like him*. Because if you don't take that invitation, someone else will, and you'll regret it."

Like I didn't already know that. Like I hadn't been torturing myself with that knowledge for over a week. My reasons for resisting him were fading before my very eyes.

"I came here tonight to help him find a job," I reminded him. "And also to... to hang out with you."

I tried to make it sound flirty, like I'd been eager to see him.

It came out sounding like an item I wanted to check off a list.

Myles lifted a hand to pat my chest. "Thank you, but no." His eyes danced. "I'm not yet so desperate as to fuck a man while he's thinking about someone else, Knox Sunday."

"What? No. I wouldn't hurt your feelings like that." I hesitated. "Not on purpose."

"Mmm. No. Because you're not cruel, you're just stubborn and criminally oblivious. So why are you hurting *his* feelings by rejecting him?"

I frowned. "It's not like that. He's going to find someone else—"

"But he's already picked you, darling. And before you tell me 'it's not like that' again, let me call your attention to the fact that Jason is talking very excitedly about something over there, yet your infant is glaring at the precise spot where my hand is on your chest. Add *that* into your calculations."

I turned my head to seek out Gage and found that Myles was totally correct. Gage *was* staring, while pretending to listen to what Jason said. I was very familiar with Goodman's "I'm nodding, but I don't actually hear you" expression.

When he caught me looking, Gage looked away guiltily. Sadly. And my heart skipped a beat.

I am in control.

All is well with me.

Oh, who was I kidding? I was nowhere near in control. I was a mess.

"Holy shit. The lust between you two is so strong I'm getting a contact high. Don't be a coward, Knox." Myles shoved the spot on my chest he'd been patting. "Go give that boy the ride of his life, or someone else will."

I hesitated… and Curtis sidled up to Gage and dropped an arm over his shoulder.

Fuck.

I strode across the living room in two seconds, ignoring

Myles's laughter behind me.

The familiar faces around me all seemed so jaded. So bored.

Gage deserved better than anyone he could find at this party. He deserved someone who'd appreciate him… and maybe… maybe I could be that someone for as long as he stayed at the orchard.

My heart pounded as I let myself imagine holding him, kissing him, *having* him.

I gritted my teeth and struggled to figure out what the hell was wrong with me.

For weeks, I'd told myself he wasn't for me. That I could walk away, force myself to stop wanting him, and we'd both move on. But it hadn't worked like that.

And I was forced to acknowledge, right there in the middle of Myles's trendy living room, that *Gage* wasn't the one who was unsure about who he was or what he wanted. He never had been. I was the one who'd been holding back, thinking it would help me stop missing him when our time at the orchard was up…

But instead, I was missing him already, when we could have been spending that time together.

In my head, I heard Dr. Travers saying, "*Befriend the things that scare you, Knox, and you'll stop fearing them.*" I had no fucking clue what that was supposed to mean. But nothing scared me like Goodman did… and fucking sounded close to friendship, right?

"Goodman." I nudged Gage's arm with mine, interrupting Curt. "I need you."

"Sure. Jason and I are done talking business. Are you okay?" He looked at me in concern.

"Yep. Fine. But it turns out you were right about… things. And I wanted to… talk to you. About those… things."

Great. This was going… great.

"I was right about… what?" Gage frowned.

Jesus Christ, did he want me to say it in front of a crowd?

"About *sandwiches*, Goodman. I've decided to embrace the happy triangles."

"E-embrace them?" His eyes widened as under- standing dawned. "Wait, *embrace* them?"

"Mmmhmm. Grab them tight," I expounded. "Put my hands all over them. Lick them. Bite them. Make them mine."

Gage's mouth formed a silent O of surprise like he couldn't think of a damn thing to say.

My friends didn't have that problem.

"Uh. Okay, weirdo." Curt snorted.

"Shut up and have some sympathy, bitch." Rod slapped Curt's arm lightly. "Knox is clearly doing low carb. Been there, done that. Don't worry, Knox. The bread crav- ings go away, and you'll be shredded as fuck in no time."

"Tried that. These cravings aren't going away," I said, staring hard into Gage's eyes. "In fact, the longer I go without them, the worse they get."

"Oh." Gage blushed. "That's… Are you…?"

"Ready to leave?" I supplied. "Yes."

I nodded a goodbye to Jason, who inclined his head and smiled.

"But Gage, you and I were just getting to— Hey!" Curt protested as I pulled Gage away.

Gage chuckled nervously, darting a look at me as we wound our way through the living room. "Okay, your friends are…"

"Assholes?" I suggested.

"No! I'm sure they're lovely when you get to know them. I was gonna say intense. Like, they were arguing about restaurants. Legit *arguing* about them. And dog spas. Rodney says if you can't afford to have a dog sitter watch your dog in your home every day, you shouldn't be allowed to have a dog. But Dustin said that's only true if you want your dog to be an elitist asshat. And things got *tense*. Also, they're very passionate about Mykonos." He wrinkled his nose. "That's in Greece, right?"

I gave him a clipped nod and led him inside to the empty front hall, where I set my drink on a flimsy table and turned to face him. "They love to one-up each other. Ignore them."

"No, it's cool. I'm sure they're really nice. But they're not like you." He winced. "Sorry. Not that you're not nice, just that you're so… *yourself*. Unapologetic and snarky and… honest. And… I'm babbling. So weird. I haven't even had a drink yet."

I wanted to tell him that I'd missed his chatter. That his babbling felt soothing, like water on parched earth. But that seemed a little excessive. He hadn't agreed to anything yet except leaving with me.

I took a step toward him. "I can be competitive in my own way," I said softly. "I like achieving things. Being the best at what I do, because that means I get to be in charge."

Gage took a step back and tried to smile. "Ah. Y-you're the alpha of the pack," he teased. "You don't need to brag, because everyone already knows you're the best. And you don't need to be an asshole because you always…" I crowded his back against the wall, and his voice was a thready whisper as he finished. "…get what you want."

"I don't always get what I want, Goodman." I braced my hands against the wall on either side of him and leaned into his space, taking in a deep lungful of his saltwater scent. Gage's breath rushed out in a startled *whoosh*. I stared into those brown eyes that danced and sparkled and held a million secrets I'd pay money to know. "But maybe sometimes. Maybe tonight, if you'll let me."

His jaw went slack, and he stared up at me cautiously. His tongue darted out to lick his lower lip, and his pulse pounded beneath my fingers. "You... We... What's happening?"

I lifted a hand to trace the softness of his mouth with my index finger. The indent of his upper lip, the pout of the lower. His breath shuddered out of him.

"Are you sure you're done talking to Jason?" I asked, my blood singing with the need to put my mouth on his.

Gage nodded like a bobblehead. "He said he'd call me about an interview. He's... he'll—"

I moved just slightly so my thigh slotted between his, pushing up against his half-hard dick. Why had I denied myself this? Denied *both* of us this? At that moment, I couldn't remember.

"*Oh, fuck.*"

"I'd like to go back to the hotel now," I said conversationally. "Unless you wanted to stay? I know you haven't even had a drink yet or that food I promised you. And it's a shame to waste this outfit." I trailed a finger down the row of buttons from his chest to his flat belly. "It's your call, Goodman."

"I... I thought you were gonna pick someone appropriate and bring them back to the hotel. I thought you were going to get laid." His voice was hopeful, but he seemed to need me to spell it out for him, and I understood why. It was my own fault for being so indecisive for so long.

I leaned in close enough to soak up the ocean scent of him, then scraped my teeth along the edge of his jaw so I could whisper in his ear.

"I am."

Chapter Nine

GAGE

"It's your call, Goodman."

"Since when?" I wanted to ask, but I was pretty sure I knew.

Knox hated change and was deeply suspicious of things that made his life easier and better. The things he fought the hardest—becoming friends with me, or updating a billing procedure at the orchard, or eating triangular sandwich halves—were sometimes the things he wanted most, but his brain needed to consider the matter slowly. Deliberately. Like a computer running a background operation.

He had to run the numbers.

He had to analyze the risk.

But then, once he actually changed his mind—which sometimes took minutes, and sometimes days or weeks, and sometimes didn't happen at all—Knox had zero ego about admitting that he'd been wrong. He'd leave the office at night refusing to acknowledge that I had a point, then come into the office the next morning talking about the new billing procedure while eating a triangular sandwich and wearing a "Gage is my BFF" T-shirt (sadly, not literally).

It was unpredictable.

It was *infuriating*.

It was fascinating. And thrilling.

And it was so fucking adorable, it made me want to kiss the man senseless… which was exactly what I did the second we got into the Lyft.

And again against the rough brick exterior of the hotel.

Then again in the elevator, and at various points in the long corridor from the elevator to my hotel room.

I didn't need to understand how his brain worked to appreciate it.

He'd chosen this. He'd picked me. His hands were in my hair, holding my head at just the right angle while he kissed me against the hotel room door and his erection jutted against my hip.

That was as much as I needed to know.

"What do you want?" I demanded breathlessly when we got inside. "Because I have a list of fantasies, but I'm willing to hit all the highlights of your fantasy list, too, obviously."

"Generous of you." He did that thing with his teeth on my neck that made my eyes roll back in my head. "But I don't have a list. We'll go with yours."

"Wait, really?" I pulled back just slightly. "So you haven't been thinking about—?"

He snorted. "*Fuck*, of course I have. But if I'd let myself get far enough to make a list, this would have happened a long time ago." He grasped my hips and let his thumbs coast over the front of my pants mere inches from where I wanted them. "I wouldn't have been able to hold back."

I personally didn't see the downside of him giving in a

long time ago, but I was mature enough not to say *I told you so*. And those thumbs rubbing slow semicircles were hella distracting.

"M'kay," I said breathlessly. "I want you to fuck me. Me on top. No, wait, you on top first. And also blow jobs. But… Okay, wait, no. I maybe didn't order the list."

Knox took my earlobe in his mouth and sucked lightly. "Inefficient," he teased in a hot whisper.

"Shut it. Okay, blow jobs first, then… *shit*. Then I want you to fuck me. Yeah?"

He made a humming noise against the tendon in my neck that sounded like agreement, and I melted against him.

"God, I love a man who's willing to take direction."

He pulled back, and the look he gave me made my insides boil. "I didn't say *that*, Goodman."

When I blinked at him, all wide-eyed, he flashed me a wicked grin and caught my lower lip between his teeth. "Go get supplies. Because once we get started, I am not going to want to stop."

Fuuuuck.

It figured the man would be bossy in bed considering how many thoughts and opinions he had about everything else. Fortunately, I was okay with this.

In fact, as I upended my toiletry bag with shaking hands to get at the supplies I'd stashed there, I decided there were definite compensations to fucking a man with good planning skills.

After a quick, unsuccessful glance in the bathroom mirror to make sure I didn't look like a crazy person—I did, I definitely did, so I had to hope that slightly crazed look turned him on—I grabbed the condoms and lube and raced back to the bed in time to see Knox kicking off his shoes and peeling off his socks.

Why did that turn me on so much? I wasn't a foot fetishist. Or maybe I was. Could I have suddenly become a foot fetishist because of Knox Sunday?

"Get over here," he grumbled. "On the bed. Shoes off."

In my haste to comply, I accidentally shot one of my shoes at the hotel room door with a loud thud while the other tumbled into the bathroom. When Knox's low laugh hit my ears, I didn't even care. Part of me felt like he was going to change his mind at any minute, put his hands on his hips, and lecture me about being too old for me or too responsible to allow this breach in proper coworker behavior.

"Clothes off," I said breathlessly, reaching for the buttons on my shirt. "Nakedness. Nakedness is happening in here. Get naked. That's on my list."

Knox stopped his own strip show to lift an eyebrow at me. "I don't understand, Goodman. You want me to get dressed? Is that what you're saying? Put on *more* clothes?"

Was he actually trying to joke? How could he possibly be so calm right now?

I stopped and glared at him. "Ha, ha. Not funny. *Strip*."

He grinned, and *God* he was so fucking sexy. My stomach swirled with a nervous kind of excitement, the way it did when I visited one of those parking lot fairs they used to set up over in Sarasota, where you couldn't be sure if the rides were safe or not. When you took your seat, you were either in for some fun or horrible, fatal injuries. Either way, it was going to be a wild ride.

My hands fumbled frantically at my buttons, but Knox stepped over and grabbed them firmly in his grip. "Stop."

I looked up at him. "I don't want to. That... that's the exact opposite of what I want. I've been waiting so long. Please don't make me stop." My pleas came out in a whisper, as if I was afraid to even acknowledge my biggest fear coming true.

Knox's hands released mine so they could slide into the sides of my hair and tilt my face to his. "I need you to take a breath, baby. Calm down."

Oh my fucking God. If he wanted me calm, he could *not* throw out the casual *babies*. But I couldn't make my lips form words to say that.

"I want you, too," Knox continued. "This is happening. Don't rush it. I want to take my time with you, alright?" He leaned in and brushed his lips lightly across my cheek before they landed against the shell of my ear. "Savor you. Taste every inch of you."

"Oh God," I breathed. "Yeah. Yes. That's better than my naked-now plan."

I felt his smile in the tightening of his cheek, but his voice was firm when he instructed, "Get on the bed."

"Mmhm." It was hard to get on the bed when I was a puddle of sticky syrup on the floor, but somehow, I made it. I crawled to the center to lie like a starfish on the smooth sheets. *Breathe*, I reminded myself.

Knox watched me with laser eyes as he continued slowly undressing himself. My chest heaved up and down with anticipation, and my dick throbbed in my pants. I'd never wanted anything more than this man. In fact, I couldn't imagine ever wanting anything as much as Knox Sunday.

I was so fucked.

"Take off your clothes, Goodman."

My eyes slid closed as the sound of my name on his tongue did things to my dick. How could someone make my last name sound dirty like that? I hadn't even told him the dirty talk part of my list, but somehow, he'd known anyway.

I pulled my shirt slowly up my stomach, feeling the soft stroke of my own fingers across the bare skin of my abs.

The sound of Knox's sharp indrawn breath made me blink my eyes open again. Heat shot between us, and I closed my eyes and groaned as I continued pulling my shirt up my chest and over my head.

"You're the hottest fucking thing I've ever seen." Knox's voice was rough, and his words were unexpected. After all this time of teasing him, of watching him ignore me and act like he didn't give a shit about me or my body, I was overwhelmed by his response to me.

"Why now?" I asked, unable to hold back. As soon as the question was out of my mouth, I regretted it. "I mean, no big. It's fine. I'm not... that's not... never mind. Let's talk about other things. Dick things. As in, I'd like to see yours. Now, please. If it's not too much trouble."

My voice sounded shaky and unsure. I hated feeling this way. As if this mattered. As if his reaction to me mattered. I'd had sex with plenty of men. I was the king of casual sex. Emperor of hookups. This should have been no big deal.

So why was I wound up tighter than I'd ever been before? My body felt like one touch from Knox Sunday would set absolutely every fucking skin cell alight.

His eyes narrowed as he dropped his shirt on the ground. "Because I didn't want anyone else at that party to have you."

Oh. Oh fuck.

"Yeah. Okay. That's a good explanation." I pressed the heel of my palm on my cock and groaned again.

Knox's eyes heated even more. "Hands off, Goodman."

He knelt on the bed and reached for my wrist before pinning it above my head and looming over me. His wide shoulders and muscled chest made me feel like a little drool might accidentally escape my open mouth.

"Yes, sir," I whispered, just to get a rise out of him.

Knox crushed my mouth with his, reaching for my other wrist and bringing it up high above my head. Once he had both of my hands pinned together in his unrelenting grip, he brought his other hand down to stroke my cock between our bodies. I arched up into him, begging him with my hips, my indrawn breath, and my uncontrollable whimpers.

I wanted him so badly, I was leaking.

Knox's big hand fumbled for the button on my pants before yanking the zipper down and thrusting his hand inside.

"Oh fuck. Knox, *fuck*." I tried to control my breathing, but his bossy, commanding schtick was really doing it for me. Who knew?

Knox did.

"Mmhm. Just like that," he murmured against my cheek. I didn't even know what he meant, but I continued to arch up into him and beg him with my body.

Take me. Have me. Do whatever you want with me.

"Knox," I said, unsure of what I was trying to say exactly.

He shut me up with another drugging kiss. I wanted to reach greedy fingers into his hair to hold him there, but he still had me pinned. His heavy body pressed me into the mattress in the very best way.

A thousand snarky comments danced just out of reach on my tongue, but I was too dazed to bring them to my lips. Maybe that was a good thing. Maybe my big mouth was better off doing other things.

"Let me suck you," I said, remembering my plan.

A low grumble escaped his throat. He liked the idea.

I pulled my hands out of his grip and reached for his pants, scrambling frantically to get them open so I could take out his dick and taste it.

"Slow down," he warned. "Remember to breathe."

I gritted my teeth against annoyance. Didn't he know how badly I needed this? How long I'd wanted him? I couldn't do this slow. I wanted it all right fucking now.

"Whoever. Invented. Zippers. Hated. Sex," I ground out, fumbling at his fly with shaking fingers.

I was never like this. So needy. So vulnerable. I told myself the problem was that I'd gone too long without sex... but it felt like a lie.

Knox's hand gripped my chin, and he forced me to look at him. "Baby, slow down, or I stop this. Do you want to stop?"

"*Motherfucker*." I abandoned his zipper in frustration. "Why should I slow down?"

My breath sawed in and out of my lungs like I was running a race. I felt my heart trip over itself the way it did when I was on the verge of a breakthrough in writing code. But it was also the same feeling I got when bad weather came up while we were out on the boat in the Key.

Excitement? Fear? Both.

Knox's face softened. "Because I'm not going anywhere. I already told you that. And if you touch my dick right now, I'm going to come in my pants. Do you need a breather? Want to recite some multiplication tables? I do that a lot."

I blew out a breath and narrowed my eyes at him. "To stop yourself from coming? I thought older guys were better at holding their powder."

"Don't get fresh, whippersnapper." His eyes darkened with desire. "I meant I do that when I can't control my breathing."

Oh. He meant the panic attacks. My chest warmed at how freakin' thoughtful he was, and I felt my tension ease.

"Seems like you've recovered now," he purred. "Are you paying attention to me now, Goodman? Is the sound of my voice making you zone out?"

I remembered teasing him about that once, back when I hadn't wanted him to know what the sound of his voice actually did to me.

"It's making me something," I whispered. "You should maybe repeat that."

Now that we were back on familiar turf, I felt my nerves settle. This was the same old Knox from the orchard. The man who lectured me about proper dish-washer positioning for efficient surface area exposure to cleansing agents, and the man who never failed to mention how much food I consumed in a day.

Knox. *My* Knox.

Despite the teasing, I hadn't at all forgotten about the giant hard cock bulging between us. I wanted it, needed it, in my mouth.

I kept my eyes on him as I scooted down the bed. Once my face was even with the bulge, I ran my fingers over the shape of it through his open pants. The soft fabric of his boxer briefs moved easily over the hardness below as I rubbed him and enjoyed the sounds he made in response.

"Stop teasing me, Goodman," he rumbled. "And if you turn the tables on me and try and tell me we need to take it slow, I'm going to call Curt and have him talk to you about Madonna's entire back catalog while I blow you, and good fucking luck orgasming when he's talking about how 'Papa Don't Preach' helped him realize he was gay."

"You're a terrible person," I whispered against the outline of his dick.

"This is not a surprise, baby. Now get to work… or I will."

I closed my eyes and smiled for just a moment. He was so fucking fun. So adorably grumpy and deliciously sexy. What was it about him that made me feel this way? Like a balloon that had been accidentally let go at an outdoor party and floated free above the celebration? Part danger, part exhilaration.

I yanked his pants down and then shoved him onto his back on the bed before pressing my face into the front of his shorts. His body heat, his scent, the hard roll of his cock against my cheek were enough to make me let out another long moan. Knox's fingers reached into my hair and tightened.

"Goodman," he croaked.

"Your threats don't scare me," I said, feeling bubbly with anticipation. I pressed my chin against his dick and moved it up his shaft. "We're going at old man speed now whether you like it or not."

I pulled away enough to rid him of his underwear. Knox's cock was thick and ruddy, sticky at the tip and heavy in my hand.

"Nice," I whispered before dragging my tongue up and down the hot skin. Knox's thick thighs tightened as I began to work his dick. I licked and sucked while palming his sac. His balls were heavy and full, furry the way I liked them and tightening with need in my hand.

I ran my other hand along Knox's thigh, appreciating the tight shape of his muscles and the sharp crinkle of the hair there. He was big and strong, much more substantial than I was, and I wanted to feel the full weight of him pressing me down as he thrust into me.

"Just like that," Knox breathed. His grip on my hair had softened, and he caressed the back of my head before brushing my cheek with his fingers. "So hot. So fucking good for me."

Hell. I wanted to be good for him. After all the time spent flirting with him and teasing him, the truth of it was, there was part of me that wanted to serve him like this. On my knees. Willing to do anything to hear his sharp intake of breath, witness the gruff and grumbly man finally, finally letting go of some of his self-control.

I could suck this man for hours. My hands roamed everywhere, memorizing the hills and valleys of his muscular frame, imagining all the different ways I could make him feel good, make him come.

The weight of his thick cock on my tongue lulled me into a lusty haze, so when Knox's hand tightened in my hair again, I blinked up at him in surprise.

"Stop. Want to fuck you." His voice was rough again, which only made me harder. I pulled off his dick and wiped my mouth with the back of my hand.

"Condom," I said, looking around for where I'd dropped the supplies earlier. They'd ended up halfway under one of the pillows. I grabbed the bottle of lube and shoved it at him before trying unsuccessfully to rip the condom open.

"Growling at it won't get the thing open," Knox said in an annoyingly calm voice.

I glared at him, only to notice a sweet kind of tender smile on his face. My heart tumbled a tiny bit. "Well, ripping it didn't work, so what else am I supposed to try?"

Knox grabbed my face in his large grip again and pressed a firm kiss on my lips. I forgot what we were talking about.

"Lie down and let me do this part," he said against my lips.

"Uh-huh," I mumbled, slumping onto the mattress and

shooting involuntary heart eyes at him. I tried blinking the little insurgents away. This wasn't a love connection. As much as I truly liked Knox Sunday, this was a hookup. I was well aware of his aversion to relationships, especially a relationship with me, so I needed to shove the heart-train back into its highly inappropriate station.

I returned his kisses hungrily until I felt cool, slick fingers circle my hole. I sucked in a breath and threw my head back, bending my knees up to my chest to give Knox as much room as he needed. I was hungry for his touch and beyond ready to feel him inside me.

When I opened my eyes again, Knox's eyes were locked on my face, and I got the impression he was taking in every detail of my reactions and crunching the data to determine what moves worked best to wring a response out of me.

Spoiler alert: all of them.

Every single way Knox touched me was the very best way. I was hard and aching for him. Maintaining my patience while his fingers began slipping inside me was impossible.

So I began low-key begging.

"'S good. M' fine. Go ahead. Mmhm."

"Too tight," he said before nipping at the tender skin of my neck. "Let me do this."

I was on the verge of snapping at him to get on with it when his finger brushed against my gland and lit me up like Dale Jennings's New Year's waterside fireworks display.

"Ohfuckingfuck," I squeaked. "Fuck. Again."

His fingers were magic-makers. They moved in and out of me, stretching and rubbing all the right places until I finally grabbed his arm in a tight grip and barked. "Fuck me, Sunday."

Knox bit his lip against a smile and hurried to slide the

condom on. When he finally slid into my body, I let out a long, loud groan. "Fucking finally. Oh God."

He was thick enough to stretch me even more than his fingers had, and I loved every minute of feeling filled up with Knox's dick. My fingers tightened on his shoulders as if I was scared he'd leave before finishing.

"Y'okay, baby?"

I opened my eyes wider to focus on him. Knox's forehead was wrinkled with concern, and tendons stood out in his neck from holding himself back.

He was so damned sweet. Always looking out for others... for *me*.

I bit my lip and nodded.

And then he began thrusting in and out of me, slowly at first and then faster as I returned to shameless begging. The tip of my dick leaked into my happy trail, leaving sticky lines every time he hit my gland and made my cock jump.

We were a sweaty, panting, humping mess, and I realized I was probably going to pass out when I came. Sex with Knox was too good, the kind of encounter that would inevitably ruin me for other hookups in the future.

Damn Knox Sunday for fucking me better than anyone else ever could. All I'd wanted was a good dicking, not this kind of crazy-ass bar-raising sex.

That's what I got for fucking a high achiever.

"Knox," I whimpered when I felt like I couldn't take it anymore. I was on the knife's edge of my release, and my brain was buzzy.

His mouth found mine again in an aggressive, possessive kiss while his hand reached for my cock to stroke it. It was all I needed to let go.

The deep jangle shot down my spine and into my balls, arching my entire body as my release took over. The sound of Knox's shout filled the space around us as he thrust a few final times into me.

The warm fluid of my release landed on my chest and stomach, and he slowed his strokes to finish me off. I relaxed into a languid puddle, barely noticing the sheets that had come partway undone from the corners of the bed and the condom wrapper that had gotten stuck to the back of my shoulder.

But I wasn't too far gone to notice Knox's intense gaze on me. It was part shock and part confusion, as if he was suddenly seeing something strange and unexpected.

Or maybe I had it all wrong and it was something more depressing.

Like regret.

I refused to consider it right then. Nothing was going to burst my damned orgasm bubble while I still lay in the glorious afterglow of the best release ever.

As long as Knox would allow it—and, quite frankly, even if he didn't—I was going to snuggle the shit out of him and sleep plastered against him like the rogue condom wrapper on my shoulder.

Because that was some epic shit, and I was going to enjoy every minute of it until the grumpy bastard kicked me out of his bed.

Chapter Ten

KNOX

I'd given up on the concept of a good night's sleep as it applied to me long before the panic attacks had ever started. I'd thought I'd made my peace with it. I told myself I enjoyed waking up in time to watch the moonlight shine in my bedroom window back in the city or to get a jump start on the barn chores at the orchard. When I got a five-hour rest, I considered it a little bit of a miracle.

So to say that I was stunned to wake up in the morning with the sun streaming in the window and Gage's gorgeous eyes blinking at me would be an understatement. I was so disoriented, I sat up in a panic, looking around for my phone or a clock.

"I knew it," Gage groaned, pushing himself up on one elbow. "You're freaking out, aren't you?"

Still half asleep, I muttered, "Fuck yeah. A little." I scrubbed a hand over my face. "What time is it? Is it even still morning?"

Gage flopped back down onto the pillow and addressed the ceiling scornfully just like I sometimes did. "What kind of Cinderella bullshit is this? I have the best night of sex

I've had in months, and as soon as the clock strikes midnight, my lumberjack lover turns into one giant anthropomorphic *regret*? What time is it, he asks? Seriously?"

"What are you talking about?" Gage's skin was perpetually tan except for the pale area where his bathing suit would have been—an area which just happened to be visible above the hem of the sheet.

The idea that, after all these weeks of guilty fascination, I could finally know the precise location of his tan lines, that I could lick them with my tongue, was highly distracting, so I wasn't quite paying attention.

"Oh, come on." Gage rolled his wrist in the air like he was beckoning the truth out of me. "Take your best shot. I'm ready. In fact, let me start you off. 'We shouldn't have had sex, Goodman. It's not you, it's me, by which I mean it's actually *you*, for some fucked-up reason I won't even pretend is logical. You're simultaneously too smart, with a bright future ahead of you that I cannot sully with my middle-aged man-pain, and also too young and stupid to know what you want. Your hair confuses me, and your footwear is against the Lumberjack Code. You eat great quantities of supper in my family's kitchen, which makes things *complicated*, for I cannot fuck men once we've broken bread together. Also, I only fuck men after they've completed an FBI background check and taken part in an elaborate blood oath ritual to avoid one-night stands with unfulfilled expectations. Also, you're a Scorpio, and the ancient prophesies say that when a Sunday dates a water sign, the world ends. Also, I'm a vampire, and you're an exceptionally tasty young human who can never know I sparkle. And furthermore, you're too good at sex, and my dick can't handle you.' I'd be willing to accept any or all of that, Knox, but don't try to put it off like—"

I lifted the sheet and rolled on top of him, and when

our warm, bare skin collided, Goodman's words cut off with a gratifying little *mmmph*.

I felt my lips twitch. "Are you done?"

"Possibly?" He looked adorably disgruntled.

"It's later than I thought. That's really all I was saying." I ran a hand through his hair, thinking *confusing* might be a damn good adjective for it.

For a lot of things.

Gage blinked up at me suspiciously. "You were actually freaking about the *time*? What the hell for?"

"Because I don't sleep well. I haven't in months. Years. Until last night."

"Oh. So, um…" He frowned and licked his lips uncertainly. "You're saying that my freak-out about your freak-out might have been… premature? You… you *didn't* wake up and regret the whole thing?"

I stared down at him, noticing the little freckles that clustered on the peaks of his cheekbones and the center of his forehead. He was so beautiful that my gut cramped with longing even as I held him in my arms.

"Hottest, most satisfying sex ever, just like you said it would be," I confirmed roughly. "All I wanted to know was how soon we could do it again… and how often we could do it before you leave the orchard." Or before *I* did.

"Oh," he repeated. His arms drifted up my sides, and his legs parted to give me more room. "So you… *didn't* want a onetime hookup?"

I shook my head, a little surprised by how much I didn't want that. "Not if you don't."

"Well, then." He licked his lips. "It so happens that I'm open to doing this an unlimited number of times. And it *also* just so happens that I'm free… now."

"*Oooh*, sorry." I shook my head sadly. "That was before

you told me you're a Scorpio." I wrinkled my nose. "Kind of a deal breaker. Fate of the world and all that."

Gage smiled his sunshine smile and brushed back a lock of hair at my temple, a move that was surprisingly tender. "Meh. Saving the world's not your job. If it's gonna end anyway, let's enjoy it while it lasts."

I laughed out loud, then slid slowly down his body and proceeded to show him *precisely* how much we could enjoy it, until his eyes clouded with lust and he screamed my name.

By unspoken agreement, Goodman and I didn't say a damn thing to anyone in the Hollow about the change in our relationship status. I wasn't the kind of guy who'd ever make my life Facebook official—the very idea made me shudder—and my family was up in my business way too much as it was.

The only confirmation I gave of pulling my head out of my ass about hooking up with Gage was when Myles texted me a *Top Gun* meme with the caption "Take me to bed or lose me forever!" and I replied with an eye roll emoji and the word "DONE."

Smug? Why, yes, I fucking was.

But I figured I kinda had a right to be smug. Goodman was the most attractive man I'd ever met. Gorgeous enough that lying on the sofa in the apartment over the barn watching his ass flex in his jeans as he hummed some pop tune and sorted laundry after our trip was an all-consuming activity.

But he wasn't just good-looking. He was also smart and tenacious and joyful. A genuinely *good man*. And just like when I'd stopped being a resentful asshole to him a few weeks ago, now that I'd given in to the charm of him, I wasn't sure how I'd managed to hold back my attraction for so long.

Sure, he was leaving soon. And yep, that was gonna suck.

But for some reason, this guy who could have had anyone had picked *me* to be with for the next few weeks, and I wasn't in any position to be turning down miracles that found their way into my bed. He was the serendipity in an otherwise utterly shittastic year, and I was gonna savor it.

"You're doing it wrong, Goodman," I called, apropos of literally nothing.

The humming stopped, and Gage turned around slowly, a pair of socks in his hands. He lifted an eyebrow. "Pardon?"

"The laundry." I gave a pointed look at his socks. "You're doing it wrong. You're sorting by item when you should sort by color."

"But…" Gage blinked down at the socks. "I *am* sorting by color."

I stacked my hands behind my head and tucked my tongue into my cheek. "Ah, I see the problem. No, I meant sorting *correctly* by color."

He scowled. "These socks are gray. They go with light colors."

"Mmm, they're a distinctly dark gray," I lied. "They should go with darks." I tapped my toe to a happy beat only I could hear. "I mean, if you wanna be *efficient*."

His expression lightened, and he looked me up and down heatedly, making my dick stir. "Wait, are you under the mistaken impression that I think you lecturing me on the most efficient way to do shit is cute?"

I pursed my lips. "Maybe not *cute*. But a competence

kink is a real thing, Goodman. And I happen to be very..."
I ran a hand over my dick and arched up into it, giving
myself some friction. "...competent."

"Is that right?" Gage threw the socks over his shoulder
without looking to see which pile they landed in and
stalked toward the sofa with a big grin on his face. "You
know, you sound a little full of yourself there, Mr. Sunday."
He bent down to press his smile to mine and added in a
whisper, "Maybe you should be full of me instead."

I grasped him by the back of the neck, pulling him
down for a kiss, and he climbed onto the sofa with his
knees on either side of my waist. His dick was already
hard, and I wanted to taste him so badly I could—

We heard the sound of excited footsteps running up
the outside stairs at the same time, followed by the
scratching of a dog outside the door.

"Gage! Uncle Knox!" Aiden yelled.

Gage jumped off me like he'd been doused in boiling
oil precisely one second before Aiden burst through the
apartment door with Sally Ann in tow.

"Hey!" Aiden said, pink-cheeked and breathless. "You
guys comin'?"

"Er... Coming where?" I sat up and pulled a throw
pillow over my lap.

Gage knelt down to rub Sally Ann's head and adjusted
himself stealthily.

"To supper," he said, in a tone that tacked an unspoken
"*obviously*" to the end of the statement. "It's Sunday,
remember? Dad's got football on, and we're grilling." And
because he knew his audience, Aiden looked at Gage when
he added, "Chicken *and* steak. And Marco made potato
salad and pumpkin bread."

"Oh, heck yeah. We're definitely coming. I just..."
Gage darted a look at me and cleared his throat. He

hooked a thumb over his shoulder toward the washer and dryer in the closet near the kitchen. "I'm gonna put in a load of laundry, and then we'll be along, okay?"

"Sure," Aiden agreed. "But Dad invited Uncle Jack over, so you better hurry, 'cause he eats a lot."

Gage nodded solemnly. "Fast as I can."

Aiden turned to me. "You coming, Uncle Knox?"

"Of course. But first… I… should…" I looked at Gage helplessly.

"Assist me. In, uh… sorting the clothes. Your uncle is just so competent." He shrugged at Aiden apologetically.

"Oh, I can help you," Aiden said cheerfully. "I sort my clothes right when I get undressed, though. Dad says that's more efficient."

Gage looked up at the ceiling and muttered something under his breath that sounded a lot like, "Baby Jesus, save me from efficient Sundays." But he smiled at Aiden. "Why don't you go along and save me some chicken, okay?"

"M'kay," Aiden agreed. But he didn't go. In fact, he sat himself down on a chair instead. "So, how was your trip to Boston?"

Gage and I exchanged a frustrated look.

"Not long enough," Gage said with feeling.

"Way too short," I agreed. "But I enjoyed what there was of it."

"Yeah," Gage agreed, his eyes dancing. "Same."

He threw a load of laundry in the machine haphazardly, grabbed the Hannabury sweatshirt I'd lent him a few weeks ago, and declared himself ready.

All the way across the shadowy gravel parking area, Aiden kept up a nonstop stream of chatter about all the things *he* would see and do if *he* were in Boston, most importantly a Red Sox game.

"I'll take you to a game next year if you want," Gage said distractedly.

"But… will you still be here then?" Aiden's forehead puckered.

"Well, Boston's only a couple hours drive. You can come down and visit me. Maybe your Uncle Knox can bring you for a visit." Gage knocked his arm into mine and grinned up at me.

I smiled back. He didn't know it, but by then I'd be in the city, too, and Gage and I could…

Whoa.

Hold the phone.

One night of fucking, and I was all *Gage and I?*

There was no *Gage and I.* Certainly not by the time the Red Sox season started up again.

The way this worked was as a short-term thing. Trying to make it into something beyond that would be… dangerous. Feelings might get involved, and that wasn't what this was.

"What's wrong?" Gage asked too softly for Aiden to hear, and I noticed I'd begun rubbing my palm absently over my too-tight chest.

"Hmm? Oh. Nothing." I dropped my hand and smiled, which wasn't hard to do when I looked at Gage, even if I still couldn't quite draw a deep breath. "I was just realizing that I really am hungry."

Gage's expression cleared. "I made you late for breakfast at the hotel, didn't I?" he whispered. "I'll make it up to you later."

I shivered and let him walk ahead with Aiden, while I hung back and took a few deep breaths to compose myself before I went inside.

By the time I got in, Webb had already set platters of chicken and steak in the center of the wide wooden table along with the side dishes. Gage sat in his seat talking with Hawk. Em and Aiden chattered back and forth about Halloween costumes. Jack helped Uncle Drew into his seat and laughed at something he said while Marco got Sally Ann.

I stood by the door and watched them for a moment, as I often did, enjoying the chaos and beauty of them, but my gaze kept flicking to Gage as it did more and more often these days. There was something torturous but kind of fun about keeping our closeness a secret from my family. It felt like the two of us were tied together. Connected in a way.

"Knox!" Gage beckoned me over. "Come tell Hawk that I am *not* dressing up as Happy Smurf with him. There are some lines a man will not cross."

I snorted and unfroze from my spot, ducking over to the sink to wash my hands. "The problem with Goodman being Happy Smurf is that people might not know he was in costume," I called, and everyone including Goodman chuckled.

I headed for my seat near the top of the table, but Webb stopped me with an outstretched hand. "Knox, why don't you sit at the far end of the table tonight. Swap seats with Marco."

I raised one eyebrow. "What for?"

"For a new perspective," he said with the same unspoken "*obviously*" in his tone that Aiden used. "A new seat will give you a new perspective on life."

Ordinarily, I'd have told him exactly what I thought of him declaring himself Seating Czar and where on his anatomy he could shove his "new perspective," but since Marco's seat was next to Goodman, I just rolled my eyes, exchanged a shrug with Marco, and swapped seats without protest.

"Mind if I sit here, Goodman?" I asked as I took my new spot.

He inclined his head regally. "I'll allow—"

"Gage, why don't you come up here and take Knox's seat, since we're changing things up?" Webb called. "That way you can talk to Uncle Drew about Florida. Marco's always wanted to go to Florida."

He had?

"Oh." Gage's disappointment was so cute I had to fight to hide my smirk. "Yeah, okay—"

"No, but Dad! Gage and I need to talk about my science project," Aiden protested.

"But your Uncle Jack needs a place to sit, son."

Jack, who'd squeezed himself in between Drew and Em, shook his head. "I'm fine here."

"You're not," Webb insisted.

"Then let Jack take Uncle Knox's seat," Em said like the born organizer she was. "And Marco can take Jack's seat."

"But Marco's already sitting," Webb countered, conveniently forgetting that *everyone* had already been seated before he started this foolishness, and that hadn't seemed to stop him.

"Did you inhale too much smoke while grilling?" I demanded.

"Gage can sit next to Drew, then Webb, then Aiden, then Knox," Em decided. "Then on this side of the table, Marco can sit by Drew, then me, then Hawk can slide down to the last seat, Jack can sit in Gage's seat at the head of the table." She nodded to herself. "It's the most efficient way."

"But—" Webb shot back his own argument, and their bickering continued.

Gage chuckled and spoke softly enough that only I could hear. "You efficient people terrify me."

"All New Englanders enjoy efficiency," I said easily. "Give it a couple more months and you'll be assimilated."

"No, I told you it's *Sundays* who enjoy efficiency," Gage corrected saucily. "And I'm not a Sunday."

I folded my arms over my chest and raised my voice to be heard. "Webb, tell me again why we're playing musical chairs? I feel like my perspective is good and fresh already."

I knew precisely why, since all of his "most efficient" plans ended with me sitting next to Jack, but I wanted to hear him say it.

Webb flushed and nodded at Jack. "To make our guest feel more at home."

"Uh-huh. And what about Goodman feeling at home?"

Webb frowned at me like I was crazy. "Gage *is* at home. He lives here."

"He's not a guest, he's one of us," Aiden agreed.

Em nodded, too. "Which is why he has to move seats," she concluded sadly.

Goodman rolled his lips together, amused and pleased and annoyed all at once.

"Turns out you *are* a Sunday, Goodman," I said softly as we stood up. "Don't try to fight it."

We all took our new assigned seats, which left Jack in Gage's spot at the end of the table between me and Hawk.

Webb and I were going to have a serious talk—by which I meant *another* serious talk—about his matchmaking one of these days, since clearly the first talk hadn't worked.

"Sorry about that." Jack grimaced. "Webb just gets an idea in his head, and…"

"I know," I said grimly. "And you don't have to apologize for my brother. If anything, I should apologize to you."

"Wait, what idea's in Webb's head?" Hawk asked as he passed Jack the platter of chicken.

"That Jack and I are going to fall madly in love because we've sat next to each other." I rolled my eyes and took the platter from Jack. "Nothing says romance like communing over a plate of dead, charred poultry, right, honey bunch?"

Jack covered his laugh with a cough. "You know it, baby doll."

"Wait, you two?" Hawk nearly fumbled a platter of steak, and his eyes ping-ponged from me to Jack again in shock and horror. "No way. That's…"

"A figment of Webb's imagination," Jack finished calmly.

I nodded. "You're a nice guy, Jack, but I'm not…" I broke off with a helpless shrug before I could finish with *"interested in anyone but Goodman."*

Jack grinned. "I get it. It'd be weird anyway. I mean…" He lowered his voice. "Webb might think he wants to see us together, but he'd freak if I ever dated one of his brothers. He got so messed up with"—he mouthed the word *Amanda*—"that he'd need to be overly involved just to make sure no one got hurt. He'd act as our straight-guy chaperone and follow us on dates to make sure I didn't get handsy in public and ruin your reputation. He wouldn't hesitate to knock on my door with a box of condoms and a YouTube video on How to Do the Gay Sex so he could educate us, despite having zero practical experience. Right, Hawk?"

Hawk didn't seem to find this funny, but *I* found it so hilariously accurate that I laughed out loud… and then choked on the bite of potato salad I'd taken, so Jack had to whack me on the back.

From down the bench, Webb beamed at us, confident his silly plan was coming to fruition.

"Hey, Knox, I've been meaning to ask… D'you remember that Eagle Scout badge you got for adding a wheel-chair ramp over at the Theater in the Hollow?" Webb called.

"God, man," Jack groaned, covering his face with his hand. "Stop."

"Uhhh… It was twenty-something years ago," I reminded him. "But I remember it vaguely."

"You had to write up a bid for all the materials and then do the work, didn't you?" Webb stroked his beard. "It was a lot of work."

"Sure." Where was he going with this? "I guess."

Webb took a bite of potato. "Do you know, that thing was so sturdy, it's still there to this very day?"

"That's… good to know," I agreed, peering down the table at Lumberjack Yenta curiously.

Em, Hawk, Jack, Marco, and Gage all stopped eating to stare at Webb, too. And while all of us except Jack looked at Webb like we suspected he'd lost his mind, Jack glared at him like he knew it for a fact.

"What?" Webb said defensively. "Knox is good at construction projects, that's all I'm saying."

I took a sip of water. "You know, I seem to recall that *you* were also an Eagle Scout. Didn't you construct a—"

"You know, Knox, it *just this very minute* occurred to me as I was telling that completely unrelated story," Webb interrupted, "that Jack needs some help building a wheel-chair ramp at his mom's place. She messed up her knee, and she's gonna need wheels for a while. It would be really neighborly if you could help out."

The man was as subtle as a sledgehammer.

"Webb Sunday," Jack muttered. "I told you I was going to hire that handyman from Two Rivers. Knox has his own work, and I—"

"I'm happy to help," I assured him. "I don't know how helpful I'll actually be since that ramp was the last time I did any construction, but Webb's right about it being neighborly." That was the *only* thing he was right about.

"Well, there's no rush. My mom's still in rehab since she hurt her hand in the fall, too, so I have a couple weeks."

I nodded. "Pick a date, and I'll put it on my calendar."

Gage leaned back so I could see him and grinned mischievously at me. "You're so efficient, Knox."

Hmph. It was hardly an outlandish thing to keep a calendar. Almost everyone did. In fact, Goodman should keep one himself, and I was going to tell him so. At great length. At the earliest opportunity.

Was it fucked-up that lectures were our foreplay? Probably. But I liked it.

A lot.

"You know, Gage, speaking of neighborly things," Marco said. "Drew and I saw Helena Fortnum at the Farmers and Artisan Market today—she sells her wildlife photography prints, you know, and her nephew makes spice racks and medicine cabinets out of reclaimed barn wood—"

Goodman's mouth pulled down in an exaggerated frown. "Huh. Remy Fortnum, the guy with the tattoos, makes spice racks?"

"Lovely ones," Drew agreed. "Nice boy."

"*Anyway,*" Marco went on, "I told her she should ask Gage to make her a, ah… whatjamacallit." He snapped his fingers. "A thing on her website that lets her sell things direct to customers?"

"Oh, a storefront?" Gage nodded. "That's easy enough."

Marco beamed. "I knew you'd say that. But then we started brainstorming about how Remy would need a website, too…"

"And it occurred to us," Drew continued without missing a beat, "that maybe we'd need something bigger than a website. More like an app. Something that all the artisans in town could use to sell their crafts."

Em nodded. "You mean like Etsy, but for Little Pippin Hollow?"

"You could call it Pipsy," Hawk suggested.

Gage froze, and I could practically see the wheels turning in his brain as he identified the problem and found a solution.

"You know," he said slowly. "That's an amazing idea. An app that connects local artisans and suppliers with local businesses who need their products and services. Like, that big bed-and-breakfast you can see from the road just south of town—"

"The Apple of My Eye," Jack supplied.

"That's Helena's place," said Drew. "She and Remy run it."

"Wait, is it? Even better," Gage said excitedly. "Does she use Remy's reclaimed wood medicine cabinets there? Does she use Sunday Orchard apples and jams from our jam kitchen when she makes breakfast? Where does she source her pumpkins?"

Drew shrugged, baffled.

Meanwhile, my mind caught on him using the word *our*, and I tried to ignore the warm, gushy, terrifying emotion that suffused my chest.

"Okay, go with me here, right?" Gage pushed his plate out of the way—a true hallmark of how seriously he was taking this idea—and got out his phone to make notes. "If she uses all local stuff and advertises that on her website for the B&B, potential guests would find it adorable and authentic, and since some people literally need to go on vacation to find any authenticity in their lives, it would bump her business. Then we could offer her a discount for using our jam products in exchange for putting a little sign up in her breakfast room about how all the products are from Sunday Orchard, which is right down the road and be sure to visit them, which bumps our... I mean, bumps Sunday Orchard's... business. And then we could put an advertisement on the orchard website about how we recommend visitors stay at the Apple of My Eye. And *meanwhile*, there's this app—"

"Breathe," I reminded him.

Gage grinned at me before taking a deep, dramatic breath and letting it out again. "I'm good, I promise! So meanwhile there's this app—"

"Pipsy," Webb, Hawk, Em, and Marco said at once.

"Right, Pipsy," Gage agreed. "And it connects even *more* businesses. Like the speakeasy bar in the old brick building right on Stanistead Road in town—"

"The Bugle," Jack supplied.

"That building used to be the town hall back in the day," Webb said, apropos of nothing.

"Yeah. Do they carry your cider, Drew?"

Drew shook his head. "Nah. Always seemed like too much work to try to sell it."

"But what would you say if you could sell it through the app to local businesses?"

Drew's grin got even brighter. "I'd say... I think I've found my retirement project."

Marco snorted good-naturedly. "If you think this means we're not vacationing in Florida, think again."

"Gage, you're a genius," Drew said happily. "I gave you a problem, and you gave us a solution that's perfect for our town."

"You guys came up with the idea! But I'd love to build that for you. How *fun*."

"Can you do that from Boston or New York, Goodman?" I asked gently.

Nine pairs of eyes turned in my direction, and I became very fascinated with my supper.

Being the voice of reason was a thankless job.

It wasn't like I wanted Goodman to go. Not even a little. But I also wanted him to remember who he was and what his long-term goal was.

"Sure I can," he assured everyone. "No problem."

Drew shot me an unhappy look.

"If you're taking requests, Gage, do you think you could help me with my website for the diner before you leave?" Jack asked.

Gage nodded. "Absolutely. I can work it around my projects for Webb. I could probably even get to it this week, if—"

Sally Ann shook herself off the floor and barked at the back door, cutting Gage off midsentence. A moment later, someone knocked.

"C'mon in!" Uncle Drew called.

A man with neatly brushed dark hair, badly tailored khaki pants, and eyes so blue I could tell the color at a distance, stepped in on the mat. "Evening, everyone. I'm sorry to interrupt your supper—"

"Hey, Mr. Williams!" Aiden yelled excitedly, getting up on his knees in his seat. "Did you come for dinner?"

I looked down the table, and Gage and I exchanged a look. So *this* was the saintly Mr. Williams?

I knew Webb hadn't forgiven him for his role in allowing Amanda to pick Aiden up from school, and I didn't blame him for being angry. But I also knew Aiden thought this guy hung the moon, and the way he smiled at Aiden made it clear the feeling was mutual.

"I'm afraid not, Aiden." He shifted his weight. "I have plans. But first I——" He swallowed nervously.

"Come sit, Luke," Uncle Drew called kindly. "We've got plenty."

"He said he has plans." Webb's voice was flat. Hard. Unlike him. "Besides, we barely had room for everyone as it is, remember?"

"Hey." I leaned behind Aiden to smack Webb's shoulder as a reminder not to be rude.

"I needed to speak to you privately, Mr. Sunday," Luke said to Webb in a rush. "If I could have just a moment of your time."

Webb's jaw ticked. "I'm eating dinner with my family. If you'd like to meet with me, call and schedule an appointment, like the one Roberta Oliver said I needed to schedule if I wanted to speak to anyone at the school."

"Thomas. Webb. Sunday," Drew admonished in a low, insistent voice.

"Middle name," Aiden whispered nervously before glancing nervously at me.

Webb leaned back in his seat. "Whatever you have to say, Mr. Williams, just say it."

Luke darted a glance at Aiden and hesitated.

"Hey, Aiden, why don't we go check your project and see if the paint's dry. Maybe Mr. Williams can stop by the barn to see it on his way out," Emma suggested, showing better sense than Webb had shown since Luke Williams walked in.

"Will you, Mr. Williams?" Aiden asked.

"Of course I will."

Luke's quiet words only seemed to make Webb surlier. The second Aiden and Em shut the back door, Webb said, "Spit it out, then."

Luke clenched and unclenched his fingers into fists. "Right. So. Your wife contacted the—"

"*Ex*-wife."

"Of course. Yes." He squeezed his eyes shut for a second. "Ex-wife. The way your custody agreement is structured—"

"Is none of your business."

"Let the man speak, Webb," Marco interrupted impatiently.

"I know you're angry with me," Luke said. "I don't blame you. I want you to know that I truly didn't understand your custody situation at the time Aiden went missing. As you know, I haven't lived in town long. Roberta—Ms. Oliver—said there was no reason not to let him go with her, and I assumed she would know since she's the principal. Clearly, she didn't know—or chose to ignore what she knew —and I neglected to verify. I take responsibility for that, and it will *not* happen again on my watch." He cleared his throat. "Which is why I thought you should know that your wife—"

"*Ex*-wife."

"Yes, sorry." Luke sounded impatient now, too. "Amanda Sunday has requested to be copied on all school communications regarding your son, which is allowed under the terms of your current custody agreement."

Webb narrowed his eyes. "Copied on school communications. And that means?"

"That she'll get copies of his progress reports, his absence reports, his report cards, and his school pictures. She can volunteer at the school—"

"She doesn't live in Little Pippin Hollow."

Luke shrugged. "Then maybe that's a moot point. I'm only telling you what I know because I thought *you* should know. And also..." He hesitated. "I learned today that Roberta Oliver's brother-in-law—or something like that— is dating your wi—ex-wife, so Roberta's not exactly impartial here. Do with that information what you will."

Webb nodded grudgingly. "Thank you."

Luke nodded. "I'll stop by the barn to see Aiden's project. You all enjoy your evening."

I looked at Gage and saw the same concern I was feeling reflected in his eyes. It was time for me to be more aggressive about offering him the legal help he needed.

I glanced back at Aiden's teacher and could have sworn I saw him glance back at Webb with a look in his eyes that went well beyond professional concern.

Chapter Eleven

GAGE

A few weeks later, the weather had gotten noticeably colder, and I was finally beginning to realize what leaf peeping meant. The fresh air invigorated me on my walk to the farmhouse to find Webb.

"Morning, Gage. What's up?" Webb slid his mug of coffee onto the table in the farmhouse kitchen, took a seat across from me, and snagged a piece of pumpkin bread from the platter between us. His thick, dark hair was coated liberally with fake cobwebs from the Halloween decorations he'd been putting up, and tiny bits of purple glitter dust sparkled in his beard.

Drew, who sat at the head of the table between us with his walking boot propped on a chair, shot me an amused look that I returned.

"Okay, I know you're busy prepping for the haunted hayrides this weekend, but I wanted to give you guys kind of a progress report so you'd know what you're spending your money on—"

"Hey." Webb held up a hand and gave me a serious look—or as serious as he could muster when he glinted under the overhead light like the love child of Paul Bunyan and a fairy princess. "There's no rush, Gage. You're doing amazing. Everything you've done already has been great."

"Agreed," Drew echoed.

"And if you need to slow down so you can work on Pipsy or another side project—"

I smiled. "I don't, I promise. But speaking of side projects, I present…" I turned around the tablet in my hands. "The Pond App. Figured that name fit since there's already a Pond Orchard and a Pond Meadow and what-not, but we can change it if you like."

Drew's green eyes crinkled. "Love it."

"M'kay, so, disclaimer. I have a ton left to do. Like, a *ton*. The scheduling part of the app is running way behind. I'm waiting for a couple callbacks from your payroll company so I can integrate *that* whole aspect. And I still need to find a workaround for your cider press controls," I told Drew.

He waved this away. "It's way too late to worry about it for this year. It's all good, man."

"Okay. But the good news is, the expense tracking section is working. And the irrigation section controls work, too—I've tested them extensively. And I set it up so that you can control all the lights in the house and the barn, though I'm thinking I should lock a lot of those features down, or else Aiden might turn on all the lights in the middle of the night just to see what would happen."

Which was understandable, really. I'd had the same "*what would happen if I…*" brain when I was his age.

Webb frowned a little. "Don't worry about that part. Aiden doesn't have a phone. He's too young."

"Well." I licked my lips. "That's the side project I was referring to. Because… what if he did? No, hear me out.

What if he had a phone where the *only* app was the Pond App?"

Webb shook his head. "I don't follow."

"The other night after Aiden came home, you half joked that you wished you could have a GPS tracker on him, remember? But you'd also want to be able to monitor his communication with, um, people outside the Sunday family. So…" I drew an old phone from my pocket and set it on the table between us. Drew leaned in to get a better look. "I bought this secondhand, and I'd like to give it to Aiden. It has a data plan but not a phone number, so he can't call anyone and no one outside the family can call him, but using the Pond App, he can text anyone in the family… and any of the employees, I guess, though I could lock that down, too, if you want. The real improvement is that I also added a GPS tracking feature to the app, so anyone who has access to the app will know where everyone else is located within a few feet. Basically, it has all the functionality you'd want him to have from a regular phone and nothing you wouldn't want him to have."

Webb looked at the phone and then back at me. He blinked slowly.

I tried not to be disappointed. "I mean, you don't have to give it to him. No harm, no foul. You're the dad. I haven't mentioned it to him or—"

"I can't believe you did this," Webb said hoarsely. "I can't believe you thought of it."

"Oh. Well." I shrugged, a little embarrassed and a lot relieved. I'd wanted to help, to feel like I was contributing to the family in a meaningful way. "It's not revolutionary or anything. There are lots of phones for kids you can buy that come set up like this. But I thought it would be cool that it integrated to the app. One-stop shopping, kinda. Here, I have it on my phone so you can see how it works."

I opened my phone and sent a quick message to Aiden's phone through the app. The notification popped up on his screen.

"Aiden is going to be the happiest kid in the Hollow when he sees this," Drew said with a laugh.

Webb nodded. "I don't know how to thank you."

"Oh, no, seriously, it's—"

"It's a big deal to me. That you went out of your way to do this for me, for Aiden, when it's not what I hired you to do? It's pretty huge."

"That's why we're keeping you," Drew said matter-of-factly. "Oh, I mean, you can go off to Boston and all, but you're coming back for regular visits. And I'm sending you care packages like Knox's dad used to do for him. Prepare for it."

I grinned. I loved these guys so much. "Will these packages contain… pumpkin bread? Or, say, those apple muffins you make with the orange juice?"

"In bulk," Drew assured me with a wink. Then he took a piece of pumpkin bread—my third piece of the morning —and put it on the napkin in front of me.

It was nice to be understood.

Knox came whistling through the back door and headed directly to the coffeepot. "Webb, were you aware that there's a terrifying horde of zombie scarecrows congregating on the front lawn with their arms outstretched toward the house? Because if you decided to invite your friends over, you should have really let the rest of us—" He broke off when he saw all three of us staring at him. "What?"

"You're… you're whistling," Drew accused.

"So? There a law against that now?" Knox scowled. "Jeez. It's a pleasant day. The tourists are gone during the week now, and I don't have to smile at all the flatlanders buying vats of maple syrup. Perkins Limited just remitted payment on a huge invoice. I feel *whistly*, okay?"

I stuffed my mouth with pumpkin bread so I wouldn't be tempted to give him a besotted smile. We'd been hiding our relationship from the other Sundays for weeks, and you'd think it would have gotten easier. Become second nature.

But no.

Every time the man looked at me, my stomach tripped over itself, my heart danced in a funny syncopated rhythm, and I felt the desperate urge to find a new adjective to describe the particular green shade of his eyes.

"What's this?" Knox stood between Webb and Drew and glanced down at my tablet. His gorgeous eyes lifted to mine curiously.

"This is an early version of the Pond App," Webb answered proudly. "Gage's app for the orchard. It has a GPS thing we can use to keep tabs on Aiden."

Knox's beard split with a quicksilver smile that was a tinier but equally thrilling version of the happy-go-lucky smile I would never get tired of. "Awesome. Is this what you've been spending all your free time on, Goodman?"

I blushed. The man knew as well as I did that I definitely hadn't been putting in very long hours on the app since I now had a *different* hobby that consumed most of my evenings. And mornings. And lunchtimes, too, when Webb and the others went to Jack's restaurant.

"I'm dedicated," I agreed.

"I told him we're keeping him permanently," Drew said lightly. "Whether he likes it or not."

"Really?" Knox sipped his coffee. "I feel like there are laws against keeping prisoners, but okay."

"I meant metaphorically," Drew said loftily. "I wouldn't

condemn the man to sharing the barn apartment with your grumpy self for the rest of his life."

"Oh, I dunno," I piped up. "Knox isn't *so* bad as a roommate. You might say I'm used to having him around." And in my bed. "And I don't even mind his lectures." Since they always ended in sex. "His bark is worse than his bite." Not that I minded the bites.

Knox shot me a look no one else could see that said he'd be pleased to show me just how bad his bite could be, and I had to stop myself from shivering at the idea.

"It so happens that I have news, too," Knox said smugly. "I just got off the phone with Jason. You remember Jason?"

"Yeah." I nodded. "Of course."

Jason had said he'd call me to set up an interview last week, but he hadn't. And I knew I was supposed to be proactive about calling him and following up, but…

Well, I'd been really busy working on the communication app for Aiden.

And helping Aiden finish up his school project, which had not only earned him an A, it had gotten me an invite from Mr. Williams to teach the kids in his class how to build some simple robots.

And I'd been working weekends at the orchard, which was still doing a serious business with hayrides, and a haunted hay bale maze, and cider donuts, even though Webb said peak foliage time was just about done.

And setting up a website for the Averill Union Christmas fundraiser, because Em was a teenaged Napoleon in a lacrosse sweatshirt who'd twisted my arm with her pretty smile and bright green eyes.

Plus, it seemed like I still had a lot left to do for the Pond App, so it was kind of pointless to go all out to get a job *now* when I really wouldn't be able to start until after the first of the year... Right?

And then there was Knox.

Knox, who occasionally threw paperclips across the desk at me when I got distracted and daydreamy, because he was thirty-nine going on *three* and had never been told you could poke an eye out with those things.

Knox, who had not only reinstated friendly erection checks, but had volunteered to help me "take care" of any erections he happened to spot because, he'd informed me, he was a "*true* friend."

Knox, who'd been making a point of leaving the office one afternoon a week to talk to his therapist, even though I knew better than to ever mention this out loud.

Knox, who was a closet stealth cuddler, pretending to fall asleep on one side of whoever's bed we happened to end up in at night, only to plaster himself up against my side once he thought I was asleep, wrap his arm around my waist, and thread our fingers together.

Knox, who'd murmured, "*Gage*," against the back of my neck that morning with such sleepy satisfaction that I couldn't even give him shit about it being the first and only time he'd called me by my first name, but had rolled him over and thanked him with an early morning beej instead.

Knox, who I was developing Capital-R Real, Capital-F Feelings for, even though I'd sorta kinda low-key pinky sworn that I could stick to the rules.

"And what did Jason have to say?" I prompted, not really giving a shit about the answer.

"Mmm." Knox chewed pumpkin bread for a second, then grinned smugly. "That he's ready to move forward with the hiring process. One of his R&D guys left, so they had this whole organizational reshuffle, and now he has an opening in his New York office." His grin got bigger and smugger than I'd ever seen it. "He said, 'Hey, so, I have this position, but I'm not even sure what to call it. I want someone who's going to do some research and find fresh, new ideas that will get our guys excited to solve problems, and ideally this person will also want to see the project through from beginning to end. Think Gage is up for that sort of thing?' I remained very calm and told him I felt confident you'd be interested in at least taking a meeting to see what he had to offer."

"Wait. Wait, what?" My heart pounded for a whole other reason that had nothing to do with Knox—at least, I was pretty sure—and I felt both excited and weirdly scared. This was more than I'd expected. It was much more like… everything I'd wanted. "In New York?"

"Yup. Right in Chelsea. Imagine yourself looking out at the city from your office." Knox practically *bounced* he was so damn excited, which was at least as terrifying as the whistling because Knox was not a bouncy person.

"Well. I won't imagine it yet because I haven't even had the interview." I smiled. "Though I appreciate the vote of confidence."

"He started researching you when Myles first mentioned your name a while back—"

"Researching me?" I echoed.

"Yep. I guess a friend of his in Florida is friends with one of your old professors, who had extremely positive things to say about you. And I managed to dredge up a couple nice things to say, too. So the interview is seventy-five percent formality, just to make sure you mesh with the corporate culture, that you're cool with the salary… All that stuff."

"Oh." I nodded with the enthusiasm I knew I should feel—and *would* feel, no doubt, once it had really sunk in. "Wow! Well. I'm happy to talk to him, obvs, but when is he looking for someone to start? 'Cause I still have a *buh-uh-unch* of work to do on this app." I forced a laugh. "And Webb said I could take my time. Right, Webb?"

"Oh yeah." Webb nodded. "Long as you need."

Knox tilted his head and looked at me like I was being weird, which I super wasn't. *I* was not the one practically vibrating with excitement at the idea that the guy I was fucking might trot off to New York months earlier than anticipated.

It was fucking *rude*, was what it was. And I wanted my morning blow job back.

"I'm sure he'll go over all that during the interview," Knox assured me. "But if he's letting you pick your own projects, I'm sure he'll be fine letting you choose your start date. Then again, I think Webb could hire someone else to finish the app if you had to start sooner. Right, Webb?"

"Well, sure." Webb nodded again. "I mean, you've gotta do what's best for you, Gage."

I folded my arms over my chest. "But it would be a pain for you to find another app developer at this stage," I challenged. "And I'd still be working on Pipsy anyway. Right, Webb?"

"Uh." Webb frowned, his gaze flickering between me and Knox. "I mean—"

"But since it'd be almost impossible for Goodman to find a dream job like this ever again, everyone in town would understand. Right, Webb?"

"I, um—" Webb scratched his head and squinted at Knox. "Guys? What's happening here?"

Knox shrugged like he was just as mystified as his brother, which was even *ruder*.

"Nothing," I assured Webb, rolling my eyes. "Just Knox, having to have the final say, even when he's being helpful." I got to my feet and collected my tablet and phone. "I'll call Jason and set up a time. Thanks, Knox."

"It's already done. Tuesday. Nine o'clock. In Cambridge," Knox said firmly. "I'll drive you down Monday, and we can stay at my condo. The guy who sublet it for the summer is out now, and the leasing company had it cleaned."

Webb frowned. "The place hasn't sold yet? Is there something wrong with it? I thought the city real estate market was a feeding frenzy."

"Er. Yeah. Usually. I guess I need to figure that out." He cleared his throat.

"We can't do Tuesday. I'm redoing Jack's website then. He wants to add online ordering functionality and bring Panini Jack's into the twenty-first century." I smiled. "Next, he needs to add delivery so I can get my grilled cheese and apples brought to the orchard."

"Oooh, good idea," Drew approved.

"Reschedule Jack." Knox took on that superior tone that I genuinely hated. "Your career takes priority over doing a favor for a friend."

"It's not a favor. It's a *job*, even if it's for a friend, okay? Besides, Jack's been stressed about his mom and busy at the restaurant. I'm not rescheduling. I'll call Jason and reschedule."

Knox chewed a piece of pumpkin bread and watched me carefully, like he thought I was losing my mind. "Whatever you want," he agreed, clearly humoring me. "Just… let me know which day you wanna go, I guess."

Why did he sound so damned disappointed? Was he that eager for me to leave?

"You know what, Knox? Why don't you—" I squeezed my eyes shut and took a deep breath. I was one angry half second away from telling him that he could fuck himself *and* his ride to Boston, but I stopped myself at the last moment as reason broke through.

Um… What had Knox done wrong, exactly? Not a single damn thing. He was following the rules we'd laid out for this relationship. I'd promised him this would be convenient. Meaningless. Temporary. *Fun.*

He'd hyped me up to his friend. He'd gotten me an interview for an incredible job in an amazing city.

And I was pissy because… he was happy for me?

Damn. Maybe I *was* losing my mind.

"I think… Thursday," I concluded.

Knox smiled. "Great."

"I, um… promised my family I'd call and check in," I lied, motioning toward the back door. I'd actually talked to my dad over the weekend, and everyone was fine. "They like to hear from me."

"Of course they do," Drew agreed.

"Webb, let me know if Aiden has questions about the app, okay?" I asked as I pulled on my jacket.

Webb nodded. "Will do. Thanks again."

I stalked out to the parking area, my boots crunching over the gravel and my stomach churning for reasons I didn't want to examine too closely. Then I realized Knox might walk in that direction to get back to the office, and if he saw me, he'd ask what the hell my problem was. Since I didn't have a fucking clue, I definitely didn't want to do *that*.

Instead, I doubled back in the other direction and walked up the rutted path toward the Pond Orchard, my phone and tablet still clutched against my chest like a shield.

Before I had time to consciously think about it, I called my dad, thinking at least his familiar voice would knock me out of whatever mood I'd fallen into, but I was surprised when my oldest brother's boyfriend answered instead.

"Gageling!" Jay said happily. "Dude, you never call, you never write, you never take part in the Whispering Key group chat."

I smiled, because only my brother Rafe could have landed himself a guy who was an award-winning musician and not only madly in love with my brother but also madly in love with the people of Whispering Key and the life they were building there.

Then I sighed.

"Uh-oh. What's happening?" Jay demanded. "Are you okay?"

"Yeah, everything's *great*." Or, like, it was supposed to be? "I'm just having a *moment*, you know? So thought I'd check in with my dad. "

"Ah. You called his house phone, and I'm over here watering plants. Your dad decided a few weeks ago that orchids were his new passion, but he also didn't want to give up his *old* passion of taking the boat down the coast whenever the mood moved him, so I'm orchid-sitting." I could practically hear his good-natured eye roll. "Living the dream over here, like the song says."

"Same!" I said with enthusiasm I didn't feel. "I mean, I will be. I've got a huge job interview coming up down in Cambridge. Probably on Thursday." I gave him the rundown about Rubicon and Jason and the incredible make-your-own job Knox had described. "And the position would be in New York."

"Holy shit! Gage! That sounds amazing, man. You've always wanted to live in New York! You are kicking ass. No surprise there."

"Yeah. Yep. Kicking all the ass," I agreed. I hesitated,

rolling my lips together, and asked in a small voice, "So why am I not more excited?"

"Wait, you're not?"

"No, I am! I totally am. I mean… gosh, yes. It's legit what I have dreamed about. If I could have hand-drawn a job, it would be this. Yup." I paused. "But also… not."

"Ahhh. You're nervous," Jay said knowingly. "That's what this is. You want it too much."

"Yeah. Probably." I ran a hand over my face. "That makes total sense. I mean, I don't *feel* nervous, but it's probably a subconscious thing."

It was Jay's turn to hesitate. "You don't feel nervous? At all?"

"Mmm… Nope." I shrugged, though he couldn't see me. "I think it's probably because Knox said that I have it in the bag."

"Knox." I heard the crinkle of leather that meant Jay was getting comfortable on my dad's living room couch, settling in for the hot gossip the same way my stepmother did. "Is that the lumberjacky guy Toby mentioned? The one who secretly wanted to bone you? Spill your guts."

I laughed. "Yeah, he's a lumberjack alright. Gorgeous and beardy and frustrating. Remind me to send you a picture. And the desire to bone's not exactly a secret anymore. Not to me, anyway. But it's super casual between me and him. Just fun, physical, sexy… casual. Because Knox has had some minor health stuff from last spring that's weighing on him, and he's thirty-nine, so he feels like he's at this whole other place in his life than me, and I'm leaving town in a couple months anyway. That kind of casual."

"Oh," Jay said seriously. "*That* kind of casual. Oh, honey."

"Huh? No. There's no 'oh, honey,'" I assured him. "It's just…"

"If you say casual, I'm staging an intervention."

"Well, it *is*," I promised. "Casual, casual, casual. But that's not the point of this call anyway, remember? I need to figure out how to get over whatever mental block I'm having that's fucking with my mind about the job."

Jay made a noise that sounded like he was laughing, but I couldn't imagine what was funny about this.

"Can you help me or not?" I demanded. "Because I've gotta get back to work—I'll be damned if I don't finish this app before I pack up for some other job. And after school, I promised Aiden—that's my boss's first grader—that I'd make Sunday Sundaes to celebrate his science fair win. And then I have a rehearsal for the Santa singalong thing at seven, and if Lonnie Duncan bitches to me even one more time about me making a better elf than a Santa, we are going to have *words*, so I need to be emotionally prepared."

Jay was silent for a moment. "Lonnie Duncan?"

"Yeah. He runs the chicken farm down the street, on the other side of Norm Avery's place, and rumor has it he rigged a pumpkin-carving contest last… You know what? Never mind. Also not the point."

"Or maybe it *is*," Jay said inexplicably. "Have you ever considered… staying in Little Apple Hollow?"

"Little Pippin Hollow," I replied impatiently. Honestly, it wasn't that difficult a name. But then I processed his words, and I snorted. "*Stay* here? Oh, hell no. Nope."

I looked up and found that I'd walked almost to the Pond Orchard. The fruit had been almost entirely harvested in that section of the property, and the perpetual apple scent in the air was overlaid with a tang of smoke, probably from the wood stove at the farmhouse. It was fucking *cold*, too. The old guys who sat around the counter at Panini Jack's predicted a monster storm before Thanksgiving.

It was still pretty, though. Now that the foliage had died back, I could see the shadowy mountains against the horizon. And the trees looked like dainty dancers who'd taken their final bow and were stretching out their long limbs toward the blue sky in preparation for a well-earned nap.

"This town is gorgeous," I told Jay sincerely. "Really. Even Whispering Key can't hold a candle to it. But man, there is *nothing* here for me. I mean, what would I do with myself? There are zero tech companies around here. Nary a skilled website designer in sight, let alone anyone doing cutting-edge shit. That's why Webb had to find an app developer all the way in *Florida*."

"Right, that's true," Jay agreed. "I mean, that could also be a sign that they need you there."

That made me pause for a minute, remembering the conversation about Pipsy and Jack needing my help, before shaking my head. "They might need me, but only because I'm here, not because they really *need* me. If I weren't here, they'd find another way to do stuff."

"I see," Jay said, in the same voice he'd used when he said, "Oh, honey." It was not remotely comforting. "Okay, so you want my help?"

"Yes, please."

"Remember that you are a brilliant star, Gage. You can shine anywhere."

"Uh. Okay?" I hesitated. "Is… is that the advice? Because I thought Toby was a shit advice giver, but maybe he's comparatively not bad at all. He told me I should fuck Knox, and that worked out delightfully… Eventually."

"I'll just bet," Jay said wryly. "And no, that was just part one of the advice. The second part is, you need to not only decide exactly *what* you want from the job, but *why* you want it. We all have reasons for wanting what we want, and when you know *why*, you'll know *what*."

"Oh, sweet Jesus. Riddles you speak, Yoda. I don't want philosophical whateveryoucallits. I want precise instructions. Preferably like the kind you get at IKEA, with that incredibly confused-looking blob-person who puzzles through each step one at a time."

Jay snorted. "I miss you, Gage." He sighed. "Right. Tiny baby step one, go to your interview. See what the interviewer says. Smart money says this guy is gonna get you so hyped, you'll be all, 'Where do I sign?' and forget we even had this conversation."

"Right. Okay. I like this. That Gage sounds very confident and badass. Step two?"

"Step two, follow your gut. If your gut says take the job, then take it. If your gut says caution, then pause and evaluate. Because if it's *really* your dream job, you won't have to talk yourself into it. And if it's not… well, there are a lot of ways to be happy and successful, take it from me."

"Mmhmm. I get you." Sort of.

Ultimately, he was right, though. I'd come here with plans and goals, the dream to live in the city and get an exciting role making a difference in people's lives through tech. Why was I hesitating? This was it—this was my chance at the big life I'd set out to find.

I would embrace it with both arms.

After I cried just a little.

Chapter Twelve

KNOX

Have you ever been wildly turned on while watching the man in your passenger's seat strum an industrial-sized bag of Cheetos with his violently orange fingers like he was auditioning to be the next Pete Townshend in a The Who revival?

Yeah, no. That would be ridiculous.

"Ah, I love that song," Gage sighed as the last strains of "Baba O'Riley" faded. He shot me a sly, sideways look. "Best theme song ever. Those songwriters over at *CSI: New York* are geniuses."

I shook my head and set my teeth. "I refuse to be baited, whippersnapper."

I'd already fallen for it when he'd asked me if I'd gone to discos when I was his age. And I'd fallen for it again when he'd asked if "compact discs" were just tiny records. I was not going to be drawn into lecturing him anymore, no matter how often he claimed it got him hot.

"You're no fun. But seriously, though, people can say what they want about The Who, but Dave Grohl was a *legend* when he played drums for them. Isn't he, like, eighty now?"

I opened my mouth to respond to this travesty... then shut it again. "Nope. I can see exactly what you're doing. You're transparent as glass. It's not happening."

"Fine, fine." He waved a hand easily. "I was only kidding."

"If you say so."

Gage snorted. "I know my hair metal bands, Knox. God."

"The Who is not *hair* metal. They were most popular in the early '70s, while hair metal wasn't really popular until the early..."

Gage burst into laughter, and I shut my mouth so fast my molars clacked.

Motherfucker. He got me again.

"Why do you even try to resist?" he wanted to know. "You have *so much* to teach young, ignorant me."

In truth, a few weeks ago, I maybe *had* thought he was young and ignorant about anything that had happened in the last millennium, but I'd been incredibly impressed by his knowledge of music and a little shocked by how alike our tastes were.

"Are you done taunting me?" I demanded. "We're barely halfway there, and I'm ready to find a field of cows and drop you in it."

"Hey now. That's cruel and unusual!" Gage leaned back in his seat and stretched out his legs, which looked miles long encased in tight, worn jeans. He picked at a fraying spot in the denim over his thigh, and my attention homed in on the tiny square of skin peeking out. "Not my fault you declined road head, Knox. That's what I had planned to keep us occupied for the trip."

I tightened my grip on the steering wheel so I could keep the truck on the road. "It's a three-hour trip, Gage."

"Your point?"

I groaned and pushed the heel of my hand against the front of my jeans, willing my cock to stay down.

Sleeping with a twenty-four-year-old was fucking torture.

I was such a lucky bastard.

"Okay, new plan," I informed him. "Practice interview questions, so you'll be totally prepped for your meeting tomorrow."

He twisted his head against the headrest. "Oh, come on. You said I have this interview in the bag."

"Jason's on board," I agreed. "But there may be other people in the meeting, too. And… look, you were all heart-eyed about the idea of Rubicon when you first met Jason, right? But then you didn't follow up with him *and* you seemed downright reluctant when I brought up the interview yesterday. I practically had to strong-arm you into coming. And I know why."

Gage swallowed. "You… you do?"

"Obviously. You haven't done many interviews, have you? Or *any* interviews? You're nervous. I get it. I've been there myself." I shrugged. "I'm sorry if I seemed pushy, but it's because I want you to have the big life you've been dreaming of, Gage. I don't want you to psych yourself out and miss your chance. Not if I can help you."

"*So* sweet, *so* frustrating," he groaned then he rolled his eyes. "This seems lame, but okay, fine. Hit me with your first question."

"M'kay. Tell me about yourself, Gage."

"*Ugh*. Okay. Well, I'm twenty-four, which means I'm young and enthusiastic. I'm a Scorpio with Leo rising, which makes me a team player. I have a college degree in applied mathematics and computer science, which means I'm a rational thinker and problem solver. And I have an intense aversion to cows, which makes me both smart and a good judge of character." He nodded once. "Next."

I blinked. "Actually… that wasn't the worst answer I've ever heard. Except the part about cows is a fucking lie when I think about what I walked in on today."

Gage rolled his big brown eyes. "Oh, please. You make it sound like it was some sort of depraved—"

"You were crooning at Diana. You were scratching her head."

"Because Diana isn't a cow, she's a heifer. She's tiny, and her eyes are all innocent, and when you scratch her forehead in just the right spot, she makes a little noise like… Ahem. Whatever. It's different, that's all."

"Ahh." I nodded. "Of course."

"Next question," Gage huffed, folding his arms over his chest.

"Right. Okay, tell me your greatest strength."

He made a face. "Jesus. Uh. I'm easygoing? And I'm kind to animals. Even almost-cows. Next."

"Not so fast. Try thinking in terms of what you're bringing to the company. Easygoing can be mistaken for lazy or passive if you don't explain it properly. Maybe say, 'I get along with most people and have a real talent for seeing others' points of view.' Though I wouldn't say you're easygoing. You're like a dog with a bone sometimes."

"Only with you, baby," Gage said breathily, fluttering his eyelashes. "And only because I enjoy the lectures. So what's *your* greatest strength?"

"Oh, that's easy. Dedication and perseverance," I said quickly. "Once I'm committed to a path, I don't give up. Which is also one of my weaknesses." I laughed self-deprecatingly, like I might in an interview. "I've worked hard to become an active listener who can make my team feel valued and heard. I've also learned to be cautious and intentional about the number of projects I take on, because I achieve the greatest return on investment for my time when I can really see a project through to completion."

"*Wowwww*. Perseverance is a fancy way of saying workaholic? Who knew?"

"I'm *not* a workaholic. 'Workaholic' implies that I have a compulsion to work, and I don't. Like I told you the other day, it's that I like being in charge. I like achieving things. I like being…"

"Say *efficient*," he whispered ardently, leaning toward me with his hands clasped expectantly under his chin.

I shoved his face away. "I like being good at my job. I like people *knowing* I'm good. They need me at Bormon Klein Jacovic, and that feels nice. Always good to have job security, Goodman."

"Needed you," he said.

"Huh?"

"Needed. Past tense. You haven't worked there for like… four months? Five? And they're probably doing okay, so…"

I winced because, as stupid as it sounded, I'd forgotten that Gage didn't know my move to Vermont was anything but permanent. None of my family did.

In truth, I'd almost forgotten myself.

And then I winced again because it *had* been that long, and they *had* gotten along just fine without me. I hadn't checked in with anyone at Bormon Klein Jacovic in weeks, and they hadn't called me either. The last time I'd seen Rick, he and his team had been dealing with a crisis that I'd had no part in resolving.

You've been too busy getting laid. You've traded achievement for cuddling.

"Sorry," Gage said, reading my mood but not understanding the reason. "I didn't mean to say it so harshly. I'm sure they *do* miss you." His voice was sympathetic without being pitying. "It's gotta be a huge mental shift, huh?"

"Mmm," I mumbled noncommittally, my mind still processing things.

"But even though the circumstances suck, it's a good thing you went home when you did," Goodman went on, trying to soothe me. "It's gotta be hard for Webb being the sole person in charge of Sunday Orchard while raising a kid, dealing with his ex, and all that. And it'll be even harder for him next year when Em's away at school. And even after Drew's ankle heals and he *could* get out to the barn to do the accounting, he probably wants to slow down and spend some time with Marco."

I blinked. "They spend nearly every day together."

"Well, yeah, but they've never been on vacation together, even after all these years. And maybe Drew would like to move in with Marco but doesn't think he can. You know, since Em and Hawk might need him closer?"

I blinked some more. I'd legitimately never considered that. In fact, I'd thought me living in Boston had been helpful, so I wasn't intruding on Drew's space or his relationship with Em and Hawk and even Aiden, who I'd been sure were all much closer to him than to me. I hadn't really considered that Drew might have been happy for me to move back or that he'd maybe started making plans because he thought I was home permanently.

Guilt settled like a rock in my gut. I needed to tell my family the truth soon, or it'd be too late and I'd be stuck in Vermont.

And would that be the worst thing? Some distant part of my brain wondered.

I slammed the door closed fast on that intrusive thought. *Yes*, it would be the worst thing. It would be... terrible. My career was my identity, and my identity was in Boston.

"Okay, next question. Where do you see yourself in ten years?"

"Running my own company," Gage answered promptly.

I snickered. "There's not a doubt in my mind that you will, baby. But don't say that in the interview. It's a little like introducing your spouse to people as your 'first husband.' Instead, you can say, 'I see myself tackling problems through a unique understanding of a business's needs, being a leader in my field, and mentoring people.' Also not a lie."

Gage laughed merrily. "Okay, now that's some finely tuned bullshit right there."

"Not really! It's like you putting a picture of your sexy lower back dimples on Grindr, LumberjackLuvr. Not a lie, just picking your best angle." I paused and leered at him a little. "*One* of your best, anyway."

He laughed again and spontaneously reached for my hand, threading our fingers together atop the console.

This... wasn't a thing casual lovers were supposed to do, but then we'd sucked at keeping things casual since the first day. We'd shared a bed all night every night and celebrated the mornings with blow jobs. We'd watched movies on my laptop late in the evening while eating "Second Dessert" which, Goodman was right, was the meal the world hadn't known it was missing.

We'd taken long walks around the orchard at lunchtime when the weather was nice and everyone else was out doing their own thing, and I'd told him stories I hadn't even known I remembered about the history of the place and my childhood there. Each time we'd ended up at the Pond Orchard so we could make out while admiring the view.

I didn't know if all that rule breaking was because Gage had never had a friends-with-benefits relationship before and didn't know how weird it was, or because he figured boundaries didn't matter since we had a big red countdown clock ticking down our time together until this job took him to New York. Either way, I was trying not to overthink things. There'd be plenty of time to get lost in my feelings—or *not*, please Jesus—when he was gone.

And honestly, it wasn't hard to be happy when Gage was around. In fact, it was almost impossible to be broody. The man was so damn excited by the simplest things in life that he made everyone around him feel excited, too.

It was a goddamn excitement *plague*, and I wasn't even trying to fight it anymore.

"Okay, next question," I said, interrupting Gage's quiet singing along to the Avett Brothers. "What's been the defining moment of your life so far?"

He turned to me in concern. "Oh, God. Are they gonna ask me deep shit like that? For real?"

They almost definitely wouldn't, but *I* wanted to know.

"You never know," I hedged. "Better to be prepared so they don't trip you up."

"Okay," he sighed. His thumb stroked the back of my hand absently. "Hmm. There are a few. My mom died of cancer almost five years ago."

I nodded solemnly.

"That doesn't really have much to do with me, though, I guess." He rubbed his jaw with his free hand. "There was the time back in eighth grade when I was in a movie theater with my girlfriend watching *Twilight*, and the big lumberjack vampire came on the screen, and I confirmed for myself that I was one hundred percent gay—"

I laughed. "Why am I not surprised?"

"—but that's also not safe for work." Gage grinned.

"I'm gonna need to hear more about that later, though."

"I will tell you in great detail," he promised. Then he cleared his throat and got serious. "I've always been into computers and technology, maybe partly because the island where I grew up had shitty internet and was so disconnected from the mainland. I saw technology as this cool thing that can connect people, and I loved that. But then a year and a half ago, I really refined my dream about what I want my role to be—not just working on other people's ideas and making money, ultimately, but making technology accessible to people and using it to solve problems. Even tiny problems, like dispensing dog treats. And what changed for me was…" He cleared his throat. "My family found a buried treasure."

He said the last bit so quickly, all the words ran together, and I wasn't sure I'd heard him right. "A… treasure?"

"Yeah. I'll tell you the story another time. I wasn't even there, but my family gave me a cut just the same. And… yeah."

Gage's fingers tightened on mine, and he darted a side-ways look up at me, checking my reaction. I wasn't sure what he expected me to say or what the "right" reaction was, but I got the feeling a lot of people had responded the wrong way in the past.

"That's probably part of what drives you to want to get a job at a solid company and learn as much as you can from them," I said slowly. "The money is a huge gift, but I bet it can feel like a huge responsibility, too."

"*Yessss*," he sighed with something like relief and relaxed back in his seat. "You know, Kanye West once said, 'Having money's not everything, not having it is' or something like that, and it's true. I want to start my own company and give people a leg up. Identify needs and fill 'em."

In my entire life, I'd never had anyone quote Kanye West at me. Was it any wonder I was so enthralled with Gage Goodman?

"That's why the Rubicon job sounds so perfect, right?"

Gage nodded. "Yeah. I don't care about having a corner office or a fancy title or being indispensable to them, though. Ultimately, it's just a means to an end. A way to learn. I mostly just want to do my own thing and be happy."

"Mmm. Don't we all?" I mused.

"*You?*" Gage grinned, but his eyes were serious. "Sometimes I don't know. I think you're as afraid of happiness as I am of cows, and it makes about as much sense."

I scowled. "That's not remotely true. I'm happy. I've *been* happy." I took my hand away from his under the pretense of switching lanes, and I kept it firmly planted on the steering wheel.

Goodman was quiet for a moment. "You know, sometimes right before breakfast or dinner, you walk in the back door of the kitchen and just stand there for a second, watching your family. I've seen you do it a bunch. At first, I thought you were just standing there appreciating them or something, but then I started to wonder if you're scared to get too close."

"To my own family?" I scoffed. "No. Jesus."

"And then there was the whole thing of you not sleeping with me for all these contrived reasons…"

"They weren't contrived. And besides, I got over that pretty thoroughly, so your theory doesn't hold water."

"You *did* get over it." Goodman shifted in his seat so he could lean over the console and press a kiss to my cheek. Funnily enough, I couldn't remember anyone ever kissing me like that before, with such sweet, simple affection. "Have I told you recently how glad I am that you did?"

He moved back to his own seat but grabbed my hand in his again, and I let him.

"I'm gonna give you remedial happiness lessons, Knox Sunday," he said like a warning. "There's hope for you yet."

"Nonsense," I told him.

But deep down, I thought if there were anyone in the world who could teach me something like that, it was him.

―――

"Really?" I lifted an eyebrow. "A whole city at your feet, chock full of experiences and excitement, and this is what you want to do tonight?"

Gage poked his head and one naked shoulder out of the blanket pile he'd made on my living room couch and cracked one eye open. "This is *exactly* what I want to do. I'm tired. As you very impolitely pointed out earlier, I was up early today communing with a baby heifer. *And* you made me go shopping with you, which was traumatizing." He scooted over and patted the couch beside him. "Come and comfort me."

The simple command made me warm inside, and I couldn't muster even the pretense of a complaint as I sat beside him, especially when he plastered his naked chest to my equally naked side and pulled the blanket over both of us. I was comfortable in the extreme—which wasn't really a thought I'd ever had while sitting in my apartment before.

I liked the place just fine—the plain cream walls, the sleek black couch, the sliding glass door to a small deck with a view of the Charles—and someday I was going to make a mint when I sold it, but it had never been the sort of space that gave off relaxing vibes. Not until Gage was there with me.

"You didn't seem traumatized when we were in the store," I noted. "Poor Jeremy, the personal shopper who overheard you giving me a friendly erection check, on the other hand, is probably traumatized in the extreme. And that was *before* you pulled me into the dressing room with you and locked the door. The poor man's pearls have probably never been clutched so hard."

Gage shook with quiet, wicked laughter. "I bet you that was not the first time he's seen a guy pull his boyfriend into a dressing room. Probably not the first time this *week*. And Jeremy looked like the sort of guy who was more likely to have his ear pressed against the door than to clutch his pearls."

The idea of someone listening to us made me shift in my seat just a little.

So did the word *boyfriend*.

This was another moment when I could have stopped and pulled back, explained that casual relationships like ours didn't use that label.

Once again, I did not. And once again, I didn't let myself think too hard about my own strange behavior.

"I've probably been banned from shopping on Newbury Street, and you're not even appropriately sympathetic," I pretended to grumble. "Jeremy will have my picture plastered in the back room of every store."

"Are you saying it wasn't worth it?" Gage rested his head on my shoulder.

I snorted. "Fuck, no. That blowjob was some of your best work." Just remembering the way he'd gotten to his knees on the carpet, his big brown eyes staring up at me trustingly, while the whole scene was reflected in mirrors all around us... I squirmed on the sofa again and tried to stealth-adjust myself in my pants.

Not stealthily enough, though.

"Reeeeally?" Gage gave me a shit-eating grin. "Even the memory's working for you, huh?"

"You inspire me," I told him, caressing his smooth, bare shoulder. "That little flick thing you do with your tongue is fucking incredible. Truly. Award-winning."

He lifted his head and pressed a kiss to the corner of my mouth, his eyes dancing in the low light. "I kinda wanna ask questions about this award. Like, how would it be judged? And who am I competing against? But instead, I'm just gonna take my prize." He wiggled his eyebrows.

"Your prize," I repeated, amused and delighted. "Would that be a blowjob of your very own?"

Gage froze for a second. I could practically hear the wheels turning in his head, which was *also* amusing and delightful.

"No," he said finally. He pulled me down on the sofa so I was lying on my side behind him with my back against the back of the sofa. "And not because I don't want a blowjob, clearly, because that day will never, ever come. But I know you'll give me one later anyway. Whereas *this* is something you don't usually volunteer." He snuggled against me, grabbed the remote off the coffee table, and sighed happily. "Ahhh. The best possible television-watching position."

"Your prize is… watching television?"

"No. *Pfft*. My prize is cuddling. The overt kind, not the stealthy kind."

I had no idea what he was talking about. And once again, I was nearly positive this move was outlawed in the Keep It Casual Handbook. But, on the other hand, it felt like the most natural thing in the world to bury my nose in the curve of Gage's neck and my dick in the cradle of his ass. And I had no choice but to drape my hand over his waist and make sure he didn't fall onto the hardwood floor because *safety*.

"Knox, look! Oh my God! This movie was one of my mom's favorites. *Desk Set* with Katharine Hepburn and Spencer Tracy. Have you ever seen it?"

I shook my head and Gage chuckled. "You'll love this one. It's about an efficiency expert—"

I groaned, and he laughed harder.

"—an efficiency expert who learns that some things are more important than being efficient." He looked up at me and grinned, gorgeous and uninhibited. "Hard to believe, I know, but give it a chance."

I was pretty sure I wasn't as hard to sell on the concept as he thought I was.

At that moment, there were a million things I should have been doing. Texting friends to catch up while I was in town so they wouldn't forget my existence before I moved back. Shooting off an email to Rick at Bormon Klein Jacovic for approximately the same reason. Calling my family to check in. Giving Gage more interview questions. Having sex as often as possible while the sexiest man in the universe was inches away from me.

But instead, I pulled the blanket higher around us,

234

buried my face in Gage's neck, and thought that being with him was every bit as exciting as anything the city had to offer. And I smiled against his skin, confident I was *acing* my remedial happiness lessons…

Never dreaming how badly I'd already fucked things up.

Chapter Thirteen

Knox pulled off the busy street onto a tiny circular drive in front of a gleaming high-rise with the Rubicon logo etched into the glass front doors. We'd left Knox's apartment just down the river almost forty minutes ago, but we'd only just managed to fight our way through traffic.

"They're gonna love you, Gage," Knox assured me as he put the car in park.

"But what if no one plays with me or shares their treats at snack time?" I asked solemnly. Hearing my first name on his lips was still new enough to give me a little thrill.

Knox slapped my arm lightly. "Shush." But then he added, "I'm just a call away if you need a ride at any point. Remember?"

I forced myself not to laugh. He was so damn cute sometimes, and ten times more nervous for me than I was nervous for myself. I was almost waiting for him to offer to come inside and hold my hand or to take me back to his incredibly expensive but weirdly sterile black-and-white condo.

If you'd told me a couple of weeks back that Knox

Sunday could be this damn adorable, I'd have said you were a liar, but the man's capacity for adorableness grew exponentially with every day we spent together.

"I'll remember," I promised.

"Seriously. I don't know who else is going to be in that interview, but you're gonna kill it."

I leaned over the console and gave him a peck on the lips. "I know I will. Breathe, Knox. I'm chill, I promise."

"Erection check?"

I laughed out loud. "Okay, I'm nowhere near calm enough to get a spontaneous erection." But when Knox glanced appreciatively down at my charcoal-gray suit pants and licked his lips, my dick gave a half-hearted throb that said maybe I was underestimating myself.

"Yeah, you're good," Knox growled. "Go on, then."

I leaned over and kissed him again, just because I could, and then I walked into the building as confidently as I could, practically walking on air.

The bored lobby receptionist took one look at me and said, "Interviewing?"

I frowned but nodded. "How'd you know?"

She rolled her eyes, handed me a visitor's badge, and pointed at the elevators. "Seventh floor. Human Resources. Follow the signs."

As I stood in the elevator, I tried not to fidget. I'd styled my hair more carefully than usual so it flopped nicely, but that meant my reflection in the chrome elevator door was so startling, I had to fight the urge to run my hand through it and mess myself back up.

I'd somehow thought that tech jobs were more laid-back, but when I'd mentioned that at the store the day before, Knox had laughed. "Not all of them. And definitely not for the interview."

When I got upstairs and the elevator opened into a

lobby that looked like the waiting area at the DMV—if all DMV patrons wore fancy suits and smelled like performance anxiety—I was glad I'd listened to Knox and gotten dressed up.

Holy shit. No wonder the lady downstairs hadn't been surprised. The whole world was interviewing. We couldn't possibly all be going after the same position, could we?

There was a reception desk up here, too, but it was unoccupied, so I headed for one of the empty chairs set against the window and asked the guy in the next chair, "Is this seat free?"

The guy shrugged, barely making eye contact.

I didn't sit down right away, though, because there was a million-dollar view outside the window of bright orange and red trees waving against a blue sky and the Charles River rushing by—the kind of view I'd only ever seen in pictures, growing up in Florida—though none of the other people in the room seemed to notice it.

"Nice view, eh?" I said because chatter was my default setting when I wasn't comfortable. "At least they gave us a decent place to wait. I bet they're hoping we'll all get seduced by the view, and then accept the job without thinking twice."

The man did look up at me then. "I went to Harvard. The view of a dirty river and a bunch of Massholes driving smart cars doesn't entertain me. The idea that you think everyone in this room will be offered a job, on the other hand, is hilarious."

Ooookay, then.

Across the room, a girl who'd been tapping her foot like a tiny woodpecker against the marble floor stopped moving for a long moment… then clapped a hand over her mouth and darted down the hall.

"Puker," my neighbor scoffed disgustedly. "Honestly, if

you can't handle the interview, why would you think you could handle working here?"

"Well, interviewing is different," I said, hoping I didn't sound like I was speaking from personal experience. "I wasn't expecting so many people, myself. Are you applying for the New York job also?"

"New York?" He snorted. "No. New York is where the R&D guys are. You don't get hired into a position like that unless you're a fucking genius."

His look suggested I was deluding myself if I thought I fit that category.

"Be honest. In your spare time, you write inspirational quotes, don't you?" I wagged a finger at him.

"What?"

"No, no, don't be modest. Beneath that impressively believable douchewad facade beats the heart of an eternal optimist. You're the guy who came up with all those damn 'Live, Laugh, Love' signs in everyone's kitchen, aren't you? You're the reason my stepmother has 'Too Blessed to Be Stressed' sweatshirts in every color of the rainbow. But don't worry. You're secret's safe with me." I traced an X over my heart.

The guy looked like he couldn't decide whether he was more confused or angry.

See that, Knox? I'm getting along just fine with the other toddlers.

I tried to ignore his attitude, but when he got called away for his own interview a minute later, his words were still echoing in my head, and I found it hard to sit still.

Finally, a woman with a pixie cut and a genuine smile came to collect me. "I'm Hannah," she said. "Jason's assistant. Sorry we're running a little late this morning. The division head is coming to town tomorrow, and every-one's scrambling."

She led me past the elevator to a different hallway,

where the marble floor became carpet and the sleek formality became a little less constrained. She knocked on a door, and when a voice yelled, "Yeah!" she winked and pushed it open to reveal a large office with a desk and a seating area by the window.

"Gage! Good to see you again, man." Jason came out from behind his desk to shake my hand, grinning hugely. His blond hair was just as ruthlessly styled as it had been the first time I'd met him, and his suit probably cost more than my first car, but with his jacket off and his shirtsleeves rolled up, he was the most casually dressed person I'd seen that day. "How's it going?"

"Good! I can't believe how busy it is out there." I hooked a thumb down the hall toward the waiting area.

"God, I know." He rolled his eyes and gestured me to one side of the lime green sofa. "I should have mentioned when we spoke that our interview weeks are a bit of a circus. You'd think it would be easier to space the new hires out, but apparently the powers that be have decided this is what's best." He shrugged and sat in one of the leather chairs facing me. "One interviewing frenzy in the spring and another in the fall, but at least that means I only have to wear my fancy suit to the office a couple weeks a year. The company's growing exponentially, which is always a good thing." His smile turned crafty. "That's why we'd love to get you on board now, so you can be part of that growth."

I returned his smile, but I couldn't help wondering, "*Is it a good thing, though? Isn't it possible to be too big or diversified?*"

He shrugged easily and stretched out his legs. "I can't lie, long-term corporate strategy is not my wheelhouse, Gage. I trust much smarter folks than me to make those decisions. But I will tell you that the strength of the company relies on our ability to innovate new products all the time, which is why they need people like you and me. Professional visionaries."

I imagined telling Knox to refer to me as *Gage Goodman, Professional Visionary* and had to fight an inappropriate giggle before I mentally slapped myself.

What the hell was I doing? This was my dream job.

I sobered quickly. "I'm really excited to hear about this position. From everything Knox said, it sounds right up my alley. I'm eager to take a project from concept to finished product, you know? I wanna learn a little of everything. And working at Rubicon would be a dream."

Jason nodded. "We're a cutting-edge company. Right at this minute, we have a team working on an app that connects to a registry for medical implants and durable medical goods so that consumers will know when there are recalls or when multiple people have reported an adverse reaction. In the future, we're hoping to have a way to monitor implants and other devices electronically to find out why and how they fail."

A little thrill shot up my spine, making me straighten in my chair. "That's *incredible*."

"It really is." He beamed. "I remember the woman who came up with the idea, too—we started at Rubicon around the same time—and I like to think she'd be proud of what we've done with it."

"Oh, my God." I blinked. "Did she... did she die?" I whispered.

"What? No." Jason hesitated. "At least I don't think? I haven't talked to her in a couple years, but last I heard, she'd moved to Montana and writes thrillers."

"Oh." I thought this through. "So, wait, when did she come up with the idea?"

"Oh, I wanna say six or seven years back, maybe?

Took nearly a year to get the project through the selection process the first time, but she was tenacious. Then we went through a couple rounds of restructuring, and it had to be approved *again*. We assembled doctors to do test groups to check the functionality. We refined it. Then more focus groups. You know the drill."

I didn't, though. It made sense that doing things on a larger scale took longer, but… years? That was a little sobering.

"Knox mentioned you guys were restructuring," I found myself saying. "That's gotta be scary."

Jason seesawed his hand. "Eh. I guess? But it's the nature of the beast, or so I'm told. Gotta keep things fresh." He winked. "Never good to get complacent. Good news for you is, this means you'll move into the New York job that much faster."

"Move into it," I repeated. "So I wouldn't be starting there."

Douchebro from the waiting area had been right.

"Well, you would. On paper. And you'd go down for meetings and whatnot. But for the first little while, you'd spend a good part of your time up here in Boston doing some onboarding: learning about our corporate culture and our clients, learning how to analyze project costs and feasibility. All that good stuff." He winked again. "Then once you're up to speed, assuming all goes well, we'll pay to relocate you."

Assuming all went well.

"So it's a little like a probation period."

He nodded. "If you like. But that goes both ways. Not everyone has what it takes to play for our team," he said sadly. "Being very real with you here, it's demanding, rewarding work. I love it. But if you're the sort of person who wants work-life balance in the first year or two…" He shrugged in a what-can-you-do sort of way. "I get the feeling you could hack it, though." He winked again. "And Boston's a great city."

It was. And—my stomach did a giddy two-step—it was closer to Vermont than New York was by a couple of hours.

Not that it mattered, since Knox and I wouldn't be together by then.

I bit my lip. Except... what if we could be?

"In any case, you're only talking about... oh, half a year. Maybe a year." He paused, considered. "Year and a half at most. But in the meantime, we'd be paying you handsomely."

He named an amount that was at least triple what I'd earn at Sunday Orchard if they could afford for me to work for them full-time.

I coughed lightly. "That's your *starting* salary?"

"Yup." He winked a fourth time. "And I haven't even told you about the employee stock options. That's why that waiting room out there was so packed, Gage. We expect a lot from our employees—long hours, some sleepless nights —but we reward that. That's our version of work-life balance."

I chuckled uneasily. "No wonder it's popular."

"I've taken a look at your resume," Jason went on. "I'm extremely impressed. Your professors had excellent things to say about you. And is it true that you're related to the guys who found the Whispering Key treasure *and* to Jayd Rollins, the musician?"

I blinked. "Uh. Yeah. Wow, your google skills are strong."

"Oh, I take no credit. It's all down to Hannah. But all of that would be nothing if you weren't extremely qualified for the position," Jason assured me, "and if Knox hadn't given you such a glowing recommendation." He winked again.

"Did he? That's nice."

Was it weird for someone to wink five times in five minutes, especially in an interview? It *felt* weird. I was pretty sure it wasn't dry eyes or a tic, either. The man seemed to think he was being charming and friendly, but it wasn't working. Especially not after hearing Knox's name conjured an image of the man in my mind—honest and scowly and *solid*, charming without ever trying. In fact, charming *because* he didn't try to be.

"Oh, it's better than nice. Knox thinks you walk on water, Gage. Went on and on about the app you're creating and how easily you fit into the scene up there in Vermont, figuring out exactly what your clients needed. I've never heard him be that enthusiastic *ever*." Jason seemed baffled by the very idea of Knox being enthusiastic. "But that's the kind of boundless energy we need here at Rubicon."

"Oh. Yeah." I nodded, more because it seemed expected than because I was really excited. "Yes. No, I can totally do that."

"Awesome." He leaned toward me conspiratorially. "Technically, today is supposed to be for first-round interviews, where we're supposed to ask all those questions about your strengths and your goals and whatnot. We're not supposed to make selections until after the next round, but I told my boss I'd already picked you. So what do you say, Gage? Would you like to join the Rubicon team?"

I opened my mouth to say a hearty *yes, of course*, but when I tried to make the words move through my thick throat, it came out sounding like a wheeze. I licked my lips to try again, when a woman knocked on the door and poked her head in.

"Jason? Sorry to interrupt, boss, but Max is asking for

you. It's urgent," she said apologetically. "And you know how he hates to wait."

"Sure." Jason winked at me once more—*seriously*—and stood up. "Two seconds, Gage. Be right back."

I smiled and nodded, but when he was gone, I stood up and began pacing the length of the small sitting area— which was only three very unsatisfying paces long.

Why was I self-sabotaging? *Jesus Christ.* I needed this job. Not the way the other guys in the waiting room did, maybe. Not because I wanted to prove something to anyone…

I turned to pace in the other direction.

Or *did* I sort of want to prove to everyone that getting money all of a sudden hadn't turned me into a dilettante and that the company I wanted to start wasn't just a hobby or a vanity project?

I turned again.

It didn't matter, because I needed to learn about running a business before I could start my own. I needed to understand how to bring a project from a dream to an end product.

I spun once more.

But would I really learn here? Jason seemed like a really nice guy, but the gaps in his knowledge were large enough to drive a tractor through. How many times had he said that he trusted people in other departments to take care of the parts of the business he didn't understand? And if it wasn't uncommon for a project to take years and years just to get into development, how long would it take for me to get that experience? Not to mention, how well would I fit with people like Preppy McDouchebag from the waiting area?

I turned again.

Still, no job was perfect, and—

"Gage! Sorry about that." Jason hurried back in and gave me a smile that seemed a bit forced. "My boss called. He needs me to jump on a couple of things before he arrives tomorrow, so I'm afraid I'm going to have to cut our meeting short." He shrugged. "Pivoting is the name of the game around here. But can I tell him that you've agreed to jump on board?"

"Oh, yeah." I nodded. "I would love to…" I broke off, my mouth gone dry. "But I'm gonna need some time to think about it first," I concluded, shocking both of us.

The moment the words were out of my mouth, though, they felt right. I felt peaceful.

I wanted to think about this commitment a little more. I wanted to talk to people I trusted and make a rational decision. I wanted to talk to Knox, specifically, since I trusted him more than maybe anyone else in my life to give me the unvarnished truth.

Jason frowned. "Is it the salary? Because I could see if we could negotiate the salary vs. bonus if that——"

"No! Gosh, no. The salary isn't the issue. It's…" I hesitated, thinking about how I could present this like my Grindr ass dimples, but Knox and I hadn't practiced what to do in the extremely fucked-up scenario where I got cold feet and choked after being offered the job I'd been gagging for. So in the end, I opted for the truth.

"It's that I've spent the summer having a certain amount of autonomy, and I need to wrap my mind around being a well-paid intern on probation for a year and a half again." I smiled ruefully. "I understand this is how companies like Rubicon work, and it makes perfect sense for you. I just want to be a hundred percent sure that it makes sense for *me*, because once I commit, I commit."

"Ah." He looked gratifyingly disappointed. "Well, fair

enough. We'll touch base in a few days, then? See if you have any more questions I can answer for you?"

I nodded. "Thanks for understanding."

I strode out toward the elevator, eager to get out into the fresh air, and nearly ran into Myles, who was heading in the same direction.

"Gage!" He eyed me up and down and grinned. "You sure clean up nice. Did you interview with Jason?"

"Yeah! Yeah, he's great. I'm gonna think about the job. Talk it over. That kind of thing." Why wouldn't this elevator come faster?

"Oh. Well, I'm sure it'll all work out," Myles said, making it perfectly clear he had no idea what I was talking about and didn't care to know.

I took out my phone and sent Knox a text. *Maybe I'll let you pick me up after all if you still want to chauffeur me.*

He wrote back immediately. *You're done already? Tell me how it went! No, wait. Tell me in person. On my way.*

I grinned down at my phone like a sap.

"If you're spending time down here while you make your decision, I know Curt and Rod and the others would love to hang out," Myles said. "Maybe you can even convince Knox to have us over to *his* place for once."

"Maybe." I shrugged distractedly and put my phone back in my pocket. "Depends how fast it sells, I guess."

"Sells?" Myles frowned. "Knox is selling his condo? Really? He's always been so proud of that place." He rolled his eyes. "I thought he was subletting it."

"Yeah, the sublease is over. But it's been on the market for a while. I mean, he's living in Vermont now, and he's way too... *particular* about things to be an absentee land-lord for long." I grinned, thinking *particular* was my new euphemism for *control freak*.

"I suppose," Myles said dubiously. "But why now when he's moving back to Boston in just a few weeks?"

I frowned. "What do you mean?"

"I mean, at the end of the year, when his mental health sabbatical is over and he's back at Bormon Klein Jacovic, where is he going to live? Wait, are you two getting a place together? Makes sense that you're gonna want something bigger than his one-bed. Once upon a time, I considered having someone move in with me." He shuddered. "But the idea of having his sneakers in the same closet as my sneakers was—"

"Knox is taking a mental health sabbatical," I repeated, not sure I'd heard right—or, more accurately, horrified to think I might possibly have heard right.

"Yes, I know," Myles agreed slowly. "He must be dying to be back, too. He was *pissed* when his boss and the other higher-ups forced him to take time off, and probably more pissed that he needed it, but he seemed to be feeling fine at my party, so all that mantra shit must've worked. I'm sure he's bored to tears up in the back end of nowhere." He smirked and looked me up and down again. "Though clearly he's found a distraction, hmm?"

The elevator doors opened while I was still too tongue-tied to respond.

"Later, Gage! Nice to see you again. Tell Knox I'll be in touch," Myles called, taking off down another hallway like he hadn't just ruined my day.

Or, okay, that was unfair. *He* hadn't ruined my day; Knox had. Because there was no doubt in my mind that Myles was right and I was not. All the broken-off sentences and unanswered questions from every conversation Knox and I had ever had about the future slotted perfectly into place.

248

Knox had been planning on going back to the city all along.

And not only was I incredibly worried about that, because I didn't believe for a second that Mr. "Push Through and Don't Talk About Your Feelings" was making the best and most responsible choice for his mental health, I was also hurt —more than I probably had any right to be—because Knox had quickly become my confidant. My *person*. My safety.

But while I'd been catching all these feels, and sharing shit about my life goals and my family, and thinking maybe the two of us cuddling on the sofa watching old movies capital-M Meant capital-S Something… Knox had kept this huge thing from me. He hadn't trusted me with it.

Despite all the snarky comments he'd made about me being a youngster, I'd never felt deep down like Knox regarded me as anything but an equal… until that moment, when it hit me that Myles, Knox's once and future fuck buddy, knew more about Knox's plans than I did.

And that *killed* me.

Adding insult to injury, when Knox's truck pulled up at the curb, my first impulse was to lean over the console and hug him tightly, to let him stroke my back and demand all the details of my meeting, to pour out all my confusion about Rubicon, and my future, and my hurt over his lie, and to let him give me one of those grumpy lectures that always made me feel better.

How sad was it that those little lectures that had once driven me crazy had become my favorite part of the day? But when he lectured about something—whether it was the right way to eat an apple, or how you should never invest in anything you don't understand, or why Sebastian Stan as the Winter Solider was one of the most underrated performances ever because the subtlety of his body language made up for his lack of dialogue—it felt like he did it because he valued me and my opinion. Like he wanted me to understand why he believed what he believed. Like he wanted me to understand *him*.

It seemed like I'd been wrong about that, too.

"I'm guessing it didn't go well?" Knox said eventually, breaking the silence. "Listen, the interview is only one tiny part of the hiring process, okay? Your resume is fucking *solid*. And I told Jason you were really good at your job. This is not a hopeless situation."

You said I walked on water, I wanted to remind him. But hopeless was a good word for how I felt.

"Even if the interview part didn't go well—"

"Can we not talk about it?" I interrupted.

"But… Gage, you always want to talk." Knox gave me a worried look I pretended not to see.

"Not today."

"Okay, sure. You're probably talked out, huh, baby? Let's go back to my place, and we can find another old movie to watch. We'll order Indian or some other kind of food we can't get in the Hollow and just chill."

His voice was as warm as sunshine, soft as a warm blanket, but I couldn't feel comforted. Even his sweet, murmured "*baby*" made my bruised heart ache.

"You can get Indian food in Little Pippin Hollow," I said woodenly. "Turmeric House makes a great butter chicken."

Knox was silent for a second. "I didn't know that."

I smiled tightly. "The great Knox Sunday doesn't know something? Are you sure?"

After a beat, he said, "Okay, did I do something wrong?"

"No. Not really. I did." I'd let myself believe in something that wasn't true. I'd broken the rules we'd set up for our relationship. I scrubbed a hand over my face, frustrated with myself. "I think I'd like to just go home to the Hollow. I'm done with Boston for right now."

We changed clothes and collected our things from Knox's sterile condo and got on the highway. Unlike the ride down, the trip north was pretty quiet. We listened to the radio and talked in generalities about Halloween and the work I'd done on Jack's restaurant website, but it was far from pleasant. Even the sky was gray, and the radio DJ talked about a storm moving across the northeast, though a warm-up would be on the way later in the week.

I could feel the weight of all the questions he was holding back—Knox wasn't a person who handled waiting well—but I didn't want to have some drawn-out, angsty conversation, especially not while we were stuck in the car.

When we finally pulled into the gravel driveway and parked, it was midafternoon, and Knox had finally run out of patience. He cut the engine and turned toward me.

"Okay, you're officially scaring me now. You've hardly spoken in hours. I offered to stop for an early dinner, and you said *no*."

I shrugged. "I'm not hungry."

"Baby, the only other time I've known you to be not-ravenous was when Aiden was missing. What gives? If I fucked up…"

I blew out a breath. "No. I told you. It was me. I got some things wrong, and I'm annoyed at myself. But I don't want to talk about it."

"But—" Knox began, getting out also.

"Gage! Knox!" Webb waved as he jogged down the steps from the back porch. "Hey! Shit, I'm so glad to see you guys! I thought you were staying an extra day?" Without pausing for an explanation, he went on. "I need a massive favor. I finally called that lawyer you suggested, Knox, and she has an opening. *Now.*"

"Wait, you called her?" Knox demanded. "Finally? Has hell frozen over?"

"I know, I know." Webb held up a hand. "I've been a stubborn ass, but it was time. Helena Fortnum met me in the frozen food aisle at the Spence this morning and casually mentioned that Principal Oliver's been talking to the teachers at the school about how terrible it is for boys to be raised by single parents, and how sometimes non-custodial parents have to fight for their rights." He gave us both a significant look. "Seems like Amanda's not going away this time. She's gearing up for a custody fight."

"Shit. I'm sorry, Webb," I said. "But I'm glad you're talking to someone."

He nodded. "Same. But Aiden's gonna be getting off the bus in about twenty minutes, Marco's at an appointment, and Drew can't walk all the way down the driveway on his boot. I was gonna call Murray, but if you two are around…"

I looked at Knox, who nodded reluctantly back in a way that said our conversation would be tabled temporarily.

"We're around," I confirmed. "Go meet with the lawyer."

There wasn't much of anything I could do for my personal problem, but at least I could help Webb with his.

Chapter Fourteen

KNOX

After my brother left, Gage decided to put Sally Ann on a leash and walk back down the driveway to the main road where the bus would drop Aiden off. I could tell by his twitchy eyebrow and stiff shoulders that Gage didn't want company, and I was tempted to push the issue, but I didn't. Not knowing what was going on in his head was driving me crazy, though.

Having Gage so close but so closed off was like the sun going behind a cloud. I hadn't realized how bright and warm his presence had made my life until that light had dimmed.

And Jesus fucking Christ, since when had I become the sort of person who thought shit like that? Since the day Gage had walked into my life, that was when.

I clomped up the steps to the farmhouse kitchen and let myself in the back door. The room smelled like vanilla candles and something cooking in the crockpot. A few dishes were piled in the sink, and one whole end of the table was covered in papers and Webb's laptop. The place looked homey. Lived-in. Comforting.

Or it should have been. But something was off. It wasn't as comforting as it usually was.

"Knox! You're back early," Uncle Drew said from a stool at the island where he sat chopping apples with his foot propped up. "How'd Gage's interview go?"

"No idea." I poured myself a mug of coffee from the pot on the counter.

Uncle Drew frowned. "No idea? But... he didn't tell you? That's not like him. Is he upset?" I felt the weight of Drew's stare on the back of my neck. "What did you do?"

I took out a spoon, mostly for the satisfaction of slamming the drawer. "I don't know why you assume him being upset is my fault."

"And what about *you* being upset?"

"I'm not. I just... have a lot of things on my mind."

This wasn't a lie. I did have plenty of stuff to worry about. For example, I'd called Rick when Gage was doing his interview, but he hadn't answered or returned my call. Since I'd been calling to reassure myself that I was still a crucial member of the Bormon Klein Jacovic team, that hadn't exactly been reassuring.

But from the moment I'd picked Gage up and seen him so distraught, I hadn't really given my own career—or anything else—another thought.

I wanted to pull out my phone and text Jason, but I didn't think Gage would take too kindly to me saying, "What the fuck did you do to the guy who calls himself my *boyfriend* that made him not speak to me *or act like my boyfriend* anymore?"

Instead, I slid onto the stool across from Drew.

Gage couldn't have been upset about the interview, I was almost sure. His references were stellar. His academic record was flawless. And Jason had been one tiny nudge from hiring Gage sight unseen.

Gage had said it was *sorta* my fault, so had Jason told him something bad about *me*? I couldn't imagine what. Gage knew I was bi and that I wasn't remotely a virgin, and anyway, Jason didn't know the stupid shit I'd done in my twenties, unlike…

Fuck me.

Myles.

I took out my phone.

Me: *Myles, did you happen to see Gage today?*

His reply was immediate.

Myles: *Yup. He told me your apartment is on the market? Dude, since when? And where will you live in January? Are you and Gage getting a place? He seemed unsure.*

Ah, fuck me *twice*.

Me: *We'll catch up soon.*

First, I needed to talk to Gage.

Aiden burst in the door a moment later, and I stood up, ready to drag Gage out to the barn apartment, but Aiden ran through the kitchen without a word and clomped up the stairs to his room.

"What's up with him?" I asked Gage, who trailed after him.

He knelt to unleash Sally Ann and seemed to hesitate for a second, and then he sighed. "Aiden's mom was there. Out by the road."

"What?" Drew demanded.

Gage looped the leash around his hand in a tight coil. "I had my phone out to track Aiden on the Pond App while he was on the bus, mostly to see how well it worked. And the bus got to the end of the driveway before I did, because Miss Thing here had to smell every blade of grass. So I expected him to start walking and meet me… but he didn't. Instead, he walked west a hundred feet or so. When I got to the road, he was talking to a woman with Connecticut plates. I called his name, and he got startled. He ran toward me, all bug-eyed, and begged me not to tell his dad." He grimaced. "He said he knew better than to go in the car with her anymore, and he didn't want his dad upset like he was last time."

"*Ugh*," Drew said. "The poor kiddo."

"Well, we can't keep it from Webb," I told him.

Gage rolled his eyes. "Yeah, I know."

"I mean, I get what Aiden's trying to do, and it's sweet, I suppose, but *man*. So misguided. It's not his job to protect Webb. Webb is an adult."

"Yes," Gage said with an edge to his voice. "I know."

"And the situation is dangerous. I know Aiden loves his mom, but that doesn't mean he should be with her. She could be endangering him. Like, actually physically endangering him. And she's for sure endangering his mental health."

Gage tilted his head to the side. "Do we really want to talk about secrets that endanger our mental and physical health, Sunday?"

I opened my mouth to retort, found that my brain had absolutely no retort coming, and shut it again with a clack.

"Uncle Drew, Gage and I have things to discuss." I grabbed Gage by the elbow and dragged him to the door. "Would you fill Webb in about Amanda when he gets home?"

"Excuse me, what if I don't want to discuss anything with you?" Gage demanded once we'd reached the porch.

"Too bad. You're wrong, and I'm going to set you right."

Gage laughed, and it was an ugly sound. "I was wrong about *something*, that's for damn sure." He yanked his elbow away from me. "Fine. Let's do this." He stomped up the stairs as loudly as Aiden and threw open the door so hard it slammed against the wall.

"Okay, first off," I began before he could. "My situation with my family is nothing like the situation with Aiden and his mom."

"Bullshit," Gage said, arms folded and nose in the air. "It's more similar than you want to admit. You lied to Webb so he wouldn't worry. You want to go back to a job that is incredibly unhealthy for you mentally and physically, even though the whole reason you came here was because your doctor advised you to!"

"That's only partly true, and I never meant for the move to be permanent." I ran both hands through my hair in frustration. "You wanna know how I ended up back in Vermont? I was at my condo, on day three of my hundred-day sabbatical, and I was already about to bang my head against the wall out of sheer boredom. You know I don't have hobbies, right? I don't have guilty pleasures. And all of a sudden, I didn't have a single fucking purpose in my life either. Legit, nobody needed me for anything. My friends were working, I'm pretty sure my job thought I was a liability, and I felt worthless. Like my life was over. And that feeling was worse than the panic attacks, because *that* felt fucking permanent."

My hands shook, and I curled them into fists. Gage was still giving me a folded-arm glare, but his eyes had softened in sympathy.

Sympathy was way too close to pity, though, so I turned away and stared out the window at the sky beyond the orchard and the hay bale maze.

"That morning, Uncle Drew called. He'd hurt his ankle, and he couldn't get out to the office to do the bills. Webb was already so busy, and the finances were *complicated*, and could I recommend someone to help them

257

out? And I... I saw a way that I could have a little value to someone, at least, while I was taking my sabbatical. So I told Drew and the others about my panic attacks. I said I needed to leave the city and destress. I asked if I could stay here, and they said, 'Hell, yes. Of course, come home.'"

"Because they love you."

I nodded without turning around. "So I packed up my car and ran back here, and after one look at the books—and I mean literally *one* peek before Webb was all, 'No, Knox, you're here to relax and recuperate'—I saw that Sunday Orchard was standing at a financial precipice. The business had been profitable, but I told you about Webb's divorce, right? When Webb had to pay off Amanda, he had to take that money from the business, which meant that he was operating without a safety net, with no money to do the kind of upgrades he'd need to stay competitive. I needed to give him the money without making it seem like a gift, since you know how fucking proud he is, so I..." I stumbled over my words. "I got the idea to tell him I wanted to buy back into the business. My dad left Sunday Orchard to Webb, because this place has always been Webb's baby and he deserved it more than I did, but I told Webb I'd changed my mind. That I wanted to pay to have a share again."

Gage sucked in a breath.

"And yeah, okay, maybe it wasn't the right thing, manipulating him," I admitted, interpreting that indrawn breath as disapproval but not wanting to turn around and see it confirmed on his face. "It worked, though. Webb took the money and let me buy in, just like I'd known he would, because he feels guilty that he 'stole my inheritance.' And that's also how he let me do the books. Because he could hardly say no to me taking care of the finances in a company I'm part owner of. And so I've been trying to get things up and running, even though the books are a nightmare. Nothing was online, and I feel like entire years' worth of data is missing, all the receipts and purchase orders are shuffled together like a deck of cards... seriously, I don't know what Uncle Drew was doing or how they've managed as long as they have." I blew out a breath. "And I've also gotten time to rest, because even at its most stressful, life here is nothing like it was back in the city. So it's been a win-win."

"Yeah, but what happens when it's time for you to go back to Boston?" Gage whispered.

I turned around finally. "I'm not leaving until I've finished sorting out the books," I said firmly. "I would never do that. And when it's time to go... well, if Drew wants to do the books again, I'll train him how to do it right, because I've got a whole system now. Or if he doesn't want to, I'll hire someone else. I'm not going to screw my family over, Gage."

Gage rolled his eyes to the ceiling. "*Obvs.* In a million years, I would never think that. I meant, what happens to *you?*"

"I... go back to work?" I replied, wondering what the trick to the question was. "I tell my family the truth, and they'll be pissed at me initially, but Drew and my brothers *will* get over it. I know they will." I thought about it for a second. "Em's gonna make me adopt a herd of rhinos or endow a scholarship or ten first, but eventually she will, too. Because they'll see that I did it for the right reasons." I set my jaw to hide my nervous swallow. "Do you?"

Gage sat very carefully on the edge of the sofa cushion. "I'm not mad that you lied to them, Knox. Hell, most of my family tells lies more often than they change their underwear, and I'm no saint myself. I probably would have done the same thing." He took a deep breath. "But I'm upset that you lied *to me*. I know we're keeping our relationship a secret from everyone, but I let myself believe that the dishonesty stayed *outside* the truth bubble we'd created, and inside the truth bubble, we were being honest with each other. That we meant something to each other, as friends if nothing else."

"Gage," I said softly, coming to sit on the coffee table across from him and picking up his hand.

"And I'm seriously fucking upset that you're not putting your health before your job," he went on. "Does Dr. Travers know you're planning to go back? Is he on board? What other changes are you going to make to compensate for the stress you'll be under? Because you can't just go back to the life you led and expect the same thing not to happen again. That's the definition of insanity."

"Baby——" I shook my head. The idea that he was worried about me was a sweet ache deep in my chest.

"No. Don't do that. Don't give me playful sex face. Don't be all '*Gage, baby*.'" He stood up and stalked to the kitchen. "You're an idiot, and you're willfully sabotaging your mental health."

"You can't talk about a truth bubble and not have me think you're adorable. Besides which, I'm doing better," I insisted. "I promise. It's not like my time in Vermont has been entirely stress-free, you know. I helped deliver a calf, which I've never done before. Aiden went missing, and I was seriously fucking upset, but I've been able to hold it together. I'm talking to Dr. Travers regularly. I'm truly okay."

"Great! Good! But have you considered that you're doing better *because* you're here? Because you have a support network that encourages you to put yourself and your mental health first, and your life is less stressful, so you have an emotional reserve? That you're finally sleeping through the night now because you're getting lots of fresh air and activity and not working sixteen-hour days? And that all that will go away if you move back to the city?"

I blinked. I… hadn't. Not really.

"Why are you fighting so hard to go back to a job that's killing you when you could stay here and be happy? Why does being happy scare you so damn much?"

"Pfft. This again? I'm telling you, it doesn't. And my job… it's who I *am*, Gage."

Gage made an inarticulate noise of frustration and glared up at the ceiling. "Dear Precious Angel Baby Jesus, maker of warm puppies and extra-slippery lube, why in your infinite wisdom did you make me attracted to the world's most stubborn, infuriating human? Why must he insist and insist and fucking *insist* that he's right until I'm ready to brain him, and then just like that—" He snapped his fingers. "—he arrives at the correct answer and pretends like he knew it all along?"

Gage stood under the kitchen light and glared at me. Fighting with me, fighting *for* me. He was the most glorious thing I'd ever seen.

"And you know what's worse than all that?" he demanded, glaring at me with his hands on his lean hips, his golden-brown hair all askew like some sort of modern sculpture. "You know what the most fucked-up part of my attraction to you is? *I think it's cute!* It is *not* cute. What's the matter with me?"

Relief flowed through me, soothing all the rough places that had appeared since he'd walked out of his interview back in Boston.

"Okay, first of all." I stood up and moved toward him, letting the gravity of him tow me in. "I do admit when I'm wrong."

"Oh yeah? Like when?" He crossed his arms over his chest.

"Like when I thought I could keep my hands off you. Fight this attraction between us. *So* wrong. See how I'm admitting it?" I took a step closer.

His eyes widened, and he put up his hand to ward me off. "No way. Stop right there. Don't do that either."

"Do what?" Despite the seriousness of the conversation, I wanted to laugh. Only Gage could make me feel so many things at one damn time.

"You know exactly what." He made a waving motion in my direction. "That up-and-down eye-fuck thing. Stop it. We haven't finished talking."

"What eye-fuck thing? *This* eye-fuck thing?" I let every damn thing I wanted from him show in my eyes.

"You're awful," he said with no heat.

"What if I did something else instead?" I kissed him softly and traced the outline of his cock through his jeans. "Would that be awful?"

His breathing hitched. "So awful," he moaned, his hands sliding up to twine around my neck. He gave a deep sigh of capitulation. "Be awful some more."

That was all the permission I needed. I pushed him back another step so he was braced against the counter and kissed him deeply. I pulled his shirt over his head, just so I could see his gorgeous golden skin on display, then sank to my knees right there on the kitchen floor, pulling his jeans down so I could nuzzle him through his briefs and inhale the heady, musky scent of him.

He was only half erect, but it was a goddamn thrill the way he hardened almost instantly when I put my mouth on him through the cotton, tracing the veins and ridges of him with my tongue.

"All this for me, Gage?" I asked, my voice already thick with lust.

When I said his name, he whimpered, and that needy little noise made my own dick throb insistently in my jeans.

"Yeah," he breathed. "Yours." Because, *fuck*, he was so sweet.

"Now take off your shirt and undo your pants so I can watch you jerk while you blow me," he commanded breathlessly, because *fuck*, he was also so *dirty*, and the one-two punch of him was like a powerful drug.

I tore my shirt off, throwing it behind me, and ripped the damn button off my jeans in my haste to get them open.

Gage laughed exultantly as the button pinged against the refrigerator door, a husky, erotic sound. "Yeah, that's it. I love how much you want me. Damn you're gorgeous, Knox Sunday. My sexy lumberjack."

He ran hot, greedy hands over the muscles in my shoulders, and I *felt* gorgeous. Powerful.

And so fucking hard I could probably have chopped down trees with my dick.

I dragged Gage's underwear down, and his cock sprang free, slapping his stomach so enthusiastically that a tiny bead of precum landed there and stretched out, leaving a single silken thread suspended in midair for a moment.

"Look at you," I groaned. "Leaking. *Wanting*. So damn sexy." The need to taste him felt more like a compulsion, so I swirled my tongue over the damp head of his dick, toying with his slit.

Gage gasped in three tiny, stutter-breaths, and threaded his hands through my hair, holding me in place. I opened my lips wider for him, and he punched his hips forward, fucking my mouth for a few strokes before holding himself deep in my throat for a long moment, then pulling back to start it all again, just the way he knew I liked.

There was an unexpected thrill in having done this with him so often that he knew exactly how I wanted it— torturously slow and thorough—just like I knew the way to make him scream was to hold his hips hard, push his leg over my shoulder, and pull his balls into my mouth one at a time while I fingered him.

"Fuck, Knox," he whimpered as he leaned back against the counter for balance, spreading his arms out like some kind of gorgeous male sacrifice to a very horny god. "*Fuck.*"

I sucked two fingers into my mouth to get them good and wet, then ran them over his entrance, toying with him for a second, ignoring the way he was trying to fuck himself back against my finger. When I was good and ready, I pressed inside him, and his whole body stilled, his mouth frozen open, like every molecule of his energy was focused on the place where I breached him.

"Ohhhhh, that's it. *Yes.* Fuckkkkk." He whimper-hummed again. "You're so good, Knox. You're so hot. You… yeah, *oh*. Thank you. Yes, keep moving just like that. *Thank* you."

Christ, he was fun to fuck. And not just because his sex-babbling once he got close was the hottest, cutest thing ever, or because no man had ever aroused me the way he had, but because no one had ever been so damn *present*, so generous with his praise, so excited for every kiss, every look, every touch, every last ounce of pleasure. Making Gage happy was the greatest investment ever, because he magnified every bit of passion and returned it a hundredfold.

I let go of his sac with a final lick.

"Fuck my face," I ground out. "I want you to come down my throat while I jerk off for you."

"Oh, hell yeah. Do it."

I decided that I needed friction more than I needed oxygen, so I let go of his hip, trusting him not to choke me too much, spit in my palm, and jacked myself with the hand that wasn't fingering him, moaning my own pleasure around his dick, feeling his answering whimpers in my balls.

I knew I wasn't going to last long—it was too damn good—but I wanted to taste his release before I came. I crooked my fingers inside him and sucked at his dick hungrily, loving the way his whimpers turned to moans. His fingers gripped my hair so hard my eyes watered, and he came down my throat with a glad cry that was totally honest. Totally uninhibited. Totally Gage.

I swallowed down as much as I could, savoring the salty-clean taste of him.

Then Gage pushed me back gently and sank down so his knees touched mine. He cupped my balls in his hand and tugged with the perfect stroke.

"Come for me, baby," he whispered excitedly, his eyes locked on mine, and we had a single moment of total, perfect communion before my orgasm hit me like a fucking freight train and I came all over both our hands.

"Oh, shit," I breathed weakly, staring into those gorgeous brown depths as the truth sank through me.

I had serious fucking feelings for this man.

And I was going to watch him walk away regardless.

Chapter Fifteen

GAGE

I was not meant to be the big spoon in a relationship.

By the time Knox and I had picked ourselves off the floor, we'd barely had the energy to stumble into Knox's bedroom, all sticky and sweaty. Knox had shucked what was left of his jeans before pulling me down and rolling on top of me, and we'd fallen asleep just like that—in a naked, tangled heap on top of the blankets—while it was still light outside.

Fortunately, nobody came to collect us for dinner, which meant no Sunday eyeballs had to be bleached from the horror.

A couple of hours later, though, when it was fully dark and quiet outside, we'd woken up to shower and eat toast standing up in the kitchen. I'd snort-laughed when Knox had stepped on the missing button of his jeans and gone hopping around the room on one foot, because I was a sympathetic individual that way.

Knox had retaliated by holding my toast in the air with one hand—the tall bastard—and not giving it back until I'd said the words "Knox Sunday is a sex god," but the joke was on him because I would have said it anyway, especially if I'd known he'd kiss me breathless afterward.

We'd ended up back in his bed, curled up with me behind him for some reason, watching a boring-as-fuck zombie movie.

Knox had fallen asleep almost right away, which left me tired but wired, sleepy but awake, lying on my side in the cramped valley between Knox's broad, warm back and the wall, unable to move his bulk without waking him.

It was a breeding ground for overthinking.

I was not an overthinker by nature. In fact, several people who shared my DNA would probably say I was an *under*thinker when it came to certain things—case in point: me ending up trapped in a bed, in the apartment over a barn-slash-gift shop, in a little orchard, outside a tiny town, an hour away from the closest city, fifteen hundred miles from home, with the lumberjack lover of my dreams, who'd heard me confess that I was upset at his lies because I'd *thought I was special to him* and had promptly shut down the conversation by fucking me senseless.

I mean, as distraction techniques went, this was a ten out of ten, and I was not complaining. But it was also a reminder that my plan of just enjoying this thing with Knox for as long as it lasted was… you know… *flawed*.

The kind of flawed that would end in great personal disappointment if I didn't start drawing some boundaries.

I pushed gently at his shoulder, hoping he'd roll onto his stomach without protest so I could make my way to my own bed, but of course, even in sleep Knox had his own ideas.

"*Mm-mm.*" He captured my hand in one of his and pulled me so that my arm was around him, curling himself into a ball to do so. It was adorable—or would have been, if I'd had big-spoon-sized arms.

"Knox," I whispered. "Move."

He didn't budge.

For a guy who used to have trouble sleeping, he seemed to have no problem when he was with me... which was both an insult and the highest possible compliment.

"Shove over. I have to get up."

He made the same negative sound as before.

I huffed out a breath. "Knox, I can't sleep like this."

Knox groaned, clearly put out, but instead of rolling away so I'd leave him be, he rolled onto his back, pulled me all the way over him so I was lying flat on the bed on the other side, then locked me in place with his thigh thrown over mine and his arm over my stomach. He made a satisfied little noise as he drifted back to sleep.

Knox the Stealth Cuddler would not be stopped.

So I did what anyone in that position would do.

I laughed.

I clapped a hand over my mouth to hold it in, but when the full hilarity of the situation—my life with the cows and the dream job I hadn't snapped up and the gorgeous lumberjack holding me like I was his teddy bear—hit me, I couldn't help myself. Giddy mirth bubbled up inside me and spilled over until I was shaking the bed with it and tears were running down my face.

"Wha—?" Knox grumbled, blinking his eyes open. "Wait, is the movie over? Did the zombies live?"

I laughed harder, and his arm tightened around me, like he wanted to pull my laughter into him... or maybe like he just wanted me to shut the fuck up and let him sleep.

"Sorry," I sighed a moment later. I sniffed and patted his arm soothingly. "Sorry, something just struck me as funny, but I'm done now. Go back to sleep, baby."

He grunted in reply, but his fingers tensed on my waist.

"Goodman? Can't sleep like *this*," Knox whined softly, repeating my words from earlier. He pushed against me like he wanted me to move, but there was nowhere for me to go while he was holding me except the floor.

"Roll over, then," I said gently.

"No, I mean… Can't sleep like *this*." He pushed against me again, but this time he gave a roll of his hips that slid his erection against my bare thigh.

"*Ohh*." I trailed my hand down his flank to grip him. His cock was sleep-warm and rock hard, already leaking against me.

"Want you so much."

Damn, his sleepy voice made my chest wobble. "Yeah?"

He fucked my fist gently. "All the time. Can't ever get enough."

I squeezed my eyes shut. Now that was some damn honesty. And I was as helpless against it as if he'd been writing me sonnets.

"Have me, then," I urged. "I want you to." I rolled over to grab a condom and lube from Knox's side table, handing the condom to him while I remained on my side and prepped myself with shaking hands.

Knox pushed my hand aside and took over the task, his fingers scissoring me open while he alternately gnawed on my shoulder, and licked my neck, and murmured sweet, nonsense words into my skin about how beautiful I was, and how special I was, and how my ass was a miracle.

The last part made me giggle silently again, and when he finally pushed my knee up and slid inside me, my laughter turned into a moan.

"Yeah. Just like that. Want to hear you happy, Gage."

Tears sprang to my eyes because that was the unlikeliest but best thing anyone had ever said to me, and the fact that it was Knox Sunday, my grumpy, infuriating not-boyfriend, who'd thought it up made it even better.

Made it *perfect*.

"I am happy," I said breathlessly. And God, in that moment, it was the absolute truth. So true that I had to bite my lip hard against all the other true shit I wanted to say that he might remember the next morning, like how much I wished it could last, how much I wanted it not to be temporary. How I'd like to be the guy he picked.

So instead, I twisted my head, searching for his lips, wrapped my hand behind his neck, and kissed him.

At this angle, Knox couldn't move very fast—more gentle nudges and glides against my prostate than our usual heart-pounding race to the finish—but that was perfect, too. It felt like every stroke was intentional. Meaningful. And I knew later on I was gonna realize that was some top-notch wishful thinking on my part, but I'd never had sex this way before—sex that wasn't just about getting off the fastest or the hardest, but about connecting and appreciating and loving on the person you were fucking—and so I was gonna suspend the hell out of my disbelief and ride this train.

He moved so my head was pillowed on his bicep, and his free hand tugged my cock in time with his slow, gentle strokes.

"So good," I breathed.

My body flushed and my toes tingled, going from languid heat to impending orgasm like a flash fire. Knox knew, because of course he did, and he moved to get more leverage, to jerk me faster, to give me what I needed... but I shook my head. "I want to come just like this. Slow. Perfect. Like we have all the time in the world." Even if our days were numbered.

"I want... *Fuck.* Kiss me again, Gage," Knox demanded.

So I did.

My orgasm rolled through me, curling my toes and then tightening all my muscles one at a time like a wave. I whimpered against Knox's lips and twisted the sheet in my fingers as I came all over his fist.

"God, you're so fucking sexy," Knox growled. "I can't — I want—"

I bent my leg up higher, twisting myself in half, and he levered himself up on his palms so he was nearly on top of me and could thrust harder, deeper.

A sliver of moonlight slid through the window above the headboard, illuminating part of Knox's face. He looked positively feral, his green eyes locked on mine, though I was almost sure it was too dark for him to see me.

"*Gage*—"

He said my name like the beginning of a question that would forever go unanswered because a second later his body locked down and he came with a shout.

"Remind me..." he said breathlessly as he nuzzled the damp hair at my temple. "Never to make fun of your yoga practice again. Ten out of ten."

I sighed happily and nodded, my eyes drifting shut despite how sticky I was.

I was dimly aware of Knox leaving the bed, then climbing back in again, wiping me down with a damp cloth.

"You gonna tell me what happened in your interview?" He cuddled me up from behind, his voice rough now from sex instead of sleep, and even though I was *done*—ass throbbing pleasantly, sated as a boy could be—my dick jumped like a happy puppy because its favorite person was getting growly.

Down, boy.

I pried one eye open and almost-whined, "Now? Really?"

"Why not now?"

"Haven't you ever heard of afterglow? *Ugh.*" I rolled my eyes and heaved a breath. "It went okay. Jason offered me the job—"

"Wait, really? Congrat—"

"—and I told him I had to think about it."

"Oh." I braced for Knox to be annoyed, to tell me I was being ridiculous and shortsighted, but all he said was, "Why?"

"Because I want something that's right for me, not something that's going to impress a bunch of people I don't care about." I hadn't even been able to articulate the thought to myself until that moment, but it was true. "And for once, I wanted to think it through before I committed."

And why was it so much easier to think things through clearly when I was talking to Knox... unless it was *about* Knox?

I see your irony there, Universe. Well played.

"And if Jason finds someone else for the position in the meantime?"

My heart beat faster for a second because I hated to *lose*, but when I thought about not working at Rubicon, I didn't feel a sense of panic or sadness.

I yawned. "If he hires someone else, then it wasn't meant for me. I deserve a job that I'm excited about."

"Good." Knox pulled me against him and rubbed a soothing hand down my back. In no time, my eyes shut, and my mind drifted.

In that hazy space between sleep and wakefulness, Knox's lips brushed my forehead. "Don't settle for anything less than perfection, love," he whispered.

Or maybe I dreamed it.

The next time I woke up, it was to a cold bed and a milky-white morning light. I threw the covers back with a groan and eased myself out of bed, stretching my hands up to crack my spine.

"Knox was right. Old age does stalk me," I muttered to the empty apartment.

The distinct chill in the air had me running toward the bathroom to turn on the hot water in the shower. Once I was clean and feeling marginally more human, I put on Knox's big Hannabury sweatshirt, jeans, and boots, grabbed some toast from the kitchen, and clomped down-stairs to the office.

It seemed like the sky couldn't commit fully to being cloudy or sunny and had stopped in this nebulous place that was neither. I understood that on a spiritual level, because I felt like I *should* be happy—I'd been offered a killer job that I might still end up taking, I'd had six orgasms in thirty-six hours and my body was practically humming with endorphins, and breakfast was probably waiting for me in the farmhouse—but I couldn't quite get there. Despite all the sex, or maybe because of it, I felt kind of fragile. I knew I needed to take a giant step back from Knox but also wanted him to, like, give me a giant hug and console me about that necessity, which would probably be counterproductive.

"Well, someone got out of bed early—" I began as I threw open the office door, but I broke off quickly because the office was empty.

Weird. Knox usually waited to walk to breakfast with me.

Maybe he was feeling off after last night, too.

I buried my hands in my pockets and walked across the parking area to the farmhouse. The wind sent dried leaves skittering across the gravel and whipped at the zombie army in the front yard.

"Morning, Gage!" Drew called from his stool by the kitchen island as I shut the back door. "Pancakes?"

"Yes, please." I'd clearly missed the breakfast rush, because Drew and Webb were the only two Sundays in the room.

"We missed you at supper yesterday," Webb said from his spot at the table. His words were easy, but his voice sounded concerned. "Knox said you were tired. Everything okay?"

That was a matter of opinion, wasn't it?

"Oh, yeah. Everything's fine," I assured him, heading for the coffeepot. "Just a long day."

"Knox wasn't giving you a hard time, was he?" Webb stroked a hand over his beard the same way Knox sometimes did. "He likes you a lot, you know. I think he just... doesn't know how to express it sometimes."

I imagined the look on Webb's face if he'd seen just how well Knox had expressed his *like* a few hours before.

"It's okay, Webb. I promise." I sipped my coffee. "Speaking of which, have you seen Knox this morning? I wanted to go over a couple things."

That sounded way more profesh than saying *I wanted a hug*, right?

Webb and Drew exchanged a look.

"Knox went out to Jack's place," Webb said, and I expected him to get that smug little matchmakey look he usually got whenever he referred to Jack and Knox in the same sentence, but he didn't.

"Ah. Working on the ramp?" I asked brightly, taking a seat across from Webb.

Webb shook his head. "That's at his mom's house. No, Jack has a money pit of his own. He says he's renovating it, though I'm pretty sure he's just delaying its eventual collapse." He rolled his eyes with teasing affection. "He doesn't usually let anyone but Hawk come near the place —probably since Hawk's too timid to tell Jack he should tear it down and start over—but they're calling for October snow this afternoon and tonight, and there are a couple holes in the roof that need to be tarped over, which is a two-person job. I would've gone, but I have another attorney meeting this morning. I offered to reschedule, but—"

"But neither Jack nor Knox would want that," Drew said firmly, "which was why Knox volunteered."

"Right. Aiden comes first," I agreed, pretending the idea of a day without Knox to distract me from... Knox... didn't leave me feeling completely blah.

"So, Knox said your interview yesterday went well?" Drew limped toward the table in his boot and set a huge stack of piping hot pancakes in front of me. "Apple cinnamon."

"They smell terrific, thank you." I took a huge bite and chewed it with total concentration, hoping Drew and Webb would move on to discuss something else, but they both watched me expectantly. I swallowed. "Yeah, it went well. The company sounds amazing, but I had a couple concerns. Like, they would want me to learn to do things their way, which is fine, but..."

"But you don't wanna become a cog in The Man's corporate machinery." Drew nodded approvingly. "Right on."

Webb rolled his eyes. "You and Gage can go tie-dye something later, Uncle Drew. Let him finish."

"No, he's right. I just don't know if I'm gonna get what I want out of the job. You guys have spoiled me, you know?"

"I think it's great that you're being particular," Drew said. "And not just because it means we get to keep you until the end of the year and have you finish our Pipsy app. Speaking of which, I've had a couple thoughts about that after talking with Norm Avery and Kathy Tinson—you know, from Tinson's Berries. Can I talk to you about that later today?"

"Yeah, of course." God. I *wanted* to stay for a few more months. I liked everything about Little Pippin Hollow— this family that had adopted me, the food, the nice people in town, the food, the mountain views that were so different from home but had become familiar so fast, the work I was doing here, the food, and Knox.

More than anything, Knox.

But if I got any more comfortable here, how would I ever leave when it was time?

My phone chimed with a call, and I retrieved it from my sweatshirt pocket, hoping it was Knox and knowing it wasn't.

"Oh." I frowned when I realized it was Jason calling from Rubicon. I quickly explained to Webb and Drew before excusing myself to step out of the room. "Jason, hi."

After a few pleasantries, Jason got right to the point, explaining that his boss was impressed enough with me to consider making some exceptions... as long as he could meet me in person.

Jason lowered his voice. "Between you and me, I think Max was impressed that you didn't accept immediately. I think he might ask you to go to New York right away after all." Then, more loudly, he said, "Would it be possible for you to come in for a second interview. Maybe *today*?"

I looked at the giant clock on the bookcase beside the television in the living room. It was just after ten, which meant I could be there by two at the latest… but I found myself curiously reluctant. I was supposed to meet with Drew in the afternoon to talk about Pipsy. And Knox would be back by then…

But he still wouldn't be picking *me* to have a relationship with, I reminded myself firmly. Not when he had his career to get back to. Which was why I needed to rip this Band-Aid right the fuck off while I still could. And what better way than by giving a second chance to the company that *had* picked me?

"Yeah, I could come down," I agreed. "Maybe by two thirty?"

"Perfect," Jason said. "We'll see you then."

I turned back toward the kitchen and found Webb and Drew standing in the doorway, watching me avidly.

"So? What'd he say?" Webb demanded.

"They want to improve on their job offer and *allay my fears*." I snorted, still not totally able to believe it. "I'm going down to meet with them today."

"Today?" Drew frowned. "Alone?"

I smiled gently. "I drove the whole way here from Florida, remember? And if I might be moving to the city, I should probably bite the bullet and learn to drive there, right? It was nice of Knox to take me the last couple times, but he, ah…" I swallowed. "He won't be doing that forever."

Drew shook his shaggy head. "It's gonna snow in a couple hours, kiddo. Not the best day to be independent."

277

He was usually so easygoing that his worried expression gave me pause.

But then I pushed right through it. "Nah. I'll be nearly to Boston by the time it starts snowing, and I'll plan to get a hotel down there tonight. I'll be back tomorrow or the next day. It'll be a good thing," I assured him. "You'll see."

Now I just needed to convince myself.

Chapter Sixteen

KNOX

I'd started out the day wrapped up in Gage Goodman, and I'd kinda planned to stay that way. We'd spent the night making love with tenderness I'd never experienced before… but it had felt strangely bittersweet, too. Like the air had been clogged with all the things we hadn't said.

I'd slept well, because I always did with Gage, but the moment I'd woken up, I hadn't wanted to let him out of my sight.

I felt like there was an invisible countdown timer running faster and faster, no matter how good things seemed between us.

In my case, I knew exactly what I'd been holding back, the words I hadn't been saying: I was falling for Gage Goodman. Hell, I was pretty sure I'd *already* fallen, hard and irrevocably, all the way to the bottom of the love pool, despite all the excuses and stern warnings I'd tied around myself like life preservers to keep myself afloat.

But how could I tell him how I felt—how could I burden him with that when he was finally ready to make the leap to having the career he wanted, whether at Rubicon or somewhere else? I couldn't. It wouldn't be fair.

Which was another reason I'd planned to spend every minute with Gage while I could.

"Y'all set over there, Knox?" Jack yelled across the expanse of blue tarp we'd laid across his roof.

I groaned. I could say definitively that I had not planned to spend a single moment of my day twenty feet in the air, on a roof with the structural integrity of a rice cracker, while the wind howled in my ears, but unfortunately for me, a random October snowstorm, Jack's crumbling yellow Victorian, and my interfering brother had conspired to make other plans.

"This side's done," I yelled, securing the last screw in a tarp-wrapped two-by-four to the roof. "You need help over there?"

"Nope. Got it secured under the eave like you told me," Jack yelled back, his voice caught by a gust of wind. "Just the last crosspiece now?"

"Yup. I'll grab it." I hurried down the ladder on my side of the house—at least as much as I *could* hurry while climbing down an aluminum ladder that creaked concerningly every time I shifted my weight.

"I need to lay off the pumpkin bread," I muttered as I finally reached the ground. I hadn't been to a gym since leaving Massachusetts.

I grabbed one end of a board I'd cut earlier and dragged it around the house so I could hand it up to Jack. "Got it?"

"Yeah. Fuck, man, you're a lifesaver." I heard the whine of the drill three times in succession, and then Jack leaned over the edge of the roof and gave me a thumbs-up. "We done?"

"Far as I can tell, we should be." I held the ladder so Jack could climb down safely. "The tarp should hold the snow out for a little while, until you can get it fixed."

Jack sighed in relief when he reached the ground. "Yep. I'll get to it one of these days. Webb thinks I bit off more than I could chew with this house, but sometimes you've gotta take a chance, right? And she's got a solid foundation and good bones, even if she's not real—" He gently patted one of the turned spindles that comprised the railing of the wide front porch, and the whole section of railing fell down with a crash. "—sturdy," he concluded with a shake of his head. "God*fucking*dammit."

"Well, I wish you luck," I told him sincerely. "Hey, if you don't need anything else, I might—"

"Can I get you a cup of coffee to warm you up before you go?" Jack asked. "Left a pot brewing in the kitchen."

I looked dubiously toward the rear of the house, and Jack laughed. "I promise, the back side of the house is way safer."

I still hesitated. Gage was at the orchard, possibly still in bed, and I was eager to get back. But then again, Webb and Drew were probably also there, so we wouldn't get a chance to talk for hours anyway.

"Sure," I agreed.

Jack led me around the back of the house and through a wooden door to a kitchen that looked an awful lot like the kitchen at home—the same scarred oak floors and white paneled cabinets. The only difference was that Jack's kitchen was filled with brand-new appliances and looked like it had been remodeled recently.

"The only room in the whole house that's done," Jack said proudly, echoing my thoughts. "Hawk did all the painting and sanded the floors while I installed the cabinets and finished the countertops. I still don't have working heat in my bedroom, but at least I can cook in peace." He smiled. "Priorities, right?" He nodded toward a solid-looking stool at the counter. "Grab a seat. You take your coffee black?"

"Yeah. Can't believe you remember."

"Eh." He slid the coffee over to me. "Occupational hazard. Anyway, thanks again for coming out here. I apologize for dragging you away from your day. I told Webb I'd be fine to wait and see, but—"

"But Webb would worry himself to death, so you just agreed?" I gave him a lopsided smile. "That's Webb. Always trying to look out for everyone else."

Jack's brow puckered, even as he smiled back. "Funny. He says that about you."

"Me?" I shook my head. "I mean, I love them all, obviously, but I lived in Boston until a month ago." I thought about it. "I mean… five months ago." Damn, that had gone by fast.

Jack made a noise of disagreement. "The way I heard it, you moved to Boston all those years ago partly *because* you wanted to take care of them. The way Webb tells the story, you told your dad to leave Webb the orchard."

I shook my head harder. "No. I mean, *yes*, it's true about the inheritance thing. But I wasn't meant to live here. I was always more interested in hard numbers than apple varietals. If I'd stayed, the orchard would have suffered."

"Whereas Webb was interested in the apples and not the numbers." Jack said this easily, casually. But I wasn't fooled.

"His heart was here," I said firmly.

"And where was yours?"

I opened my mouth, then shut it again. "Boston. Naturally. I was focused on my career." I lifted an eyebrow. "And I've done fairly well at it."

"Oh, no doubt." Jack sipped his coffee and leaned back against his refrigerator. "And then you sent money home so Reed and all the younger kids could go to school. And you bought your way back into the business when you came home. Am I missing anything?"

For some reason—probably because I'd been hanging around with Gage so much—I wanted to argue with Jack. Lecture him. His facts were correct, but I felt like he was drawing a conclusion that wasn't true.

"Seems about right," I said lightly. "You know how it goes. Family is family." I took a big sip of coffee and set my mug down with a clack. "I should really be getting back."

"Sure. But seriously, thanks again for coming."

"Anytime." I smiled ruefully as I stood. "Don't tell Webb I said that, though, or he'll have me out here twice a day."

"No shit. Hawk and I were talking about that just yesterday. Webb's my best friend, and he means well, but he's oblivious." Jack shook his head with a grin and trailed me toward the back door.

Privately, I thought Webb was not the only oblivious one. Jack seemed to feel sort of big-brotherly toward Hawk, but I wasn't sure Hawk's feelings were quite so platonic.

"In particular," Jack went on, "Hawk thinks it's hilarious that Webb doesn't seem to have noticed that you and Gage are in love, and I can't decide if it's my duty as his friend to fill him in or just let him keep bumbling along." He grinned.

Meanwhile, I stopped short in the doorway with one foot in midair.

"You… Wait, what?"

"Oh, no, I was kidding! I'm not gonna say shit. It's your business. Yours and Gage's. I'll let you be the ones to tell him," Jack assured me, misunderstanding the reason for my shock. "I just think it's kinda weird that Webb hasn't sensed it. Like maybe all the shit with Amanda has, I dunno, made it harder for him to spot romantic love, even when it's happening right in front of him?" He wrinkled his nose. "I worry about him sometimes, you know? I hope he finds a woman who'll love him."

I couldn't think about Webb at that precise moment. I set my foot down—*inside* the door. "You think I'm in love with Gage."

Jack blinked. "Uh. Yes. Are you not?"

"No, I—" I hesitated, my heart beating hard. "I am." I couldn't deny it. "I just didn't know it was so... obvious."

Did Gage know, too? Had he sensed it?

I felt like I was thirty-nine going on twelve. *Did he like me? Did he know I liked him?*

And why was I even surprised anymore? I hadn't been able to control my emotional response to the man since the day he'd arrived and literally hurtled himself into my arms. He made everything seem so simple. So possible.

So terrifying.

"Ah. Well, I mean, it's not *that* obvious—" Jack paused for a second. "Actually, I'm lying. It's super obvious to anyone who has eyes and a brain... assuming they haven't also been fucked up by their ex-wife leaving them, and their mom dying when they were a kid, and their former stepmom leaving their dad, and therefore conditioned to believe that being happy and in love is a precursor to doom because love isn't permanent. In other words, to anyone but Webb." He shrugged. "But, hey, congratulations anyway, man. I haven't gotten to know him that well, but Gage seems pretty awesome. And he clearly cares about you a lot." One side of his mouth quirked up in a half-smile.

I couldn't return it.

In fact, I was pretty sure I needed some of Dr. Travers's breathing exercises, stat. Wouldn't it be just my luck to have a panic attack over a revelation like this?

"I've gotta go," I told Jack, and then I strode... half jogged... full-out *ran* for my truck, needing to get back to the orchard and Gage immediately.

Gage cared about me *a lot*.

I mean, I knew that.

I'd known that.

Of course I did.

He showed it time and time again in the way he'd always turned *toward* me no matter what, the way he'd made himself vulnerable to me, the way he'd smiled and teased and laughed and shared his joy with me. But after talking to Jack, it felt like clouds in my mind had blown off, leaving the bright, shining truth staring me in the face.

Gage cared about me... *a lot*. And what had I done for Gage?

Gage had wanted to be friends. I'd denied him.

Gage had wanted me. I'd come up with every excuse to keep him at a distance.

Gage had called me his boyfriend. I'd blown it off.

Gage had been honest and open with me... and I'd given him lies and technicalities, half-baked justifications and rationalizations.

Gage lived his life honestly and fearlessly. He'd befriended my nephew and helped my brother, he'd gotten to know nearly everyone in Little Pippin Hollow personally, and he *liked* them—even the ones who cheated at pumpkin carving.

He was smart. He was kind. He was brave as fuck,

because he knew the risks of loving unreservedly and he took them anyway.

And I loved him.

I felt a thrill of fear that was all out of proportion to those three little words, but I didn't step back from it.

Because loving him wasn't something I should fucking *hide* like it was a terrible secret that would burden him. It didn't have to be a burden at all unless I made it one. It didn't have to come with strings unless I tied them on myself. And it didn't have to end in disaster, even though, like Jack said, Webb had been conditioned to think of it that way...

And so had I.

Because I'd watched the same poor examples of relationships he had. I'd watched as my dad had been heartbroken twice and while Amanda had not only left Webb, but abandoned her own son.

Love did end in disaster. At least... at least that was what I seemed to have internalized somehow.

This realization was terrifying, though. Which was real? Were those examples the right ones—that love really was mostly destructive and cruel—or were those anomalies? Was true love actually possible? And if so...

If so, could I have it with Gage Goodman, the most amazing, annoying, adorable, snarktastic, stupid T-shirt–wearing, cowphobic sweetheart to ever walk the earth?

As I drove down the twisty mountain road toward the orchard, I could hear Gage's voice in my head asking me why I was so scared to be happy. I'd denied it, because in some areas I *was* happy—things like work and casual friendships. The things I could control.

But when it came to the things that mattered more—the *people* who mattered more—I was a chickenshit because I had no control at all. So I'd tried to pretend that living away from the Hollow all these years was the practical choice, just like I'd tried to pretend that keeping things casual with Gage was the smart choice.

And Jesus Christ, all those months of therapy and I hadn't made a breakthrough this huge, but one cup of coffee in Jack's house of ruin had done the trick. Or maybe it was Gage who'd done it, by showing me over and over that love and friendship weren't zero-sum games.

I loved him. I repeated the words to myself, and it was easier this time. It felt *good.*

And Gage deserved to know it. Even if he didn't feel the same. Even if he left Little Pippin Hollow eventually anyway. He was a miracle who'd appeared in my life out of nowhere. And he made me want to have faith in something for the first time in a long time.

The drive home felt a billion times longer than it should have, even though the roads were mostly empty. The first flakes had begun to fall, and though none were sticking to the roads yet, the trees with their slightly faded foliage were getting iced over. The storm seemed to be coming in a lot faster than predicted, and I was really hoping Gage would be amenable to just taking a snow day to lie in my bed and watch the flakes fall through the window.

I realized giddily that he probably hadn't ever had a snow day growing up. I wanted to spend his first one with him.

I pulled into the gravel area right outside the gift shop barn and parked the truck haphazardly. Webb had done the smart thing and kept the shop closed for the day, so there wasn't a single other car in the lot.

That should have been my first clue that something was wrong, but I missed it.

I slammed the truck door closed and raced around to

the back door and into the office like a kid on Christmas morning, beyond eager to see Gage.

I threw open the closed office door. "Hey, Goodman, what do you say we—"

But the office was empty. The lights were off, and Gage's laptop was gone.

I grinned. *Perfect.* Gage had already decided to work upstairs, meaning I wouldn't have to convince him at all.

I jogged back outside and saw Hawk wave from the back porch of the farmhouse. "Knox, hey! Come over."

I lifted a hand in greeting but didn't slow down as I took the steps to the apartment two at a time, holding the railing so I wouldn't slip on the quickly accumulating snow. "Yeah, later!"

He probably wants to know how Jack was, I thought with a smirk. And I understood why, because in a full 180-degree, who-the-hell-am-I-anyway about-face, I'd become a sap who was in love with love.

I'd fought it and fought it and fought it, just like Gage had said, and then I'd changed my opinion all at once. But I wasn't pretending the change was my idea—this was all thanks to Gage Goodman.

I tried the doorknob, but it didn't budge, which was unusual unless Gage and I were fucking. I got out my keys and unlocked it, wondering what Gage had thought he needed privacy for. I had a few ideas, and they all made my stomach clench in anticipation.

But I could tell the moment I opened the door that the place wasn't occupied. No Gage, no laptop, no heavy coat on the peg by the door.

Damn it. He was over at the farmhouse eating lunch. I groaned as I shut the door again, preparing myself to be polite and civil to my family and not literally drag

Goodman out of there by his pretty, just-fucked hair so I could do unspeakable—

"Knox." Webb greeted me at the bottom of the stairs, along with Hawk, who looked subdued. "Y'okay?"

"Yeah, I'm great." I grinned. "Better than I've been in a while." Acknowledging the truth apparently did that for a person.

Webb's mouth pulled down, like he hadn't expected that response. "Everything went well at Jack's, then?"

I rolled my eyes. "Webb. I love you, but you have to let that die. There's nothing between me and Jack but friendship, okay? I'm…" I started to tell Webb about my revelation, but I stopped myself. Gage deserved to hear it first. "Is Goodman at the house with Drew?" Another thought occurred to me, and I winced. "Please tell me he didn't go to town for lunch."

Webb and Hawk exchanged a look. "You haven't checked your texts in a while, have you?"

I patted my pockets for my phone and frowned. "No. The service up at Jack's place is for shit, so I shut my phone off before it killed itself trying to find a signal. Why? What'd I miss?" My pulse kicked up instinctively as I skimmed my texts. Two from Webb and one from Hawk fifteen minutes ago asking me to call home. "Where's Goodman?"

My brothers exchanged another look, and I wanted to shake them both.

"He's gone," Hawk said softly. "To Boston."

"No he's not. We just got home yesterday."

"He got a call earlier from the interview guy," Webb began. "They wanted to improve their offer. Move him to New York right away. They wanted him down in Boston ASAP."

"Fuck." I pushed a hand through my hair. "Why didn't he wait for me?"

Webb tilted his head in an accusatory way. "You tell me. Because Drew suggested that he shouldn't go alone, and Gage said something about you not always being around to help him, and I know you two were fighting yesterday, and Gage looked *sad* this morning, and I swear to God, if you ran off my programmer, Knox, I'm gonna be *pissed.*"

"Oh." I rubbed at the ache in the center of my chest. The idea that I'd made Gage sad, that he'd thought he couldn't rely on me, killed me.

He hadn't even texted to say he was leaving.

I'd fucked this up. I'd messed up completely.

My brain began a loop of awful possibilities, and in that moment they seemed as real and unavoidable as the earth's turning. Gage wouldn't listen to me if I apologized or told him how I felt. Gage had moved to New York and wouldn't say goodbye. Gage was driving himself in the snow and he was going to get hurt.

I couldn't stop it. I couldn't control any of it.

My heart rate kicked up to marathon-sprinting levels and I started panting as my lungs forgot how to expand properly. I was almost sure I was going to vomit.

Hawk put a hand on my arm. "We delayed him as long as we could. He only left twenty minutes ago, and he's running an errand for Uncle Drew on his way out of town, so I bet you can catch him!"

My mind latched onto the fact that he'd left twenty minutes ago. If I hadn't stayed for a cup of coffee, I wouldn't have been too late.

I gripped the railing of the stairs with a palm gone damp as my vision throbbed like a pulse. A line of heat—the kind that burned so hot it felt momentarily cold—crawled down my arms and legs until my fingers and toes went numb. I could practically feel the blood pooling in my thighs and my muscles prepared to run or fight or lift trees... if only I could figure out how to *breathe*, damn it.

"Knox," Webb said firmly but calmly. He was right beside me somehow, propping me up, though I hadn't even noticed him moving. "Knox, you're having a panic attack. Come on and sit on the step right here. Perfect. Now breathe with me. That's right—in, then hold, then—"

I held out a hand to ward him off. I did *not* need to be *breathed with*.

Webb backed off but didn't go away completely. He stayed right beside me and kept encouraging me. "Okay, you've got this. Keep going."

I tried hard to focus on Webb's face and the sound of his voice, to mimic his deep, even breathing, although the white noise in my head was astoundingly loud and I felt like I was falling, falling, *falling* into infinity.

"All is well with me," I told him in a raspy voice. "*All is well with me.*"

"It is," Webb confirmed. "Keep breathing."

Several minutes or hours or years later—I honestly had no clue—Hawk said, "You're doing great. Now name five things you can feel or hear or see around you, Knox."

I swallowed. I knew what he was doing—that this was a standard panic attack response—but I wasn't sure how he knew to do it.

"The snow," I croaked. "The barn. Th-the step underneath me. The ground under my boots."

I wasn't falling. The ground was solid, and my brothers

were standing by me. I was finally able to take a deep breath of sweet, sweet oxygen.

"That's only four things," Webb prompted. "Not five."

I blew out a shaky breath and lifted my head to frown at him. "Seriously? You're giving me shit for not counting properly? I don't think that's a standard response for panic attacks."

Webb gave me a half-smile. "It was distracting, wasn't it? I got some pamphlets from Dr. Paget in town and one suggested that an amusing distraction could help."

"*Amusing*, not *annoying*," I said wryly.

"Eh." He shrugged. "The pamphlets don't know what distracts you like we do."

I closed my eyes briefly and ran both hands over my face. My family *did* know me. I didn't know who I'd thought I was fooling by pretending that my mental health was my problem to handle alone.

"Come on," Hawk said. "Let's go upstairs. You need to relax for a bit."

"I can't now. I have to find Gage," I told them. "I have things to tell him, and I'd like to do that before he agrees to take a job." I wanted him to know I wanted to be with him, whether it was here in Vermont, or in Boston or New York, or… hell, anywhere.

"Rest first," Hawk said, more insistently than he'd ever said anything to me before, and in my head, I heard Goodman saying that worrying about your brothers was a two-way street. "Trust us, Knox."

I sighed and let them lead me upstairs, where Hawk made me a cup of tea while I changed out of my sweaty clothes and Webb kept up a constant stream of nonsense chatter while I sat on the sofa and drained it.

If I'd ever doubted how much Webb loved me, hearing my taciturn brother voluntarily begin a conversation about what color he might paint the barn—debating only with himself all the while, since neither Hawk nor I had an opinion—then segue into bitching about how Aiden's teacher had moved right next door—"when he doesn't know *shit* about proper orchard management!"—then move into the Averill Union Beavers' chance of clinching a football playoff spot without pausing for breath proved it beyond a shadow of a doubt.

Finally, I set my cup down on the table. "I've got to go. I need to find Goodman if I can."

Hawk tilted his head and watched me like he was trying to gauge if I was capable of making that decision.

"I'm okay. I promise. I…" I hesitated, then volunteered, "After a panic attack, I feel tired but wired. Like you might after a run or a workout. I'm safe to drive."

Hawk and Webb exchanged a glance.

Webb nodded. "Okay. Because you *do* need to find him, if only so you can apologize for whatever put that look in his eyes earlier. And you need to tell him you love him." He grimaced. "And this convo is done not a minute too soon, because I've run out of words."

I blinked. "Wait, you know that me and Gage…?"

"Are a giant romantic *thing*? No, Edwin Knox," Webb said, lifting an eyebrow. "Drew filled me in on his suspicions this morning after you left for Jack's, which was necessary because my *brother* had been trying to keep it a secret."

I winced. "I know. That's my fault. And Gage leaving is my fault, too, because I…" I imagined Gage telling me to be honest. To trust Webb to handle it. "I was planning on going back to Boston at the end of the year."

Webb rolled his eyes. "Yeah, now that I *did* know."

"Wait." I narrowed my eyes. "You knew? But…"

"Dude, yes. We all did."

"Yep." Hawk nodded. "Even Emma. Maybe even Aiden."

Webb rolled his eyes. "You've had one foot out the door the whole time you've been here. Why do you think I've been pushing you to do Norm Avery's financial planning and marry my best friend? God, why do you think Drew keeps finding receipts from the Great Depression and putting them in boxes for you to sort? We knew you were thinking to leave, and we wanted to give you a reason to stay. If going back to Boston is what'll truly make you happy and *healthy*—" He touched his temple. "—then go. Nobody wants to hold you back, Knox. But if there's a part of you that wants to come back—if there's a part of you that would like to be here full-time for real—we wanted you to know that we want that. You have a place here waiting for you, and we miss you when you're gone." He clapped my shoulder. "*I* miss you."

Wow. I swallowed. "I don't know what to say. I…"

"Don't say a damn thing," Webb scoffed. "*Christ*. I've had all the talking I can take until after Thanksgiving at least. Go get your man and talk to *him*. He probably wants to hear it."

"And bring him home," Hawk said softly.

I nodded confidently. "I will."

But as I pulled back down the driveway through the heavy snow and headed for the highway a little faster than I should have, I directed a glance at the roof of the truck.

"Quick reminder, Lord, that I do not live in Grey's Anatomy-land, or Downton Abbey-land. I do not require a car accident to add drama to my day, because I'm plenty fucking good at that all by myself. Though if you were looking for an opportunity to practice the walk-on-water shit, maybe you could give me a sign that'll help me find the man I love, preferably before there's six inches of snow on the ground?"

But then my phone let out a strange chime, and I remembered in a flash that I didn't need to follow a sign from above… because Gage had already given me a signal I could follow.

Chapter Seventeen

GAGE

In retrospect, I was beginning to believe my trip to Boston had been a miscalculation.

In my defense, I blamed the lumberjacks.

First, there'd been Webb, giving me minute-by-minute weather projections while I got my suit out of the closet in the barn-apartment and threw my toiletries in a bag. It was almost like he'd been *trying* to get in my way as much as possible, ensuring that a ten-minute packing sesh turned into a thirty-minute dance marathon as we stumbled around each other.

Then Hawk had come home from the morning rush at the restaurant, and he'd come upstairs to "help" also, which had mostly involved him begging me in his sweet, bewildered voice to repeat every detail of the conversation I'd had with Jason—*twice*—but I couldn't get cranky because no decent human could get cranky with Hawk.

Then they'd both insisted that I say goodbye to Drew, since otherwise he might be so upset I'd forgotten him that he'd trip over his boot and break his other ankle... which was extremely unlikely, of course, but once the idea was in my head, I'd decided it would probably be best to err on the side of caution.

But then Drew, who was a lumberjack, too, albeit of the older, devil's-lettuce-loving variety, had been worried about what Aiden would think if I left without saying goodbye. He'd insisted that I take a minute to leave the boy a farewell letter—which had seemed really melodramatic, considering I wasn't going off to war and would, in fact, be back by Sunday at the latest—so I'd compromised by texting Aiden through the Pond App and prepared to leave.

Except then Marco had come rushing in, gasping for air like he'd run all the way over from his house next door, and breathlessly begged me to teach him how to use the Pond App just in case "anyone in the family" went missing while I was gone. That was such a horrifying thought, I hadn't been able to leave without giving him a basic rundown on how the app worked and how everyone in the family with the app installed could see where anyone else in the family was, as long as they had their privacy settings configured right.

Webb had insisted I take a coffee in a to-go cup to keep me awake—despite it being eleven in the morning and me being perfectly well rested—and had brewed me a fresh pot.

But then Drew had implored me to wait for his pumpkin bread—*"with the chocolate chips you suggested, Gage!"* —to come out of the oven so I could have a snack for the road to go with my coffee… which, admittedly, hadn't been a hard sell, since it had been a minute since breakfast and I'd been quite peckish.

Then Hawk suggested I bring a blanket in the car, just in case I got stranded—because people in New England packed emergency shit in their cars like that in winter—so

I'd waited while he fetched a blanket from his own room, which had taken about as long as if he'd knitted it for me himself.

But when Marco had asked if I needed to pee before I left because "you never know when the urge might hit you while you're on the road," I'd had *enough*.

No more snacks, no more blankies, no more final pees. I'd gotten in the car and left…

Well. Sort of.

I mean, when Drew had limped out onto the porch after me and begged me to take a loaf of the pumpkin bread to Betty Ann Wolff, the head of the Little Pippin Hookers on my way through town—"because she'd kill herself trying to come and fetch it in this snow, Gage!"—I might have agreed.

And when I'd stopped to deliver it, I might also have gotten sucked into "stepping inside to enjoy a slice with a lonely old woman, dear," but in my defense, Betty Ann's green eyes had reminded me of Knox's and I couldn't argue.

It was only after I'd gotten down her driveway and headed toward the highway that I remembered one very large, lumberjack-shaped oversight.

I hadn't told Knox I was leaving town.

I'd planned to! I *had*. My intention had never been to flounce away or to leave in a huff, because I wasn't flouncy or huffy or angry at him at all anymore. It wasn't his fault I'd broken the rules, right? It wasn't his fault I'd smashed them to smithereens and wanted *more*.

I'd tried calling him, but his phone had gone straight to voicemail, and I hadn't known quite what to say in a message other than, "Hey, I'm purposely leaving before you get home and volunteer to chauffeur me because I don't think I could handle spending time in your truck with you again while all this unrequited love juice is flowing from my pores," which I thought maybe sounded just a tiny bit desperate.

I'd been so discombobulated, I'd gotten halfway down the snowy, deserted road toward the highway before I'd remembered that texting was a thing and I could send him a message, but when I'd pulled over into one of the scenic overlooks on Route 26 and opened my phone, the Pond App had already been open from my impromptu tutoring session with Marco, and I'd realized maybe there was something better than texting. Maybe I could message him through the messaging section of the Pond App as a way to remind him that I was still part of the orchard and that I'd be back.

Back at least for a while.

Back at least long enough to say goodbye.

Me: *Hey! Your phone was going straight to voicemail, so I'm messaging instead. I had to head to Boston for a second interview, and I'll be staying at a hotel tonight. Call me if you want!*

I debated for a full half minute about adding a heart emoji before deciding I didn't like the person I was becoming—second-guessing and overthinking were not my favorite or my best, thank you very much—so I'd added the heart and hit Send. Then I'd immediately thrown the phone onto the passenger's seat so I wouldn't be tempted to watch it and pulled back out onto the road.

It felt odd driving down this road without Knox. It was strange how quickly you could get used to something and how fast you could come to miss it. Case in point: both sides of the road out here past the Apple of My Eye Bed and Breakfast were lined with cow fields interspersed with scenic overlooks, and I was feeling nostalgic for *both* those things.

Yes, me, feeling sentimental attachment to *bovines*.

How lowering.

I wondered if maybe this was what Knox had been looking to protect me from back at the beginning with his "Gage, I don't want to hurt you" schtick. He'd known I'd fall for him, and he'd known he wouldn't pick me, and I hadn't listened, and…

Damn it, I was crying. Actual salty fluid leaking from my actual eyeholes, and no one was showing me pictures of sad puppies while Sarah MacLachlan played "Angel" or anything.

This day got worse and worse.

I reached down for a napkin to dry my stupid eyes—one of the twenty-seven napkins Drew had packed with my pumpkin bread—and in that literally *one second* that my eyes were off the road, a giant *beast* galloped into my path. I swung the car left into the opposite lane to avoid it and found myself sliding all over the road despite there being only one inch of snow on the ground.

I hit my brakes hard, and the whole car juddered and slid, juddered and slid, in a super-dramatic fashion, until I ended up on the other side of the road, facing back in the direction I'd come, with my two passenger-side wheels in a ditch and the car tilted at a crazy angle.

Meanwhile, the cow that had sauntered into my path watched me judgmentally from the other lane.

"*Oh, holy shitballs,*" I said out loud. My head felt stuffy, and everything smelled metallic, and I couldn't stop shaking, and I needed to pee—Marco had been right!—which made me start laughing hysterically and then cry some more. *"Holy shit, holy shit, holy shit."*

I'd almost *died*. Or okay, maybe not, but it was as close

as I'd ever come. My entire life had flashed before my eyes —all the people I loved, all the good times I'd had for the past twenty-four years—and the biggest, best part of it was Little Pippin Hollow.

With Knox.

I gripped the steering wheel—squeeze, release, squeeze, release—with both hands as my heart pumped pure adrenaline through my body.

What was I doing? What the actual fuck was I doing, heading off to Boston to *maybe* get a job I'd *maybe* love?

I *had* a job I loved.

I had a place to live and people I cared about who liked and cared about me. I had a purpose. I was making an impact on people's lives *already*, in a way that didn't require me to put my ideas through a committee first.

I heard Jay's voice in my head saying, "Follow your instincts. There are lots of ways to be happy and success-ful," and I realized that I didn't need to go out in the world and seek that, because I already had it. I'd found it. It was *mine*.

I could seek-no-further.

Knox had interpreted that story entirely wrong—which should not have been surprising, I thought with a quick burst of affection. He'd taken that tale to mean that you were supposed to go taste the apples on everyone else's tree to assure yourself that you had the best, because to him, being happy was asking for trouble. But it was okay to be content with the apple you had. In fact—

"Okay, cute and delightful baby Jesus, I'm being sincere this time. Please do not let this tendency to think in apple metaphors be a permanent condition. Amen," I murmured.

Because otherwise Knox wouldn't let me live it down.

Knox!

I dove for my phone to call him, to text him, to commission a skywriter—did they have those in Vermont? If not, I'd import one—so I could get him a message.

I loved him.

I. Loved. Him.

And he could fight it and fight it and fight it, but I was willing to risk everything I had that in the end, after he'd crunched the numbers and analyzed the data, he'd recognize the rightness of it.

We were meant to be together.

The phone had fallen down on the floor when the car slid, and the first time I lunged for it, I nearly strangled myself with my seat belt. I took off my belt and dove across the console searching for it, ass in the air and head in the wheel well, when suddenly my door was wrenched open and big, strong hands were reaching for me.

"Gage? *Gage, baby.* Oh, fuck. Are you hurt? Stay still, don't move. I'm calling an ambulance." His hands pawed at my legs and ass, any part of me he could reach, assessing me for damages and ready to knit me back together himself if he had to.

"Knox? Oh, God, you're here. Let me up. Let me up! I'm fine. I promise. I'm not hurt. I was just looking for my phone." I held the device up triumphantly. "I was going to call you. How did you…?" I shook my head. "How are you here?"

Knox dragged me from the car and set me on my feet in the snowy street like I weighed nothing. His big hands patted me through my down jacket like he couldn't quite believe I was actually alright. "I got your message. I… I tracked you with the Pond App. I was going to find you. Bring you back home to the orchard or offer to take you to Boston myself if you really wanted to go, but then… "

His questing hands reached my face, and he cupped

my jaw gently, running his thumbs over the freckles on my cheeks the way he sometimes did. His green eyes were huge and shining with an emotion that would have made my heart speed up if it hadn't already been sprinting like crazy. "When I saw your car tilted off the road, and you upside down like that, I... I..."

"I know," I said, trying to soothe him as much as I could, despite my own jangling nerves. "But I'm okay. Everything is okay."

"I've never been so scared," Knox admitted. "I thought maybe I was too late."

"No." I shook my head wildly. "Not too late. I'm not going to Boston. I mean, I *was*, but then that cow leaped out into the road like a fucking panther, all teeth and claws and *arrrrgh*, and it scared the shit out of me, and I thought I might die, and I ran off the road, and I decided I was being an idiot and I needed to head back. I needed to find you and tell you that I..." I took a deep, shuddering breath and wrapped my hands around his wrists, holding his palms against my face. "That I love you."

His lips parted in shock, but I kept talking because I needed him to hear me before he pulled away. "No, no, listen. I know you don't feel the same way just yet. And I know you don't want to make promises you can't keep because you don't want to let me down. But it's too late to protect me, okay? So don't do that thing where you're gonna walk away so I can save myself because I don't need saving. I love you. I'm in this. A hundred percent. And I... *I pick you*, Knox Sunday. In the apple orchard of life, you are my Seek-No-Further. And I love every grumpy, loving, sexy, protective, overopinionated, adorable, infuriating, encouraging, gorgeous, dumbass bone in your body. And it's okay if you don't pick me back yet. Because I have faith enough for the both of us. You are the man I want, and—"

I ran out of air and had to suck in another breath… and that was when he kissed me.

Knox's lips molded to mine as he pushed me back against the side of the car, and his mouth moved against mine—gently at first, like I was a beautiful, precious thing, and then more forcefully, like I was a beautiful, precious thing *he'd almost lost* and he needed to claim me.

"I love you," he said the instant he pulled back. "I didn't want to interrupt you, 'cause you know I love when you talk, but I need you to know that. I pick you, too, Gage Goodman. I don't know how I got lucky enough to have you in my life, but I will *always* pick you."

I lifted on my tiptoes, wrapped my arm around his neck, and kissed him, too, loving the feel of his beard against my lips, his hands on my face, his heart beating against mine.

When he finally lifted his head, I felt dizzy, like I'd been shaken up in my own personal snow globe, and I grinned up at Knox's gorgeous face, just fucking delighted with the surprises life had had in store for me this day.

"I regret to inform you," I said with as much fake-sadness as I could muster, "that this entire loving scene was precipitated by a *cow*."

I glanced to my left, and Knox glanced to his right. The cow still stood in the road, a lonely witness to our love.

Knox whistled low. "Just *look* at the fangs on that thing. It's a miracle you survived."

"Did I mention the part where you're infuriating?"

He smirked. "You mentioned the part where you love me."

I shook my head. "Sadly, the cow factor invalidates this whole proceeding," I informed him. "In order for this love declaration to be binding, we're gonna need to reenact this. *Sans* cow." I shrugged. "I don't make the rules."

Knox lifted an eyebrow and wrapped his arms around my waist. "I could get behind that, I suppose… as long as we can do it without cars sliding off the road." He shivered just a little and lowered his head to kiss me again before pressing our foreheads together. "In fact, without snow, period."

"I don't know, I kinda like the snow," I said softly, leaning back in his embrace so I could watch the flakes fall dreamily around us.

Knox stared at me for a beat, heat kindling in his eyes. "Or we could find shelter and try it without *clothes.*"

"Ohhh." My eyes widened, and I straightened up. "Fuck, yes. Baby, I like the way you think. You're on," I agreed. "Let's go."

Knox wrapped his arms around my waist and spun me in a circle. "Christ, I love you. In thirty-nine years, you are the single best thing that's ever happened to me."

"Just wait and see how the next thirty-nine go." I wiggled my eyebrows. "You ain't seen nothin' yet."

Chapter Eighteen

KNOX

"We'll call for a tow truck as soon as we get home," I promised Gage as he buckled himself into my truck and set his duffel bag at his feet. He looked damp and bedraggled and pink-cheeked and perfect, and it was all I could do not to haul him against me right then and there. "As soon as we get you home and warm," I amended, tucking his car keys in my pocket.

"Home," Gage repeated slowly. "Home?"

I was so in love, so besotted, so drunk on relief and high on the feeling of being the luckiest bastard in the universe that even Gage's repeating thing was adorable.

"Home," I agreed. "To Sunday Orchard? Where we live?"

"Riiiight." Gage licked his lips. "Except... that's far away. And the weather is bad."

Ah, I hadn't even thought about that. I took his hand in my own larger one and brought it to my lips for a kiss. "I promise, baby, I've driven in snow for decades. I know what I'm doing."

"Riiiight," Gage said again. "But the Apple of My Eye

Bed and Breakfast is just there." He pointed out the windshield up ahead. "Exponentially closer. And, you know, if we go home, Webb is gonna wanna know where my car is, and Drew is gonna be all worried about me being in wet clothes, and Marco's gonna make us a hot toddy, and Aiden is going to want to build a snowman, and… I *love* that. I cannot tell you how much I love that. But, um, at this exact moment, I was sort of thinking…"

I flipped on my blinker and pulled into the parking lot without another word.

"Who is this reasonable man who looks like my Knox Sunday?" Gage wondered.

"Your Knox Sunday, huh?" Little carbonation bubbles of joy were fizzing up in my stomach, and I thought that if this was what true happiness felt like, I'd never actually experienced it before that moment. And I still wouldn't have, if not for Gage.

"My Knox Sunday," he confirmed, and just looking at him, I knew he felt the same joy I did.

When we parked, I grabbed his bag before he could, then went around the truck to help him down, partly because he was still a little jittery and mostly because I was. We giggled our way up the front steps of the old Victorian house like a pair of drunks and walked into…

"Oh. Wow. That's…" Gage stammered. "Apples."

There were apple clocks on the apple wallpaper and apple figurines on apple-shaped shelves. On the table in front of the apple-printed sofa sat an apple-shaped teapot.

"I forgot it was like this," I told him with a snicker. "I haven't been here since I was a kid."

"I don't think it's changed much since then," he whispered back. "Or at all."

"Gage!" Helena Fortnum called from behind the front

desk. "Full moon tonight. Come to drink some hooch and get naked with me?"

Gage's eyes widened, and he looked from me to Helena and back again. I saw the moment he realized that the bed-and-breakfast had been a strategic error, and we'd have been better off taking our chances with my family.

Fortunately, I wasn't nearly as polite as Gage was.

"We need a room, Ms. Fortnum," I said firmly, stepping in front of him. "Gage's car slid off the road a few yards down, and we need to escape the storm for a little while. We'll also need to call Hiram about coming to tow the car—"

She raised an eyebrow. "Just the one room?"

Suddenly, I felt about eight years old, which was the last time I'd been on the receiving end of that eyebrow. "Er. Yes, ma'am?"

"Mmmhmm. So you've decided to make an honest man of our Gage?" She pursed her lips.

Gage snickered and pressed his face against my back.

"I have. I very definitely have. Which is why we need a room," I persisted, loving the feel of Gage's laughter vibrating through my skin. "Before Gage catches a chill in his wet clothes."

Ms. Fortnum's face broke out into a wide smile. "I always knew you had it in you, Knox Sunday. Leave Gage's keys with me and I'll call Hiram myself." She winked. "I'll tell them to send the bill to Sunday Orchard."

"Perfect," I agreed.

She held out a key, but before I could grab it, she feinted left to catch a glimpse of Gage. "Gage, I never did tell you what sort of student Knox was, did I?"

Gage moved around me, curiosity caught. "No, ma'am, you never did." He side-eyed me. "I still say it was paste eating."

I stuck a single finger in the beltloop of his pants right above his ass and hauled him back against me.

"It *wasn't* paste eating," I growled, and his breathing hitched.

"He was the protective one." She winked at me over Goodman's head. "The one who'd give up everything to make sure everyone he loved was safe and happy. To make sure he didn't let anyone down. I'm glad he has someone looking out for him now."

I blinked at her, stunned, for one beat and then another while Gage beamed up at me.

"I can see that," he said softly. "And I promise, I will."

We stumbled down the hall and into our room, shedding our clothes as we went.

"Did you know you can actually experience hypothermia indoors?" I asked, yanking his shirt off.

"Which is why you're... undressing me?" Gage asked with his signature cheeky grin.

"It's important to get these wet clothes off. We need to get you warmed up." I moved my hands to his waistband and tried to focus on removing his clothes instead of memorizing every inch of his still-tan skin with my hungry eyes.

"I'll trust your expertise in this," he said, lying back on the bed and wiggling his butt a little to help me peel his pants off. I bit back a groan as he continued. "Because in Florida, we get naked for the opposite reason."

I closed my eyes for a moment as the image of him stretched out naked on a sunny, sandy beach flashed through my mind.

"Christ," I muttered under my breath. I was going to

have to add "See Goodman naked on a beach" to my bucket list.

"You're cold, too," he said with a little mischief in his eyes. "Maybe you need the same hypothermia treatment you're giving me."

I met his eyes and saw everything I'd ever wanted in them. Affection, desire, humor, intelligence... joy.

Gage Goodman was full of joy. He radiated it even when he was shivering and covered in goose bumps. I loved that about him. He made me happy, *period*. And I was going to do everything I could to make sure he was just as happy.

I pinched his ass before leaning in to kiss his cold lips. His laughter faded into our shared kisses while I did my best to warm him inch by inch with my hands on his bare skin.

We tumbled around on the bed, kissing and touching and pulling off the final pieces of clothing before we were completely naked and plenty warmed up.

"Want you," Gage said breathlessly. "I didn't... I didn't let myself hope for this, and I want to feel you... make love to you... knowing it's real. Maybe that sounds silly, but—"

"It sounds amazing," I said in a rough voice. This was all too good to be true. "I'm sorry I fought it... you and me. *This*. It was..."

Gage brushed my hair back from where it hung in my face. "Scary?"

"Terrifying," I breathed. "I can't control it. I worried that I wouldn't be enough for you and you'd want to leave. I worried that I'd hold you back."

"From what?" he asked, wrapping arms and legs around me to keep me close.

"Having everything you ever wanted. Making a big life for yourself... Your dreams."

Gage brought my face down until our foreheads pressed together. "I see it's time to begin reenacting our declarations. I love you, Knox Sunday. I fell in love with your happy-go-lucky smile before I even knew you. You *are* the dream. You *are* my big life."

I couldn't say anything past the lump in my throat. Instead, I kissed him gently and tried to pour my heart out through my kisses. I moved my mouth down his body to worship as much of him as I could reach with my lips and tongue. When I finally had him breathless and begging, the way I liked, I flipped him over and shoved his knees under him while raining kisses down his spine.

At this point, Gage's ability to make sensible words was completely gone. The noises he made were muffled by the pillow but encouraging. I loved bringing him pleasure. And I selfishly enjoyed using his strong, sexy body for my own pleasure.

I spread his tight ass cheeks apart and licked over his hole.

Gage let out a surprised *meep* sound.

"This good?"

"Good, yes. *Gnfhhh*," he said as I dove back in with his approval.

His body was warm and soft, pliant and willing. I indulged myself with a long, lingering taste of him. In addition to his usual sea-salt scent, he also smelled a little like the snow and the pine trees around the bed-and-breakfast.

I wondered if he would always keep some of the Key embedded in his skin or if he would gradually begin to smell like everything I loved about living in Vermont.

Someone had already turned on the gas fire in the fireplace opposite the bed, and I felt the warmth of it bathe my bare back as I continued to satisfy myself with Gage's body. With every swipe of my tongue over his tender entrance, I felt my dick throb harder and harder.

"Baby, you ready for me?" I asked. He was sprawled flat across the bed with his ass in the air. His messy hair and dazed eyes made my heart squeeze tightly in my chest.

"Get inside me *now*."

I wanted to laugh. Being with Gage made me giddy and light. He reminded me that I was *not* my job, that I was so much more than my professional successes, that as long as I had him, I knew I was exactly where I was meant to be.

"Home and permanence," I whispered. Just like Webb had said, damn him.

"Knox? Are you waiting until I'm as old as you are? Because that's not how math works, baby."

He made me so damned happy.

I ran a hand up his spine and followed the trail with kisses. "You're gorgeous and sexy," I murmured into his skin. "And I want to spend my life giving you things to feel joyful about."

Gage turned over onto his back and peered up at me. His face was flushed with pink from exertion now, rather than cold, and I wondered if I'd ever seen anything more beautiful.

"You make me feel like I've finally found the place I belong," he said, echoing my thoughts perfectly. He reached out to grasp my hand, pulled me down on top of him and clasped the sides of my neck. I felt the warm, hard press of his cock against my stomach before he wrapped his legs around me. "I'm happiest when I'm with you," he added softly.

I leaned down and kissed him slowly at first, but within seconds, the intensity skyrocketed and my cock thrummed insistently to get closer to him, to get inside of him and hold him tight.

As I fumbled with the condom, I thought about a time, hopefully in the near future, when we could get tested and go bare. Just thinking about it made me even less coordinated until Gage started giggling.

"Need help?"

"Shut it, Goodman," I muttered.

"Shall I fetch you some reading glasses, old man?"

I couldn't hold back a snort. "Kids today think they're so funny."

"Hashtag LOL?"

I shoved his knees up toward his shoulders and met his eyes. They danced with joy and teasing, my favorite Gage expression. "Make your old-man jokes now," I suggested, pressing inside his body and trying not to groan in satisfaction at the tight squeeze. "I dare you."

"Knox," he said on a gasp. "Oh God, yes. Just like that. Fuck."

Once I was fully inside him, I leaned closer and nipped kisses on the side of his neck while he adjusted to me. Gage's fingers played in my hair, and he whispered words in my ear about how good I felt, how grateful he was that I'd come after him, and how much he loved me.

Making love to Gage Goodman made everything else in my life fade in comparison. My job, my friends, all the things I'd once found important. As long as I had Gage… I had everything I needed. Happiness, contentment, fun, joy.

"Love you so damned much," I murmured as I began moving in and out of him. "Thank you for coming back to me."

His eyes were damp, so I brushed my lips underneath them to catch the spill.

When we both finally came in a tangle of limbs and staggered breaths, I felt all of my stress and worry finally settle.

It didn't go away—I wasn't fool enough to think there was an easy fix for it, and I knew I needed to continue to take my mental health seriously—but I knew I would have someone on my side as I battled it in the future.

"You know," I murmured sleepily. "I practiced a whole speech on the way here."

"You practiced?" Gage sounded delighted.

"Naturally. I wanted it to sound right. I wanted it to be…"

"Efficient?" he teased.

"Convincing."

"Baby." He lifted his head and kissed me. "I was already convinced."

"Mmm." I kissed him back. "Convenient, that."

"But, you know, you shouldn't let your speech go to waste." He stacked his hands on my chest and rested his chin there. "I find myself with free time and open ears."

I snickered. "Well. First, I was going to talk about all the ways you make me a happier person. A better person. A less afraid person. About how your joy is contagious. About how it doesn't matter that I'm older than you because I learn things from you every damn day. About how amazing it is—literally, Gage, I'm amazed—that you know I'm a grumpy, anxious ass and you like me anyway—"

He laughed.

"And then, I was going to tell you that I like how I can talk to you about things I can't say to anyone else. And how you showed me that my job isn't my purpose in life. And how you introduced me to the concept of the trust bubble, and I want to be back inside it."

Gage shut his eyes for a moment and shook his head. "You never left it."

"But really, the main point I wanted to make was that I love you. And I don't want to spend a single day without you. So we can go to Boston or New York if you want that. You can redecorate my condo, or we'll buy a new one. I'll pick out all your suits. Maybe I'll do some consulting—"

"Consulting?"

"Yeah. I…" I swallowed because it was still hard to say the words even though I knew they were right. "I'm not going back to Bormon Klein Jacovic. I loved that job, but… it's not a job I can do well if I want to have time for other things in my life. Like handling the books at Sunday Orchard. Like staying connected to my family. Like helping my boyfriend build his multi-kabillion-dollar Pipsy empire while he takes over Rubicon single-handedly. Like building a life together with him."

Gage huffed out a disbelieving laugh. "God, baby. But I don't want the Rubicon job. I'm calling to cancel the interview. I want to stay in the Hollow. Because I finally figured out that I can learn all I need to learn right *here*. But I don't want you to give up your dream either."

"What is it you told me not twenty minutes ago?" I asked lazily. "Something along the lines of 'You *are* the dream'?"

"Probably. Sounds intelligent."

"Well, I feel exactly the same. I'll pick you every time."

"And I pick Little Pippin Hollow," he informed me, this man I loved with my whole heart, who loved me back in equal measure, and I felt the rightness of *that* choice settle into me, too. "This is where we belong."

I pushed back his tangled mop from his face and leaned up to kiss him. "Then this is where we'll stay. For good."

Epilogue

GAGE

~about four months later~

Beale: *Hey, everyone! Sorry to hijack the group chat, but I've got a little limpkin over here who needs some extra love this weekend. Anyone wanna volunteer to help me out?*

When my brother's text hit my phone, I was already sitting outside The Bugle, Little Pippin Hollow's most beloved town bar, with my breath fogging in the air as I tried to get a cell signal. Since all my family and friends got together for football games every Saturday (and Sunday, plus the occasional Monday and Thursday), text chatting or FaceTiming at halftime meant I could talk to all of them at once, which was handy. Since Ernest, the owner of The Bugle, happened to serve the best collection of hard cider in all of New England, this meant I could be adequately prepared to converse with the strange collection of personalities on the Key, which was even handier.

Still, when I read Beale's text, I had to wonder if the half glass I'd drunk before coming outside was a little stronger than usual, because I couldn't fathom what the hell he was talking about.

It turned out I was not the only one.

Dad: *Beale, son, we've all been there. But maybe the Whispering Key Party Planning Committee Group Chat isn't the best place to talk about your limpkin. Have you and Toby talked to Doc Mason? Maybe he could prescribe something.*

Dale Jennings: *Nooooo. Don't let Big Pharma anywhere near your limpkin, buddy! I've got a guy who can hook you up with some supplements that'll get your limpkin saluting the flag. Gel coated STEEL, my man. (Gel coating helps the digestion.) Call me.*

I laughed out loud. Dale Jennings and his questionable supplements were a Whispering Key legend.

Lorenna McKetcham: *Beale, you were right to ask for an assist—sometimes getting some volunteers to help out is exactly what a man needs to recharge the old limpkin! It's Senior Discount Night at The Crab Emporium, otherwise me and George would be over to help. Man's been frisky ever since his hip replacement.*

I snorted. If I ever needed a reminder of what I loved and missed about the little Florida island where I'd been born and raised, all I had to do was open the group chat.

It was also a really important reminder of why I lived far from Whispering Key. Here in the Hollow, people were every bit as neighborly and supportive, but not nearly as interfering or as eccentric.

I mean, unless they were conspiring to make Knox stay in town. Or to prevent me from leaving…

Okay, yeah, they could possibly be considered interfering. *Hmm.*

I looked down the hill at the snow-covered Town Square with its spindly-branched trees and empty gazebo and frowned. Someone, somehow, had shoveled perfect concentric rings around the gazebo maybe six feet apart, forming a snowy crop circle.

Then I remembered Katey Valcourt, who'd knitted Webb a pair of homemade socks for Christmas even *after*

Webb had explained that he didn't return her feelings because, she'd informed him happily, everyone needed a hobby and having a crush on him was hers.

And Helena Fortnum, with her hooch and her, um, apple décor.

And Lonnie Duncan, the so-called Pumpkin Carving Champion, who had a chicken called The Matron that made most of his life decisions. ("Sorry, Sheila. I really like you, but The Matron says it's not gonna work out.")

Hmm again.

Okay, evidence suggested that Hollowans were also, in their own way, every bit as eccentric as the Whispering Keysters I'd grown up with. Maybe the only difference was that they were *my* brand of strange, which was why I'd grafted myself into life here so seamlessly.

Beale: *A limpkin is a majestic BIRD, people. Goodness!*

Ahhh. This made total sense, since my brother was all about wildlife rescue. It also happened to be the perfect setup for a joke, and I couldn't resist.

Me: *You're saying your limpkin is… majestic? Weird flex but okay.*

Toby: *Gagelet!! Precious, how are you?? How is your delightful lumberjackian paramour?? (Yes, I am deliberately turning the conversation, and the first person who changes it back will be dis-invited to the Super Football Day Feast at Beale's and my house. Do not test me. *staring eyes emoji)*

Me: *I'm doing great! Knox is doing awesome! And I think you mean the Super Bowl?*

Dad: *Hahaha. Yeah, he means Super Bowl.*

Fenn: *Super Football Day. *laugh-cry-emoji*

Mason: *He definitely means Super Bowl. But at least he knew it was football?*

Toby: *I'm referring to the football-themed Hors d'Oeuvres Banquet so extensive that it will be enshrined in legend and, indeed,* become part of the collective consciousness of our island, so that generations from now, the names of those who were disinvited will be spoken in voices of hushed pity. But please, you guys, keep talking about how I don't know sportsball. It's totes fun!

Dad: *Do you know, I've always privately thought it should be called Super Football Day?*

Jay: *Same! Exact same. Mason and I were just talking about that the other day.*

Rafe: *Toby, are you making that artichoke feta dip?*

Toby: *A double batch.*

Rafe: *Then as mayor, I'm officially declaring it Super Football Day on Whispering Key.*

Jay: *(You guys, he just banged the kitchen counter at your dad's house like he had a gavel!!! *laugh emoji The mayor thing has officially gone to his head.)*

I snorted. But to be fair, I'd had Toby's feta artichoke dip when we visited the island last month, and I'd declare a holiday for it, too. In fact, I was planning to make a batch for our Super Football Day party back at the orchard, and I'd told Marco I might or might not be willing to barter if he ponied up his precious shortbread recipe.

"Gage?" Knox stepped out the front door and immediately clocked me where I was perched on the porch railing. "You okay, baby? It's fucking freezing out here and you don't have a coat."

I slid my phone into the front pocket of my sweatshirt —the sweatshirt that Knox no longer even pretended was his—and leaned back against the porch railing. I looked up at the love of my life, the man who made me smile each and every day, the man who was my *home* every bit as much as this town was, and scoffed loudly. "*Pssht.* You flatlanders with your sensitivity to the cold. Honestly. Ernest's right about you."

Knox leaned against the railing beside me and folded

his arms over his chest, which would have been a lot more intimidating if he hadn't also been fighting a smile. "Oh, really. And what does the bartender have to say about 'us flatlanders,' pray tell?"

"That you can't tell your applewine from your English," I said smugly.

Knox looked up at the porch roof. "Nearly a billion gay men in the world, Jesus, and I had to end up falling in love with the one who can make apple cider varietals sound like dirty talk? Really?"

I snickered and tugged at the hem of his bulky sweater until he scooted close enough for me to lean my head on his shoulder. "You had to end up falling in love with the one who got so excited about helping Uncle Drew with his retirement project that he became just the *teensiest* bit obsessed with cider. But on the plus side, Ernest says anyone who knows cider as well as I do is clearly a native of the Hollow, no matter where he happened to be born—"

"Oh, well as long as an authority like *Ernest* says you belong here." Knox rolled his eyes even as he wrapped his arm around my shoulder.

"Unlike certain folk," I interrupted, wrinkling my nose, "who had the 'overwhelming good fortune' to be born in the Hollow and then 'absconded to parts unknown—'"

Knox snorted. "Boston is hardly parts unknown—"

"Which was like giving up your right to citizenship in the Hollow forever," I concluded sadly. "According to Ernest."

"That's… fascinating, but it doesn't actually work like that," Knox said with the trademark grumpy expression I loved.

"Mmm. You sure?" I twisted my mouth to one side doubtfully. "Ernest's not just the bartender, he's also the mayor, remember? *And* his bar is the old town hall." I nodded at the Historical Society plaque affixed beside the door which, aside from the "The Bugle, Est. 1767" sign on the front lawn, was truly the only thing that made the building look like anything besides an old, white clapboard Colonial house. "So, like... I'm pretty sure Ernest would know, baby."

"I'm positive. Citizenship is about where you live and are registered to pay taxes, not some ridiculous cider-based eligibility test. And furthermore, you don't get to ban someone forever just because—"

"Tell me more," I whispered huskily, fluttering my eyelashes at him. "Educate me, Daddy."

Knox closed his eyes and shook his head. "I hate you."

"But not as much as you love me!" I laughed. "And, good news, Ernest says I can convey citizenship on my spouse, so when we... Uh."

Shit. I had definitely not meant to say that.

I cleared my throat. "You know what? I think I hear the second half of the game starting. I was out here chatting with the fam, but I'm done now. So weird how you can't get a signal inside the building, eh? But you're right, we should go back inside. *Brrr.* Chilly. Does it look like snow to you? Hurry before we're stuck out here in the blizzard." I pushed ineffectually at his muscular arm.

He refused to be budged. "Mmm. Wait just a minute there, Goodman. Finish your thought. Are you offering to marry me so I can... become a citizen of Little Pippin Hollow?"

"No. Ha! As if. *No.* We've only been together for, like, four months! A third of a year. And I'm only twenty-five, Knox. That'd be... it'd be..."

Crazy. Scary. *Perfect.*

My pulse increased with excitement and no fear whatsoever, but I forced myself to calm the fuck down. Before we got together, Knox had been unsure about getting into a relationship at all.

He was joking. Joke. Ing.

Sure enough, when he looked at me his eyes danced. "Hey, if we did, would that make me a naturalized citizen of Whispering Key, too? Because your dad offered to take me out on the boat when we were down there last month, but I'm thinking maybe I should get my *own* boat since I'm a citizen. Can I be part of the group chat? Should we ask the mayor? He'd probably know."

I narrowed my eyes. "I see what you're doing and you're not funny."

"Except I kind of am." He smiled his happy-go-lucky smile and I melted into a puddle of Gage-goo right there.

"You kind of are," I agreed. "And as my boyfriend, you can be part of the group chat whenever you want." I patted his chest, mostly for the excuse to touch him. "Their shenanigans might piss you off constantly, though, fair warning."

"Nah." He leaned in and ran his cold nose against my jaw, making me shiver. "I'm calm as the orchard in winter these days."

"Yeah." I teased with a happy sigh. "And all because you found the love of a good man."

He laughed. "I was gonna credit the weekly therapy sessions, consistent meditation practice, good coping mechanisms, total lifestyle change, and having a patient doctor who's worked to get me on a good combo of medication even though it's taken months." He turned and wrapped his arms around my waist. "But all of that has gotten me to a place where I can appreciate and return the love of a good man, and build a future with him, which is pretty crucial."

"Aw." I leaned into him. "I was joking and you got all serious. I love you."

"I love you, too. And I appreciate you giving me that jokey out, but I don't need it. You're it for me. So if you ever *do* want to seal that deal, baby, and become an efficient Sunday for real, you just let me know."

I gaped at him. "Wait. *Wait.* Seriously?"

"Serious as your newfound love of cows," he vowed.

Knowing how fond I was of Diana, that… was very serious indeed.

He kissed me and it tasted like laughter. "I can see I've broken your brain, Goodman. It's fine. We don't need to decide anything tonight. We have forever, so there's no need to rush to get——"

Hawk threw the door open, his face pale and his eyes huge. "You guys need to come inside. Webb accidentally got *married*!"

Accidentally?

Knox stared at Hawk in shock, but me? I grinned hugely.

"Come on," I told Knox, tugging him by the hand. "This I have to see."

It turned out that life in Little Pippin Hollow might actually be weirder than any other place in the world, and way more exciting than any big city.

And there was nowhere else I'd rather be.

Wanna see how Webb ended up married? Check out *Hand-Picked*, coming early next year!

Wanna catch up with all the folks on Whispering Key? Start the series with Off Plan!

Also by May Archer

Licking Thicket series (with Lucy Lennox)

Thicket Security series (with Lucy Lennox)

Sunday Brothers series

Love in O'Leary series

Whispering Key series

The Way Home series

M/F Romance written as Maisy Archer

About May

May lives outside Boston. She spends her days raising three incredibly sarcastic children, finding inventive ways to drive her husband crazy, planning beach vacations, avoiding the gym, reading M/M romance, and occasionally writing it. She's also published several M/F romance titles as Maisy Archer.

For free content and the latest info on new releases, sign up for her newsletter at: https://www.subscribepage.com/MayArcher_News

Want to know what projects May has coming up? Check out her Facebook reader group <u>Club May</u> for giveaways, first-look cover reveals, and more.

You can also catch her on Bookbub, and check out her recommended reads!

Printed in Great Britain
by Amazon